Mystified

sometimes the truth isn't pretty

Julia Ash

DEDICATION

*With gratitude and love
to my husband Rick
for cheering "Hollywood, Baby!"
whenever I needed it most.*

ഒ ൚ ൞ ൜

ALSO BY JULIA ASH

THE ELI CHRONICLES

a dark fantasy series

The One and Only (Book #1)

"And while the zombie action is exceptional, readers
will likely find themselves rooting for the messy demise of Ox,
whose lechery boils from the page." – *Kirkus Reviews*

The Tether (Book #2)

"It seems there is never a dull moment, with plenty of twists
and cliffhanging chapters." – *The BookLife Prize*

The Turning Point (Book #3)

Writer's Digest HONORABLE MENTION
(Self-Published E-Book Awards, 2020)

BookLife by Publishers Weekly SEMI-FINALIST
(The BookLife Prize, 2020)

"Ultimately, Ash's ability to weave together multiple genres
into a well-paced synthesis of science fiction, fantasy, and horror
(with appealing dialogue and welcome moments of humor)
makes this futuristic series a genuinely one-of-a-kind experience."
– *BookLife Reviews*

"Ash plots a twisty, surprising course through this extravagantly
inventive material, always guiding readers to what matters most
in any of the crisp, tightly written chapters."
– *The BookLife Prize*

"It is never too late to be what you might have been."

~ Mary Ann Evans, Novelist
(Pen Name: George Eliot)

Mystified

sometimes the truth isn't pretty

Julia Ash

1

JULIETTE ANNABELLA PARKER stood near the edge of her parents' pool, entranced by the long brown hair rhythmically swaying at the bottom of the deep end. She ran her fingers through her own wet hair, not sure why. Maybe because Jules was the only person with long brown hair at the Parkers' estate.

Touching the skin across her neck, she winced, feeling the moist sting of a wire thin abrasion. The wound confused her, along with everything else, but she didn't have time to make sense of her peculiar disorientation.

Whistling distracted her.

Looking up, Jules saw their groundskeeper. He was walking around the corner of the mansion, holding his cellphone while heading toward the pool. She noticed his creased forehead as he neared the water and focused on her inflatable lounger, now barely afloat. He stopped whistling, eyes tracking toward the deep end.

Next to the thick locks of hair, something dark had also sunk to the bottom and was sprawled out beside the drain cover.

"My purple towel," Jules shouted to Garth from the other side of the pool, trying to ease his apparent worry.

Thunder growled in the distance.

Skies above the western shore of the Chesapeake Bay had darkened, streaked with angry veins of crimson and green. Thrust eastward by a chilled wind, the midday storm arrived as forecasted.

Instead of acknowledging her towel comment, Garth leaned over the edge and seemed to peer more intently into the water.

"Christ!" he yelled, tossing his cellphone onto the deck and diving into the pool fully clothed.

She startled at his explosion of energy.

Immobilized, Jules's mouth gaped open. The only thing she could do was watch.

As she tried to see through the dark turquoise water, an army of bubbles frantically retreated to the surface, fleeing whatever terror it had encountered below.

Lightning flashed as a bolt struck in the middle of nearby Gibson Island. Seconds later, a clap of thunder boomed, forcing the residual rumble to race east, sweeping over the bay towards them.

Jules was scared. Terrified. But not about the weather.

"Hurry, Garth!" she pleaded, racing over to where he had entered the pool. A closer look might explain what was unfolding.

Fixated on the deep end, Jules saw blurred images begin to take shape on the bottom. The water cleared. Garth was tugging and yanking at a figure, a female, located close to the drain.

How could Jules have missed someone joining her in the pool?

A tinge of guilt prickled her skin. Her heart hammered in her chest. Swallowing hard, she pushed down a wave of nausea.

Garth finally broke the surface and kicked toward the wall, pulling the body behind him. Reaching the side, he pushed the girl's torso up and out of the pool. The teenager fell hard on the pavers, face down, arms straight by her sides; but she didn't make a sound. Her legs dangled in the water, unmoving.

Panting, Garth lifted himself onto the pool's concrete edge. Turning toward the girl, he bent down and locked his arms under her armpits before hoisting the rest of her from the pool.

Long hair masked her face.

In their odd embrace, with the girl pressed against his chest, he walked backwards, moving her over the pavers in an awkward dance. The tops of her feet scraped against the stone tiles.

"Please, God, no!" Garth cried.

After he lowered the teen onto the grass, placing her on her back, Jules began to register details. The victim wore a periwinkle bikini.

Jules's mind was jumbled, but not enough to miss the likeness.

Slowly, she glanced down at her own bathing suit. *Periwinkle.* Her favorite color on any palette.

Garth brushed hair away from the victim's face.

Familiar blue eyes stared at nothing.

Hot liquid raced up Jules's throat. This time, the force was too great to suppress. She threw up, smelling chlorine mixed with water.

Dizziness caused her energy to hiccup. To short circuit. Probably from exhaustion. From shock.

The body on the grass was *hers.*

She remembered, then, though her memories were sketchy.

Someone had been strangling her.

Had been trying to drown her in the pool.

Who could've hated her that much?

2

Friday, August 13, 2027
The Parkers' G&G Estate: Hickory Thicket, Maryland
(Two Days *before* Juliette's Death)

SITTING IN DARKNESS in front of her loft's paneled window, Jules tried to erase the mental picture which regularly haunted her daydreams: a scorched, lonely hell where Mother stoked the flames.

A blank canvas, even for a night, might give her hope.

After all, having friends was what Jules longed for. Obsessed about. So much so, that constantly reminding herself she didn't have *any* tightened her chest and caused her heart to shrivel.

A raisin popped into her thoughts.

That was it; her heart had become a petrified raisin.

Thankfully, hardly anyone recognized her misery or her loneliness. Jules worked tirelessly to project a façade of aloofness. Better to have teens her age believe she was overly confident and standoffish than learn the ugly truth.

For those who weren't intimidated by Jules's attitude?

Mother intervened.

As soon as the brazen got too close, they'd feel the heat. In the end, no one was interested in getting burned, so unless Jules's maternal warden dropped her diamond-studded blowtorch or her father miraculously emerged from the flickering shadows holding buckets of water, nothing would change in the friend category.

Stiff from sitting in place, Jules repositioned herself on the chair. She squinted, attempting to focus on something, anything, beyond her parents' pool and patio area below. On clear nights, she could see across the Chesapeake Bay to the twinkling lights on Gibson Island. The lights were mesmerizing, making it easy for her imagination to escape from her bedroom. From her hellish boredom.

Not tonight.

Dense fog painted her third floor view a milky black.

Equally disappointing, crickets and cicadas were speechless. Not even a brackish breeze ruffled her nightgown or stirred the curtains in her room. Friday the 13th was a flop. Where were the superstitious happenings like seeing ghosts drift across the lawn with the mist or hearing eerie sounds bubble up from the marshes?

Instead, the night was comatose. One faint heartbeat from death.

Planting her elbows on the windowsill, she supported her chin with the palms of her hands and released a lengthy sigh while slumping her shoulders.

Jules was adept at theatrics, performing at the crème-de-la-crème level. No real surprise since exaggeration and pageantry were synonymous. As the newly crowned 2027 National Miss Junior Teen beauty champion—the "nation's darling" as reporters called her, she had perfected the art of hyperbole at age 15, both in body language and speech. In fact, turning the subtle into the sensational had earned her hundreds of coveted crowns throughout her childhood.

Mother said most teenagers her age didn't have a victory library.

Jules had two.

Illuminated by crystal chandeliers, the adjoining trophy rooms featured rows of shelving halfway up each wall. Jeweled tiaras, bronzed dress shoes, and dried flowers embellished all the shelves while framed scholarship certificates, sashes, and photographs of Jules with important people covered every inch of wall space. In the largest library, a marble pedestal was showcased, supporting a sculpted bronze bust of none other than Jules wearing a crown.

She rarely stepped foot into the rooms.

The enclosed garden and her loft were the only domains on her parents' Glitz and Glamour Estate she genuinely cared about.

In the distance, backyard floodlights from the estate next door turned on, though the light was trapped in mist, forming halos around each fixture.

Their new neighbors to the right—actually, their *one* neighbor since marshlands bordered the Parkers' property on the left—were a mysterious bunch who kept to themselves. A perfect fit for Hickory Thicket.

If only the floodlights next door meant somebody had gone outside, but the landscape remained as lifeless as when she had started her nightly vigil. By now, Jules had been staring out her window for nearly two hours, despite the fog which had engulfed their waterfront acreage, concealing the bay, their narrow beach, and most of their garden, pool, and mansion.

At dusk, Mindi Maxwell (Mother's uber obnoxious personal assistant) had served her dinner in her loft. Beef Wellington. Medium rare. Jules hadn't bothered to protest eating by herself, earlier than usual, in the confines of her bedroom and en suite.

Did it really matter *when* she was locked in for the night?

Wasn't like Dad had come home. As a detective for the Rock Hall Police Department, he claimed he simply *had* to work nightshift at the station to tackle piles of paperwork. She wasn't about to question him, though the real reason he stayed away seemed obvious.

On the good side, eating in seclusion meant she could avoid Mother's enumeration of the rules, especially number thirteen: *Avoid distractions*. Mother was convinced that subjecting oneself to distractions and outside impurities, like having friends who harbored contagious thoughts and promoted competing allegiances, would pollute the body in the form of blemishes, wrinkles, and blotches. All of which soured an audience. Namely, pageant judges.

In Jules's wishful-thinking rulebook, friends were distractions who helped tire the mind and body in a healthy way.

Which meant, she wasn't close to being sleepy.

Alone all day, she had done nothing but prepare for tomorrow's interview and photo shoot with *Beauty World* magazine. Not exactly a formula for exhaustion. That, and she had swung open the window screen at nightfall and carefully dumped all but a tiny sip of her *stea,* watering the potted cherry tree positioned on the patio below her, some 35-feet down.

Stea was the nickname she had given to the spiked tea Mother concocted to address Jules's insomnia. The nightcap, which was no secret in the Parker household, was a combination of caffeine-free white tea for anti-aging, a brimming shot of dark rum, crushed zolpidem for sleeping, and honey to mask the sour burn of the drug.

The real secret was that on most nights like this one, Jules disposed of her *stea*.

Constance Parker controlled just about all of Jules's life, but not her insomnia. Not her afflictions.

Someday (someday soon, Jules hoped), she would gain enough courage to exert herself even more. To become her own person.

She heard sounds downstairs.

A click. A jangle from clanking bracelets.

Had someone opened the pantry door leading to her private staircase? Were they making their way up the steps?

Holding her breath, Jules turned her head toward the locked door behind her, trying to determine if she had actually heard something.

Sure enough, the 20th step released its warning groan.

Mother was coming.

3

Friday, August 13, 2027
The Parkers' G&G Estate: Hickory Thicket, Maryland
(Two Days *before* Juliette's Death)

JULES TIPTOED ACROSS the hardwood flooring and quickly tucked herself under the sheets. She shifted onto her right side to avoid facing Mother when she entered the bedroom.

The knob turned, releasing the lock. The door creaked open.

Light from the fixture over the staircase fanned into her loft and brightened the space.

"A queen, sleeping on her side, rules nothing but facial creases," Mother snarled.

Jules rolled onto her back. "Yes, Ma'am."

"Sometimes I think you intend to sabotage our success."

"Your success is too important to me."

"Juliette Annabella," Mother said, placing her hands on her hips. "Was that a sarcastic tone? May I remind you? Sarcasm is ugly. Do you understand?"

Mother always asked questions which didn't require an answer. *Do you understand* meant Jules had touched the electric fence and Mother was about to flip the switch.

Jules nodded anyway. At least her response was safer than words.

"We agree, then," she announced to Jules, claiming her victory before moving on to the next subject. "Tomorrow morning, Mindi will drive us to Washington, D.C. at eight o'clock sharp. Breakfast is in the sunroom at seven. Now get to sleep. Your mind needs to be crisp. This interview is a tremendous opportunity."

"Can't we go by ourselves? Why does Mindi need to take us?"

In all honesty, Mother showed off in front of her hand-selected protégé. A break from the theatrics would be nice.

"*My* job is to determine whether we should drive or be driven, young lady," she huffed at Jules. "*Your* job is to obey your handler."

Mother strolled to the window as if an audience watched. She tilted the chair backwards and dragged the rear legs over the flooring until the chair rested by the mahogany table where Jules completed her homeschooling assignments.

"Good heavens, Juliette! How many times must I repeat myself? Always leave a room the same or better than you found it."

"But I haven't left."

On the makeshift runway formed by the light, Jules could see Mother's eyes narrow.

"Do you understand?" she repeated. More slowly this time.

"Yes, Ma'am."

"Excellent."

Her "Queen Mother," a former Miss America and a runner-up Miss Universe (to…*she who must never be named*), model-walked to the door with her chin held high. Before reaching for the knob, she stopped. "You seem wide awake. Did you drink your tea?"

"I did."

As far as Jules was concerned, there was enough truth in her answer to be acceptable. In anticipation of Mother's nightly question, she had intentionally taken a miniscule sip before dumping the concoction out the window. Thank goodness Mother never asked if Jules had consumed every ounce of her tea.

"I am locking the door again," Mother said, "to ensure you have no distractions." She added in her stage voice, "Tomorrow, Queen Juliette, you shall glitter like a royal's prized jewel!"

The door clicked shut.

Mother depressed the button lock on the knob.

Darkness and solitude returned like a comforting childhood blanket.

Jules waited until she no longer heard footsteps. The light over the staircase turned off, signaling the coast was clear. Tossing off her sheets, she lowered herself from the bed and tiptoed to her window.

In three short years, Mother wouldn't be able to control or isolate her. Jules would become a legal adult. Then, no one could prevent her from having as many "distractions" as she wanted.

After destroying the rules posted around her loft, Jules would leave her parents' estate. Maybe she'd use her pageantry winnings to go to college for agriculture. Or perhaps she'd get her hands dirty right away, working for a nursery or in the fields of an organic farm. One thing was certain; she planned on wearing jeans, work boots, and hardly any makeup because planting in her garden was where she had always felt the most natural. The most alive.

Standing in front of the window, she returned to her night watch, fantasizing that the mystery family who had moved next door included teenagers. She had no doubts she would make a good friend. In fact, when Jules was 12, she almost had one. Lila Lovelace was in pageantry, too. A competitor in the same age group.

Back in 2024 on a chartered flight to LAX in Los Angeles, Jules and Mother encountered Lila and her handler who insisted that she and Jules exchange seats on the plane, allowing the adults to converse over cocktails. Mother protested, at first, but must have gotten thirsty for alcohol and gossip because she changed her mind.

The unprecedented opportunity had given Jules five hours to talk privately with Lila, setting the foundation for a promising friendship. But their relationship was abruptly hampered two weeks later when she overheard a conversation between both mothers after Lila had invited Jules to spend the night. Mother had whispered that her daughter was a bedwetter—had never outgrown the dreadful malady, so a sleepover was out of the question. Not that Jules didn't have empathy for those who suffered from the condition because she absolutely did. It was just that Jules's bedsheets were always dry.

At the following pageant, Jules had snuck a moment under Mother's radar to confess to Lila that she wasn't a bedwetter, that her actual afflictions were asthma and insomnia. Mostly wide awake at night, Jules had no trouble making it to the bathroom in time. In truth, Mother wouldn't let her sleep over because Jules wasn't *allowed* to have friends. Lila believed her. In fact, she was the only person outside of the G&G who knew an inch of Jules's milelong truth.

Jules's mind snapped out of her reverie when a lone racoon scurried across the lawn, close enough to the garden's entrance that the motion sensor light clicked on, casting a glowing bubble of mist around the gate area.

The masked racoon paused and quivered, as if detecting a predator, before scampering toward the marshes for safety.

To Jules's right, a swirl of fog grabbed her attention by the loblolly pines, those planted years ago to form a natural fence line between her parents' estate and the property next door.

Her heart pounded in her ears.

Goosebumps rose on her arms.

Maybe the night was finally waking up.

Freezing in place in the pitch black, she widened her eyes to capture as much light as they could take in.

A person emerged from the trees and stirred the mist while walking to Jules's enclosed labyrinth-like gardens. Upon arriving, the figure stopped and clutched the iron gate.

The intruder stood motionless, facing away from her, for what seemed like forever.

Jules willed herself not to move. Not to breathe.

Maybe the trespasser wouldn't turn around and see her.

4

Friday, August 13, 2027
The Parkers' G&G Estate: Hickory Thicket, Maryland
(Two Days *before* Juliette's Death)

TRUITT WINDSOR STOOD in front of the entrance to the coolest, most badass garden he had ever made a habit of sneaking into. Enclosed by eight-foot-high brick walls, his neighbors' botanical paradise was magical, to say the least. Inside, sculpted shrubs, decorative walls, and well-placed water structures created a maze worthy of a royal family. And he wasn't kidding.

Veggies, fruits, herbs, and flowers—his posh neighbors were growing everything, including envy.

Because of the thick fog, Truitt had considered abandoning his nighttime adventure of intruding into the labyrinth and challenging himself to accurately identify each plant variety. The idea of skipping his visit was short lived. Going to the garden was an easy win, despite the fog, because if he had stayed indoors, he would've been bored to death.

Isolation was already messing with him.

Cognitively, Truitt seemed to be in slow motion, drifting around in his own internal fog. He was spending more time daydreaming about the past than living in the present. Solution? He had to force himself to stay active, to snap out of his strange lethargy.

That's why five minutes earlier, he had released his house's backdoor, anticipating the familiar bang that had always inspired his Mom to shout at him to *close* the door instead of letting it slam against the doorjamb. Over time, the rule infringement had become a playful ritual, one he treasured more than he had ever realized.

Tonight, like every night since his family had moved to Hickory Thicket two weeks ago, the screen door had made no sound at all. Consequently, no snappy banter had followed.

Not even a cricket chirped to acknowledge him.

Truitt kept forgetting that their new house—more like a French country-styled mansion—didn't include the old bones and warmth of his childhood home. Someday soon, he hoped he'd settle into his upscale digs like a comfortable chair that embraced him. Right now, though, the home was stiff and cold, making him feel everything *but* welcomed.

Turning left from the back of his house, he had headed to the swath of loblolly pine trees separating his parents' property from the one called G&G. By August standards, he might've described the night as chilly, though his navy football jersey was all he needed. Nevertheless, the cooler temperatures had him thinking about fall. In fact, in his former life back in Bishopville, football practice would've started.

As he stood frozen in front of the garden, he thought about time.

On his way over, he had glanced at his wristwatch. The hands were stuck on 8:27. A slight crack flawed the crystal face. Kids his age always laughed at his nostalgic appreciation for outdated technology. He didn't care. He shrugged every time someone called him an old man in a teenager's body.

What he *did* care about was that he had forgotten, once again, to see if his Dad would help him find a jeweler where he could get his wristwatch fixed. The vein running across its face didn't bother him. All the 40-year old watch needed was a new battery.

His forgetfulness proved he was out of sorts. The move had clearly affected his stress level. Maybe this was what depression felt like…a heavy weight turning everything that used to be easy and second nature into something overwhelming.

At the garden's iron gate, he clasped a picket and sucked in a breath. He desperately wanted to break out of his emotional funk. Exploring seemed to help.

That's when he felt eyes blazing down on him.

Could it be the girl? The one he had seen every evening and night as she sat on the other side of her third-floor window, staring out at the bay? Apparently deep in thought, she never seemed to notice him, though he avoided being out in the open.

Even at a distance, Truitt could tell she was beautiful—long brown hair and porcelain skin. He wasn't a peeping Tom or anything like that. He was simply a night owl who paid attention to details. Never mind he was trespassing on her family's property.

Ironic if she had *finally* noticed him on the foggiest night of the century. Go figure.

No need to react quickly. If she was staring at him, he'd turn when he was good and ready.

More than once, Truitt had thought of introducing himself, standing below her window and hollering up to her. After several days of thinking about saying hello, he still hadn't opened his mouth.

In addition to his absentmindedness, he was acting oddly shy and awkward. Did depression do that, too? He had never had problems with girls before. They always seemed interested in what made him tick. His Dad said being a magnet for attention came with the territory. Quarterbacks were natural born leaders, and that fact alone drew people in, including young ladies his age.

Hickory Thicket wasn't exactly buzzing with female fans. Or *any* fans, for that matter.

In fact, year-round residents who lived off Eastern Neck Road, about five miles south of Rock Hall, probably wouldn't consider their estates being part of a neighborhood. Teenagers weren't hanging out in a cul-de-sac, listening to tunes, sipping cheap beer, and talking about rivals in their high school football conference.

Truitt missed living in Bishopville, a town inland from Ocean City, Maryland. Leaving behind his medium-sized high school wasn't easy either, not by a long shot.

Going from *popular* to *do you even exist* was his hardest adjustment.

Even his longtime friends (those he'd had since kindergarten) were proving that *out of sight, out of mind* was more than a catchy phrase. Someone had put those despairing words together for a reason—one reflected in his current circumstances.

Worse, the prospect of making new friends was beyond doubtful.

MYSTIFIED

Rural-rich Hickory Thicket was smaller than small, given the dot on the map wasn't even big enough to have its own post office. Which might be why the few residents of HT (that's how he referred to his new hometown) pretty much kept to themselves, something his parents were craving these days. They had come into some money (significant if anyone asked him) and wanted nothing more than to chill. Maybe they were relieved to leave behind the demands of football. In HT, there were no athletic boosters, no training regimens or Friday night lights, and no pontifications over possible college scholarships to Big Ten universities.

The only chatter came from crickets.

Yuppers, his parents, Abigail and Darren Windsor, had abruptly changed lifestyles to "save their marriage," or so he had overheard them whisper privately one night. Neither of his parents had ever asked Truitt what *he* had wanted to do. Maybe they felt they had sacrificed enough for their only child. Which was true. No arguments from him.

Seventeen and about to head into his senior year, Truitt wasn't calling the plays in the Windsor household anymore; so on second down at the five-yard line, minutes from halftime, the moving vans came anyway. His parents dropped the ball before the snap, forcing a play change: a permanent time out.

The Windsors walked off the field. Game over.

Truitt squeezed his eyes shut, forcing back tears. When would he stop thinking about the past? Revisiting what *shoulda, coulda, woulda* only drained his energy more.

The past never changed; no do-overs.

Formulating a new game plan was his only Hail Mary. He needed to start living in the present again.

Pulling the gate toward him, Truitt slowly turned and glanced up at the girl's window. What the hell did he have to lose?

His heart fisted and pummeled his chest.

As he spotted her image in the window, standing in the dark on the third floor, he was 100-percent sure she was staring at him.

Time to disappear in the labyrinth.

5

AS IF CEMENTED in place while surrounded by the darkness of her loft, Jules peered at the mystery person who stood by the garden's entrance. Jules didn't breathe or swallow. Or blink.

The stranger was a teenager, a male.

As he opened the gate, he swooshed the fog. Before entering, he gazed in her direction. Right smack at her window! Had the trespasser known she was there all along?

She nearly gasped out loud.

The light by the garden's gate illuminated him. His hair was dark and short, fashioned in a one-inch buzz cut. His skin, brown. He wore jeans and a jersey touting a name and number on the back, printed with white decals. Probably an athlete. If she had to guess, he looked slightly older, like 16 or 17, but that might have been her imagination in wishful-thinking mode.

The neighbors' floodlights shut off at the same time the gate's light dimmed down.

She flinched.

Only darkness remained, along with a chill that nipped at her forearms.

Using the blackout to her advantage, Jules moved to the left side of her window. Pressing her back against the wall, she inhaled. Fainting would benefit no one. She relied on her pageantry training and the rules: *Steady breathing calms the anxious soul.*

A sudden gust of wind sent her opened curtains into a messy dance of flapping and twirling above her head. Turning sideways toward the window while remaining hidden, she glimpsed at the sky, noticing a tear forming in the moving layers of clouds and fog. The breach revealed a patch of starry skies, allowing the waxing moon to momentarily cast its rays.

Finding courage, she tilted her head forward and focused on the garden's entrance. The gate swung back and forth with the wind's arrival, clanking against the iron frame, unable to click into a closed position.

Whomever she had seen was no longer in sight. He had entered the garden. *Her* garden.

How dare he! In fact, Jules was going to find out who the teen was and what his intentions were.

Rushing to her bed, she reached for the dinner knife which she had recently acquired and stashed between her mattress and box-spring. The only good thing about door locks was she knew how to pick them. Using the blade with mastered precision, she retracted the bolt and opened the door.

Sneaking out was her only option because Mother would never approve. Not even in broad daylight with a chaperone. Which meant, Jules couldn't get caught.

In the dark, she listened for movement downstairs. Nothing but quiet.

Jules tiptoed down the stairs, skipping over the 20th step. At the bottom of the staircase, she slowly opened the door. Both the pantry and kitchen were dark. Mother had already retired to her master suite on the other side of the house.

Walking cautiously to the kitchen's backdoor, she slipped outside to the patio.

Fog had coated surfaces like a heavy dew, and Jules felt the wetness of the pavers on her bare feet. A gust annoyingly fluttered her nightgown and for the first time, she realized she hadn't changed into something more appropriate, like *way* more. Too risky to backtrack. Thankfully, she still clutched her dinner knife which could serve as a deterrent if she pretended that she knew how to wield it.

Running on the grass toward the garden, she felt tiny beads of moisture dampen her skin and hair. At least the fog masked her nightwear.

In front of her garden's entrance, Jules grabbed the gate and stopped it from clanking against the frame. She looked back at the mansion as lights in the master suite turned off.

Aloneness might have shaken other kids, but not her. She was well within her comfort zone.

Except for her nightgown.

Closing the gate behind her, she considered her options. The garden divided into three sections, each meandering in a maze-like fashion before leading to the garden's secluded center which showcased a large circular fountain and concrete benches with clawed feet. The left passageway featured vegetable and herb plantings; the right, fruits; and the center, flowers and greenery. Like a labyrinth, no one could see beyond the path they were on, not that it mattered on a foggy night. In addition, each lane had turnoffs leading to special displays in dead end nooks.

When her parents wanted to show off for guests, they would flip a switch on the garden wall or from the house to artfully illuminate the gardens. Good thing Jules didn't require lights to navigate the lanes. She knew the gardens even better than the rules.

If Jules were an intruder, she'd select the fruit pathway, since it was easier to pick fruit from its stem, consume it, and leave the garden without any evidence. On the vegetable side, hardly anyone had the desire to chow down a raw eggplant or squash.

Following the pebbled pathway, she entered the fruit lane. The wind's arrival hadn't affected the thick blanket of fog protected within the garden walls. However, the dark, milky coverage was even more desirable since her dampened nightgown had begun to cling to her legs.

Every now and then, moon rays tried to illuminate her pathway, but the suspended droplets of moisture shielded direct light. She had to admit, knowing precisely where she was on the trail was more challenging than she'd anticipated. Jules stopped walking and squatted, reaching to her left where she imagined the now fruitless strawberry plants would be. Running her palm over the ground, she felt mulch instead of leafy plants. She had spread wood chips under the two blueberry bushes, located before the strawberry patch, apple trees, and birdhouse.

Jules heard a twig snap.

"Who's there?"

She clenched her dinner knife.

No one answered.

Slowly, she straightened her legs and stood. A breeze ruffled her nightgown, mid-section. The wind had probably entered through the drainage grates positioned every six feet at the base of the brick walls.

Fear no one and no thing, she repeated to herself.

Jules reached out in search of a blueberry branch. Touching the leaves shaped like elongated ovals, she confirmed her location. She was halfway through the fruit trail.

As she moved forward, moist pebbles against her bare soles helped guide her on the path. With her right hand clasping the knife, Jules kept her left arm extended, sweeping it back and forth from the front to her left side like a windshield wiper. She hoped to snag the wooden pole supporting their Purple Martin birdhouse since it marked where she needed to turn left.

When her left hand brushed against the roughness of the birdhouse's wooden pole, Jules felt relief. She was almost to the fountain which operated around the clock. In fact, she heard the water cascading over the top scalloped bowl and splashing into the reservoir in the massive basin below. The sound reminded her of pelting rain hitting their mansion's metal roof.

Jules had concentrated so intensely on not taking a misstep in the dark that she had nearly forgotten her reason for entering the garden in the first place: the intruder. That's why she had risked poking an eye, stubbing a toe, being the main entree for mosquitos, or having Mother track her down and escort her back to her prison disguised as a home.

"Is anybody there?" she asked, raising her voice over the steady splash of the fountain.

She felt a chill. The mist had soaked her.

Jules shivered. Her teeth chattered.

Pebbles crunched in front of her, somewhere near the fountain.

Instinctively, she raised her knife. Goosebumps on her arms were on full alert.

"You shouldn't be out alone at night," a male voice said from behind her.

From *behind* her?

Whipping around, Jules only saw a thick cloud of fog.

"You mean, out *alone* at night with a…thief? A trespassing jerk?" she snapped, her heart throbbing in her throat, making it difficult to swallow. "Come out where I can see you."

The intruder emerged from the mist.

"Can you see me now?" he asked.

"I have eyes."

"Ouch," he said. "Did you get up on the wrong side of the bed or something?"

Why-oh-why couldn't a ray of moonlight shine on her blade to make it look ominous instead of the laughingstock of weaponry?

"Who are you?" she insisted.

"The new guy next door." He bobbed his head. "Truitt Windsor. And you are?"

"Jules. Jules Parker. Why are you in my garden?"

"I enjoy the night. And let's face it, not a whole lot is happening after sundown in Hickory Thicket. On the bright side, your garden is totally cool. Sorry if I frightened you."

"Come closer."

The trespasser named Truitt took several steps toward her. He was tall, like six-foot something. His shoulders were broad and even in the dullness of the charcoal light, he looked physically fit.

"Stop there," she ordered when he stood a few steps from her.

"You lack social skills, don't you?" he pressed.

How odd for him to question her social adeptness, of all things. Jules knew precisely how to work a crowd. Then again, that was when she was on stage or walking the runway—when actress Juliette Annabella had the pageant judges leaning forward in their seats, eager for her next word, gesture, or facial expression.

Could her new neighbor have figured out, so easily, that she was clueless when it came to making friends?

When she didn't answer, he added, gazing at her dinner knife,

"Do you intend to stab me?"

He smiled, revealing dimples in each cheek. Conclusion: Truitt Windsor was way cute.

Jules started feeling conscious of her appearance. However, now was not the time to project weakness or a lack of confidence. No. To retain the upper hand, *she'd* be the one asking questions.

"How did you make it to the center of my garden? In the dark? In the fog?" she asked.

"Probably shouldn't admit this, but I've been coming here every night for two weeks, since we moved in next door. I know my way around. Tonight, I took the vegetable route."

"I hadn't pegged you as a zucchini snatcher."

Curling his lips, he delivered a full smile.

No white lies needed. His smile could instantly melt ice cream. The kind that was spoon bending frozen.

"Actually, I'm partial to miniature heirloom tomatoes. You know...tomatoes are really in the fruit family. They form from flowers and are filled with small seeds. You've planted them in the wrong section."

"Says the uninvited jock."

"You like labels. I get it. I had a coach like that once. He called me plenty of things, but never Truitt." He scratched his chin. "Interested in walking on the beach? Or maybe swimming?"

A brief flash of light somewhere near her house caught Jules's attention. Maybe Dad had come home from the station. Maybe Mother had discovered her missing and was suiting up for the hunt.

"I have to go," she said, accidentally emoting worry instead of confidence.

He glanced down at her bare feet. "Let me guess. You have a wicked stepmother and you've lost your glass slippers."

"Warmer than you think."

"Hey. Before you go, I was wondering," he said, rubbing his neck and grimacing. "Will you be around tomorrow?"

"Are you hurt?"

"Stiff neck," he answered. "I play football. Or should I say... *played*. About tomorrow. Want to hang out?" He eyed her nightgown. "You could even wear shorts and a T-shirt, if you wanted."

This time, he delivered a crooked smile that probably made other girls swoon from gasping and weak knees.

"Sorry. My Saturday is already booked," she said. "As the winningest junior teen in beauty pageantry, I'm going to be interviewed on TBC. Live, airing at one o'clock."

"TBC?"

She rolled her eyes. "The Beauty Channel. Two-hundred and forty-six on your remote."

"Huh," he said, running his right hand over his hair. "Never watched that channel."

"Don't worry, you only have to be beautiful if you're *on* it. Anyone can watch."

"Double ouch."

Actually, Jules hadn't set out to wound him. She wanted nothing more than to learn about the new teenager next door, to see if maybe they could become friends, even if they had to hide their relationship from Mother. Sadly for Jules, starting a friendship was like learning a foreign language without a book or teacher. Where did she begin?

Instead of venturing into uncharted territory, she resorted to her standbys: being snarky and standoffish. And relying on the rules when she was out of her comfort zone.

Turning east toward her house, she faced away from Truitt. Without saying goodbye, she began to leave, deciding to take the flower path back to the entrance gate. Her shoulders were back, chin up, while applying her runway gait for full blown attitude.

Leave them wanting more.

6

CONSTANCE PARKER SIPPED her espresso at the dining table in the sunroom. She had come downstairs early, before anyone else, to focus on the day ahead, especially on her daughter's extraordinary opportunity to further broaden her fan base.

In truth, Constance was not at all concerned about the image her daughter would project during the interview with *Beauty World*. As Juliette's handler, she had selected her daughter's outfit ensemble, from her undergarments to the smallest accessory.

Make no mistake: Constance had calculated the desired effect that every minute detail would generate.

Indeed, in the game of beauty, winners understood that absolutely everything created a perception, whether it was true or not.

Control the perception, control the outcome.

Constance Isabel Reyes Parker was a winner.

When Juliette joined her for breakfast in the next few minutes, she would be wearing a silk pants suit in periwinkle blue. The skinny-styled pantlegs were straight, snug, and to the ankle. Her tailored tunic, custom fitted to flatter her daughter's elegant and mature physique, donned faux-diamond buttons encircled with white pearls. Her ornamented shoes would be four-inch-high sandals with heels lined in her suit's fabric.

Around her neck, Juliette would be wearing her platinum necklace, the one given to her by Constance's mother, Madam Beatrice. The pendant fashioned prongs which mounted an exquisite two carat, three dimensional heart-shaped diamond in its center. Her earrings would be large pearls with a linear drop of diamonds.

Juliette's image would be stellar.

Pearls symbolized incorruptibility while diamonds reflected purity. And periwinkle blue connoted calmness and everlasting love. Not to mention, the color matched Juliette's eyes.

Image earns crowns.

Constance preferred this rule over her own mother's *beauty is everything* and *good breeding and wealth are paramount.*

There were implications to Beatrice Reyes's adages that felt harsh. For instance, if Constance had not been blessed with jet black hair, green eyes, high cheek bones, a long neck, and a tall shapely stature, would she have been *nothing?* If her deceased father, with an impeccable pedigree, had not been the sole heir to a filthy rich aristocrat from Spain, would his only daughter, Constance Isabel, have been *nothing?*

Despite being at odds with several of her deceased mother's philosophies, Constance proudly admitted she had adopted her mother's fierce determination to control every detail, impression, and dramatic moment she could.

Which meant, Constance was concerned about that which she could *not* control. Namely, how her daughter would respond to interview inquiries on the fly.

Sure, Juliette answered random questions in competitions all the time, but everyone knew the types of questions pageant hosts asked: *What makes you different from other teens in this competition? How would you dispel the negative image associated with pageantry? How would you make the world a better place?* All standard fare.

Today's interview presented a higher risk.

The interviewer, also the editor of *Beauty World,* had a daughter who participated in the same pageantry circuit as Juliette. Of course, Juliette consistently outperformed Lila.

Hopefully, Victoria Scarborough would consider the negative consequences of trying to embarrass Juliette during the interview. There would be extreme backlash if Victoria attempted to make

Juliette appear unworthy as the 2027 National Miss Junior Teen crown holder. Extreme backlash, indeed.

Constance's husband strolled into the sunroom, heading straight to the brewing machine. After placing his tall Washington Nationals mug on the tray, Finn would press French roast, black, like he always did, even though there were 18 options.

After 21 years together, 16 of them married, she could recite every move in his routine. Then again, he was habitually predictable.

"Good morning, darling," she cooed.

He continued to concentrate on the selection panel as if he had never seen it before. Finally, he pressed start and turned toward her. "You said something?"

Constance rarely repeated herself. Doing so would deprive a poor listener from developing incentivized self-discipline.

"What time did you come to bed?" she asked instead, already knowing the time, but wanting to gauge his honesty.

"Two-ish, I guess."

Precisely 2:17 a.m., which was close enough to forgo a correction.

She stared at him for a moment. He was still delicious eye candy. His premature silver hair made his blue eyes radiant. At 39, clean cut Finley Charles Parker was as gorgeous as when she had met him at a high school football game. His officer uniform and array of weaponry wrapped around his waist only accentuated his attractiveness and strength, but they could not compensate for his growing lack of interest in *her*.

His aloofness was insulting.

Not only had the fountain of youth blessed Constance, her Glitz and Glamour Estate was *her* nest egg. She paid for everything in their upscale world. Absolutely everything. In fact, if they had been living off *his* pitiful salary, no doubt they would be struggling to pay a mortgage on a middleclass rancher. In a freaking neighborhood. Driving an American-made station wagon. Please.

The least her pampered Finn could do was *act* interested.

Constance heard the pantry door open, followed by sandals clicking on the floors.

Juliette came into view, pausing under the walnut beam accentuating the sunroom's entrance. As if rehearsed, her daughter performed a slow pirouette, giving Constance time to inspect her.

Finn's face brightened. "My God! You're gorgeous, Jules!"

All details conformed to Constance's instructions, except for her daughter's brown hair.

"I thought we had agreed on wearing your hair down," Constance questioned, refusing to mimic her husband's sappy tail wagging.

"My hair *is* down. I just used a barrette for my long bangs."

"You made this decision on your own…because?"

"Although my loose hair projects openness like you said," Juliette explained, "I wanted to avoid flicking my bangs from my eyes while on camera. That would look sloppy. Which might lead viewers into thinking my answers are just as haphazard as my hairstyle."

Constance smiled. Her daughter was anticipating reactions, a skill which beauty contestants should never underrate. At that moment, she felt enormous pride.

"Ease up, Connie," Finn snarled at her. "Let our daughter be a kid and wear her hair the way she wants, for God sakes. She's only fifteen."

"So she can forever mirror her father?" Constance snapped. "A child at nearly forty?"

He briefly closed his eyes and shook his head. His way of telling her to shut up.

Juliette sat at the table and scooped fresh fruit onto her plate.

"Did you remember your crown and inhaler?" Constance asked her daughter.

"My crown is in its case, ready to go. My inhaler's in my purse."

Constance glanced at her smartwatch: 7:05 a.m. Her personal assistant was late. Again.

Stepping into the room, Chef Evelyn looked half-baked as always. She was topped with stringy blonde hair, boasted a belly resembling rising dough, and wore her pristine whites—the buttons barely able to contain her plumping breasts.

"Excuse me, Ma'am," Chef Evelyn started. "Is there anything else I can serve you for breakfast?"

"No, thank you," Constance answered. "However, in the future, please remember that when we must attend an obligation, French toast is not appropriate. Syrup stains."

"Of course. I apologize." She nodded her head as she turned toward the kitchen.

Like a messy whirlwind, Mindi raced into the sunroom, practically tackling the chef. "Forgive me, Constance," she said, in between breaths. "Traffic was horrendous."

Most police detectives were hard to read. Not her husband. His eyes widened in disbelief at Mindi's traffic comment since they lived in rural Hickory Thicket. Heavy traffic might constitute a flock of Canadian geese waddling across the narrow lanes of Eastern Neck Road while horns honked to hurry the feathered stragglers along.

At any rate, Constance appreciated that Mindi had tried to steer her audience into a particular direction, albeit with a pitiful white lie.

The verdict was still out on her assistant, but in some ways, the recent college graduate reminded Constance of her youthful self. With long black hair, Mindi even looked a bit like Constance, though her assistant's eyes were wheat colored and her height was three inches shorter than Constance's five-nine.

"What is in your hand?" Constance asked, eyeing the brown paper bag Mindi held.

"Oh." She stretched her arm in Finn's direction, clutching the top fold of the bag. "I made brownies last night and remembered how much Mr. Parker enjoys them. These are for him."

"How very, utterly thoughtful of you, Mindi." She glared at her husband. "What do you have to say in response to such a deliciously lovely gesture, darling?"

Finn took the bag from her assistant. "Yes. Very thoughtful. Thank you."

Could Mindi have an infatuation with her husband? Constance would have to pay attention.

Her personal assistant sat down at the table and loaded French toast onto her plate, smothering it with syrup. Mindi Maxwell still had a lot to learn.

"Juliette Annabella," Constance began, knowing the addition of her middle name would signify to her daughter that she meant business. In fact, she had waited to broach what she was about to say until Mindi was present, since her personal assistant was the information's source.

"Yes, Mother?"

"Did you get enough sleep last night?"

"I did."

"Were you aware that a dinner knife has been missing from our collection? For several days?"

7

FINN HOLSTERED WEAPONS on his tactical duty belt. In comparison, his wife's words were her ordnance and she packed high caliber artillery, 24/7. Discharging rounds as if shooting at a firing range, Connie didn't hesitate to wound anyone landing in her sights.

Worse, she possessed an endless supply of ammo.

As Finn stood by the bay windows beside the sunroom's dining table, gazing out at the Chesapeake, he listened to his wife take aim at their daughter. His temperature rose. From his experience, Connie wasn't making idle chit chat with Jules about a freaking dinner knife gone missing. His wife had a purpose to her question.

She always had a purpose.

"You could buy an entire flatware manufacturer if you wanted to," Finn interrupted, before his daughter could answer. "Why don't you cut out the drama and make your point?"

With narrowing eyes, Connie's face flushed crimson. Maybe his comment had gone too far, and he was about to regret his boldness.

"It's okay, Dad," Jules said, intervening and looking so mature for a teenager. She turned her gaze from him to his wife who sat across from her at the table. "How can a knife be missing when the cutlery in question is in my loft?"

"And why, pray tell, would a dinner knife be in your sleeping quarters?" Connie asked.

"Two reasons, I suppose. First, you insist that I eat dinner in my loft. At least you equip me with all the necessary cutleries. Thank you for that, Mother."

Finn jerked his head toward Connie, narrowing his eyes to make sure she understood his accusation. Was she still isolating Jules in her bedroom? Making her eat dinner alone?

Given he had added the nightshift at the station, parttime—anything to earn extra cash and to minimize the time he had to spend on the estate, his loaded schedule made it difficult to monitor the situation at the homestead. However, his demands had been crystal clear: His wife was not to treat Jules like a fashion doll, like a possession which she could lock up at night when playtime was over. Christ Almighty. His daughter was a living, breathing teenager!

He sighed, feeling defeated.

What had made him think Connie would've listened this time?

She never did.

In his heart of hearts, Finn knew that he should broach the subject again, that he should put his foot down. Now was not the time. Soon, though. He'd get the nerve…soon.

"And second," Jules continued, eyeing her mother's personal assistant, "Mindi takes away my tray, including my utensils. I think you refer to this, Mother, as shared responsibility."

Finn couldn't help smiling. If his wife's mouth was her weapon, his daughter's skin was a bullet proof suit—impenetrable; add to that her astuteness which served as a deflective shield. Nothing seemed to rock Jules emotionally. If it did, she never let on. She was always the unflappable one in any situation. Fearless in her resolve. Consistently the adult in the room.

Mindi lifted her face from the sweet pull of her French toast, looking shocked at the implication that she was, in fact, partially culpable for the misplaced knife.

"I…I…," she stumbled, licking the lingering syrup from the corner of her mouth. "I'll count the silverware from now on. Before leaving the loft."

Mindi had clearly ratted on Jules, as if his daughter had some sinister reason for keeping a dull dinner knife. Connie's assistant obviously thought snitching would help her suck up to his wife.

"Excellent." Connie placed her linen napkin down by her place setting. "I suppose this matter should be resolved at another time, since my intention was not to sour our morning."

Too late. The morning already tasted like straight lemon juice.

Bottomline, Finn lived in Crazy-town, pure and simple.

Not for long, though.

The white lie that his and Connie's marriage was smooth sailing was about to crash into the rocks for all to witness. His *real* truth was in Chestertown where he had secretly put a 20-percent down payment on a riverfront condo, purchased in Jules's name (though his daughter wasn't aware), with him as her custodian. He would never touch his daughter's banking accounts and investments which were stockpiling all her pageantry winnings, not that he even could, since none of her assets included his name as a co-signer. However, her stash of money was all the collateral the condo association and bank lender needed to ensure that "she" could pay "her" monthly mortgage.

Paperwork had been a breeze. Finn knew how to forge Jules's signature and a notary worked at the police station. Besides, he had signed most of the documents online.

To his surprise, mortgage fraud wasn't that difficult, but Finn was no criminal. He harbored no mal intent. These were the lengths required to keep his plans under the radar.

Thankfully, Connie wouldn't be monitoring the filing of settlement papers associated with their daughter, as she'd never expect it. Liquid assets and investments would have been another story; his wife (as Jules's sole financial custodian) monitored them all.

Finn pushed aside any guilt he might have felt, given he was using his daughter's success for his own benefit. He believed she would understand. Jules wanted him to be happy. He simply couldn't risk her disapproval or worse, having her tell her mother.

Until his situation leveled out, he was confident Jules wouldn't find out. It wasn't like she had access to the Internet. Virtually or in the flesh, Jules remained "offline."

What she didn't know wouldn't hurt her.

Still, he couldn't deny that there were two hiccups in the process which elevated his risk that things might not go as planned.

Most obvious was that Finn had no clue how he'd make the condo's mortgage payments which started next month. A divorce wouldn't help. He had signed a prenup. One with teeth.

Secondly, he had to negotiate for the down payment and closing costs with an "underground" lender. The $75 grand came from a former high school acquaintance who had become a high-powered loan shark, charging a ridiculous 12-percent interest on the principal.

Finn had no other choice but to work with the asshole.

That's what someone *had* to do when married to a woman who controlled all the purse strings and had moles planted in every nook and cranny of the community.

There was no going back.

Finn had received his down-payment loan five days ago.

Anyway, he had finally let go of the sadness which used to overwhelm him every time he revisited memory lane, remembering the woman Connie used to be. The woman *before* she had inherited $617 million (three weeks prior to their wedding day) from her daddy who had spent most of his years in Europe rather than in the States where he "kept" his wife and child. Talk about parental distancing.

Connie was no longer the girl Finn had bumped into at a Kent County High School football game. Even though she was homeschooled, like Jules, she had attended the big Thanksgiving rivalry game with her only friend, Deanna Mae Anderson, who had grown up two estates down from her in Rock Hall. Not looking where she was going, Connie bumped into him on the stadium steps, sending his popcorn into the laps of onlookers.

When she had smiled at him—with an angelic innocence, his future flashed in his mind. In every frame, he saw Connie standing beside him. However, *beside* wasn't how his dream had materialized. More like Connie led him by a pronged choke collar hooked to a short leash. Who would've known the word *partnership* was missing from his wife's extensive vocabulary?

Finn snapped out of his preoccupation with "All Things Constance," noticing Mindi's empathetic eyes staring at him—wide and concerned. Her expression conveyed that she, too, felt his pain; required, as they both were, to endure the Queen Mother.

Really? What was Mindi, 22 or 23? Employed by Connie for a

mere month? How could Mindi understand a damn thing?

She locked eyes with him.

Wait.

Could her expression be one of interest? Like, *let's get together and share horror stories?* He couldn't read her, except to acknowledge that her vibes were sending mixed signals. On the one hand, Mindi had tried to get Jules in trouble. Bad move if she had hoped to impress him. On the other hand, she had brought extra brownies to the house…just for him. Interesting.

That, and she couldn't take her eyes off him.

Maybe women would still find him attractive. Wasn't like he hadn't *been* with other women; but it was different when the one-nighters came with a price tag, and he had to pay up.

A spark of excitement ignited within him. But only for a second.

He had his own "rules" to abide by. Rules like: *Where there's a spark, there's fire.*

Truth was, Finn had become a cop to keep sparks from igniting into something bigger, into something ugly, where people got hurt. Even killed.

He recalled his Mom's warning about Connie: *Remember son, 'hell hath no fury like a woman scorned.' Especially if the fiery scorn should come from a woman like Constance.*

Fiery was right.

Perhaps Finn should've become a firefighter.

8

Saturday, August 14, 2027
Beauty World Headquarters: Washington, D.C.
(One Day *before* Juliette's Death)

AFTER THE PHOTO shoot, Jules took her place on the stage where a television crew would be filming her *Beauty World* interview. Sitting in a chair, she followed instructions as a makeup artist lightly powdered her forehead and a stylist adjusted her intricately ornamented silver crown, reclipping the headpiece onto her hair.

Jules glanced around the studio. Mother was nowhere in sight. She had left to track down the production manager to demand that he lower the stage's temperature, fearful that the overhead lighting would make Jules perspire once filming started. In addition, she had told Jules that it was highly irregular not to have an idea, immediately prior to going live, about the questions the interviewer would ask. *Unacceptable,* Mother had snarled before storming off.

On a more pleasant note, the studio platform was quite homey, featuring two Victorian chairs upholstered in gray velvet, angled toward each other. A coffee table stood in between the chairs and potted tropical plants flanked each end of the half circle.

Jules was surprised Mrs. Scarborough had not taken her seat during the touchup session. Usually, an interviewer sat and stimulated small talk to break the ice, making sure their guest felt comfortable before broadcasting began. But Mrs. Scarborough wasn't around.

"Five-minute warning," the lead videographer announced.

The makeup artist and hair stylist collected their supplies and walked off the stage.

Scanning the studio again, Jules hoped to spot Mother who always gave her a thumbs up prior to any event or competition. However, she continued to be a no show in the audience apron—the chairs positioned in front and around the sides of the stage. She also wasn't standing beside one of the many curtains decorating the stage's periphery. Strange.

"Two minutes and counting."

Jules stood, planning to find out where Mother was. Where the interviewer was.

"Please stay seated, Miss Parker," the cameraman said. "We're in countdown mode."

"I don't even have an interviewer!" she countered, her heart accelerating.

At that moment, Mrs. Scarborough flounced across the stage, outfitted in a lime-green dress that no one, not even an alien on Mars, could've ignored. And her exposed cleavage was as deep as a Himalayan gorge. So much for Jules being the focal point.

Stay composed, Jules urged herself, sitting down again. *Let others sweat.*

Mrs. Scarborough lowered herself in the chair, crossing her legs.

"Are you nervous?" she asked Jules.

The videographer gave the one-minute warning as she contemplated the oddness of Mrs. Scarborough's greeting, if one could call it that.

"Should I be?"

With a wicked smile, Mrs. Scarborough whispered, "Only if you are vulnerable, my dear." She raised her pencil thin eyebrows and then winked.

The 10-second countdown was underway. Jules took a deep breath, reminding herself to focus, stay calm, and collect herself. Most of all, to exude that she was enjoying herself.

"Three, two, one," said the cameraman, pointing his finger that they were now live.

After a cheery introduction, coupled with an unenthusiastic mention that Jules was the 2027 champion in her age category, the questions began.

"Your mother has earned many top beauty titles," Mrs. Scarborough started. "Did she influence you to participate in pageantry?"

Jules smiled, displaying maximum lip-curl since she was prepared for the question. She breezed through the answer, making sure her flattery of *the* Constance Parker landed at the level of Nobel Prize for Mother of the Year.

The topic of earnings was next. Mrs. Scarborough mentioned Jules's first national victory as a two-year-old, when she had won $50 thousand. "Your winnings continue to be lucrative twelve years later," Mrs. Scarborough noted, with an edge to her voice. "Why, just last month, a panel of judges crowned you as the top junior teen in the nation. Congratulations are in order!"

"Thank you so much, Mrs. Scarborough. Being National Miss Junior Teen is an incredible honor. I hope to inspire other girls and young women to embrace pageantry. The experience is a wonderful springboard; your name and title can advance causes that will make the world a better place."

Mrs. Scarborough paused long enough that the silence felt unnatural.

Jules wondered if her answer had been sufficient.

Leaning closer to her, Mrs. Scarborough unleashed another question, one loaded with negative implications. "Were you aware that your mother went to college with one of the judges who scored your performances in Florida? At the competition? Or was their relationship intended to be hidden from the public?"

Jules's emotions leapt from slightly uncomfortable to full blown anxiety. She fisted her hands—maybe the camera wouldn't notice. Taking a breath, she also hoped that suppressing her stress wouldn't kickstart an asthma attack. Her purse and inhaler were in the green room.

What Jules *wanted* to say was that Mrs. Scarborough had bushels of her own dirty secrets. She was the mother of Lila, the runner-up at the same junior teen competition. Many people didn't know Lila Lovelace was Mrs. Scarborough's daughter because of Lila's stage name. In addition, Lila had contracted a hired handler instead of her mother. But Jules knew.

Mrs. Scarborough was a hypocrite. She was no different than Jules's mother; they both flaunted their clout to influence others. Clearly, Lila's mother was using her position at *Beauty World* and as an interviewer to attempt to sway the audience into thinking that Jules hadn't earned her crown ethically. That bias had resulted in elevated scores.

Emote positivity; suppress negativity.

"As a beauty pageant icon, Mrs. Scarborough," Jules said, smiling and trying to regain her composure, "Mother knows many wonderful people, both nationally and internationally. Some, she's even shared the same campus with, like at Cornell University which enrolls twenty-five thousand students annually."

Jules teetered on the line between cordial and defensive.

Thank goodness she spotted Mother at last, sitting in the front row. Imperceptible to others, Mother slightly shook her head. Jules interpreted that to mean she should respond in general terms to the personal attack. *Defend the forest, not the bark.*

"Thank you for raising the issue of connections, however," Jules said. "If competition rules forbade judges from knowing *anyone* in the pageantry world, including attending the same college campus, judges might not understand what it means to be beautiful on the inside and out.

"Hopefully," Jules continued, "most people agree with me that interpersonal connections are extremely important to pageantry and can occur without giving rise to bias in contestant scoring. Connections, for example, have enabled my mother, and other beauty matriarchs—perhaps you as well, to raise tremendous amounts of money for important causes such as United Way, the March of Dimes, Mothers Against Drunk Driving, and the like."

"Yes, I suppose."

Mrs. Scarborough's eyes narrowed. Her attack wasn't over.

"Speaking of important causes," she said, "you are a teen spokesperson for the Humane Society. Mercy me! Cats and dogs must be racing up and down the halls of your home! How many pets have you personally adopted?"

Lila. Lila knew Jules didn't have any rescues. Mother wouldn't allow pets. Lila must have told Mrs. Scarborough to use this fact against her, but it didn't make sense. Lila was a teen spokesperson for the American Cancer Society, and it wasn't like *she* had to have cancer in order to raise money to help wipe out the disease.

If only Jules could defend herself by making this point about Lila, but she couldn't. She'd come off as argumentative. Sassy. Disrespectful. And that wouldn't please Queen Mother.

Instead, Jules internalized her frustration, making her hands shake. Her chest tightened and she felt her first wheeze.

Jules remembered: *Answer the question you wish you were asked.*

"Yes, I am a proud spokesperson for the Humane Society," Jules said. "We must reduce the number of unwanted animals by promoting the importance of spaying and neutering. Did you know that between six and eight million cats and dogs are taken to shelters each year?"

Jules looked straight into the camera. "In addition, we have to strengthen laws against animal cruelty, holding those who would hurt or neglect animals responsible for their actions. Please visit the Humane Society website if you would like to adopt, help, or donate. Together, we can make a better life for our most vulnerable furry friends."

"Once again, Juliette, you have provided a perfect segue," Mrs. Scarborough said.

Bringing her bent arm to her mouth, Jules coughed, trying to open her airway. She locked eyes with Mother, long enough to convey she was in trouble.

"Humans are vulnerable as well," Mrs. Scarborough said. "For example, I understand you suffer from insomnia. How do you manage such a dreadful affliction? Drugs? Medicinal marijuana, perhaps?"

Jules had also told Lila about her struggle with sleep, though she hadn't intended the information for public consumption. Thank goodness she had never mentioned her *stea*.

"Insomnia is a sleeping disorder which affects one in four Americans," Jules said, beginning to feel lightheaded. Beads of sweat had formed on her forehead. She resisted drawing attention to the moisture by wiping it away. "I meditate and..."

Jules attempted a shallow breath.

"Are you all right, Juliette?" Mrs. Scarborough asked. "You're looking quite pale."

Sounds became muffled and Jules felt as though she were drowning. Sinking in an abyss.

As everything blurred, one thing was clear: The rules existed for predictable environments governed by strict regulations, like a pageant competition. Jules's epiphany was that the untamed *real world* was more indicative of Mrs. Scarborough, where people wielded personal agendas and trampled others to reach their goals. In a predatory culture, the rules were as worthless as politely asking a starved mountain lion to find food elsewhere.

Jules gasped for air, but none filled her lungs. She slumped onto the floor.

Her crown toppled off her head.

Weird how she pictured her pants suit, grateful she wasn't wearing a dress.

She tried to blink, not knowing if she had. Her brain was hiccupping. Shorting out.

What had she been thinking about anyway?

The rules. That's right. She had been evaluating their worth…or lack of it.

All the rules did was make her look fine on the outside. Temporarily at best, because on the inside, her body was attacking itself. That's what hiding one's emotions did. Made a person sick with ailments like insomnia, depression, and stress induced asthma.

If she survived, she would change somehow.

Darkness swallowed her before she could figure out *how*.

9

TRUITT SAT WITH his parents at the table in their kitchen nook, overlooking the cobalt blue of the Chesapeake. The reflection of the afternoon sun glistened off the bay's choppy surface. Frothy foam collected on their private beach. Even from inside, he could hear their American flag, clipped to a backyard pole, thrashing in the wind.

Lunch was a simple salad topped with grilled chicken breasts. His place setting was empty. Not hungry. Hard to believe, since during football season, he had always been ravenous, starved for proteins and carbs: breakfast, lunch, and dinner. With snacks in between.

At a quarter past one, Truitt wondered how Jules was doing in her televised interview.

In last night's fog and darkness, he couldn't tell her age, but he guessed she was younger than him. That was fine. Truitt couldn't handle being interested in a girl right now, even one as pretty and sassy as Jules Parker. But a friend? That piqued his interest.

He was over being lonely. Tired of being down in the dumps.

Jules might be the positive catalyst he needed.

The next time he saw her, which he hoped would be that night, maybe she'd agree on his suggestion to take a dip in the bay—in darkness, adding to the adventure. Living by the water, she *had* to know how to swim. After all, her parents had a large, inviting lap pool in their patio area.

If swimming didn't interest her, maybe they could walk on the beach by moonlight, looking for pieces of polished glass that had washed up on shore.

Truitt rubbed his neck.

Was it his imagination, or was his injury getting worse? Even his cheek hurt.

"I'm so cold in this house and it's August," his Mom said, putting down her fork. "Maybe we should've stayed in Bishopville. I miss the warmth of our home."

Truitt wasn't going to argue.

"You have to get acclimated to the moisture in the air, Abby," his Dad countered. "We're right on the water here. Give the place time. It's only been two weeks."

Not only that, but warmth was within reach.

"This problem I can solve," Truitt said. "It's way warmer outside than inside." He got up from his chair. "Here. Fresh air will take away the chill."

Unlatching the window was a huge mistake. A gust blew it open, slamming the panel into another glass pane.

Somehow the glass remained intact.

With the crash, his Mom nearly bolted from her chair, pale and trembling. Her eyes widened and her mouth opened as if she might scream. She was so edgy. Thankfully, his Dad placed his hand on hers to calm her, while urging her to remain at the table.

"Relax, Mom," Truitt echoed, recognizing that his mother was experiencing her own emotional funk. "I didn't mean for that to happen. Sorry."

"Everything's fine," his Dad added.

After shutting the window and securing the latch, Truitt sat back down at the table.

"You have to forgive us, son," his Mom pleaded, tears racing down her cheeks. "We feel such guilt about everything. Including moving here. Moving away from your friends, from football. We thought a new start would help us, but we know you're having trouble with our decision."

"Don't cry, Mom," he said, his heart aching from her confession. "For as long as I can remember, you've always put *me* before anything else." He shrugged his shoulders. "Let's face it; I haven't been the easiest kid. So now it's your turn. And you and Dad are doing better here."

"Truth is, the move isn't working out as we'd hoped," his Dad admitted, his head drooped forward.

Truitt tried not to let his thoughts surface, but he couldn't help thinking that maybe his parents should've analyzed the pros and cons of moving to HT before the ball snapped into play.

Regardless, he had to convince them he was adjusting to the move. For sure, that would help his Mom.

"Listen," Truitt said. "Last night, I met a girl who lives next door. She seems nice and might even hang out with me. With a friend, I'll bounce back. No worries."

"We love you," his Mom said. "Always and forever."

"Back at you." He smiled.

Truitt would've considered the conversation a breakthrough, except his parents still weren't looking him in the eye. Not since moving to HT.

Guilt was a bitch.

10

Saturday, August 14, 2027
Driving from Washington, D.C. to Hickory Thicket, Maryland
(One Day *before* Juliette's Death)

JULES RESTED HER head on Mother's lap in the rear seat of their Maserati Quattroporte sedan, as Mindi drove them back home from Washington D.C. and the disastrous *Beauty World* interview which had been broadcasted on live television.

According to Mother, after rolling the fallen Jules onto her side, she was able to administer her daughter's bronchodilator (via her inhaler) to help open her airways.

Cameras had kept rolling.

The experience was surreal. Not the asthma attack. Or the fact that videographers had recorded her near-death experience for all to witness. No, surreal was the fact that Mother was now running her fingers through Jules's hair while Mindi chauffeured. Since Mother was seldom nurturing, Jules never wanted the moment to end.

"Are you able to sit up, Juliette?" Mother asked abruptly. "My silk skirt is horribly wrinkled."

At least Jules would always cherish the brief display of affection.

"Sure." She raised herself and straightened her hair. "Please be honest. Will I be the laughingstock of TBC and *Beauty World?*"

"Heavens no! You have solidified your reign as the nation's darling of pageantry." Mother ran her palms over her royal blue pencil-skirt, trying to smooth creases. "Victoria hurled insults at you like Goliath, even bullying you into an asthma attack, but you turned the tables, killing *her* with kindness. Well done, Juliette." She glanced up from her skirt, locking eyes with her. "You are royalty through and through. A queen, *naturel.*"

"My attack wasn't *staged,* Mother."

"I am well aware. The optics, however, are worth celebrating, especially since they unfolded authentically."

"And the fact that I didn't *die?* Is that worth anything? Perhaps a measly high five?"

"No need to introduce sarcasm into our analysis, Juliette."

Turning her head toward her side window, Jules watched the landscape blur by, blinking hard to fight back tears. She felt like a stage prop used to advance everyone else's goals. Mother, Mrs. Scarborough—they were all the same: users.

What had shocked Jules most was Mrs. Scarborough's visceral conviction to hurt her publicly. It didn't seem to matter that Jules was just a kid. A teenager. Or that in Jules's mind, pageantry was similar to an innocent hobby like horseback riding, tennis, or painting. One, that she didn't even choose for herself or wholeheartedly enjoy.

Then again, most hobbies probably didn't earn significant money. Maybe earnings were the factor that had put her on a collision course with the Scarboroughs.

The outside world clearly did not know Jules at all. They only saw the optics, as Mother had mentioned. Underneath the façade, however, Jules was more than a stage prop or an actress playing a role for an audience. More than monotonous rules. *More* than Mother's vision of her as a beauty queen, continuing the Miss America legacy of *the* Constance Parker.

"Dollar for your thoughts," Mother probed.

"Don't you mean *penny* for your thoughts?"

"Raise the bar. Dream bigger, Juliette."

Conversation rarely strayed far from one rule or another. Did every household obsess over rules, or was that just hers?

She reached inside her purse and retrieved her inhaler. Placing her lips around the mouthpiece, she pressed down on the canister, sucking in the aerosol and holding her breath.

"A response?" Mother pressed. "I will not repeat my inquiry."

Jules exhaled, already feeling relief from her tightening chest. "I was thinking how scary Mrs. Scarborough was when she looked into my eyes during the interview. I saw daggers, as if she hated me. As if she wouldn't mind if I were dead."

"What Victoria *hates* is that her precious Lila consistently underperforms—always the bridesmaid, never the bride." Mother held her hands above her lap, inspecting her nail extensions. "Victoria Scarborough relies on her daughter's winnings to sustain her lifestyle now that she is divorced. Ironically, if Lila died, she might easily be able to do just that."

"What does *that* mean?"

Even Mindi glanced at them in the rearview mirror.

"Life insurance, of course," Mother stated, matter of fact.

"I have no clue what life insurance is," Jules said.

"Quite simple, really. A life insurance policy allows beneficiaries to cover their living expenses in the event that a wage earner in their family dies. Some policies are in the millions."

"Do you and Mr. Parker have a life insurance policy on Jules?" Mindi asked.

"Hello!" Jules raised her hands for emphasis. "I'm right here. Very much alive."

Mother patted her leg. "Nothing personal, Juliette. This is business." She gazed ahead at the rearview mirror. "Life insurance is precautionary, and may I add, completely customary in pageantry. Yes, we do have a policy. Finn and I would be foolish not to."

"Shouldn't you be putting energy into keeping me *alive?*" Jules felt like she might need another hit of albuterol. "You know, instead of making sure you'd benefit from my death?"

"You are not going anywhere, Juliette Annabella. Your work is far from over."

Was Mother going for…heartwarming?

"Now in reference to Victoria Scarborough," Mother continued. "Never doubt my tenacity. She will regret her attempt to make you look less than stellar on national television. No one, especially not *that* cheaply augmented, poorly Botox-ed, lime-green fruit of a woman, will best you or Constance Isabel Reyes Parker."

Whenever Mother referenced herself in third person, using her full name, someone was about to pay. Dearly.

11

Saturday, August 14, 2027
The Parkers' G&G Estate: Hickory Thicket, Maryland
(One Day *before* Juliette's Death)

FINN STARED AT his email inbox with utter disbelief.

His life was turning into a shitshow without toilet paper.

The orange and pink sunset had teased him into thinking he'd have an enjoyable evening. Connie, Jules, and Mindi had stopped for dinner on their way home from D.C. For once, he was home alone, absent the acrid atmosphere of embittered spouses competing for the same oxygen. In his book, a celebration was in order.

After opening a bottle of reserve Cabernet—the good stuff, he had lounged in an Adirondack chair on the lawn edging the beach. Watching barges navigate up and down the channel, he had savored the tannins in the wine as they warmed his veins.

Being on the precipice of his new life tasted divine.

However, the wine's bold richness turned to vinegar after he had entered the house at nightfall, deciding to check his office computer for new emails.

Un-fucking believable.

His loan shark had sent him three identical messages, precisely 10 minutes apart, as if he required a response to stop the annoying bombardment.

Forget the wine glass. Finn raised the bottle to his lips and guzzled the Cab.

The email read:

Finn,

Change of plans. For business reasons, I'm recalling my loan of $75k. Sorry man. These hiccups happen. This may pose a hardship for you, so I'm agreeable to the following: Drop off half ($37.5k) in a certified check on Monday, August 16. The balance is due on the 23rd. I'll reduce interest from 12% to 8% (or $6k) due to the recall. (Add the interest to your payment on the 23rd.)

Hey, don't be late. The shark in loan shark is there for a reason. LOL.

Rip Riley

So much for a high school acquaintance helping out a fellow classmate. Bottomline, Finn was beginning to hate rich people. Connie had inherited all of her fortune, yet she greedily held on to every dime as if she had worked her fingers to the bone, earning the wealth herself. On the other hand, Rip had actually labored for his prosperity. Unfortunately, his success was on the backs of financially desperate people, and he made no apologies for it.

The computer pinged and Finn nearly jumped out of his skin. Another email. The exact message he had first received a half hour ago. What the hell was he going to do?

In Finn's limited arsenal, the only option he could afford was calling Rip.

He used Rip's number to Skype him on his office computer, since it had a large monitor. Finn was confident he'd accept his request. After all, Rip gave the strictest fidelity to his money.

"Hey," Rip said. "I gather you saw my emails. I know the news sucks. Sorry, man."

For being a prick, Ripley Riley was attractive—the rugged model type. No doubt, his good looks drove his clientele into agreeing to any terms he dished out.

Upon meeting Rip, the first topic of conversation usually involved his name and why his parents had chosen it. Rip never hesitated disclosing that Maine's Ripley Rock near Kennebunk Beach was where his parents had conceived him. He delivered the story using his hook—his larger than life smile.

Romantics probably pictured a blanket spread out on a smooth flat rock, complete with a picnic basket of cheeses and fine wine. Not at all Finn's image. He pictured a jagged boulder covered in poison ivy, with seagulls flying overhead—squawking and laughing as they prepared to empty their intestinal cargo on the two fools below who had overtaken their rocky perch.

"There's no way I can meet that timeline," Finn finally said. "I only received your cash five days ago. And the down payment on the condo was wired to the bank yesterday."

Rip's steel eyes narrowed. "Nonnegotiable. How you meet the new deadline is your business. Personally, I'd start by asking Constance for help. You could probably strike some sort of a deal with her. But truthfully? Your private haggling is of no interest to me. You're a cop. You know how this works. Deliver my check on Monday or suffer consequences."

"Is that a threat?"

"I'm a loan shark. Fairly certain your detective skills can figure out the answer."

"You'll get your money as soon as I can get it," he countered. "In terms of finding leverage over me, don't waste your time trying to intimidate me. I've got nothing that matters."

"Nothing?" Rip scratched his facial hair. "Lenders never loan money to people who have nothing to lose, Finn."

The asshole disconnected.

Of course, Finn did have things that mattered. One in particular: Jules. But Rip wasn't a hardcore criminal; he was simply a dick who blew hot air up his own filthy rich ass. He and Rip had gone to high school together for God sakes.

Still, he'd have to find a way to pay Rip back while keeping his condo under the radar. Hocking his opulent wedding band might be a good start. Anyway, detectives never wore diamond studded bands on duty, especially not bands with five carats worth of blue diamonds. While he was at it, maybe he'd throw in his cufflinks. They would bring in a pretty penny, too.

His chest tightened.

Taking another swig of the wine, Finn turned around and nearly choked on his mouthful.

Christ Almighty.

The groundskeeper was standing in the doorway, for how long he didn't know.

Had Garth overheard his conversation?

Seen his loan shark on the computer screen?

12

Saturday, August 14, 2027
The Parkers' G&G Estate: Hickory Thicket, Maryland
(One Day *before* Juliette's Death)

RICH PEOPLE ALWAYS harbored a secret or two…*thousand.* At times like these, Garth Harris didn't regret his adequately average income. Not one bit.

Garth didn't mean to sound negative. He was actually quite grateful for the nine years the Parkers had employed him as their groundskeeper. On the day after high school graduation, Mrs. Parker had called him. She knew a friend of a friend of a friend who had considered him a reliable handyman. His employment at an affluent summer camp on the Chester River had probably earned him the kudos. It was there he had maintained grounds and structures.

His job with the Parkers kept him on the straight and narrow. By that he meant, out of trouble. Garth had plans beyond the Glitz and Glamour Estate. He aspired to earn a college degree in business management and open a nursery someday. From his first day of work at the G&G to the present, he had never wavered from his goal. What earnings he hadn't spent on his truck or apartment rent in downtown Rock Hall, he had put away in a savings account.

According to his most recent calculations, this would be his last year with the Parkers. In the winter, he would enroll at Chesapeake College at the ripe age of 27.

Although Mrs. Parker gave the orders and paid him, he favored Mr. Parker's personality. The man was laid back and seemed to want his daughter to be a normal kid. But one thing bugged him: Mr. Parker ignored a lot of crap that went down at the homestead. What guy—a police officer, no less—would turn his back on his daughter when his whacked-out wife treated the girl no different from a possession, from a pretty dress-and-play doll?

What guy would act like nothing questionable was happening at the G&G?

Guess he could also call himself out on that one. The "doing nothing about it" part.

What was the expression? *It takes a village…to ignore crazy shit.*

Hopefully, the kid would turn out okay, but his latest orders suggested Mrs. Parker was diving deeper into the twisted, weedy world of cray-cray.

And she no longer stood alone on that special planet.

Based on the Skype conversation Garth had just witnessed on Mr. Parker's large computer monitor, positioned on a table behind his boss's formal desk, Mr. Parker was sinking into some deep shit himself. Why was he borrowing money from a loan shark when Mrs. Parker was rolling in dough? Could their marriage be on the rocks?

That would suck. Jules's troubles would get much worse with a split on the horizon.

If only the kid was 18, he'd get her out. At 15, though, taking her from her home would be kidnapping, even if she agreed to leave with him. Wasn't like Garth could call a Parker relative to give them the lowdown, to ask for help. The Parkers had none. The only other option would be to contact Social Services, and with the high and mighty, *that* would spark a media circus. No one would emerge without permanent scars.

Truth: In some situations, the only resolution was time.

Right?

Besides, it wasn't like his employers were beating their daughter.

In Garth's humble opinion, Jules would grow up and give them all the finger as she slammed the door behind her. Sayonara.

"Are you going to stand there forever?" Mr. Parker snapped. "What do you want?"

His boss never sounded curt. Had to be the red wine talking.

"Oh, sorry," Garth said, shifting weight from one leg to the other out of awkwardness. "Didn't want to interrupt while you were conferencing. But my toolbox. I left it in your office."

"Can't it wait until tomorrow, Garth? Why are you here so late?"

"Got a text from Mrs. Parker, from the road."

"What the hell does she want?"

"She's insisted I change Jules's bedroom lock from a doorknob mechanism to a deadbolt with a key. Also ordered me to install a barrel bolt on the outside of the door. I'm to complete both tonight. She was crystal clear."

Mr. Parker looked genuinely baffled. "Why the changes?"

"Apparently, Jules uses a dinner knife on the lock to sneak out at night."

"There it is," he said, mostly under his breath. "The freaking dinner knife saga."

"Excuse me?"

"Did Mrs. Parker mention why she thought Jules was sneaking out? I mean, it's not like there are any kids to hang out with."

"Your wife told me Mindi caught a glimpse of a teenaged boy running along the beach at night. He had come from next door. Had run onto this property before heading toward the water."

"Of course…Mindi."

"Anything else, sir?" Garth asked, hoping Mr. Parker would challenge the order.

"Isn't a deadbolt and barrel lock, installed on the *outside* of Jules's door, an even greater safety risk? In the event of a fire?"

Bingo! Reality was finally igniting inside the man's brain.

Garth nodded. "Give me the word and I won't do it. Maybe you could talk with Mrs. Parker and explain the dangers. Her request is a major code violation."

Mr. Parker stared at him in silence, clearly considering his suggestion.

"Let me ask you something, Garth. And be honest. Would *you* want to speak with my wife? Want to challenge her instructions?"

Garth knew where this was going. In fact, there had been something *else* he had wanted to tell Mr. Parker but wouldn't, in fear of his wife's wrath. "I'd prefer not to," he admitted.

"Then you understand my quandary." Mr. Parker rubbed his

temple as if trying to dispel the guilt of it all. "Wait. I have an idea. How about buying one of those roped fire escape ladders for her loft's window? Jules could keep the ladder hidden under her bed in case of an emergency."

Garth smiled. He hadn't thought of that. "Not sure they have one in the thirty-foot range. Do I have your permission to get one custom made?"

"Absolutely. I'll get you cash to pay for it."

Turning, Garth began to walk away, feeling relieved.

"Keep this *our* little secret," Mr. Parker called to him. "All of it," he added, no doubt referring to his earlier Skype call.

Yup, the rich always kept a secret or two...*thousand.*

13

Saturday, August 14, 2027
The Parkers' G&G Estate: Hickory Thicket, Maryland
(One Day *before* Juliette's Death)

JULES COULD NOT wait for the day to be over. What a nightmare. And now she had to wait to change into her nightgown and crawl under the sheets because Garth was adding new locks on the outside of her loft's door.

Her maternal warden always made countermoves to stay one step ahead. Not even Jules's near death experience eased her resolve.

Garth stopped tinkering.

Standing on the outside of her doorway, he motioned for her to join him on the staircase's landing. Sort of weird. Why not talk with her in her room?

When she stepped over the threshold, Garth closed the door, just short of shutting it. He raised his index finger to his lips and released an elongated *shhhhh*.

"Your mother will have my head if she finds out I've told anyone this," he whispered, "especially you. Promise not to rat on me?"

She nodded, wondering what additional fortifications Mother had insisted on.

"While you were gone today, your mother made me install a hidden video recorder in your bookcase. Second shelf, beside *Pride and Prejudice* to be exact. She only used to have a few cameras around the mansion. Now they seem to be everywhere."

"Seriously?" she mouthed.

"And the cameras capture audio, too," Garth explained. "Her command center is in her walk-in safe, the one behind the shoe rack in her wardrobe room. A computer is recording everything, twenty-four-seven."

If Jules ever had any doubts that she was a prisoner in her own home, the doubts were gone. She could no longer make excuses or deny her dire reality.

How would she survive in this hellhole until she was 18?

"Anyway, thought you should know," Garth continued. "She wants every nook and cranny under her watchful eyes. In fact, I'll be installing more cameras tomorrow afternoon, especially outside."

"*Outside?*" she asked softly. "I thought we already had security cameras outside."

"Only at the driveway's entrance gate and near the front door. Now your mother wants cameras in the pool area and throughout the garden." He looped his index finger in small circles near his temple, the universal sign for *she's out of her mind*. "I'm really sorry about all this."

"You're only doing your job. Don't worry about it."

"Not all my news is bad," he whispered. "Couldn't tell your Dad about the cameras, but I did mention the locks. Got permission to get you one of those fire-escape ladders. Have you seen them? They come rolled up. After you secure the handle hooks on your sill, you let the ladder fall to the ground. Voila! You climb down, safe."

Garth was the closest person she had to a friend.

"Thanks for thinking of my safety," she said.

"Actually, your father suggested the ladder."

That was a new one. Except for the few barbs Dad exchanged with Mother about what constituted acceptable parenting, her father was pretty much hands off. He wore blinders to limit his view, to make himself feel better by pretending everything was hunky dory.

"It's our secret then," Jules whispered, winking.

Garth twitched his eyebrows and chuckled. She knew exactly what he was going to say next, since he had created an adage that he liked to repeat with her.

"The rich," he said quietly, "always keep a secret or two…"

"*Thousand!*" they murmured in unison, silently laughing afterwards.

Ten minutes later, Garth finished installing the locks. "Anything I can get you before I, *umm,* lock the door?" he asked.

She shook her head and was grateful he would even ask.

Nodding, he closed and locked the door. *Click. Click.* She heard his footsteps descend the staircase. The light that had crept through the door sill became dark.

Flipping switches, she turned off the lights in her bedroom loft, bathroom, and walk-in closet. No way did she want the hidden camera to capture her changing. Besides, the partial moon cast enough light for her to see. She'd undress in the darkest of shadows.

Unlatching Nana Bea's heart necklace, she left the prized jewelry on top of her dresser. She'd return the heirloom to her wall safe tomorrow. Likewise, she didn't bother to place her silk pants suit in the dry-cleaning hamper, so she draped the ensemble over a chair.

Tomorrow.

After changing into her nightgown, she brushed her teeth in front of her vanity. Even in the dark, she could see the silhouette of the printed rules taped to her mirror. She eyed them with disdain. Had the rules lessened Mother's obsessive control? Protected her from people like Mrs. Scarborough? Prevented an asthma attack? Or helped her sleep? Were the rules getting Jules closer to being the person *she* wanted to be?

She despised the stupid rules, which she knew by heart.

1. Trust and obey your handler
2. Practice, practice, practice (the 3 P's)
3. Embrace your destiny (God made you with purpose)
4. Raise the bar for yourself (dream bigger)
5. Image earns crowns
6. Fear no one and no thing
7. Steady breathing cleanses the anxious soul
8. Emote positivity; suppress negativity
9. Make the unintentional seem intentional
10. Answer the question you wish you were asked
11. Sarcasm is ugly

12. Be whom others expect you to be

13. Avoid distractions

14. Ignore insults; never be contrary

15. Retribution is the job of your handler

16. Control the perception; control the outcome

17. White lies are the desired truth; use them wisely

18. The truth is in you; sharing it is a choice

19. Tears win every interview

20. Stay composed; let others sweat

21. Walk and talk like a queen (you are royalty)

22. Defend the forest, not the bark

23. Leave them wanting more

24. Leave a room the same or better than you found it

25. Sleep rejuvenates (slumber on your back)

Some rules made sense; Jules admitted that. But others were making her sick physically—especially, *be whom others expect you to be*. More than that, absolutely none of them had changed her circumstances from unbearable to normal. Not one!

Everything was getting worse.

Pulling the rules free from the tape on her mirror, she walked into her bedroom and tossed the sheet onto the floor. She didn't care if the camera captured her defiance. Of course, in the morning, she'd have to return the sheet back to its spot. She didn't want her hair pulled or her lower back pinched to bruise.

Mother was an expert at hiding the marks of "retribution."

Prior to turning in, Jules gazed out her window. Unlike the previous night, her view was crystal clear. The moon caused shadows from the trees to dance on the patio and grounds. At the same time, fireflies were holding an aerial party, showcasing their blinking sparklers as they twirled and fluttered in the breeze. The lights twinkled on Gibson Island.

"Hey!" Truitt waved his hands as he emerged from the pines. "Join me outside!"

Was he out of his mind? Her heartbeat was like a hummingbird's, and she couldn't help but look in the direction of the bookshelf. No doubt the lens was capturing footage.

Maneuvering her body so she was facing away from the camera, Jules raised her index finger to her lips. His wince indicated he understood.

Instead of calling to her, he waved his arm, urging her to come downstairs.

Holding her finger in front of her, she hoped he'd interpret she wanted a minute.

He scanned his surroundings to make sure no one had spotted him before nodding.

Jules needed to write down a message and get it to him.

The rules, printed on durable index paper, would work. Tomorrow, she'd formulate a white lie about what had happened to her bathroom copy.

In the dark, she picked up the sheet from the floor and took it to her table where she did schoolwork. Using a pen in the moonlight, she wrote on the back of the piece of paper:

Truitt,

Wish I had freedom like you. Then we could hang out tonight, but I can't. Maybe tomorrow?

Anyway, I have things to tell you. Secrets.

Soon,
Jules :)

Sharing secrets seemed like a good catalyst for friendship.

After making a paper airplane, Jules opened her window screen and held her plane in the launch position. She waited to receive a nod from Truitt, indicating he was ready.

When he bobbed his head, she released her airplane.

The wind carried it to the garden's entrance where it crash-landed.

Jogging over, Truitt retrieved her aircraft and unfolded the paper, reading her message. Giving her a thumbs up, he delivered a smile that made her stomach swoop and spiral as if she were riding a rollercoaster.

How lucky was she to finally have the opportunity for a real friend? One way or another, she'd figure out a way to see Truitt tomorrow.

Stuffing the plane into his hoody's pocket, he turned and grabbed the garden's iron gate. Smiling, he waved goodbye.

Jules tucked herself into bed, hoping sleep would arrive quickly and soundly. She actually felt excited about what tomorrow might bring.

Maybe Sunday would be a day she'd never forget.

Sometime past midnight, Jules's eyes flew open.

Her heart raced.

She gasped for air.

Flames were consuming her loft, creeping up her walls and crawling across her ceiling. The heat was blistering. Falling embers burned her skin.

Water began seeping in through cracks in the drywall. Such a relief. Until the seeping became *gushing*, resembling burst pipes or a breached dam.

The sheets tangled around her arms and legs like vines. The more she moved, the tighter they twisted. She held her breath. All the while, water filled her room, rising to the brim.

Even if she could've freed herself from the clutch of her linens, she couldn't have escaped anyway. Not without a window ladder.

Jules woke from her nightmare; perspiration soaked her sheets.

The last vision from her dream terrified her. The printed rules were the only things which had survived.

14

Sunday, August 15, 2027
Hidden Creek Trailer Park: New Yarmouth, Maryland
(Day *of* Juliette's Death)

BROCK NOLAN MISSED being somebody, the kind of somebody he had been in college lacrosse. Getting his ass tapped by teammates, his coach, and fans as they told him *good job* meant something. In addition, he had grown accustomed to eating in a special dining hall, served a hoity-toity meal that usually included a juicy steak. Most of all, he liked how girls didn't hesitate dishing out tasty treats when he was hungry for something other than food.

Too bad college athletes had to get good grades to stay eligible, even when they were consistently the team's MVP at matches. In high school, grades were easy to acquire. He had his ways. Not so much in college. His GPA had fallen to 1.5 or maybe a tad lower (statistics weren't his thing). His academic advisor was a bitch who had wanted to prove to the universe that one person, namely *her,* could play by the rulebook. She wanted to place him in a mandatory tutoring program, to be his heroine—the one who saved an underprivileged trailer-trash white kid from himself.

Yeah, right.

He dropped out.

Fuck Miss Goody Two Shoes. Fuck higher education.

As a former "middie" in lacrosse, he knew how to play both ends of the field—that's what midfielders did, with a do-or-die attitude.

If college was out, something else was in. One way or another, he

60

was going to matter.

Brock had hooked up with Constance Parker first. Not the kind of hook up he fantasized about because there was no denying she was sizzling hot, even at 39. In fact, if he was brutally honest, he wanted her bad. Real bad. And to get there, he'd do anything to please her.

She had a sweet spot for him, too. Initially, he called her Mrs. Parker but just last night, after her return from D.C., she closed the distance between them. As they stood by her pool at midnight, discussing her need-to-know about any street chatter involving her dickhead husband, she insisted he call her Constance. And as he was leaving, she even referred to him as *darling*.

Brock's father was the only person who knew he worked for the richest woman in the Rock Hall area. Thankfully, his Dad was a drunk who lived in the shabby trailer, two down from him. His old man wasn't going to spill the beans. No one wanted to talk to him anyway. And Brock had no plans of buying him more toothpaste. Poor hygiene was an insurance policy.

With his second employer, Brock had to watch his step to make sure he didn't mess up. Rip Riley seemed all nice and charming on the outside, but there was something about him that kept Brock on his toes. The man reminded him of a guy who patted and cooed over a cat and then the next day, poor kitty was floating in the pool. Maybe the cat hadn't purred to his liking.

As a private employee for both Constance and Rip, Brock ran errands, the type of errands they didn't want anyone else to know about. For example, he had followed Mindi Maxwell, Constance's personal assistant, three weeks prior to Constance hiring her, to make sure Mindi didn't have any skeletons that might make her ineligible for the job. The actual assignment was harder than the ask since Brock knew Mindi. They had "a thing" in high school.

Jobs for Rip were more high risk.

As a loan shark, Rip needed Brock to put the squeeze on clients who weren't paying up. Standard stuff mostly. In the dead of night, Brock slashed tires, broke into homes, tossed things around, and "relocated" pets—things like that. Rip had explained that getting physical with deadbeats was a last resort, but Brock assured him that all his boss had to do was ask.

As a former lacrosse player, Brock was "fast and furious," baby. Rigged out in a jacked 22-year-old body, he had absolutely nothing to lose. Nothing.

Both of his employers paid him enough, under the table, so he was able to move out of his Dad's hoarding heaven and buy his own double wide in Hidden Creek Trailer Park. And just last month, he had purchased a used F-250 truck with a super cab. His ride was badass, complete with offset wheels that stuck out below a healthy amount of tire clearance in the wheel wells. Basically, an athletic stance that warned everyone on the road to fuck off.

What made Brock chuckle, making him feel a bit superior if he was honest, was that Constance and Rip weren't aware that he worked for both of them. Each thought their connection to Brock was exclusive. How rich was that?

For the first time since his dual employments, he was going to share a tidbit of information from one employer to the other, strategically landing in Constance's good graces. Not that he wasn't already. Just that he was a greedy bastard who wanted...*more*.

See, Rip had given him a heads up that they might have to play hardball with Mr. Parker regarding a loan recall for some condo down payment. Bring it on. Not only did Brock hate cops, but he hated good looking po-po who were banging his cougar love-interest.

Brock could've mentioned the condo/loan situation to Constance last night, but he wanted to give her the impression he had worked for the info. Worked hard for it, just for *her*.

The time was 8:00 a.m. which was way early for Brock. Constance, however, was a morning person. Besides, she had given him the green light to contact her anytime, day or night.

On his cellphone, he wrote and sent a text:

Constance,

Stayed up late investigating. I've learned some info that might be of interest to you. Mr. Parker has put a down payment on a unit in Chestertown's Wilmer Park Condominiums, off South Cross Street.

Not sure what this means but thought you would want to know.

Brock

Brock could see on his phone that Constance had read his message. His heart raced thinking about how she might respect him more. Depend on him more. *Want* him more. After all, he was delivering on her request only eight hours after she had made it.

Proving his loyalty was his only mission. Truthfully, he'd turn over every stone for her.

Unfortunately, some hopes blew up on the runway before ever taking flight.

Old news, but thanks.

That was all Constance wrote.

Had to be a record for turning limp.

Constance hadn't even included his name. And how had she found out about the condo? She must have another mole.

Fucking-A.

He felt his temper ignite over his contempt for Mr. Parker. That cocksucker of a cop must have gotten the condo to take women there at lunchtime.

Brock's grandfather used to call that *afternoon delight.*

Pops always said that the best thing about lunch with Grams was he always got dessert afterwards. As a child, Brock walked in on them one time, wondering why they were eating dessert in the bedroom. Pops was eating all right, but it was a different kind of honey pie.

When it came to Brock's chances with Constance, he should've felt relief that Mr. Parker was eating more than glazed donuts. Instead, he felt pissed off, though he wasn't sure why. All he knew was he deserved respect. He was *somebody.* Somebody important.

If people didn't treat him right, they were going to be sorry.

15

Sunday, August 15, 2027
The Parkers' G&G Estate: Hickory Thicket, Maryland
(Day *of* Juliette's Death)

THE MORNING AFTER the *Beauty World* interview crisis, Mindi made sure she sat across from Finn at breakfast in the sunroom. Who wouldn't want to look into those mesmerizing blue eyes? Or imagine his six-pack abs tucked under his tight fitting police uniform? Even bolder: Daydream about what he might be willing to do with those handcuffs clipped to his belt?

As Mindi wolfed down her omelet, she tried not to stare. Letting Constance know she had the hots for her husband, even though the woman literally hated him, might encourage the Queen Mother to become territorial. Mindi would never benefit from that scenario.

Only one alpha lived at the G&G: Constance. And she marked all her possessions as a warning to those who might want what was hers.

When Constance's cellphone pinged with a text, she picked up the cell and fired off a response. Who would be texting her boss at 8:00 on a Sunday morning?

Still, the distraction gave Mindi a second to glance at Finn. Just so happened, he was sipping his coffee and looking straight at *her*.

Holy moly, the man could cream jeans without touching her.

The Queen Mother laid her cellphone on the dining table, face down. "So, Juliette," she started, eyeing her daughter who shockingly sported tousled hair and circles under her eyes. "How was your sleep last night?"

Every morning at breakfast, Constance badgered her daughter, otherwise known in Mindi's private journal as Beauty Brat or BB Jules, about how she had slept. Way to make sure her kid never forgot she was an insomniac. These people were ridiculous.

BB Jules went into the whole pointless shebang: fire in her loft, followed by flooding. No way out, *yadda, yadda, yadda.* Translation? Last night, poor little rich kid from Castle Privileged had a night terror. Like *that* was surprising for an insomniac.

Even BB Jules's tears had gold flecks in them.

If only the kid would cry Mindi a river. Or die. That would work.

Mindi had every intention of walking down the aisle with a divorced Finley Parker—her sexy hunk of blue. What did Constance always say? *Raise the bar for yourself (dream bigger).*

"It will please you, then," the Queen Mother told BB Jules when her sob story finally ended, "that I am giving you a vacation from your daily duties, only for today."

Ordinarily, Sundays (the national day of rest) meant nothing to the woman, so this bit of news was significant. Mindi wondered what was up. Maybe the announcement meant Mindi would also get some time off. Babysitting, more like hovering, was weird when the kid was 15. At that age, Mindi had already lost her virginity on her high school's lacrosse field.

In pure drama-queen fashion, BB Jules paused with her fork midair. Her blue eyes bulged. "Really? The whole *entire* day?"

"Correct," Constance said. "I have an appointment in D.C. with Orin Yates, president of the National Miss Pageant Association. Victoria Scarborough is about to learn the consequences of mistreating my daughter. The incident will not go unpunished."

"You're meeting on a *Sunday?*"

That was precisely the question Mindi had. As Constance's personal assistant, Mindi had synchronized her cellphone with her boss's. There was no meeting posted with Orin Yates of the NMPA. On a Sunday, no less. And "the incident," as the Queen Mother now called the infamous interview, had only happened yesterday.

Mindi's Momma always said: *Skunks don't stink to smell themselves.* Skunks sprayed when they were scared of something.

Whatever Constance was up to, it wasn't with Orin Yates; she wasn't scared of him at all. No, the foul odor wafting from her boss was too strong to be about the NMPA president. Besides, why would the Queen Mother need to travel into D.C. for a meeting? By herself? A simple Skype or phone call would have efficiently initiated a complaint.

Constance had to be hiding something.

"Can't we just let the interview go?" Beauty Brat whined. "I don't want to draw any more attention to it. The incident was embarrassing. Who faints on live television?"

In deliberate slow motion, Constance lowered her heirloom coffee cup onto the table. "What is done is done," she said. "Now is the time to move forward and make the best of it. And the *best* option is to play the sympathy card. Quite frankly, I had forgotten how much attention sympathy garners. It is truly an underutilized gold mine."

"People may not react the way you're hoping, Mother."

"Pardon the expression, but hog wash. My cellphone has already been inundated with texts and emails expressing shock over your horrific treatment and terrifying health scare." Constance re-engaged her coffee cup, raising it to her magenta painted lips. "The iron is sizzling hot, Juliette Annabella. And we shall not ignore the opportunity to pounce."

"Any suggestions on how I should spend my day?" BB Jules asked her mother.

Either the kid had lost her ability to think for herself or she was sucking up, reinforcing the power her mother wielded. Both possibilities were gag worthy.

Finn forked a bite of home-fries. "Do whatever you want, kiddo," he said. "Enjoy the sunshine. The outdoors. I'll be working at the station until four o'clock. Let's take a walk on the beach when I get home."

Constance sneered at him. "The question was posed to *me*, darling." When everyone stopped chewing and breathing, she added, "I agree with your father about enjoying fresh air, but under no circumstances will you expose your skin to the sun. Lounge under the pool house awning, apply plenty of organic sunblock, and read a book. Mindi will serve you tea before noon so you can relax comfortably, enough to sleep. You certainly need it."

"A dip in the pool sounds good, too," BB Jules said.

"I intentionally did not include swimming," the Queen Mother countered. "Chlorine is harsh on the skin and hair. Besides, swimming is far from your best skill."

"Probably because you rarely let me enjoy the water."

BB Jules was abnormally defiant this morning. The teenaged boy Mindi had seen from a distance, the one jogging on the beach at night and loitering near the garden, was probably emboldening her.

"I have an idea," Finn said. "Invite the new kid next door over for the day. He could keep you company. And when it comes to pool safety, two are better than one."

Practically spitting her espresso across the dining table, Constance locked eyes with Mindi, making sure she interpreted her insinuation. Constance thought *she* had spilled the beans to her husband about the teenager next door. Not true. But why the hell would it matter?

Oh yeah. The woman was a control freak.

The Queen Mother glared at him. "How do you know there is a teenager next door?"

Finn tapped the badge on his chest. "Detective, Connie. I like to know who's who in Hickory Thicket. Kind of my thing, right?"

Mindi was good at reading people when they were telling the truth or spewing stench. At the moment, the air reeked of straight up deception. Clearly, someone else had informed Finn about the teen who had moved in next door. Had to be the kiss ass groundskeeper; Constance had told him because of the locks.

Not to mention, Garth favored one of his bosses. The one overflowing with testosterone.

Being on Team Finn was the only similarity she and Garth had in common. Which presented another problem altogether. When her alarm had been triggered during her first week at the G&G, when Garth barely looked in her direction—which was unheard of, she understood: Without careful attention, the groundskeeper might very well become her competition.

Beauty Brat was about to open her mouth, but Constance held up a finger to silence her. "Permission to invite company is *not* granted," she stated. "Mindi will remain on the premises until my return for dinner at six. She will ensure you obey my wishes. Understood?"

Fucking fireballs to hell.

Mindi's hopes for the day sunk out of reach.

Finn stood from the table, intentionally leaving his chair untucked and cockeyed (a pet peeve of his wife's). "Looks like you have everything under control, Connie."

He walked to the brewing machine for his usual refill prior to leaving for work.

"I'd like to get started on my day," Mindi said, hating that she was essentially asking for permission. "Earlier, I picked flowers from the garden. I'd like to place the arrangements around the house. If you agree, of course."

"Sounds splendid," Constance said. "We need to spread more cheer around here. And when you finish, I would like to reconvene to review instructions for the day."

"Certainly, Ma'am."

Mindi decided a coffee refill was in order for her as well.

At the brewing machine, she rubbed her shoulder against Finn's arm, making sure he couldn't tell if the touching was an accident or her intention.

Looking up at him, Mindi smiled. Not the kind of smile that said, *Have a nice day.*

More like the kind of smile that conveyed she was picturing him with his clothes off.

Lying naked next to her.

16

Sunday, August 15, 2027
The Parkers' G&G Estate: Hickory Thicket, Maryland
(Day *of* Juliette's Death)

TODAY HAD TO be the luckiest day in Jules's life. For the first
time since she could remember, Sunday was actually going to be a day
of rest. How sweet was that?

No locked doors. No lengthy to-do lists. No alarms ringing to
manage her schedule.

FREEDOM.

Yes, with Mother out of town and Dad at work, "new" Jules had
the chance to initiate changes in her life. To put herself first, in a
normal teenager sort of way.

She had only asked Mother about what she should do during her
"free" day to convince her that the status quo was chugging along as
usual. In truth, Juliette Annabella Parker planned on hanging out with
Truitt Windsor.

The prospect nearly made her giddy. *Nearly* because any display of
excitement might cause Mother to suspect that Jules was planning on
having the witty, cheek dimpled, smile dazzling, six-foot-something
"distraction" over to their pool.

Somehow, she'd deal with Mindi Maxwell's unwanted babysitting
by finding a way to negotiate with her. If Mother could manipulate
Mindi, Jules had a shot at doing the same.

"Would you please place a vase of flowers in my loft, Mindi?"
Jules asked, as Mother's personal assistant was leaving the sunroom

with her coffee cup.

Mindi nodded, turning left toward the kitchen.

Time to distract her maternal warden. Jules needed to get Mother obsessing over something *other* than her daughter and the promised day off. Queen Mother had a nasty habit of holding out a juicy carrot and then yanking it away. Jules couldn't let that happen, not when the best-day-ever was within her grasp. No, the reset version of Jules had to advocate for herself. In her dysfunctional family, stoking more discord might be the perfect diversion.

"I think Mindi is infatuated with you, Dad," Jules whispered.

"That's ridiculous. I could practically be her father."

"Precisely how many men has age stopped, darling?" Mother asked, using her voice like the sharp edge of a honed knife. The room was instantly hotter.

"My eyes are only for you, dear wife."

"And your heart?" Mother asked.

Dad's silence was like a dousing of frigid water.

"Sadly predictable," Mother murmured.

"Speaking of surprises, Dad," Jules started, before he left the sunroom. "Did you know that you and Mother have a life insurance policy on me? In case I die?"

Scrunching his eyebrows, Dad tilted his head as if flipping through his memory bank.

"He remembers, Juliette," Mother answered instead. "As I mentioned yesterday, having a policy is standard practice. I should not need to repeat myself."

Jules expected her father to blow a gasket. Expected him to be surprised by the revelation. But absent a defensive reaction, perhaps he had known all along.

"I'm curious," Jules said. "How much am I worth to you...*dead?*"

Dad raised his eyebrows. Only, his expression didn't look horrified. More like his eyebrows were inviting an answer—intrigued to learn the amount at the same time she did.

"You are quite proficient in mathematics and business, Juliette Annabella, so your tone is inappropriate," Mother scolded. "Clearly, we do not *need* money from an insurance policy. More than obvious. Again, having a policy is merely a good business practice in the unlikely event of a tragedy." Gazing at Dad, she added, "Have I explained the matter accurately, darling?"

The conversation was taking an odd turn. Completely unexpected.

"You have," he agreed. "But I see no harm in sharing the amount. After all, without Jules, there is no pageantry business. She has the right to know about affairs which involve her."

"I am astonished!" Mother raised her chin, something she did to remind her opponent she was superior. "I have always found you to be a minimalist when talking about personal *affairs*. Yet, here you are, encouraging full disclosure!"

"Are we changing subjects, Connie?"

"The policy with Transnational Life is for four million," Mother blurted.

Jules tried to hold herself together. Four *million* dollars?

"How much are my total earnings and investments worth?" she asked.

"Approximately eight-hundred-thousand."

Standing, Jules began to shake. Her chest tightened. "You mean, I'm five times more valuable *dead* than alive? What a perfect message! Thank you so much."

The math felt terribly wrong. Why was the life insurance policy on her so much higher than her worth—which happened to take over a decade and a half to accumulate? Even though the insurance "reward" undoubtedly accounted for future winnings, she couldn't deny the twists in her stomach. Or the acid bubbling up her throat.

She, the *child* of Finley and Constance Parker, was nothing more than a business asset.

Turning away from the people who were supposed to love her, Jules bolted out of the sunroom.

She needed her inhaler.

"Wait!" Dad called after her, but she kept running, not hearing his next words.

Tears cascaded down her cheeks as she stormed through the kitchen and pantry, as she raced up her private staircase to her loft. Her lungs screamed for oxygen. When she reached the landing, she stopped in her tracks despite her wheezing.

For some reason, her door had closed. Maybe Mindi had shut it after delivering flowers?

Jules pushed open the door and froze.

Wearing the diamond necklace from her Nana Bea, Mindi stood atop the platform located on the right side of her room, gazing at herself within the three panels of full-length mirrors configured like a bay window. Mother's personal assistant caressed the heart-shaped diamond with her fingers, gently touching the pendant as if the act wasn't a violation. As if the precious heirloom was hers to fondle.

Lunging for the inhaler on her nightstand, Jules clasped the device and administered two hits in rapid succession. She held her breath, locking in the vapor, until she felt her chest relax.

While Jules was trying to avoid another full-blown asthma attack, Mindi had unclasped her Nana's necklace and returned it to the dresser, beside a newly placed vase of flowers.

"Don't make a big deal about this, Jules," Mindi barked.

"That's just it. I haven't made *any* deal with you, big or small. Which means, you have no right trying on my things without permission, especially something as special as my Nana Bea's necklace."

"Your Nana Beatrice is dead. The necklace belongs to you."

With cheeks flushed, Jules stepped toward Mindi, not sure what would happen when she reached the bitch's personal body space but quite confident it involved pain.

"Stop," Mindi said, defensively holding her hands in front of her. "I only wanted to see how the necklace looked on me. I wasn't going to steal it."

"Right." Jules huffed. "That's like taking someone's car for a joy ride and when you're caught, you tell them you were only taking a test drive, curious how the vehicle handled." Jules walked over to her dresser and retrieved the necklace, clasping it around her own neck. "Here's my advice, Mindi. Earn your own life. Envy is ugly."

"Let's talk about envy, shall we?" Mindi reached into her pants pocket and pulled out a folded sheet of index paper. "Look what I found in the garden this morning…"

The rules. Her note to Truitt.

"Wish I had freedom like you," Mindi recited from Jules's writing. "Sounds like envy to me. Right? And wouldn't your mother just love

to know that her little Beauty Brat plans on sharing *secrets* with the boy next door? With a complete stranger?" Mindi placed her finger on her chin and closed her eyes as if deep in thought. "I predict Garth will be installing a steel door next, as well as bars on your windows. Perhaps even accessorizing you with a chastity belt."

Feeling better, Jules smiled as her resolve returned.

"Is this funny?" Mindi asked.

"More like ironic. See, we both have damaging information on each other. Make no mistake, your greedy fingers are as egregious as my unauthorized note."

Such a flat out lie. Queen Mother adored when others envied what she *had,* and they *wanted.* Thankfully, Mindi was new to the game. Perhaps she hadn't learned this truth yet.

"Which means," Jules continued, "we have the perfect opportunity to negotiate over things like babysitting me today. Should we begin by stating our conditions?"

Mindi was speechless for a moment, probably getting her demands in order.

At last, Mother's assistant answered. "Go on. I'm listening."

17

Sunday, August 15, 2027
The Parkers' G&G Estate: Hickory Thicket, Maryland
(Day *of* Juliette's Death)

MINDI WAS EAGER to hear Beauty Brat's proposal. In truth, she hadn't expected to initiate her plans until Thursday, when Constance had scheduled an appointment in Annapolis. Her boss had already informed Mindi that she wouldn't require her attendance.

Might an even better opportunity be presenting itself...early?

Negotiations could prove beneficial. After all, the checkmarks for today were adding up. Why wait? Constance would be hours away, returning at dinnertime; Finn had just left the estate for a full day of work; Garth would arrive on the property at 1:00 p.m. (which might end up being perfect timing); and Chef Evelyn was already gone until 3:00 p.m. since the Queen Mother had cancelled lunch. Not to mention, the housekeeper had Sundays off.

August 15th was promising.

The unknown was if Mindi, herself, was ready.

One misstep and all her plans would collapse.

"My conditions are practically effortless," BB Jules started. "You get time off, away from here until three o'clock. In turn, we'll keep our infractions a secret between us. But right after Mother leaves, we'll need to sneak into her walk-in safe; I know the code. We'll erase the incriminating evidence." She pointed to her bookcase. "Given your confused expression, coupled with the necklace incident, you obviously aren't aware that everything in this room, including our current conversation, is being recorded on a hidden camera."

"A hidden camera? In *here?*"

Damn it. Shock had driven Mindi to unintentionally express her surprise. So much for priding herself as the Queen Mother's confidante and protégé. Now Jules would conclude Mindi wasn't in "the know" and she'd be right.

"If we don't remove the footage," BB Jules added, "we'll both be screwed."

Another problem reared its ugly head, in terms of Mindi's goals: Beauty Brat was smart beyond her years. Her perceptiveness, in fact, would be a huge issue when Mindi hooked up with her father. At least Mindi had already decided how she'd remove the threat. No one, including little miss brainiac, was going to stop her from getting inducted into Finn's private fraternity—the "him and her" club.

Impressive amounts of smarts were *not* exclusive to BB Jules.

She'd prove it. Today, not Thursday.

Right now, though, she had to focus on the unexpected problem: potentially having Constance see and hear an *unfiltered* Mindi. The prospect terrified her. To the bone.

"You make a good point," Mindi said, ready to play. "As far as my conditions go…if I agree to yours, then you'll have to abide by mine. Promise to drink your tea when I give it to you. In addition, cheerfully consent to all my instructions—out loud, like only actress Juliette Annabella can pull off.

"Finally," she continued, "I'll need you to insist on having a sports drink—the perfect accompaniment for a relaxing day by the pool. Of course, I'll need to run out to the store in Rock Hall and will only be gone a short time." Mindi shrugged, like she didn't care which way negotiations went. "If I'm satisfied with your performance, I'll develop instant amnesia about the whole note incident."

BB Jules tilted her head. "Why would you care?" she asked. "I mean, once Mother is gone, why does it matter if I *do* or *don't* drink her disgusting concoction? Or agree to her list of demands, which we know she'll give you before she leaves?"

"Pardon me for saying so, but your mother is paranoid. That's why she collects and compares footage from multiple camera sources."

"I'm not following."

"There's a hidden camera in the kitchen," Mindi stated plainly. "I know about it; Garth doesn't. Garth knew about the camera in your bedroom; I didn't. This is how your mother gauges authenticity within her staff. She compares what she hears in rooms where the person knows there's a camera against what's recorded in rooms where the person is unaware."

"Wait. If Garth didn't install the camera in the kitchen, who did?" BB Jules asked.

"The Queen Mother has her own private grunt—someone who comes to the mansion at night and does the work. A person who knows the security codes. I'm not privy to their identity."

"Rather risky when my Dad is a gun-toting police detective, don't you think?"

"A detective who regularly works the nightshift," Mindi corrected. "And you certainly wouldn't know, locked away in your loft. Your mother doesn't miss a trick. She may preach *defend the forest, not the bark,* but I've never met anyone more obsessed with the tiniest of details. She's the only woman I know who could easily get away with murder. Living with a cop, no less."

Mindi worried her comment about murder might have gotten a rise from BB Jules, throwing their discussions off course, but thankfully, the brat remained on topic. Maybe she agreed.

"Getting back to your conditions," BB Jules said. "What you're saying…is that you want Mother to witness you taking charge of me, captured on the hidden kitchen camera. As far as she knows, I'm not aware of *any* cameras in the house. Which means, Queen Mother will be uber impressed by how you get me to comply with her wishes while I'm gushing with respect for you. Who knows? You could even earn a raise over our epic exchange.

"Regarding the sports drink," she continued. "Our documented conversation will give you an acceptable reason, at least arguably, to leave the estate. And how will cameras indicate how long you're gone? They won't. Garth told me there aren't any cameras in the pool area. Not yet. He's installing them this afternoon. So I'll just confirm, if asked, that you brought back the sports drink and were here with me by the pool. How on target am I?"

"Crosshairs."

Mindi shook hands with Beauty Brat before heading downstairs.

Sure enough, Constance handed her a list of orders.

After the Queen Mother left the estate at 9:00 a.m., she and BB Jules expertly erased the captured footage of their exchange in the loft. Working quickly, they copied video of her empty bedroom and spliced in the duplicated footage to fill the void. Only someone fishing for a tiny flaw might spot the editing.

They moved into the kitchen for the second act.

Mindi positioned herself in front of the camera; after all, she was the lead in their production. It felt good knowing the footage would capture BB Jules's back instead of her annoyingly pretty face.

She picked up Constance's written list. "My first instruction," Mindi said aloud, "is to: *Give Jules the tea I've prepared and watch her drink all of it. The poor child needs to relax.*"

Beauty Brat was about to pick up the teacup.

Mindi stopped her.

"Wait. Your mother leaves your sleeping meds in this little fancy pill box." Mindi lifted the lid and sure enough, two sleeping pills were in the bottom, like they were every evening.

After crushing the pills, she sprinkled them into the tea and swirled the cocktail to dissolve the drug. Microwaving the cup, Mindi enjoyed the aroma of the warm rum perfuming the air. She remembered sneaking sips of her parents' rum and replenishing the bottle with water to hide the deficit. But what parent actually *gave* their kid alcohol every single day?

"Now, please do as your mother says," Mindi instructed, acting for the camera. "Drink all of it; this minute if you don't mind. Your mother is extremely worried about your difficult night last night. She wants you to have a relaxing day."

BB Jules picked up the teacup. "I haven't told you this lately," she said, "but Mother is lucky to have someone as loyal as you. Thank you, Mindi."

What a performance. A little excessive, but acceptable.

Beauty Brat downed her tea like a pro, though she slightly grimaced when she finished.

The rest of the script unfolded flawlessly.

When Mindi drove away from the Glitz and Glamour estate, her car's dashboard clock read 10:04 a.m.

At the time of her departure, BB Jules had been lying on a lounge chair, under the awning closest to the pool, practically asleep.

Time was the only thing Mindi cared about.

Would there be enough of it for her plans?

Smiling, she decided the day might rank as one of her best.

18

Sunday, August 15, 2027
The Parkers' G&G Estate: Hickory Thicket, Maryland
(Day *of* Juliette's Death)

TRUITT THOUGHT SEEING Jules might be challenging, given the rules printed on the paper airplane she had released from her window last night. Although he'd lost the airplane somewhere in the garden, he had read the ludicrous litany of directives. All 25 of them.

Jules's parents clearly controlled their daughter's every move, including how she acted.

Who told their kid to *be whom others expect you to be?* Or encouraged them to use white lies? Or approved of crying for effect? And what the hell was a "handler?"

To him, the rules sounded way high on the creep factor pole.

Another thing. Jules's parents had to be clueless about how their rules might stunt their daughter's emotional growth. How would she ever develop into her own person?

Mr. and Mrs. Parker were treating Jules like a family puppet.

Even though Truitt's parents had decided to move to HT, they didn't force him to *act* a certain way. To the contrary. They knew he was having trouble adjusting and they felt guilty about it. Everything was in the open. Painstakingly authentic.

What kind of sicko advice was *emote positivity; suppress negativity?*

If he talked to Jules today, maybe some of the secrets she promised to share would shed light on her situation. Would she tell him she was miserable? Trapped? Scared?

Maybe she'd say she had a ticket out of Loony Lane.

On the other hand, if the rules had influenced her whole upbringing, she might not know they were callous and flawed. She might even defend them. Think they were normal.

From his hidden spot among the loblollies dividing his backyard from G&G's, Truitt surveyed the Parkers' mansion and grounds. Being alone with Jules was his only option, so he was abundantly cautious.

He could see her lounging under the pool house awning.

After 15 minutes of watching her, he suspected no one else was home. Made sense since he had observed four vehicles leaving the property earlier that morning; one was a police cruiser, probably Jules's father because more often than not, he watched the vehicle return to the mansion in the early morning hours.

Weatherwise, if he wanted to hang out with Jules, he couldn't hesitate. Blue skies wouldn't last. Local forecasters were predicting thunderstorms around noon, and he thought it was already half-past ten, maybe later. He tapped on the face of his wristwatch out of habit. Still no movement.

Walking onto the decking, he stared at Jules as she was lying on her back, asleep on the lounge chair. She was even more beautiful than he had thought, based on their foggy encounter in the garden. She was pale, like the sun had never touched her, making her skin porcelain perfect. Flowing over her shoulders and onto her chest, her brown hair was shiny and curled at the ends. And her body— showcased in a periwinkle bikini—was…developed. Hot, if he was locker room frank.

Maybe she was older than he had first thought. One conclusion was beyond dispute: The Beauty Channel was definitely for people like Jules Parker.

"You can't be *The Princess and the Pea*," he teased. "You're sleeping too soundly."

She struggled to open her eyes.

When her lids raised and she focused on him, she gasped.

Truitt took a step back.

"Sorry. You frightened me," she said, sounding groggy. She raised the back of her lounge chair. "Are you into fairytales or something?

You referenced *Cinderella* in the garden."

"Guilty." He smiled. "I'm drawn to anything nostalgic."

"Like that antique device around your wrist? I suppose it's better than a sundial."

"Nostalgia has time limits, you know," he said, winking. "Sundials are classified as ancient, not nostalgic, since the first one was created by the Babylonians in 1500 BC. Not to mention, they're a bit clunky to carry around and set up. And you're screwed when it rains. I just need to get my wristwatch fixed. Then I'll be ticking like a treasured flashback."

"You're a historian, too." She yawned. "Sit down before your old bones ache."

He sat in the chair beside Jules's deck recliner. "You're yawning. Am I boring you, Princess? Making you sleepy?"

"Historians should know their royal hierarchies, Peasant. According to Mother, I am Queen Juliette. I command you to respect my position and title, thank you very much."

"Rule number twenty-one: *Walk and talk like a queen. You are royalty.*" He pinched his chin. "However, I believe you require some schooling yourself. Surely you can tell that I am a nobleman. A prominent baron, in fact."

Truitt hoped his wit and photographic memory would impress her. Jules was a good match for him. She didn't seem nervous or gawk at him like he was a chocolate velvet cream pie about to become the main course. He also appreciated her snarky sense of humor. Her boldness drew him in.

"Well, Baron Windsor," Jules said. "You left my sheet of rules in the garden, and I almost got in trouble."

"Oh man. I wondered where they had gotten to. Sorry."

"I managed the situation. But now you know one of my secrets. Queen or not, I'm forced to live by ridiculous rules, most of which, I don't respect."

A relief. At least, they were on the same page about her rules.

"What do your friends say about your rules?" he asked. "Do they worry about you? Or are freakish rules commonplace in the wonderful world of pageantry?"

"Did you say...*friends?* Prohibited by unlucky number thirteen:

Avoid distractions."

"That sucks." He rubbed his neck, but only for a second so she wouldn't press him again about his injury. He wanted to spend time learning about *her.* "Tell me, Queen Juliette. I've been dying to know. What other secrets do you want to divulge? Your age, maybe? I'm seventeen. Heading into senior year."

"I'm older." She smirked. "Fifteen going on twenty. And homeschooled."

After chuckling, Truitt listened as Jules told him about the interview on TBC, where the interviewer had stressed her into an asthma attack. She also disclosed that her parents had jointly taken out a life insurance policy on her, in the event she died. For four million effing dollars! Sounded like a wicked temptation derived by the devil himself. Even more disturbing, her mother *locked* Jules in her loft each night and recorded her every move with what the woman thought were hidden cameras. Dang! Talk about bizarro.

Her parents had trapped Jules in their horror flick.

"Anyway, as my actual elder," she said, close to slurring and barely able to keep her eyes open, "if you...if you have any suggestions on improving my circumstances, I'm all ears."

Without thinking, Truitt massaged his neck again. "Have to chew on that one. I don't mean to sound insensitive, but I've never encountered a friend who has parents quite like yours."

"What? There aren't any deadbeat parents in the black community?"

"Deadbeats come in all colors, Jules. I just don't know any."

"I suppose my circumstances *are* uniquely pathetic," she said, adding another yawn. "By the way, you never told me exactly how you injured your neck. A football game? At practice?"

"Injuries happen anywhere, anytime." He was intentionally vague, so he switched subjects by telling her that his parents had forced him to leave behind his childhood home, high school, and beloved sport, much to his chagrin. Then he added, "Mind if I ask why you're so tired? Maybe from the ordeal yesterday? I mean, stress really makes me sluggish. Just wondering."

He tried not to wear shock on his face as Jules explained the concoction her mother made her drink every night and even during the day *as needed*. "Hey, here's some instant advice about what you call *stea*," he said sternly. "Don't drink it. Ever. Promise me."

"I know. I know," she said. "I usually don't. There were extenuating circumstances this morning. Drinking it was necessary."

"More advice," Truitt said. "You seem beyond sleepy. More like drugged. Better stay out of your lap pool which, if I do say so, is gargantuan." He stretched his neck, as best he could, to take in the massive swimming pool. "Jeez. It even has a deep end. How deep?"

"Twelve and a half feet."

A flimsy inflatable lounger was near the pool's edge.

"Your parents go all out," he said. "Except for pool loungers. That one's seen better days. Don't even consider using it. Best to stay under the awning to sleep off the effects of your spiked tea." Truitt pointed toward the pool. "Besides, your skin would burn out there in a hot second."

"Such a bossy baron. One with astounding talents, nevertheless. Your resumé will read: injured historian lifeguard with a tomato fetish, a keen eye for matters of dermatology, an appreciation for drugged insomniacs, and counseling skills at the perfection level."

"You left out my science nerdiness."

"My, my! You *are* well rounded."

"Seriously though," he scolded. "Don't be cavalier about safety. Totally not worth it."

A gust of wind blew several leaves into the pool.

Standing from his chair, he walked over to the side of the pool where a skimmer was. Picking up the long aluminum handle, he began scooping leaves into the netted basket.

"Don't bother," Jules said. "Our groundskeeper is coming this afternoon. Besides, it's supposed to rain. A thunderstorm, I think. So I'm sure more leaves will sink to the bottom before the day is over."

"Better than dying slowly." He regretted saying that. Depression, if that's what he was experiencing, was making him morbid.

Jules winked at him. "Says the foreboding historian lifeguard who loves science and dabbles in dark realism."

Truitt listened beyond Jules. Maybe the wind had carried sounds across his yard into the Parkers' pool area. "Did you hear crying?" he asked, looking toward his parents' estate.

"Crying?" Jules tilted her head. "I don't hear a thing. Why? Is something wrong at your house?"

"My Mom has been going through a tough time. I better get back home and check on her."

"And neglect your lifeguarding duties? Leaving your queen unchaperoned and subject to her own careless whims? What kind of perfection is that, Baron Windsor?"

Putting down the skimmer, Truitt left the basket out over the water for the groundskeeper to finish. His mother needed him. No time to be thinking about himself. He could get to know Jules later.

Before leaving, he'd clear something up.

No more joking around.

"Here's some dark realism. I'm not as perfect as you wish." He started to walk away. "Stay out of the pool, please. I mean it. I'll be back in a few."

19

Sunday, August 15, 2027
The Parkers' G&G Estate: Hickory Thicket, Maryland
(Day *of* Juliette's Death)

JULES WOKE ON her deck recliner as if she'd been moved, while napping, from the unpleasant stickiness of the Delmarva Peninsula in August to the suffocating humidity of a tropical rainforest.

A coating of perspiration varnished her body. Her hair was wet and matted. Skin, blotchy red. The air was thick, and saliva swam in her mouth. Worse, she felt clammy and shaky, symptoms that usually meant she was about to get sick to her stomach.

Even though Truitt had suspected she was experiencing some sort of *stea* overdose, she disagreed. Mother had a precise formula for the concoction and Jules had never had this type of reaction before.

Instead, maybe she hadn't eaten enough of her omelet or drank sufficient orange juice at breakfast and was having some sort of a blood sugar issue.

A strong gust rippled the pool water.

Looking toward the Chesapeake, Jules saw white caps on the bay. Building thunderheads marked the western horizon.

Leaves somersaulted across the backyard. Rising above the brick walls of her garden, the crowns of peach and apple trees swayed. By the pool's edge, her inflatable lounger glided over the patio pavers until a decorative bush snagged it. At the same time, the G&G's crested flag flapped to life and the canvas awning shook and quivered above her.

The wind should've cooled her off, especially since the shade protected her, but Jules's temperature was at the roasted turkey level.

From the far side of the pool deck, coming from inside the mansion, she heard a vibrating clank in the kitchen.

Had someone dropped a tray or pan on the floor?

"Mindi?" she called. No one answered. "Garth?" She paused and then added, *"Anybody?"*

Nothing.

The wind through a window must have knocked something down.

She thought about Truitt's warning to stay out of the pool. Wise as his advice seemed, he had no idea how hot she was. Besides, she must have slept for at least a half hour, which meant he would be returning any minute after checking on his mother.

No doubt, he might get annoyed by her blatant disregard for his instructions. Maybe her defiance could serve as a test. If Truitt was a control freak like most people in her life, then he'd probably get angry by her quick float in the pool. Perhaps even furious.

So be it.

Today, she was making decisions for *herself.* Her new beginning.

Beyond the awning, a ballooning cloud, wearing a darkened gray face, blocked the sun and cast a massive shadow that inched across the backyard.

Jules rose from her recliner and wobbled with dizziness.

What was wrong with her?

Steadying herself by clutching the back of a chair, she waited until the wave of nausea passed. She picked up the towel she had been lying on; it was heavy with moisture.

Taking a few steps with the towel draped over her forearm, she stopped. First nausea. Now, the telltale signs of an asthma attack. Her chest was tightening. Throat, narrowing. She wheezed as she took a breath. Figures she had left her inhaler on her night table in the loft. Before getting it, she'd try the pool. Cool water might ease the onset.

She glanced at her skin. Great. She hadn't remembered her sunblock either. No worries. At most, she'd float ten minutes.

Walking to the inflatable lounger, Jules wondered if Truitt might have been right. Maybe Mindi *had* given her too much zolpidem. But why? She made the concoction every night. And in terms of getting along, their morning collaboration had been their best. In fact, a secret alliance between them might prove beneficial. Why would Mindi risk everything with a hostile act? Not to mention, intentionally overdosing Jules would have consequences, especially from the almighty Queen Mother.

Mindi wasn't the sharpest knife in the drawer, but she wasn't completely dull either.

Another loud noise came from the house.

This time, it sounded like glass breaking.

Whatever. Jules was going to cool off and prevent an asthma attack regardless of who was rummaging through their kitchen. Anyway, Mother always had people coming in and out of the house for this reason or that. Jules had probably missed someone's arrival while sleeping.

More nausea reminded her to hurry.

After grabbing the plastic float, she shuffled to the pool's steps and clutched the rail with her free hand. As she stepped down and her feet lowered into the water, she gasped, surprised at how cold it was. Instead of being unduly drugged, perhaps she was coming down with the flu and had a fever.

Figured she'd get sick on the only free day of her existence.

Jules placed the lounger flat on the water and spread the towel over the top. Plastic felt awful against her skin. She chuckled. No tiny vegetables required; she had found her catalyst for *The Princess and the Pea* syndrome: plastic.

As she arranged herself on the float (lying on her back and stretching out length-wise from one end to the other), pool water rushed to cover her stomach. Truitt had accurately assessed the lounger; it needed more air. However, in her woozy state, she welcomed it. The water was refreshingly cold. Her towel had become saturated, too, spreading relief up and down her backside.

Jules coaxed herself to relax, picturing her bronchioles opening wide. Her lungs, expanding to full capacity.

Mental visualization was working. Wheezing subsided.

Returning sunshine glistened off the pool like glowing fairies dancing and leaping on the water's surface. Closing her eyes, she enjoyed how the sparkles glittered through her eyelids.

She listened to the flapping flag, enjoying the rhythm.

A few seconds later, she felt as if someone was staring at her. Just a feeling, but she was usually right. Anyway, having people gawk at her wasn't a big deal. She was a beauty champion. One who had absolutely no energy to get out of the pool and investigate.

Instead, her thoughts drifted to Truitt as she gently rocked with the wind while floating on her lounger.

Truitt was funny and good looking and seemed like a doting son. Dreamy, really. But not without a dash of eccentricity. Or a touch of mystery. Like…what had he meant when he said he wasn't as perfect as she wished? Was he a wolf in sheep's skin?

Jules was curious about something else. What could be happening over at the Windsors to make his mother so darn weepy? And why had his parents yanked their son from his childhood home and everything he had really enjoyed?

Something seemed slightly off with Truitt and his family, but she couldn't put her finger on it.

Nearby, a bird's upbeat melody caught her attention. Was the tune from a Carolina chickadee?

She'd have to listen more closely.

But then…

Was it seconds later? Minutes?

She remembered feeling better, listening to a songbird.

And now…

Now, she was *in* the water. Completely submerged.

Her heart pounded in her ears.

Confusion jumbled her thoughts. Panic swept over her body.

Something pressed on her head. Pushing her down.

Holding her down.

She thrashed. Twisted. Flailed.

Was her situation *real?*

Was she truly in physical…*danger?*

The horrible burning in her lungs wasn't fake.

Neither was her descent to the bottom of the pool.

Please, God! She didn't want to die.

She couldn't die. She was too young!

Her legs kicked against something. Against *someone.*

Pressure. She felt pressure around her neck.

Someone was *choking* her. Forcing her deeper.

Her lungs screamed for air.

Jules did what she always did when she needed a breath.

She inhaled. Gasped. Gulped. Anything for oxygen.

Water rushed in, filling her lungs like ten-pound weights.

How could this be happening?

She was scared.

Exhausted.

More thrashes.

Until…

Until the person drowning Jules released her.

She could save herself. At last.

If only…

If only she had an ounce of strength left.

But she didn't.

Everything felt heavy.

Her body stilled.

She sank downward. In slow motion. Her arms extended to her sides. Suspended in a liquid heaven.

Oddly at peace.

She saw no final images with her family. No laughing together. No rapid fire memories of special childhood milestones. No hugging or saying *I love you.*

When the blanket of darkness came, a snapshot of her loft was the only vision which flashed into her thoughts. Jules was in her comfort zone, sitting in her pitch black bedroom, staring across the bay at the twinkling lights on Gibson Island.

Very much…

Alone.

20

Sunday, August 15, 2027
The Parkers' G&G Estate: Hickory Thicket, Maryland
(Day *of* Juliette's Death)

AFTER REGAINING CONSCIOUSNESS, Jules watched as their groundskeeper rescued her body from the pool, moved it to a patch of grass, and lowered her on her back.

Without hesitation, Garth straddled her and started compressions.

She stood feet away. Frozen. Observing. Remembering that someone had been strangling her in the water, trying to drown her.

The shock was immobilizing.

On the grass, her body still wasn't moving.

Was she? Was Jules...*dead?*

"Shit, shit," Garth cried, repeatedly pressing down on her chest.

Water swelled and cascaded from Jules's mouth.

Rolling her body onto its side, he struck her back. More water spilled from her lips.

"Come on! Come on!" he urged, maybe even demanded. He sounded more desperate than she had ever heard him. "Breathe, Jules. Do it, damn it. Breathe!"

Lowering her on her back again, he continued compressions with greater force. With wild eyes and a crazed resolve.

"Where the fuck is my cellphone?" he shouted.

A boom of thunder shook the ground. Clouds had deepened into angry shades of charcoal, red, and green. Electricity was in the air.

Thankfully, Garth's cellphone was where he had left it. Near the pool's edge. Near the spot where he had plunged into the deep end.

Determination recharged Jules. Energy coursed through every blood vessel—if that was even possible in her current state. Regardless, she had to help Garth save her *real* body.

Jules raced to the cellphone, scooping up the device in a whirlwind of energy and tossing it onto the grass beside Garth.

Despite his look of shock, he grabbed the cellphone and dialed 911. He quickly explained the crisis to an emergency operator, ending the call with, "Hurry! Please! She's unresponsive."

Minutes passed, maybe ten. Jules wasn't sure.

A siren sounded in the distance.

As Garth continued applying compressions to her body's chest, Jules realized she wasn't going to wake up. The fact that her spirit was at the scene meant something. Meant her attacker had been successful. He, she, or they—Jules had no clue. All she knew for sure was she had been *murdered*.

To think, today was the first day of Jules's teenage life that she had abandoned the rules, that she had decided to think for herself. Make her own decisions. Break free from Mother's shadow. And most importantly, become healthy on the inside and out.

A predator had destroyed her anyway.

She was mystified.

The question piercing her heart was who could've hated her that much? It wasn't like she was allowed to have friends. Friends who could have devious motives. Friends who might let jealousy consume them. Or who projected their self-hatred onto an innocent victim.

Jules didn't have any friends.

Except one. Except for her secret friendship with Truitt Windsor.

A siren blared; an ambulance was racing up their long driveway.

Jules's eyelids blinked rapidly. Her heart raced.

Turning her head, she looked toward the Windsors' estate. Something moved among the swath of loblollies separating the properties. Something fast. Then all she saw were the trees.

Fear overwhelmed her.

Most murders were committed by people who knew their victims.

Could Truitt have returned while she was resting in the pool? While she floated on her inflatable lounger?

21

Sunday, August 15, 2027
The Parkers' G&G Estate: Hickory Thicket, Maryland
(Day *of* Juliette's Death)

FINN WAS QUESTIONING Daisy Smithhisler regarding the whereabouts of her deadbeat son in relation to the break-in at the medicinal marijuana depot when he heard the dispatcher over the radio. A possible 11-44 (fatality). Body found in pool. White female. Ambulance requested.

What constricted his throat like tightening vice grips was the address. The 911 emergency was at the G&G.

As he sped from Rock Hall to Hickory Thicket, flashing his cruiser's red and blue lights, he rehashed morning conversations of who was going to be where and when. His vehicle's dashboard read 1:23 p.m. which meant three people were on estate grounds: Jules, Mindi, and Garth.

The victim's description in the radio dispatch was *white female*.

The victim couldn't be Jules. No way.

Finn remembered at breakfast, Connie had expressly forbidden Jules from taking a swim in the pool, and his daughter followed her mother's orders. Unlocking her bedroom door with a dinner knife, to sneak outside at night, was notably out of character. Jules was no rebel, though. Her natural disposition was to please. She was an amenable conformist.

Not to mention, why would *anyone* at the G&G swim during a severe thunderstorm warning? Jules certainly knew better.

With an increased heartrate, sweat beaded on his forehead. Clenching the steering wheel, his palms became slick.

What if the victim *was* Jules?

Christ Almighty.

Before his daughter had left the dining table that morning, Connie suggested she drink that damn concoction—the tea mixed with alcohol and sleeping pills. His wife wanted her to consume the hideous brew sometime before noon so Jules could rest "comfortably" under the pool house's overhang.

Had Jules swallowed that crap?

The pills came with a prescription, but not the rum. Then again, teenagers might spike their own tea. Especially when an opportunity presented itself. Absolutely no one would be shocked. Anyway, a small trace of alcohol might not even register in an autopsy.

Another thought assaulted him.

Regardless of who ended up being the victim, when detectives swept the house for possible evidence, they'd find the door locks on the *outside* of Jules's loft. How could he explain that? Would he have to throw Connie under the bus? Confess that his filthy rich, trophy of a wife was a narcissistic control freak who imprisoned their daughter every night? And sometimes during the day?

Of course, he'd also be admitting that he, a law enforcement detective, turned a blind eye.

Shit.

Finn pounded the steering wheel about what they'd find. About *why* was he thinking of defending the scene instead of worrying about his daughter. *If* the victim was even Jules.

Maybe the deceased would be Mindi. He could live with that.

He shook his head to clear it.

Why was he certain the victim was dead?

His gut.

His gut told him so, and his intuition was rarely wrong. He suspected that the dispatcher had reported a "possible" fatality at his estate for *his* benefit. She knew he'd hear the broadcast.

Fuck.

He had to collect himself.

Racing up his driveway, his speedometer registered 50 miles per hour. With any luck, a tire would slip off the asphalt, catching an edge and sending his cruiser into a large pine. Dying instantly would help him avoid awkward questions which would undoubtedly come his way. Why not let the burden of truth fall on Connie? After all, she was the bewitching matriarch of their dysfunctional dynasty. Of their diabolical lair. She deserved to feel the heat.

He pulled into his spot and pressed the ignition button to shut down the engine.

Great. Chief Keller had parked his vehicle beside two cruisers.

Before opening the car door, Finn deeply inhaled while putting on his issued cap. Whatever had happened, his life was about to implode. Once again.

The cloud ceiling ripped open.

As he stepped from the patrol car, rain pummeled him. He ran around the corner of his house, darting toward the group congregating on a patch of grass beside the pool decking. Included were Chief Keller, detectives Lopez and Smith, and his groundskeeper Garth Harris.

In the center of the cluster, a black tarp covered a body.

Everyone looked at him. Their eyes conveyed shock, uneasiness.

"Let's go under the awning, Finn," Chief said, sounding fatherly.

Finn ignored him.

Squatting, he folded back the top corner of the tarp.

In that hellish fucking moment, Finn emptied. He was alive and dead at the same time.

Flashes of holding his tiny daughter in his arms for the first time, his perfect bundle of potential, made his heart ache so fiercely his legs shook violently. *His* Jules. His precious, astute, beautiful, articulate, and fearless daughter was lifeless before him. Gone. Taken from him.

He dropped to his knees, about to topple over.

Lopez and Smith lifted him to his feet.

"Take him to the pool house," Chief ordered. "The overhang will block the rain." He covered Jules's face with the tarp. Rain made a harsh pelting sound against the plastic. Thunder rumbled.

Under the canopy, Finn's coworkers helped lower him onto a recliner as Keller took a seat in a nearby chair. His boss leaned forward, resting his elbows on his thighs. Supporting his chin, he used his weathered fingers to rub his eyes and caress the stubble on his chin and cheeks.

Garth stood in a darkened nook where the awning met the back corner of the pool house.

"I'm so sorry, Finn," Chief started. "My heart tells me to give you a minute to grieve, but my law enforcement side reminds me the clock is ticking. As you well know, evidence and timeliness are everything in solving a homicide. We can't let either get cold."

Finn's heart nearly stopped. He looked up, glaring at his boss. "Did you say…*homicide?*"

"There's a thin white line of broken skin around your daughter's neck. Could mean strangulation. There's also a skimmer at the bottom of the pool. Perhaps from a struggle? Then again, the wind might've blown it into the water. When the storm passes, we'll retrieve it. Send the skimmer to the lab for fingerprints. The natural oil from any prints should remain intact."

Finn glared at Garth. "Did you? Did you *hurt* her?"

"Now hold on, Finn," Chief cautioned. "Mr. Harris called-in the emergency. Said he found Jules in the deep end. Her hair was stuck in the drain. After he freed her and placed her on the grass, he didn't stop compressions until we arrived."

"Then Jules's death could've been an accident?"

"Accidental drowning can't be ruled out, not yet. But with marks on her neck, we're required to initiate a forensics investigation," Chief said. "Jules's body will go to OCME in Baltimore. An autopsy will hopefully give us answers."

A tear cascaded down Finn's cheek. "Wait." He remembered. "Where's Mindi—my wife's personal assistant? She was supposed to be watching Jules while Connie was out of town." He looked at Garth. "Was Mindi here when you arrived?"

Garth stepped into the light. "No, sir. As best I could tell, Jules had been alone."

"Maybe you'd better call this Mindi and find out why she's not here," his boss said. "Speaking of calls, Constance needs to be notified. Best ask her to come home right away."

Finn's fingers were shaking as he speed-dialed his wife.

The call went immediately to voicemail.

Instead of leaving a message, he texted Connie to call him back as soon as possible.

The rain stopped as quickly as it had started. Departing thunder rumbled east of their estate and brightening skies were across the bay to the west.

"We're going to get to work," Chief said. "Stay here so you don't miss your wife's call."

The team, including Garth, walked away toward Jules's body.

As Finn waited alone, his mind explored possibilities like The Academy trained all detectives to do. Only this time, the suspected homicide was in his backyard. The victim was his daughter.

Rip Riley was the first suspect who entered Finn's mind. Yesterday evening, Rip had threatened him by saying, *lenders never loan money to people who have nothing to lose.* But if Rip had killed Jules, the loan shark would have destroyed the only leverage that could've motivated Finn to pay him back quickly. Rip was smarter than that.

Unless, of course, killing his daughter was a warning that Finn would be next.

Hard to believe the guy might commit murder for a mere $75 grand. That amount was chump change for a loan shark of his caliber. At any rate, public knowledge of Finn's dealings with Rip would have significant consequences. Beyond Connie's reaction and her learning about the condo, Finn's association with a loan shark highlighted his desperation for money.

He stared at his cellphone.

Jesus. Why wasn't Connie returning his freaking call?

Contacting the station's front desk, Finn asked the deputy on duty, who was already crying over the news of Jules's death, to track down the NMPA president, calling his D.C. office and home in search of Connie. The officer agreed to call Finn when she got any answers.

Sitting in the recliner watching Chief Keller direct his officers in securing a possible crime scene, Finn's mind drifted. Only, he wasn't proud of what popped into his head.

In terms of Jules's life insurance policy, he and Connie were equal beneficiaries. Would a homicide delay the payout? Clearly, his two-million-dollar cut would resolve quite a few financial issues. And as insensitive as the subject matter seemed, timing wise, the truth was that Finn *hadn't* killed his daughter. He loved Jules. He'd give anything to turn back time.

His stomach churned when another likelihood surfaced: He'd be a suspect. His financial woes, coupled with a monetary reward that depended on his daughter's death, and the fact that he had committed mortgage fraud to acquire the Chestertown condo using Jules's name, might land him on the most wanted list.

Finn imagined the scandalous headlines. His career ruined.

Another tear raced down his cheek. This time, in response to his grim future.

His cellphone rang.

Wasn't Connie. The call came from the station.

"Parker," he answered.

"I tracked down Orin Yates," the deputy said. "He was home. Seems Mrs. Parker Skyped him this morning and launched a complaint about some Scarborough woman who interviewed your daughter yesterday…" She paused, as if waiting for him to put two and two together.

Finn was too tired for puzzles, even simple ones. *"And?"*

"Yates never had an in-person meeting scheduled with your wife. He hasn't seen her."

Closing his eyes, Finn slowly exhaled.

What the hell was his dear wife up to?

22

Sunday, August 15, 2027
The Windsors' Residence: Hickory Thicket, Maryland
(Day *of* Juliette's Death)

TRUITT HID BEHIND a loblolly tree between the properties, trying to remain undetected. The flashing lights of police cars in the Parkers' driveway had immobilized him like a hypnotic trance.

Confusion coursed through his veins.

When had he left his house? How long had he been standing in the trees watching? More than an hour? Less?

Maybe if he recalled what he'd been doing last, his short-term memories would return.

His Mom. He had been helping her inside the house, in their den.

The memories flooded back.

After hearing his mother cry, Truitt had left Jules under the pool house awning to return home. Once in his den, he had looked at the wall clock; the time, just after 11:30 a.m.

Turns out, his Mom's meltdown had been about a framed family photo that was supposed to be on one end-table and had somehow ended up on another. Ever since his family had moved to HT, Truitt's mother acted overly obsessed about where all the trinkets and knickknacks were supposed to be. The tiniest change to her environment would set her off, making her feel out of control.

Truitt remembered kneeling beside his Mom's recliner, holding her hand to soothe her. He admitted that he had been looking at the photo—his favorite. Last November, his team's halfback had snapped the family shot after Truitt had broken his conference's quarterback record in his junior year, no less. Even with Truitt's recent difficulty remembering details, he'd never forget his record: 5,761 yards passing, 425 completions, and a whopping 83 touchdown passes. In fact, he was ranked third in the nation for the greatest single-season QB performance in high school *history*. Hell yeah.

In the photo, his Mom and Dad stood on either side of him after his conference's championship game, while he still donned his blue jersey, boasting a few grass stains. His mother held a bouquet of flowers. Their smiles always made Truitt tear up. The photo had seared their happiness into his mind forever. Nothing could ever take that moment away.

After relishing his brief visit down memory lane, Truitt had unintentionally placed the framed photo on the wrong table. He promised his Mom he'd pay better attention in the future, putting everything back precisely as he had found it. Scout's Honor.

During Truitt's confession, his Dad had been standing behind his mother's chair, massaging her shoulders. "I think it's time we get help, Abby," his Dad had whispered.

With tears taking the place of words, his Mom nodded.

Truitt's relief had been overwhelming.

Back in Bishopville, in his childhood home, Truitt had been self-centered and that was putting it mildly. Why deny the truth? Everything had been about *him*.

Of course, his parents had enjoyed a lot of perks from his success. Abigail and Darren Windsor were *the* football parents, not just at his high school, but in the conference. Dang, in the state of Maryland. Perhaps on the entire East Coast.

Everyone near and far went to them for advice. *What protein drink helps your son? Which works better after a game, icing or heat? Where do you buy a size 14 shoe? How does your son make Honor Roll every quarter?*

Truitt was the center of his universe.

Not to mention, the attention made him feel privileged. No lie: He'd use his cellphone to call his Mom from his bedroom and tell her he was hungry, joking that her food service was slipping. Calling in meal orders made him feel like royalty.

Forget being a baron. Truitt had been a KING—all caps intended.

Laundry? Dirty clothes fell to the floor wherever he undressed. He never even made his bed. Ever. His Mom did everything for him inside the house. His Dad, everything on the outside. Truitt's job was football and grades. And occasionally letting off steam.

He was a celebrity, and he milked every ounce of his fame.

When his parents took back their lives by moving to HT, Truitt's inflated self-worth sprung a leak.

With newfound humility, he couldn't help feeling partially responsible for his Mom's instability, for her wild emotional spikes and paranoia. No doubt, she was mentally exhausted.

She wasn't the only one.

Truitt continued to experience his own unraveling of sorts, like when he blacked out during emotional stress. He wasn't sure if "blacked out" was the right term. His episodes didn't involve fainting or anything physical as far as he could tell. More like an instant onset of oblivion; a lapse in time that he couldn't account for.

In the present, at least Truitt had recalled what he'd been doing inside his house before standing among the swath of pine trees and acting dazed by the flashing lights. But had he done anything else after leaving his house, besides spying on his neighbors?

What also escaped him was why officers were in a huddle beside the pool area. In the rain. A short toss from where he had left Jules.

His mind was uncomfortably blank.

If only his Dad had taken him to a jeweler in Rock Hall to finally get a new battery for his wristwatch. Then maybe he'd be able to keep track of time. Surely his watch could help.

When officers broke from their tight circle on the grass, Truitt saw a black tarp. Was it covering a...*body?*

A gust of wind briefly folded back one side of the plastic, long enough for him to see a person underneath. A girl.

A teenager who looked like Jules. Only, dead.

He gagged and retched on the pine needles.

Whether he could keep track of time or not, another truth was brutally painful. One that continued to plague him: *The past never changed. No do-overs.*

As he rubbed his neck, a tear raced down his cheek.

And in a blink of an eye, his mind blacked out again.

23

WHILE ROCK HALL'S Chief of Police spoke with Dad under the awning, Jules lingered around her body. Seeing her shape under a veil of black plastic was surreal.

Sadness overwhelmed her.

Dreams of leaving the G&G, of going to college or working in horticulture, had died with her. If she had known her lifespan would end abruptly at 15, she might not have been so patient at riding out her incredibly screwed up childhood.

Look at what her tolerance had yielded: *death!*

Someone had murdered her. Drowned her in her parents' pool.

At the very least, following ridiculous rules and being a prisoner in her own home should've afforded her a long life. Kept her safe. In all seriousness, hadn't she earned that much?

Laughable was Mother had constantly referred to her as a queen.

A *queen?* What a joke.

Jules had stopped complaining about the disingenuous title. No point, since Constance Parker did and said what she wanted, relentlessly. Protests meant nothing to her.

Not even placing a crown on her daughter's head had disguised the obvious. Jules's actual station in life was at the bottom of the royal hierarchy. From day one, she had been born a peasant, forced to coo on demand by her obsessive ruler, *the* Queen Mother.

Fancy clothes, sparkling jewelry, makeup, and perfected manners were camouflage.

What confused Jules was why she hadn't woken up in Heaven after her death. Instead, her spirit was hanging around the G&G—a place she mostly loathed.

Weren't the meek supposed to be Heaven bound?

She remembered a passage from *The Beatitudes* in the *Bible*. One in particular: *"Blessed are the poor in spirit, for theirs is the kingdom of heaven."* And even though Mother touted that Jules's birthright entitled her to Grandfather Reyes's aristocracy, she had never felt privileged. Inside, she considered herself insignificant. Lowly. Without a voice.

Surely, Jules should've qualified for celestial paradise as a downtrodden spirit.

In books, she had read about souls getting stuck on Earth as ghosts. Stuck, until they resolved some issue which had haunted their biological lives.

Maybe, just maybe, she was supposed to find her murderer.

Drifting toward the pool house, Jules wondered if anyone would notice her. She didn't know much about ghosts but thought some manifested to the living—to those who had a sixth sense, second sight, or extrasensory perception.

As she approached the group which had reconvened under the awning, Dad crossed his arms in front of him.

He placed his hands over each sleeve, rubbing his biceps. "The storm dropped the temperature. I've got goosebumps," Dad said, through chattering teeth.

"You're upset and soaked," the chief responded. "Let's go inside the house and look around. Besides, it's probably best if you're not here when the OCME van arrives."

Dad's skin paled.

Not surprising. Their house hid secrets he wanted to keep.

While Garth offered to stay in the pool area to help the other detectives, Chief Keller and Dad walked toward the kitchen door. Jules followed, concluding they hadn't detected her presence. Or weren't admitting to it anyway.

Inside, the silver tray Mindi used to deliver Jules's *stea* every evening was upside down on the hardwood flooring. A broken piece of her teacup lay on top. The fall had scattered the remaining pieces of porcelain on the floor beside the kitchen island.

Jules had a brief flashback. She remembered hearing sounds earlier, while floating in the pool. Now they made sense: a vibrating clank; a crash of breaking china. The unsolved mystery was *how* the tray and teacup had toppled over.

"Was there some sort of disagreement here?" the chief asked Dad. "Between you and your wife? Perhaps over Jules?"

"Really? Are you going to start playing like I'm a suspect, Sam?" He raised his eyebrows. "Between you and me, I have disagreements with Connie every time I'm in her presence. We hurt one another with words, not silver and fine china. And we do *not* take our distaste for each other out on our daughter.

"As far as arguing over her?" Dad continued. "Sure. Sometimes Jules was the topic of our fights. We're typical parents; have different ways of doing things. And you, of all people, know how much I loved my daughter. Adored her.

"Since you're turning procedural on me," Dad added, with a sour face and tone, "I was interviewing Daisy Smithhisler about her pothead son when I heard the dispatcher over the radio. Prior, I ate my usual eleven-thirty lunch at the Bistro. Include *that* in your report, Chief."

Jules was standing near the pantry's entrance when she heard Dad refer to himself and Queen Mother as *typical* parents. Seriously? Was he really going to perpetuate the masquerade, even after her death?

How would pretending they were a normal family help catch the murderer who had ended her life?

"I heard you say *you* loved your daughter," the chief followed up. "Did Constance feel the same about Jules? You know how mothers and teenaged daughters can be."

"Not going to dignify your question with an answer. For God sakes, we just lost our daughter. Connie doesn't even know yet."

"Got it." The chief rubbed his chin. "How about that personal assistant of your wife's? Mindi, I think you said? Maybe *she* argued with Jules."

Dad keyed the touchpad on his cell. "Texting her now. Telling her to get over here."

Jules and Mindi *had* exchanged words after breakfast, but the only way Mindi could've had anything to do with the mess on the kitchen floor—or with Jules's death, for that matter—was if she had come back, after leaving the estate to do who knows what.

A gust blew through the open window over the sink, making an eerie whistling sound.

From his pocket, the chief withdrew latex gloves and a baggy. "Who knows? Maybe the wind knocked this stuff over." He secured the gloves onto his hands. Squatting, he collected large fragments of the teacup and placed them into his baggy. "Better analyze a few pieces. Learn whose fingers had touched this cup." Chief Keller stood. "Mind showing me Jules's bedroom?"

Dad took a deep breath, briefly closing his eyes.

"Is there a problem?" the chief asked.

"You mean other than the fact that my daughter's dead and I'm going to see her bedroom for the first time since her passing? Since her possible *murder?*"

"Sorry, Finn." Chief Keller scratched his bald head. "You're usually the one conducting these kinds of interviews. My bedside manners are rusty."

Dad led him up the narrow staircase to her loft. The 20th step creaked.

"Kind of secluded, isn't it?" the chief asked.

"A teenager's dream."

"If you say so, my friend."

Jules followed behind them.

"I get what you were saying earlier," the chief said. "The temperature *is* chilly."

At the landing, her father quickly pushed Jules's door wide-open, maybe hoping Chief Keller wouldn't notice the locks. They walked inside her bedroom.

Jules's silk pants suit was still on her chair, draped over the back. At that moment, reality deepened: Life could stop in an instant— before clothes even made it to the dry-cleaning hamper.

Treading over to her bulletin board, the chief scuffed his combat boots on her flooring, leaving several black streaks on the wooden planks. He focused on a copy of the rules, one Jules's mother had pinned into the cork. He stood in silence, reading the print.

"Interesting stuff," the chief said. "I take it your wife was Jules's...handler?"

"Common term for a manager. Yes."

"Got it." The chief looked around. "I think we should tape off Jules's room and get a forensics team in here. That okay with you?"

"Absolutely."

If Jules could move Garth's cellphone as he performed CPR on her body, maybe she could affect the loft's door by making it move, by drawing attention to it. She wanted to witness how Dad would explain the locks. Gauge where her father's words fell on the truth spectrum.

Harnessing the energy that coursed through her "veins," Jules concentrated on releasing the electrical charge from her hands. And just like that, the door began to slowly swing on its hinges, enough to get the chief to notice.

"I'll be straight with you, Finn," Chief Keller said, walking toward the door. "This house gives me the creeps." He examined both sides of the wood slab and looked up at Dad. "Why is there a deadbolt on the *outside?* Supplemented with a barrel bolt?"

Jules's heart felt like it was pounding in her chest, which was over-the-top ironic.

"This loft was used as a storage attic before we converted the space into Jules's bedroom and en suite," Dad explained, not missing a beat. "We never bothered to remove the locks."

Her father was a liar!

Chief Keller bent down and pinched something between his fingers. He brought the specimen to his nose and sniffed. "Interesting. A small woodchip." He locked eyes with Dad again. "What did you keep in there? The Mona Lisa?"

"More like Monet and fine jewelry, but you've got the picture," Dad answered.

They stepped out of her loft and back onto the landing above her staircase.

Not only did Jules have to deal with hovering in a world she no longer belonged to, but she had to listen to her father outright lie.

The truth stung before it numbed.

Then again, why should she feel shocked?

How different was turning a blind eye to flat out lying about her abuse? Both choices were enabling. Both caused sadness and anger deep within her core.

She slammed her bedroom door so forcefully that a hanging picture rattled on the wall across from the stairs.

Even Dad flinched.

24

Sunday, August 15, 2027
The Parkers' G&G Estate: Hickory Thicket, Maryland
(Day *of* Juliette's Death)

AS MINDI DROVE on the graveled roadway leading out of
Hidden Creek Trailer Park, after a visit with her former high school
sweetheart, she heard the ping of a delivered text on her cellphone.
The time on her Volvo's dashboard read 2:34 p.m.

She would've avoided glancing at her cell while driving if her tires
hadn't been crunching over stones, barely registering 10 miles-per-
hour. But given she drove faster in the parking lot of her
Grandmomma's nursing home, navigating around gray-tops clutching
their walkers and inching along the asphalt, she didn't hesitate to read
the message.

Finn here. Need you at the G&G. Immediately.

Fucking fireballs to hell.

And now Brock was calling her.

After Mindi returned home from college, Brock Nolan was her
only friend in the area. The only one she confided in. Of course, Finn
would replace him; that was already in the works.

Until then, Brock was sly and crafty, devious even, and Mindi
needed his perspective for advice. Besides, he was like a worn out
stuffed animal from childhood. The toy no longer sparked an urge to
cuddle but remained hard to throw away.

Good or bad, history was like glue.

She answered Brock's call by pressing the touchscreen on her car's center console. "I'm being summoned back to the estate."

"Turned on my police scanner after you left," Brock said. "There's a code one-hundred at the G&G. Officers found a dead body. Imagine that." He chuckled. "Someone drowned your Beauty Brat in the pool. Being considered a crime scene."

Hence, the text from Finn.

Pulling over on the grass, Mindi put her sedan in park and let it idle as she collected her thoughts. She hadn't noticed a woman walking her leashed standard poodle on the same side of the road. The annoyed woman raised her hand in protest as she walked her dog into the stony roadway and around the car.

Fuck the bitch. Mindi had more important matters on her mind.

BB Jules was officially dead.

Deeply inhaling, she repeated to herself: *Steady breathing cleanses the anxious soul.*

Shit would be hitting the fan.

Maybe she should've felt more than anxiety, but she didn't.

"Don't admit you came here," Brock continued over the car's speakerphone. "Or ever saw me. No matter what. We agreed."

"Shut up and give me a minute to think," she said.

The Queen Mother obsessed about time and would expect her personal assistant to account for every minute away from the property, especially since Mindi had disregarded her orders to stay with BB Jules. *Especially* now that her daughter was found dead.

After leaving the G&G that morning, Mindi had purchased a sports drink for Beauty Brat at the Rock Hall convenience store, keeping with the plan recorded by the kitchen's hidden camera. She had her receipt. The stop had taken longer since cars and patrons crowded the parking lot, no doubt due to the highest ever lottery jackpot. Mindi left the store around 10:40 a.m.

A trip to her apartment was next. She stayed for about an hour before heading to the police station, arriving at 11:50 a.m. The officer wearing a "Walker" nametag would remember Mindi. Anyway, the note she handed over, the one securely sealed and addressed to Finn, proved she had stopped there.

Of course, Mindi would provide Constance with a bogus explanation as to what the note said. A thank you to Finn for scheduling the Volvo's oil change (an estate vehicle) seemed reasonable enough, since he had actually handled that for her.

Twenty minutes after delivering her note, she arrived at Brock's.

The three-hour block between leaving the police station and arriving back at the G&G would be the time frame in question. She'd say she had returned to her apartment after the station, instead of the truth: that she was at Brock's. But to prove she had remained in Rock Hall and hadn't returned to Hickory Thicket, she'd need more than her word. She'd need evidence.

"You still there?" Brock asked. "Did you hear me?"

"I'll head back to the convenience store first," she said, her heart racing.

"Before heading to the G&G? Why?"

"Couldn't be any timelier for the ticket strategy you told me about. I'll buy something else, too. Something that explains why I needed to return. This will work. My whereabouts will be traceable, and they won't point to you or the G&G."

"You'll be cool when the cops question you, right?"

Brock's obsession with staying under the radar annoyed her. He didn't even have a job. What was he so worried about? No one at Castle Privileged knew he existed! *Her* ass was the one on the chopping block. Not his!

"Your concern for me is underwhelming," she snapped, as she ended their call.

Earlier, while at his trailer, she had asked Brock to school her on being more manipulative—on learning how to "manage" obstacles others mistook as insurmountable. After all, if Mindi had any hopes of luring Finn away and surviving the Queen Mother's wrath, she had to bolster her skills.

Since the largest jackpot drawing in lottery history was tomorrow, Brock had mentioned purchased tickets as an overlooked alibi. Apparently, Brock had a cousin who worked for the lottery system. She had explained to him that each ticket's code identified the location of purchase. And with the time included, each ticket functioned as a footprint.

Meaning, a criminal might have a trusted confidante buy a ticket for him at the time of a planned robbery. Once the ticket was turned over to the criminal, he could verify his whereabouts.

Of course, the strategy only worked if the cops didn't catch the perp within 24 hours of the crime. According to Brock, that's how long most convenience stores kept in-store security footage before erasing it. If cops caught the suspect *after* 24 hours and he furnished the lottery ticket, he'd hold a piece of evidence supporting his innocence since someone can't be at two places at one time.

A store couldn't prove, without footage, that the criminal was never there. That he never purchased the ticket himself.

Brock had also shared an option if someone was working alone and needed a similar time clock to account for a shorter period, like an hour. Only requirement? A slow line.

Lady Luck was on Mindi's side.

When she pulled into the convenience store's parking lot again, the line was even longer than when she'd bought the sports drink earlier that morning. Patrons snaked through the glass doors, spilling into the lot in a curvy line.

As per Brock's instructions, the first step was stopping a person who had just purchased a ticket. Thankfully, the man fitting that description was a senior and his age might mean he wouldn't be in a rush. Turns out, the old gray-top had bought two tickets for a total of four dollars. He claimed he had waited in line for nearly an hour.

Mindi struck a quick deal by offering him $50 for his tickets.

Smiling and clutching his crisp bill, he started shuffling back toward the end of the line.

Twenty-one people—mostly end of summer tourists if she had to guess—were waiting in line to buy tickets. In typical Rock Hall fashion, nothing moved faster than sloth speed.

Inside the store, Mindi grabbed a box of tampons. Her period had stopped two days ago. Being desperate for feminine products, however, was a perfect "emergency." After receiving Finn's text, she simply *had* to return to the store to avert a bloody disaster. Not to mention, the topic of menstruation and cramps always shortened a conversation. Who wanted to probe deeper into that topic? Best of all, no one was actually going to check if she was bleeding.

The lottery ticket would place her at a location other than Brock's double wide or the G&G, during a time frame when she needed proof of her whereabouts. And even though there would be plenty of suspects ahead of Mindi in the drowning of BB Jules, attending to the details now (when maneuvering was easy) might save her when intense scrutiny came *later.*

She entered the express lane—the one not selling lottery tickets to keep regular customers from bitching. After paying for her items, she asked for a receipt.

"I bought two lottery tickets earlier," she told the cashier, holding up her slips to the security camera, enjoying the acting. "I was so excited that I forgot what I came here to buy!"

"Tell someone who cares," the guy griped, while handing her the receipt and looking to the person behind her. "Next..."

Good for the cashier that Mindi had somewhere to be. Otherwise, she might have waited for the bastard to get off work. Then, she'd "accidentally" run him over in the busy parking lot. As he moaned about how unfair it was for him to die in the prime of his freaking life, she'd chuckle and remind the prick to *tell someone who cared.*

On the way to her car, the old man waved at her from the lottery line. Fucking fireballs. Hopefully, he suffered from dementia and wouldn't remember their transaction come tomorrow.

Driving to the estate, she reminded herself to think of her Grandmomma's inevitable passing. Not because she wanted her to die. Only because imagining her death would open the flood gates when Mindi pretended she was hearing about the brat's drowning for the first time.

She wondered if Constance would've returned to the G&G by now. No doubt, the Queen Mother would have to decide what to do about the video cameras hidden around the mansion. She'd need to address her surveillance system *before* the cops discovered it and followed the breadcrumbs to Constance's secret surveillance setup in her walk-in closet.

Paranoia wasn't a great look during a murder investigation.

At least footage from the kitchen would show that Mindi's last exchange with BB Jules was amiable. But that damned tea. Thank goodness she had read Constance's written instructions aloud for the camera. The evidence would be indisputable: Her boss had directed her to give the brat that cocktail. The order was on paper.

What could Mindi do? She worked for the woman and didn't want to lose her job. And she had assumed that Constance would know best, as far as her daughter's wellbeing was concerned.

If cops ever got their hands on the recordings, hopefully authorities would clear Mindi of any wrongdoing. Clearly, both parents approved of the tea, but maybe she'd intentionally omit Finn's knowledge of it. After all, what good were her plans if her sexy hunk of blue was behind bars?

When Mindi arrived at the house, she decided to knock on the front door, located slightly off center, nearest the right wing. The move might emphasize her employee status instead of looking like she was an intimate member of the family.

Projecting a healthy distance from the inner core seemed wise.

Someone caught her attention among the pine trees separating the properties. The figure looked like a male—the very same teenager whom BB Jules had undoubtedly met in the garden, after she had snuck outside. The one to whom Jules had written a note, promising to disclose secrets.

The *same* boy Mindi had seen jogging on the G&G's beach.

Smiling, she knew precisely how she'd contribute to an investigation of Jules's drowning.

If her Detective Parker was a wolf, the kid named Truitt had just become raw lamb.

25

Sunday, August 15, 2027
The Parkers' G&G Estate: Hickory Thicket, Maryland
(Day *of* Juliette's Death)

CONSTANCE WAS PRAGMATIC, especially under enormous stress. Observers had difficulty understanding her stoicism which was why she had learned to cry on demand: to ease their minds that she was not completely heartless.

In the course of her beauty career, Constance had adopted an empirical approach to cause and effect, keenly studying people of all demographics to accurately anticipate their expectations and reactions to a variety of stimuli. Those, like her, who had developed a strategic playbook on the human psyche were at an advantage in life. In fact, every woman who had ever won the Miss America title possessed a similar craft, though certainly not at Constance's level of mastery.

Control the perception; control the outcome.

Driving her Maserati toward her Glitz and Glamour estate, she recalled the time when a pageantry host had asked her to describe herself in one word, in one second. *Empathetic,* she had blurted out, widening her eyes to display sincerity, knowing full well that *empathetic* was what judges would yearn to hear from a contestant blessed with disproportionate beauty and abundant wealth. In truth, the word that should have left her red lacquered lips was *calculating.*

Of course, *calculating* was far too ugly to earn a crown. Precisely why every successful beauty queen, politician running for office, or Hollywood elite acted like they were everything *but.*

How deliciously decadent.

In Constance's current situation, being calculating meant she would project "the grieving mother" while holding herself together on the inside. After all, she had i's to dot and t's to cross. Absolutely nothing came before Constance's reputation. Her image was all she could hope to save. In contrast, Juliette Annabella was already dead.

Yes, Constance was unapologetically pragmatic.

Thankfully, she shared her Machiavellian approach to self-preservation with her best and only true friend, Deanna Mae, who lived with her emotionally frigid, industrial tycoon of a husband on a waterfront estate in Delta Heights, north of Rock Hall.

Before puberty, she and Deanna Mae had made a pact to protect each other's reputations from their future indiscretions, perversions, and culpable pleasures. They had sealed the deal in an exchange of blood and their contract with one another had never failed.

Over time, she and Deanna Mae craved nothing because they could afford everything. They became bored from satisfying their every whim. Instead, exhilaration blossomed from planning elaborate ruses to cover their tracks, which they simply referred to as "contingencies."

Constance's supposed trip to Washington, D.C., had required such a contingency.

As part of their ruse, Deanna Mae visited a posh boutique on Connecticut Avenue in Washington, D.C. to coincide with Constance's claim she would be meeting with NMPA President Orin Yates and shopping afterwards. Joining Deanna Mae was another close friend—a woman who could pass as Constance's body-double from a distance, a woman who retained a few of Constance's credit cards and was equally thirsty to escape the boredom of privileged living. Also, Constance knew one of her not-so-little secrets which motivated her to toe the line.

During contingencies, Constance and her body double dressed identically. Today, they donned a French bun covered by a Carolina Herrera floral scarf, a white tunic blouse and silk black pants, Dolce and Gabbana sandals, magenta lips, and Cartier Paris sunglasses.

In on their duplicity, the boutique owner was a mutual friend of all three women: Constance, her body double, and Deanna Mae.

Money, as long as it continued to flow, forged inseparable alliances.

For several hours, Deanna Mae and Constance's body double enjoyed shopping at the boutique, making several purchases over the course of their visit. Half-past noon, they dined at Le Diplomate for a late brunch. Constance's credit card picked up the bill for two lobster omelets and four mimosas. The ladies might have considered the day drab if it were not for the fact that they were players in an iniquitous performance.

Oh, the twisted amusements of the filthy rich.

When Constance's darling husband called at 1:40 p.m. and followed up with a text, her heartrate had spiked. Adrenaline made her fingers tremble. Not from fear, but from the prospect that the contingency might elevate in importance. At that moment, Constance directed Deanna Mae and Constance's body double to return home, while remaining at the ready for further instructions. After all, travel from D.C. to Delta Heights took two hours on average.

An hour later, her bitchboy grunt called and the contingency shifted classifications to bona fide. Brock had heard over his police scanner that Juliette had drowned in their pool. This, despite the fact that Constance had expressly forbidden her daughter to swim.

In truth, Juliette Annabella had been getting more rebellious by the minute, disregarding her handler *and* the rules.

Compartmentalize, she reminded herself before anger consumed her.

With the news, Constance had called Deanna Mae back. Her best friend was halfway home. They agreed to meet at their regular secluded rendezvous for contingencies—one void of security cameras. Once they had connected, Deanna Mae gave Constance her receipts, credit card, and boutique purchases: two Valentino cocktail dresses.

Pulling into her driveway, Constance's smartwatch read 4:02 p.m. She deeply inhaled like a performer about to take the stage.

After parking, she pulled off her sandals. Why ruin them unnecessarily? Besides, mud between her toes would look uncharacteristically desperate, which was far more believable when coming home to a driveway congested with police cruisers than projecting runway elegance.

She opened her mansion's front door, clutching her boutique bags and sandals. Finn, Chief Keller, two detectives, Garth, and Mindi were standing in the foyer, as if ready to depart.

"What the hell is going on, Finn?" she asked, tears beginning to stream down her cheeks.

Her husband wrapped his arms around her and whispered the dreaded news to her ear, as she slumped to the floor, having held her breath long enough to faint.

When Constance regained consciousness, she was lying on the velvet couch in the parlor.

Sam Keller delivered the chronology of events.

"Where is Juliette now?" she cried. "I want to see her."

"I'm sorry," Finn said. "There were marks on her neck. Protocol requires the chief to proceed as if Jules's death was a homicide. Her body is already in Baltimore for an autopsy."

The thought had never crossed Constance's mind.

Her cheeks flushed.

"Absolutely not!" she said, standing and stomping her right foot. "No one will butcher our daughter. Mourners will expect an open casket. My God, Finn! Juliette was a beauty queen. A renowned national champion. Her looks were everything!"

During her drive home, Constance had pictured the service. Her daughter would lie in repose, wearing a white gown of innocence, as she delivered a heart-wrenching eulogy inspiring wailing and generating copious amounts of sympathy. Attendees would embrace the grieving mother. The occasion would be epic, and the media would immortalize the event.

A closed casket was *not* in her vision.

"I tried calling you, Connie. You didn't answer. Where were you?"

Her bastard husband was all too eager to learn if she would incriminate herself.

She shivered. Why was the parlor so frigid? Were her nerves getting the best of her?

"Orin Yates preferred a video conference over an in-person meeting," Constance started. "However, I elected not to cancel my planned shopping spree with Deanna Mae. She was looking forward to our engagement. So I went to D.C. anyway."

"Your cellphone," Finn pressed. "You didn't respond to me."

"Apologies, darling. I always mute my phone while shopping and dining. I simply forgot to unmute it. And I was having such fun with Deanna Mae that I never checked for messages."

Mindi began slithering out of the parlor.

"Wait!" Constance snapped at her. "Where were you when Juliette Annabella needed you? I had instructed you to remain by her side."

"Mindi went to buy your daughter a sports drink at Jules's request," Sam Keller said. "She made a number of stops before...*umm*...developing menstrual cramps. I'm sure Finn will give you the details of her whereabouts."

"Take tomorrow off," she told Mindi. "We can discuss this matter when you report for work on Tuesday. Besides, a little downtime will serve us all well."

Her personal assistant nodded and left the room.

"Sounds like a good idea," Sam said. "In fact, we'll clear out to give you folks a chance to grieve in private. We won't be back until the medical examiner has determined a cause of death. Just keep everyone out of Jules's room. We've taped off the area."

"Before you go," Constance said. "If Juliette's death *is* a homicide, then offer a million dollar reward for information leading to an arrest and conviction. Please publicize this."

Finn's mouth almost dropped open. "One *million?*"

"Is money *a problem* for you, darling?"

"No. No, of course not."

"One more thing, come to think of it," the chief said. "Have you witnessed the teenager next door hanging around your daughter?"

"Only Mindi has seen him thus far, from a distance," Constance answered.

"We plan on questioning Truitt Windsor. At this early stage, he seems to be our prime person of interest. Best to stay away from him. Better keep the doors locked, too."

26

Tuesday, August 17, 2027
OCME Lab: Baltimore, Maryland
(Two Days *after* Juliette's Death)

MONDAY HAD BEEN a complete blur for Jules.

Tuesday was a different story. Energized and refreshed, she popped into the medical examiner's office within the OCME laboratory facility in Baltimore. Dad and Chief Keller were already there, waiting to hear the results of her autopsy.

Undetected by anyone in the room, she stood beside a potted plastic palm tree in the back corner. The blinds were closed. Eye-squinting fluorescents buzzed from the ceiling.

In order to figure out who had murdered her, Jules wanted to hear the doctor's findings firsthand, but she wasn't quite sure how she had known the time of the meeting or where it was taking place.

One aspect of being a ghost was becoming crystal clear. Her subconscious played a significant role. Sometimes, she consciously decided where to go. Other times, like this morning, her subconscious popped her into where she *needed* to be.

Her clothes fell into a similar category. When she appeared in the office, she was wearing comfortable jeans, a T-shirt, and work boots. Her subconscious had made a great choice because her outfit would've appalled Queen Mother. *Business meetings require professional attire.* Jules smiled. She was beginning to appreciate the benefits of being a ghost, especially since she had no choice but to exist as one.

Dad and Chief Keller were dressed in their law enforcement

uniforms. Facing away from her, they sat in chairs in front of a large desk cluttered with stacks of papers.

On the other side of the desk sat a man in a white lab coat. With his peppered hair pulled back into a ponytail, he sported round framed glasses. The nameplate on the desk identified him as Dr. Quade Zappa, Medical Examiner and Lead Forensic Pathologist.

After Dr. Zappa's condolences, the meeting began.

"As part of the autopsy," the doctor started, reading from a paper on his desk, "I conducted thorough external and internal examinations, as well as submitted fluids for a toxicology report. Based on body temperature, rigor, livor mortis (or skin discoloration), and stomach contents, I'm approximating the time of death between eleven a.m. and one o'clock p.m. on August the fifteenth." He raised his head and locked eyes with Dad. "My most inconclusive finding in your daughter's case was determining the manner of death.

"For one thing, the decedent's toxicology report is concerning," he continued. "Your daughter's blood confirmed twelve milligrams of zolpidem, which is a sedative."

"Jules was an insomniac," Dad said, nodding.

"A normal dosage for her body type is five milligrams...or less, taken at night, not during the day," Dr. Zappa said, ignoring Dad's comment. "At this toxicity level, your daughter was likely experiencing extreme drowsiness and depressed respiration. Her impairments would have been visible and may have included slurred speech and a lack of coordination."

Truitt had been right. Her *stea* had been unusually potent.

But why? How in the world could Mindi benefit from her death?

"My daughter died of an overdose then?" Dad asked.

"Detective Parker. My conclusions aren't presented in an interactive format," Dr. Zappa scolded. "If you don't mind, I prefer my methodical, uninterrupted approach to delivering my findings. May I continue?"

"Sorry. Please go on."

The doctor looked down at his report again. "Your daughter's Blood Alcohol Concentration was .02 percent, which wouldn't be significant alone, but coupled with zolpidem, would have further compromised her. As we know, intoxication and swimming can easily result in accidental drowning.

"In terms of the decedent's causes of death," Dr. Zappa continued, "I found hypoxemia and cerebral anoxia, both standard in drowning victims. However, with a partial ring visible around her neck, marked by a thin abrasion, I also found evidence of asphyxia."

"My daughter was an asthmatic," Dad piped in.

Dr. Zappa narrowed his eyes, probably since her father had already disregarded his request to keep quiet during his report. "Though it is highly probable that water inflated her lungs while she was still alive, suggesting the manner of death was, indeed, accidental drowning while intoxicated, it is also possible that even in her impaired state, she was defending herself against strangulation and involuntarily inhaled the pool water.

"In either scenario," the doctor added, "learning if she knowingly overdosed would be helpful, though you may never be able to verify her intentions, unless she kept a journal or diary, or had told a friend of her plans."

Knowingly overdosed? Jules would never!

Listening to the men talk about her, when she was present in the room, was difficult. She had things to say, to contribute, like telling them a hidden camera in the kitchen recorded Mindi *giving* her the spiked tea. At the time, Jules had no clue it was stronger than usual.

"There's always the possibility someone intentionally drugged her to make drowning her easier," the doctor said. "Or perhaps someone found the victim in her physically compromised state and took advantage of the opportunity. I'm merely voicing conjectures."

At least the doctor was mentioning more likely scenarios.

"Got it," Chief Keller said. "We'll explore every angle."

Dr. Zappa handed the report to the chief while looking at Dad. "This may bring you and your wife a bit of comfort, Detective Parker. It is my opinion your daughter became unconscious quickly.

"In conclusion, I'm temporarily classifying her manner of death as 'undetermined' while noting a possible homicide. Which means your department has an investigation to conduct. Obviously, we need more information in order to submit a definitive finding."

"It's settled. The case will remain open," Chief Keller announced.

"I'll pull together an investigative team, which may include another department's assistance, to take a closer look at the scene." He turned to Dad. "I'm thinking you can expect us at the G&G tomorrow."

"That works."

"By the way," the chief said to Dr. Zappa, "A broken teacup and skimmer were collected from the scene. We retrieved the skimmer from the bottom of the pool and the lab found two sets of prints, one from their groundskeeper—who's cooperating—and one unknown set. We're running the mystery fingerprints in our database to see if there are any matches."

The skimmer sparked a memory.

Jules remembered Truitt had been scooping leaves from the pool, using the skimmer, as they chatted on the morning of her death. She had told him not to bother because a storm was coming. *More leaves will sink to the bottom,* she recalled saying.

The fingerprints had to be *his.*

At the time, Truitt had said something strange to her. What was it?

Her temperature started to rise, absorbing energy from the room.

"Your AC is working overtime," the chief said. "I can practically see my breath."

As her memory began to crystalize, her spirit became charged like a live electrical circuit.

"The thermostat's literally dropping as we speak," Dad commented, looking shocked as the green numbers on the mounted wall unit lowered with each blink.

Truitt's odd words echoed in Jules's mind. *Better than dying slowly,* he had said.

In a sudden rage, she released all the air from her lungs. A bizarre sensation, since she no longer had real lungs. Not physically anyway.

A stack of papers on Dr. Zappa's desk took flight like giant-sized confetti.

"What the hell?" Dad said.

The doctor stood, trying to snatch a few papers midair. "Welcome to my world."

"What's that supposed to mean?" Chief Keller asked.

"I work with victimized corpses. Sometimes they decide to join the conversation."

27

Tuesday, August 17, 2027
The Parkers' G&G Estate: Hickory Thicket, Maryland
(Two Days *after* Juliette's Death)

FROM THE DEN'S wall of windows facing the Parkers' backyard, Mindi watched from a distance as the Queen Mother reached for the garden's iron gate with her right hand while clutching a basket handle in her left. The mansion still cast a shadowy blanket over the backyard landscape. At 9:30 a.m., the sun hadn't risen high enough in the sky to bask the lawn with its warm glow. As a result, cool tones gave the impression the atmosphere might be refreshing.

Mindi knew the sticky truth. Humidity was off the charts.

Yet, there was the former Miss America, taking a morning stroll to pick roses, if Mindi had to guess. A vision of tranquility. Probably not a bead of sweat on her.

How could Constance look and act so freaking nonchalant? The woman had cameras hidden throughout the house! Didn't she worry about investigators coming any day now to scour her daughter's room and the spaces she frequented, searching for evidence? Worry, that they'd find the cameras and request the recorded footage? Worry, that they'd learn about the tea concoction Constance prescribed for her daughter?

Focus. That's what Mindi needed to do. She had her own worries. Like maybe Beauty Brat had kept a diary or journal. A lot of people did. And if BB Jules had one, Mindi was certain it would include unfavorable entries about none other than her mother's personal assistant. After all, the only time they had ever gotten along was two days ago, on the day of the brat's death.

Mindi had every intention of finding Jules's journal, if one existed, before investigators did. This morning was the perfect opportunity to search. Apparently, her sexy hunk of blue had left the house dreadfully early for Baltimore, where he and the chief were meeting with the medical examiner about Jules's autopsy. Chef Evelyn had driven off into town to beat the tourist crowds in the grocery store, and the housekeeper was cleaning in the left wing where the master suite was located. With the Queen Mother in the garden, Mindi headed for the pantry.

Speaking of journals, she had set her own ablaze yesterday, in Brock's backyard where he kept an old industrial barrel behind his double wide to burn things. Incriminating things. Certainly, her journal had qualified. She never held back when she penned her hopes, dreams, and vivid fantasies. That's what journals were all about. Since Mindi had written…*I wish Beauty Brat was dead*…way more than once, and now the object of that repugnance was, in fact, *dead,* damage control became her priority. Searching for Jules's possible diary was equally urgent.

After climbing the stairs, she clutched the banister and stared before stepping onto the landing. BB Jules's door was shut, sealed with a crisscross of yellow crime tape stuck to the frame. The image was so final. The brat was really gone.

Reaching into her pocket, she grabbed latex gloves and put them on. Loosening the tape was easy, just as putting it back would be.

Once inside the loft, Mindi started her search within Jules's drawers, using her fingers to probe for a journal between the garments. She found nothing. Rushing around the space, she looked over, under, and in between everything, lifting pillows and the mattress and box spring.

Beads of sweat accentuated her strenuous efforts. In addition, she simply had to avoid Constance catching her in the act. Picking roses only took so long.

Empty hangers in the walk-in closet began to rattle. The temperature in the room plummeted. Fucking fireballs to hell. Couldn't anything be normal in Castle Privileged?

Her cellphone pinged with a text. Her heart sputtered.

Finn here. About the note you left at the station.
I'll be at the Bistro tomorrow at 11:30 a.m.

Her sexy hunk of blue's meeting must have ended, and the first thing he did was contact her! Unfortunately, Mindi couldn't afford to daydream until later. Right now, she had to hurry.

After foraging like a starved rodent through articles of clothing and boxes of keepsakes, she found no journal, notes, or writings of any kind. The brat had only kept a few congratulatory cards from other contestants, as well as a dozen letters from dead Nana Bea.

Leaving the loft, she returned the crime tape and removed her gloves, stuffing them into her pocket. Almost to the bottom of the staircase, the worst possible scenario happened.

Constance opened the door at the base of the stairs.

"And what, pray tell, are you doing in my daughter's stairwell?" Constance asked, using her *I'll eat you up and spit you out* tone. "Absolutely no one is to have access to her loft."

"I had hoped to get a moment alone in her room, to privately pay my respects before investigators rummage through her things. But the cops, I mean, detectives have taped off her room, so I wasn't able to go inside. I certainly didn't mean to appear...intrusive."

The Queen Mother preferred a polished vocabulary.

Constance stood to the side of the door, providing room for Mindi to slide by her and walk into the pantry. Her boss closed the door and turned to face her. "I gave you the day off yesterday. But make no mistake. My disappointment in your actions could not be higher," she said. "You disobeyed several of my orders and now Juliette Annabella is dead."

"Several?" Mindi only knew of one: leaving the property.

"I instructed you to *give* Jules the tea I prepared, not to *add* more zolpidem. Her tea already included the proper dosage. You can imagine my horror, my shock, as I watched the camera footage showing you include her evening pills as well! No doubt the autopsy will find that Juliette had alarming levels of the sleeping aid in her bloodstream. Which means you, darling Mindi, may be the very reason my daughter perished."

Mindi felt a chill race up and down her spine. Her stomach contents rose to her throat.

"That was an accident!" she cried, her heart palpitating. "I always crush her pills and add them to the batch of tea you've made. You must have *wanted* me to misunderstand!"

"And now you sound like a frantic child who just got caught with an empty cookie jar, far too busy accusing others instead of wiping the crumbs from your messy little fingers."

Clearly, Constance was going to throw her under the bus. If Mindi stood a chance of avoiding her own demise, she had to regain her composure and level the playing field.

"How clean are your fingers, Constance?" Mindi asked. "Before you go on one of your outings, I've heard you whisper the word *contingency* when speaking with your friend from Delta Heights. What does that mean, exactly?"

Constance raised her chin. "An incidental expense, of course."

Mindi was going to be mincemeat if she couldn't convince the Queen Mother to play together. Nicely. Without drawing blood.

"In light of your negligence," her boss continued, "is there any reason why you should remain as my personal assistant? What benefit could you be to me now?"

"On the surface, you have a funeral to plan. I can help make it legendary," Mindi said, appealing to her boss's pragmatic side. "Closer to the bone, we should work together to manage our secrets. Like you always say: *Control the perception; control the outcome.*"

Until Mindi fulfilled her plans, she had to keep her enemies close.

Her boss slightly tilted her head. Was she annoyed or impressed?

"Let me warn you, Mindi," Constance growled. "Perception is a delicate creature. The difference between 'accidental' and 'intentional' is one brittle whisker. Cross me, and you will learn how very fragile your future truly is."

Mindi took a shallow breath. She might actually have saved herself. Temporarily.

"Is that understood?" Constance pressed.

"Yes, Ma'am."

"Excellent."

28

Tuesday, August 17, 2027
The Parkers' G&G Estate: Hickory Thicket, Maryland
(Two Days *after* Juliette's Death)

AT NIGHTFALL, CONSTANCE lit candles in the den and turned off all the lights. Sitting in her favorite chair, she gazed out across the backyard, watching nearby fireflies and comparing them to the distant twinkling lights on Gibson Island. Raising her glass of exquisite cognac, Hennessy Paradis to be exact, she sipped and savored the dark chocolate, orange, and vanilla notes, accentuated by a pleasantly lingering dash of peppery spice.

Constance was in a solemn mood. Never had she felt so alone.

Not even their daughter's death could keep her husband home. Finn had left Glitz and Glamour and had gone into the station for nightshift duty. Unbelievable. He would rather work at his two-bit job than console her. Adding salt to the wound, he had declined Chief Keller's offer to be involved in Juliette's case, even though having him part of the investigative team could help steer the hounds away from *sensitive* areas. Was he too clueless to comprehend that his secrets were as much at risk as hers?

Regardless, her darling Finley had elected to remain on the sidelines. How very, utterly worthless.

To herself, she could admit that she had contributed to Finn's unwillingness to take a stand on anything. From their courtship to marriage to parenting, and especially regarding finances, that was precisely how she had wanted him to be: hands off, in terms of decision making. Constance had always insisted on taking the lead, having no interest whatsoever in compromising on one bloody thing. And since she controlled *her* wealth and everything else around them, he possessed no bargaining chips. Over time, Finn had become increasingly aloof and disengaged. In other words, a spineless coward.

Flashes of lightning strobed in the night sky.

At least the cognac diluted the sour taste of her wretched Tuesday.

Her earlier encounter with Mindi had provoked her to take two actions.

First, Constance realized she had no choice but to submit, to authorities, a thumb drive of the video recordings involving her daughter. She would hand over the drive tomorrow. Choosing to keep them secret would only give her personal assistant leverage over which to negotiate, and Constance would not stoop so low as to give Mindi equal footing. Hell would freeze over first.

Thankfully, video captured from the kitchen gave Constance the upper hand. Footage showed Mindi had misunderstood her directions about "giving" versus "preparing" the tea. The verdict was still out in terms of how Constance would promote her assistant's actions to detectives. Was adding more zolpidem accidental or intentional? Mindi had certainly given Constance plenty of evidence suggesting her assistant was insanely jealous of Juliette.

Without question, Constance's opinion on Mindi's motivations would be highly influential with investigators, especially with Sam Keller, whether Finn was on the team or not.

Footage filmed in the loft was not as instantly advantageous. One small sentence in the recorded film required alterations prior to handing over the thumb drive.

After Finn had left the property for his nightshift, she had summoned Brock for help.

Fortunately, Constance had not positioned the hidden camera in Juliette's loft to record images of the door. Therefore, no one could see Garth installing the new door locks; they could only hear him. As he was leaving the room, he had asked Juliette the following: *Anything I can get you…before I lock the door?*

The reference was problematic, to say the least.

Brock recorded over the misstep. *Before I lock the door* became *before*

I shut the door.

More lightning flashed over the bay, accompanied by deepening rumbles of thunder.

Under her oversight, Brock had prepared a thumb drive for authorities. Afterwards, he expertly wiped all the video files from her laptop and helped return her walk-in closet to pre-surveillance status. The young man was proving to be an asset.

All the cameras throughout the house remained in place, and she continued to capture footage on most of them, with the exception of the loft's which she no longer needed. Constance had to treat her cameras as customary—a privilege and right of the rich. She had nothing to be ashamed of. The Glitz and Glamour was her private estate and she managed it as she pleased.

While Brock was still at the mansion, she initiated her second plan of action.

She needed more leverage on her personal assistant in the event that Mindi became an even greater adversary. And Constance knew precisely how to gain an advantage. Brock would execute Constance's orders tomorrow morning, immediately after Mindi reported to the estate for work. Constance would text him, indicating the coast was clear to proceed.

Sipping her cognac, Constance spotted a shadowy figure racing across the lawn toward the garden. Had her mind played a trick on her? Standing from her chair, she neared the glass wall and used her left hand as a visor, hoping to eliminate the glare from the flickering candles.

She was right! Someone was running toward her garden, trespassing. The intruder had come from the right, from the pines. No doubt the figure was that teenager from next door, the one Mindi had reported as pestering Juliette and encouraging her to disregard the rules.

Constance placed her cognac glass on the coffee table and raced to the garden's light switch on the wall. Flipping the switch, the interior of the garden formed a bright dome of light above the brick walls. The iron gate was swinging back and forth.

"How dare he step onto my private property without permission!" she shouted aloud.

Grabbing her cellphone, she threw open a French door and ran outside. As she jogged toward the garden, she realized she probably should have removed her heeled sandals. Then again, no one maneuvered better on heels than Constance Parker.

Inside the walls of the garden, she hollered, "Where are you, young man? You come out this very minute!"

She continued on the fruit track, intending to head toward the fountain area. Somehow, as she was making a left turn at the Purple Martin birdhouse, she rolled her right ankle and fell hard onto the pebbled pathway. When her body hit the ground, her cellphone launched from her hand. She cried out in pain.

A flash of lightning and a boom of thunder was all that answered.

Rain suddenly fell in hard sheets, pelting her back and drenching her hair and silk blouse.

"I will have your head on a stick!" she warned.

Soaked, goosebumps erupted on her skin. She tried to stand, but the pain was too severe. Instead, she used her arms to inch her body toward her phone which had landed at the beginning of the watermelon patch. Just as she reached for her device, the garden lights turned off.

"Do you know with whom you are toying?" she shouted.

With a valiant stretch, she clutched her cellphone and texted:

I need you. Now. I have fallen in the garden.

As she waited, sprawled out on the stones, she rested her head on her arm and cried. About a half hour later, feeling waterlogged and frozen, she felt warm arms scooping her up.

"Always my rock," she whispered, as he raised her into his arms and carried her from the garden to her mansion.

29

Wednesday, August 18, 2027
The Parkers' G&G Estate: Hickory Thicket, Maryland
(Three Days *after* Juliette's Death)

TIMING WAS ALMOST perfect for Truitt to sneak into Jules's loft to see if she had left behind any clues. Maybe in a diary?

Some students from his high school back home had admitted they kept one. They wrote entries about kids they liked, kids they hated, or how their parents had made them door-punching angry by saying the most dreaded word in a teenager's life: *no.*

Friends had even confessed they entered secrets, those they'd never dream of whispering to others.

If Truitt wanted to avoid falling deeper into his emotional sinkhole, he had to keep busy. Sadly, his new friend—the one he'd been counting on to help rescue *him*—was gone. He was alone again.

Moving forward, he'd at least have purpose if he searched for the missing puzzle pieces of Jules's final day and hour.

Her death raised so many unanswered questions. Had Jules died by accident? By being self-indulgent and careless?

Or, had someone intentionally overdosed her? As part of a nefarious plan to end her life?

He only hoped he wouldn't black out from stress while in the Parkers' house. His episodes were striking more frequently, getting harder and harder to ward off.

Not knowing where he'd been or what he'd done was beyond disconcerting.

From his current hiding spot behind the pool's mechanical outbuilding, he observed Mrs. Parker as she lay on the very same deck recliner where Jules had rested on the day of her death. That detail didn't seem to bother Mrs. Parker. Under the awning, Jules's mother sipped what looked like a Bloody Mary. A stack of towels was under her right foot, elevating her bruised ankle.

Given her injury, Truitt wondered if he had handled himself properly the night before. In truth, he hadn't been "toying" with Mrs. Parker at all. His primary motivation was to avoid a confrontation with her in the garden. Or anywhere. She wasn't exactly neighborly.

The reason he had turned off the garden lights was to buy time for his escape. In darkness. Which he'd done successfully. But just because he had gotten away didn't mean he had stopped watching.

A half hour later, some guy arrived in a light-colored truck. After parking, the man jogged into the garden only to emerge carrying Mrs. Parker to the house.

Since the night had been rainy, details were scarce. Truitt knew for sure the guy was white skinned and didn't walk like Mr. Parker.

He sighed. More mysteries to make sense of.

Shaking his head, Truitt reset his focus. He had to stop daydreaming or he'd squander his chance to search inside Jules's loft.

About to leave his hiding spot for the mansion's kitchen door, he heard footsteps over the pavers. He froze in place. The female approaching Mrs. Parker was her assistant.

Luckily, Truitt was close enough to hear their exchange. Jules's mother ordered her younger look-alike to go into Rock Hall to purchase extra newspapers, since Jules's obituary would appear in today's edition.

The assistant asked if she could stay in town for lunch before returning to the G&G. Mrs. Parker agreed.

After the assistant drove down the driveway, Truitt made his way into the house and up to Jules's loft. He carefully loosened the crime tape and stepped inside the room.

Standing in her space, knowing she was dead, was heart wrenching. He wasn't kidding.

No blackouts, no blackouts, he repeated to himself until he calmed.

Truitt got to work searching Jules's things but found nothing.

About 20 minutes in, he felt a chill down his spine. Someone was watching him. Turning toward the walk-in closet, he flinched. A figure was standing there: Jules. Only as a...ghost.

His heart skipped a beat, but he didn't freak out. He had seen ghosts before. Sometimes, they even talked to him. Since none had ever attempted to harm him, why be frightened? A monstrous linebacker trying to sack him was far scarier.

Standing at the closet's entrance, Jules wore shorts, a T-shirt, and her hair pulled back into a ponytail. She was drop-dead gorgeous, though he needed to remember to use a different expression now. Still, he wondered why she hadn't passed on. Why she was stuck.

"When the cat's away, the rat will play," she snarked.

"Why are you here?" he asked. "Not here, here. I mean, on Earth in general?"

"Wait. You can *see* me? *Hear* me?"

"Yuppers. You're not even my first ghost." He winked.

"Not the time to be flirty. How did you find my loft?"

"What can I say...I excel at floorplans and spatial relations."

"Tell me what you're looking for," she said, bossier than ever.

Truitt shared he was searching for clues. He wanted to help solve the unanswered questions associated with her drowning. Figure out if anything sinister had happened to her.

"Sinister? First, I was drugged," she snapped. "Then Garth found me dead in my pool with a thin abrasion around my neck. Someone strangled me! Is that *sinister* enough for you?"

"I'm sorry, Jules."

"You know what *I'm* sorry about? I'm sorry you never came back to the pool like you promised. I'm sorry you didn't turn out to be Cinderella's Prince Charming—someone who could've saved me from my killer. Thanks for nothing."

"I...I've been having these blackouts. From stress," he confessed. "I had one that day, after I left and helped my Mom. The next thing I knew, the police were on your property, and you had drowned. I wish, more than anything, I had returned in time to protect you."

"Blackouts?" She took three steps back from him. "Could *you* have killed me during an episode?"

"You're not serious."

"All I know is that the police found two sets of fingerprints on the skimmer which may have been used in my murder. One set is from Garth and the other, from an unknown source. We both know you handled that skimmer. Those other prints are yours, Truitt."

"Doesn't mean I harmed you, Jules. I would never. You have to believe me!"

She pointed over her shoulder to the bookcase. "Let's not forget that my mother's hidden camera is probably filming you this minute. Shouldn't you be trembling with fear?"

"My parents have persuasive lawyers. Trust me."

The temperature in the loft started to plummet like a polar vortex. "Trust *you?*"

The hangers began to move and clank together on the rods in her closet. One launched his way and nearly struck him.

"Get out of here, Truitt Windsor," she seethed. "Do *not* come back. I couldn't trust you in life. I certainly can't trust you now. Our friendship is as dead as I am!"

30

Wednesday, August 18, 2027
The Parkers' G&G Estate: Hickory Thicket, Maryland
(Three Days *after* Juliette's Death)

JULES HAD TO remain active to keep her mind off Truitt. Instead of feeling the sting of a lost friendship, she listened as the lounging Queen Mother spoke to their chef under the pool house awning.

After downing two Bloody Mary's before 11:00 a.m., Mother announced she was ready to confront the neighbors about their trespassing son whom she had every intention of pressing charges against. She ordered Chef Evelyn to fetch the golf cart.

"Didn't you tell me, Ma'am, that the police urged you to stay away from the new neighbors?" Chef Evelyn asked. "At least until they've interviewed and cleared the young man?"

"Are you lecturing me?" Mother questioned.

Chef Evelyn dropped her head in a bob of submission. Her untamed blonde hair temporarily covered her face and reddening cheeks. "Sorry to overstep, Ma'am."

Poor Chef. She tried to help a woman who didn't even know she needed any.

As the chef walked away to follow orders, Mother put on her kimono to cover her bikini. Picking up the hand mirror on the table, she brushed her hair and applied a fresh coat of lipstick.

Fifteen minutes later, the chef drove the golf cart under the overhang and helped Mother climb into the driver's seat. Chef Evelyn handed her a cane for walking, advising her to use it once she arrived at their neighbors' mansion.

Jules had a change of plans. Even though she and Truitt's budding friendship was over, she was mega curious about the Windsors and why his mother was always teary. Was she worried because her son was blacking out? Worried about what he might be doing during those time voids? Like possibly *killing* the girl next door?

Tagging along, Jules watched as Mother parked the golf cart on the Windsors' lawn near the front entrance. Bare footed, she hobbled to the front door using her cane.

The rules still haunted Jules: *Control the perception; control the outcome.*

Clearly, Mother was working the stage.

A tall, handsome man, probably Mr. Windsor, opened the door before Mother even knocked. "I saw you drive up," he said. "I'm Darren Windsor. May I help you?"

"You certainly may," Mother answered. "I am Constance Parker, your neighbor, and I wish to complain about your son's behavior."

"There's been a misunderstanding," he said. "Please come in."

Jules drifted into the house behind Mother.

Mr. Windsor led them into a den with a high cathedral ceiling supported by timbered beams. Flames roared in the gas fireplace, which was odd for August, especially at lunchtime.

"Abby," he started. "Our neighbor, Constance Parker, is here."

Mrs. Windsor stood from her recliner, letting her blanket fall onto the leather seat. A box of Kleenex was on the end table, next to a pile of used, crinkled tissues.

"Forgive my attire," Mrs. Windsor said. "I wasn't expecting company." She pointed to the couch. "Please, have a seat. May we get you something to drink?"

Mother declined. "Let me get straight to the point. Your son has been trespassing on our property. Just last night, I chased him after he entered our garden. I tripped in the process, spraining my ankle."

"I'm sorry you got hurt, but you're mistaken about our son," Mrs. Windsor said, her voice shaking. Glancing at her husband with glassy eyes, she reached for a new tissue.

Truitt quietly entered the room, standing near the back corner, refusing to make eye contact with Jules. He looked nervous. Totally an appropriate reaction because he was about to have his head handed to him. He had no clue how vicious Queen Mother could be.

Despite their falling out, Jules felt sorry for him.

"I have not misunderstood or made a mistake, thank you very much," Mother snarled. "And I am not the only person who has seen him. My personal assistant has also witnessed your son prowling on our private property. Illegally, I might add."

Mrs. Windsor began to visibly tremble. Reaching for the arm of her recliner, she lowered herself into the seat, on top of the blanket, and wiped her eyes with a tissue.

"This cruel attack is upsetting my wife," Mr. Windsor said.

Cruel attack? His comment didn't fit the conversation. No wonder Truitt had blackouts. His parents were nuts. Blackouts were probably the only way he could escape the madness.

"Have you seen my bruised ankle?" Mother questioned. "Your son's behavior caused this! In fact, I would classify *my* injury as a 'cruel attack.' No doubt my lawyers will have an identical interpretation. Do you understand?"

The electric fence was crackling hot, and Mother was about to flip the switch to on.

Mr. Windsor moved behind his wife's recliner and rubbed her shoulders as she wept.

"Our son died eight months ago, Mrs. Parker," Truitt's Dad said.

The words wafted in the air, lingering, before Jules was able to absorb them.

"Excuse me?" Mother said.

"You heard me. Our son died in a single car accident last December. It would've been minor—nothing but a small dent on the fender, except the driver-side airbag was faulty and broke Truitt's neck. Our world ended with his death. We only moved here in hopes of healing. Turns out, grief isn't attached to a zip code." He wiped a tear from his cheek. "Sometimes, we even feel his presence. Right here, in this house."

In total shock, Jules turned toward Truitt, only he was no longer standing in the corner.

A French door leading to the backyard flew open, by itself, and crashed against the wall.

Mrs. Windsor screamed.

31

Wednesday, August 18, 2027
The Parkers' G&G Estate: Hickory Thicket, Maryland
(Three Days *after* Juliette's Death)

TRUITT STORMED FROM his parents' den, trying to avert an emotional blackout.

When his Dad announced his son was dead and Truitt watched Jules process the news, the shade of nothingness had tried to lower, tried to force him into temporary oblivion. But Truitt refused to let the void swallow him. Remaining in the present was crucial because after he calmed himself, he needed to explain to Jules why he had never confessed he was a ghost.

The main reason was that every time he thought of telling her, the intention quickly fizzled. Being a ghost muddled the mind, blurring the line between who was living and who was dead. Not to mention, Jules played a major role in the matter. Alive *and* dead, she perceived him as *real,* as solid flesh and blood. This triggered his selfishness, not that he wasn't *trying* to think of others first. Sometimes, he just caved.

Truth: He wanted Jules to think he was alive. Who would want to spoil that feeling? The feeling he belonged among the living again.

After fleeing his house, Truitt arrived at his special place in the Parkers' garden: among the tomatoes. While other kids his age snacked on candy and chips, chased with high-test soda, he had been an heirloom tomato junkie, growing his own in a raised garden bed back in Bishopville. Chocolate cherry, indigo rose, Vesuvio Piennolo, and yellow pear teardrops—he loved the different shapes, colors, and levels of sweetness, so standing among the cages and stakes supporting ripe tomatoes felt comforting. He couldn't actually eat them anymore, though he got pleasure from his memories.

One fact about the heirlooms was depressing. The tomatoes around him probably wouldn't grow old on the vine. They'd face a harvest whether they wanted one or not. He could relate.

"Tell me something," Jules said from a position behind him.

He flinched.

"Why did you look real to me?" she asked. "I get why you do *now*, but why before? When I was alive?"

He smiled before turning around. First, the fact that Jules had followed him made him beyond happy. A good sign if he hoped to restore their friendship, which he longed for more than anything. Second, she always cut to the chase with him, blurting out what was on her mind instead of treating him like someone deserving of deceptive filters—those she admitted she used in pageantry. Instead, she made him feel special by being unabashedly authentic. Which included being vulnerable, something she tried to hide with others.

He pivoted to face her. "Sorry I didn't mention I'm a ghost."

"You didn't want to freak me out. I get it. But why couldn't I tell on my own?"

"I'm thinking the phenomenon goes hand in hand with color."

"Color?" she asked. "You mean like a white person thing?"

"Dang, Jules! Not everything involves skin color. I meant the *science* of color."

"Then hit me with your scientific nerdiness. Help me understand."

"Apply the concepts of visual perception and energy," he said. "The similarity is there. That's because color is a visual perception of light reflected off an object, like the reflection of light that makes these cherry tomatoes appear to have solid red skin. And don't forget, light is a wavelength of energy. Conclusion? People can have different interpretations of light's energy. For example, my Mom always called my bedspread purple, even though I saw blue."

"You're saying people perceive ghosts differently, too?"

"Exactly. Rare as it is, a few people can see the energy of spirits in the same way they see the solid red of a tomato. That's you. Others, like your mother and Mindi, perceive brief glimpses of a misty red, similar to an intermittent hologram. At a distance, these holograms can appear normal-ish.

"Additional factors contribute to whether we'll be seen," he continued. "Most ghost encounters happen at night or when people have lost their inhibitions, like when they've drank too much alcohol. Or even during that halfway reality between sleep and waking up."

"The morning of my death," Jules said, "I remember something. You frightened me as I woke up under the pool house awning. For a moment, you appeared blurry."

"Right then, I thought you might realize I was a ghost. Especially since you were drugged."

"I didn't, though."

"Have to admit, I was happy your perception of me didn't change," he said. "Anyway, the majority can't see or feel our presence at all. Except for people like my parents who detect us with other senses, like feeling a temperature drop or being super aware of when we move stuff."

"Speaking of temperature drops…when I'm tagging along, people get cold. They even shiver. Is that real or perceived?"

"Real. Simple physics. We need energy to visit this dimension. Heat is energy. To appear, we pull the heat from our environment and sometimes the people around us are left with the residual chill."

"What about *our* senses? I seem to have them all intact, except for taste since I can't eat. Are my experiences real or imagined?"

"Mostly real. Our energy doesn't have a body, but we're still analyzing aspects of our redefined existence as if we were still alive. Touch, sight, hearing, and smell…we experience them all. We're even able to detect temperature and humidity."

Truitt enjoyed answering her questions. He felt needed.

"About moving stuff," she said. "I launched a hanger at you. The sensation felt like I was able to harness and release the energy I'd collected. Is that how it works?"

"Yuppers. At least, that's what I've learned over the last eight months as a ghost."

"You feel so real to me," she said, touching his arm.

"Maybe not *all* your rules were loony. Number sixteen deserves some respect."

"Control the perception; control the outcome?"

"I'm thinking you've always wanted me to be real, and so I am." He winked and delivered his half-smile that formerly made girls blush. Maybe Jules wouldn't ignore his flirting this time. "I didn't want the feeling to end. Can't argue that having you perceive me as real felt more flattering than knowing you were attracted to some dead guy."

"How *did* you die? The long story, please."

His attempt at being playful had fumbled. She was keeping him on task.

"My parents," he started, no longer having a legitimate reason to avoid the subject, "they wanted me to come home after our football banquet. It was a snowy Friday night in early December. But spoiled kids don't always listen. Most times, I did what I wanted. Why not? That approach had always worked out for me. Anyway, I wanted to go to the after party more than going home."

The truth pained him since he constantly dreamt of what his life might have been like if he had made a different decision. "To get there, I drove on a back road, only going twenty-five miles-per-hour. I remember feeling surprised. Snowfall had gotten heavy. Roads were treacherous, but I wasn't afraid. I was a star quarterback. I knew how to stay in the pocket."

"Your Dad said you died of a faulty airbag."

He nodded. "When my sedan slid off the road and bumped a tree down a slight embankment, the airbag deployed. Debris tore into my cheek and the force broke my neck."

"I'm hoping you didn't feel any pain?" she said, half asking, but more like half wishing.

"At first, I woke up in calmness. I could hear the soft patter of snow landing on my car, the steady squeak of my windshield wipers, and the purr of my engine." He released a tear that he'd been fighting to hold back. "I knew things were different for me, though. Nothing below my waist hurt, not that I could move anything. But I still remember the intense burn of my right cheek. I could feel the warm wash of blood running over my skin. My neck throbbed, ached."

"Now I understand why you rub your neck."

"My last memory," he said, nodding, "was wanting to know the time. How long had I been bleeding in the car, off the road, in the snow? Would my parents be worried? The airbag covered the dash, and I had no clue where my cellphone had landed during the accident. I looked down, hoping to see my wristwatch. A sharp stabbing pain overwhelmed my neck—so much worse than if someone had actually inserted a knife. That was it. Lights out."

Truitt showed her his wristwatch. "The airbag struck me at exactly eight twenty-seven."

Sadly, a new watch battery would fix nothing. Sometimes he had trouble remembering. Or maybe the challenge was *accepting* it.

"The next thing I knew," he continued, "I was standing beside my vehicle as a police cruiser arrived. Only, the officer couldn't see me. I was a ghost. Even now, the flashing lights trigger the events of that horrible night. The night, I should've listened to my parents."

"So sad," she said. "Was the airbag company held responsible?"

"They settled with my parents quickly, out of court, making them sign a nondisclosure agreement. I've listened to my parents talk about it since. They regret the decision. At the time, all they wanted was to start over somewhere else, to put the pain behind them."

"Why didn't you pass on? You know, go to Heaven?"

"Two words: scared shitless. See, everything in my life had been about me. At my death, I was frightened to learn my destination. Would I be climbing a ladder of white light or pulled underground through a manhole of darkness? Apparently, God must have wondered where I belonged, too, so I remained here. Thought I'd use my time to change for the better. Helping my parents was a good start. Now I can help you, too."

She looked at him with those wide blue eyes that could heal a broken heart.

"Help *me?*" she asked.

"Find your murderer. Unless you still consider me a suspect?"

"I'm not a ghost expert like you," she said, "but ghosts can't possibly have fingerprints, so those on the skimmer aren't yours. Anyway, I never should've accused you. I'm sorry."

"No worries. We've both made mistakes."

"It makes sense I'm still on Earth to unravel the mysteries behind my death. I mean, if we can identify my killer, we might be able to save someone else from having the same horrible fate. And if I don't try, I'm pretty sure the unknowns would haunt me for eternity."

"I hear that," he agreed. "Isn't it interesting how we've lived such contrasting lives? I came from modest means compared to you. Yet, I expected everyone to treat me like football royalty—a king. My parents were my staff. Friends, my subjects. *You* came from big money but had virtually no rights, even though your mother labeled you a queen and decked you out in all the trimmings. In reality, you were her plaything, her doll. Guess we all need to get to know the real person behind the façade." He reached out and shook her hand. "Pleased to meet you. I'm self-*ish*. And you are?"

"Self-*less*." She smiled. "But I'm interested in a name change. *Normal* sounds good."

"I like it. And we'd better get started. I've been here for eight months, but who knows how long before time runs out for either of us. Any ideas on where to begin?"

With a new purpose, his positive energy was off the charts. More importantly, he shared that purpose with a companion—someone he could help. Someone who could also help him.

"Let's visit Lila Lovelace," Jules said. "Tonight. When she has the best chance to see us."

"Lovelace?"

"That's her stage name, but she's a Scarborough. And I want to know if Mrs. Scarborough or Lila hated me enough to kill me. I mean, is that why Lila shared my secrets with her mother? So she could use them against me in the *Beauty World* interview? Was that the precursor to making me go away forever?"

"Sounds like a plan." He reached out his hand to her, hoping she'd accept the invitation. "Until nightfall, want to hang out by the fountain?"

When her hand wrapped around his fingers, his heart reacted. Had it skipped a beat? Taken a free fall? Done a loop de loop?

"Ironic, don't you think?" she asked.

"What?" He hoped his whole heart thing hadn't been too obvious.

"I got my first friend after I was murdered."

Okay, good. She hadn't noticed.

"Death has a twisted sense of humor," he said.

32

Wednesday, August 18, 2027
Rock Hall Bistro: Rock Hall, Maryland
(Three Days *after* Juliette's Death)

MINDI ARRIVED EARLY at the Bistro to ensure she sat at her sexy hunk of blue's usual table in the restaurant's back corner.

The hostess protested at first, obviously loyal to her regular customer from local law enforcement, but when Mindi explained she'd be dining with Detective Parker, the woman sat her, albeit reluctantly. Finn clearly preferred dining alone. Or was it more like the hostess didn't want him to eat with anyone else?

Either way, arriving ahead of him meant Mindi could place the drink order. She smiled at her cunningness. The Queen Mother should consider adding another rule: *Control the cocktail; control the sex.*

Hard to believe Constance had agreed to let Mindi lunch in town. Permission allowed her to scrap the "flat tire" excuse after fulfilling her chore of purchasing newspapers. She could forgo intentionally soiling her favorite button-down shirt dress, a tailored fit in light blue silk. Ruining the garment would've been a necessary but expensive sacrifice required to explain her delay in returning to the G&G.

Mindi was also pleased she had chosen a classy look. After all, she and Finn would start off in public. Besides, the man was responsive to women who advertised sophistication over solicitation.

The bell attached to the Bistro's door jingled.

Everyone dining looked up as Finn strolled in. He took off his police-issued peaked cap and somberly nodding to familiar patrons.

Some touched his arm as he passed them by, sharing their condolences in hushed voices.

As Finn approached the table, she felt her first rush of warmth between her legs, causing her to tightly squeeze her thighs together to contract her pleasure muscle. The man was so damn good looking she could orgasm on anticipation alone.

He sat down, placing his cap on the table.

"What's on your mind, Mindi?" he asked, skipping the small talk.

She fingered the stem of her full wine glass. "Sip your beer first, unless you're in a rush."

Pushy women were also Finn's type. He had married Constance, hadn't he?

"I'm on duty."

"No one is going to judge you, Finn. You've lost your daughter. Ease the pain for a minute and relax. You deserve it."

He locked eyes with her. Maybe he was trying to figure out her motive. Maybe he was wondering if he should surrender to the inviting pull of alcohol.

Lifting his pint glass to his lips, he took several swallows.

"What's in this beer?" he asked.

"A Steamroller. You're probably tasting the added rye whiskey, but it has some other goodies as well. Do you like the flavor?"

"Sure, but it tastes strong and again, I'm on duty."

She scanned the restaurant for dramatic effect. "Doesn't look like much is happening in Rock Hall. Crime wise, I mean."

"Except for my daughter's unsolved...*murder?*"

"I didn't intend to sound insensitive. But my understanding is you've opted out of the investigative team. Otherwise, you'd be heading to the G&G soon. That's what Constance said."

Definitely the right thing to mention.

Finn picked up his glass and downed the contents. Holding his hand in the air, he got the hostess's attention and pointed to his empty glass. The twenty-something nodded and scurried to the bar with her tongue hanging out.

Silence fell between them until the hostess delivered his fresh drink to the table. Mindi took the opportunity to order herself a whiskey on the rocks. The hostess's eyes widened before glancing nervously between her and Finn. Yeah, she got it.

Her Constance comment must have really pissed Finn off because he guzzled half of his new drink before putting the pint glass down.

"You requested this meeting," he said. "What do you want?"

"To see if I could help in any way. No doubt, you're grieving. And with the chilly relationship you have with your…"

"Wife."

"Yes, with Constance. I thought maybe you could use a shoulder to lean on. We're all in this together." She subtly licked her lips, hoping he'd interpret the act as sexy over desperate.

Thankfully, he gazed at her as if unbuttoning her dress, starting at the top and continuing down until the tabletop blocked his view. Perfect. The drinks were diluting his resolve.

Slightly spreading her legs under the table, she pressed herself against the hardwood seat until she felt another pleasure spasm. Hopefully, she wouldn't leave behind a streak of moisture on the chair when she stood to leave.

As she filled him in on preliminary plans for BB Jules's funeral service, he finished the rest of his enhanced beer. Fifteen minutes later, he rolled his eyes while shaking his head.

"That's just great," he snarked. "Now I'm buzzed. Driving is out for the moment. Fuck."

Shifting her eyes to her cocktail glasses, she hoped he'd gaze in their direction. He followed her focus. The wine in her goblet was untouched, and she'd only taken one sip of her whiskey. "I know someone who's straight line sober. Want me to drive you to the G&G or the station? After all, I encouraged you to…relax."

She had already guessed his answer. Resisting a smile was difficult.

"No. I'll just sit here and drink water for a while."

She placed a $100 bill on the table and stood. "Nonsense. I'll drive you around. I have bottled water in the car. At least *my* way, you won't attract attention."

As if leaving with a beautiful 22-year-old woman wouldn't raise eyebrows! Her argument was pathetic. For someone sober.

Mindi walked with him to the Volvo.

Once she was driving, he kept his police cap off and slouched in the passenger seat, probably trying to stay incognito. Occasionally drinking from a water bottle, he rambled on about what a sucky year he was having. The worst ever. *Yadda, yadda, yadda.*

When she parked in her lot, he stopped talking.

Confusion marked his face. "Where are we? Why have you stopped?"

"Sorry, but when a girl has to pee, a girl has to pee." She pointed ahead. "My apartment. Come up with me. I'll be brief and there are more water bottles in the fridge."

Mindi thought he might protest, but he opened his car door instead. He was catching on and obviously wasn't interested in resisting.

After helping guide her sexy hunk of blue up the flight of stairs, she unlocked her door. They entered her one-bedroom apartment.

"Kitchen is straight ahead. Help yourself to the water," she said. "I'll be a minute. After I pee, I'm going to change into something more comfortable before heading back to the G&G."

"Hurry. I need to return to my cruiser."

Mindi didn't want to lose momentum and give him time to regain a conscience.

Impressed with her tactics thus far, she headed for her bedroom with confidence. She had learned so much from her boss—the woman she despised. The woman who had everything Mindi wanted.

After unbuttoning five buttons, allowing her lacy bra to show, she called out. "Finn? Would you mind helping me for a moment? I can't unclasp my necklace."

She was standing at the foot of her bed when he arrived at her door. Finn froze. Except for his eyes. They wandered over her body.

"You're not wearing a necklace," he said.

"I'm not?" Placing her palms on her chest, she caressed the tops of her breasts before moving her hands up to her neck as if searching. "Oops. You're right! What was I thinking?"

Leaning on the doorjamb, he smiled for the first time since she watched him enter the Bistro. Her goal was in reach.

"Are you extending an invitation, Ms. Maxwell?" he asked. "To have sex?"

She unbuttoned one more button. "Quite impressive! No one would ever doubt you're a detective. You don't miss a clue, do you?"

"Call me a stickler," Finn said. "I prefer a consensual yes. We can sex tease after."

"Hard fucking doesn't leave much energy for teasing, Detective. But sure, I'm voicing my consensual yes. The only question left is…what are you going to do about it?"

Finn was surprisingly fast. He aggressively marched from the doorway to the bed. Before she could say something else clever, he placed his hands on the opened seams of her dress and yanked them apart with brute strength. The remaining buttons popped loose and fell to the floor.

Oh well. Her silk dress had become a casualty after all.

Clasping her waist, he lifted her, tossing her on top of the comforter. She landed on her back. He reached up and clutched her thong undies. With unbridled aggression, he pulled them down her legs and over her feet, letting them drop.

Grabbing her legs, he spread them apart to the point of almost hurting. He stared at her exposure like a wild animal. "So you like to fuck hard, do you? Careful what you ask for."

For the next hour, he pounded and sucked and pounded and fingered and pounded again. He didn't seem to care where he thrust himself into, only that he performed with force.

When they finished, sweat and bodily fluids covered them from head to toe. She had orgasmed so many times, she'd lost count.

Before they washed off and dressed, she was grateful for a small assurance. Mindi had asked Brock to sweep her apartment in search of hidden cameras. The Queen Mother was more obsessed with them than ever. Mindi needed to be smart and cautious. Especially now.

Brock had assured her that her place was clean. Thank God!

33

DESPITE BEING DEAD, Jules was on cloud nine hanging out in the garden with her one and only friend. For the first time in her existence, she was starting to understand the special connection between BFFs. They were free to talk about anything. Free to be themselves without judgment.

A convoy of vehicles raced up the driveway toward the mansion.

"Must be the forensics team," Jules said. "Detectives plan to search for clues today."

"I remember, but isn't their timing like throwing the football at the same time the clock runs out? What's the point? I mean, you died three long days ago."

Tilting her head, she smirked. "I'm not sure about the football part. What I do know is this is Hickory Thicket. Moving too quickly is more of a penalty than taking it slow. And in their defense, I guess they wanted to confirm my death as 'suspicious' before deploying the troops. My autopsy results were only completed yesterday."

"Always empathetic. Hey, want to add some chill to their investigation?" He winked.

"Why not? I could use some heat right about now."

"On second thought, some things we hear might be upsetting."

"Nothing could sting worse than our deaths, right? Everything else is glitter."

Jules led the way as they drifted from the garden into the house and eventually entered the sunroom. She instantly felt a boost of energy circulate through her being—a warm electrical charge that made her feel alive.

Picking a corner from which to observe, she and Truitt stood motionless.

Mother sat at the dining table, having changed from her kimono into leggings and a matching onyx tunic. No makeup. No jewelry. No fancy hairstyle (her long black hair was pulled into a ponytail). She personified the perfect image of a mourning Queen Mother.

Sitting across from her, Chief Keller brandished a tablet and pen. The other detectives had already headed to the loft carrying supplies, including boxes and plastic bags.

The chief had finished his condolences and was commenting on Mother's ankle injury, wishing her a quick recovery. "Anymore, my bones ache from the cold," the chief added, rubbing his arms. "An early fall is coming. There's a chill in the air. Can you feel it?"

Ignoring the pleasantries, Mother handed him a thumb drive. "We have security cameras throughout the mansion. I have compiled footage that may assist in the investigation."

"Maybe your cameras caught that boy next door?" the chief asked. "The one who's been lurking around? We're heading over there after we wrap up here. He's a person of interest."

Jules glanced at Truitt. She knew what was coming. Knew how hard it would be to hear the words *died* or *dead* or *deceased* out loud.

"Not necessary," Mother told Chief Keller. "The intruder wasn't him. Apparently, our neighbors' son died last December."

"Wow. I did not know that." He jotted down a note. "Anything helpful on the footage?"

"Most impressive, Sam!" she said, using an excitable tone appropriate for a child. "You have pinpointed the precise reason behind my giving you the thumb drive. Never mind that I mentioned this fact a moment ago."

Without pausing for a reaction, Mother continued by explaining that after her husband shared autopsy findings with her, she had reviewed all the footage collected. Shockingly, she had discovered video of her personal assistant administering twice the prescribed dosage of zolpidem in her daughter's tea, on the very morning of her death.

Jules understood *how* she had received too much of her sleeping meds; she just didn't know *why*. Was it an accident born of confusion? Of miscommunication? Or had Mother, Mindi, or both of them tried to make the overdose appear to be a mistake?

"So you're implicating Mindi Maxwell?" Chief Keller asked. "Suggesting she deliberately overdosed your daughter?"

"Instead of a tablet, perhaps you should carry a recorder with you, Sam." Mother narrowed her eyes. "Then, you could refer to my precise words. Nevertheless, I will respond to your questions by reminding you that it is *your* department's job, not mine, to formulate implications that can be proven or dismissed."

"Got it," he said. "Oh, and while I'm on official business, mind calling me Chief? It's more professional that way." He rubbed his bald head. "Curious: Have you let your personal assistant go? Maybe filed for a restraining order? Something like that?"

"Of course not...*Chief,*" Mother said, sounding like his title was a furball in her throat. "We live in a country where one is presumed innocent until proven guilty. Unless Rock Hall has a different philosophy? Under your leadership perhaps?"

"Don't be curt with me, Connie."

"Mrs. Parker," she corrected.

He nodded his head, as if acknowledging Mother had bested him. "One more question before I join the team upstairs. My cousin's friend has a kid in pageantry. Apparently, she's won several crowns. Nothing like Jules. But still, she's accrued quite a bank account. Can you believe the kid's parents have a life insurance policy on her? Anything like that happening here?"

Mother gave her spiel about the common practice of life insurance, announcing Jules had one, too. Her words were like nails scratching across an old chalkboard.

"Obviously, *I* do not need the money," she added. "The department can verify this fact without difficulty. I simply adhere to customary practices for the pageantry world."

"You emphasized *you* don't need the money. Would that include Detective Parker?"

"Our monies are legally separate, Chief," Mother said, smiling. "I am certain you can determine his financial health just as easily as mine."

"Got it. Might Detective Parker be on the life insurance policy as a beneficiary?"

"He is."

"How much did you say that policy was worth?" the chief asked.

"A recorder would most definitely assist you, Chief Keller, for I had not disclosed the amount." She reached for a set of papers which had been face down on the table, like she had anticipated the chief raising the subject and was ready for it. "A copy for you." She handed the papers over. "The policy is for four million. Finn and I are equal beneficiaries. As I mentioned before, I plan to use one million as a reward to the person or persons who provide information leading to an arrest and conviction. I will donate my remaining portion, another million, to the Humane Society. As you may be aware, Juliette was a teen spokesperson for the non-profit."

Mother's apparent generosity was having no effect on Jules. She knew Queen Mother's words were only advancing a desired perception. Instead, the insinuation that her father might have financial motives associated with her death was curious, but not in a good way.

"What do you think Detective Parker intends to do with his half?" Chief Keller asked.

"He's *your* employee. Ask him yourself. I try to avoid speculation."

"Interesting. I did not know that either." The chief rose from his seat, signaling the interview was over.

In contrast, Jules's confusion was far from over.

She looked at Truitt, her eyebrows tense. "Why would my Dad *need* money?"

34

Wednesday, August 18, 2027
The Parkers' G&G Estate: Hickory Thicket, Maryland
(Three Days *after* Juliette's Death)

CONSTANCE WAS SEETHING. Her cheeks had likely become hideously blotchy. Luckily, no one was near her to witness them. The only people remaining at the mansion as evening approached were Mindi and Garth and she could care less about them.

After Mindi had returned from her extended lunch with flushed cheeks and wearing a new outfit, Constance had sent her into the kitchen to clean silver and clip Juliette's obituaries from a stack of newspapers. She had tasked Garth with unclogging the sink in the parlor's powder room.

While her staff fulfilled their assignments, Constance had remained in the sunroom, stewing about her interview with Sam Keller. His arrogance was unacceptable.

The supercilious Chief of Police had failed to remember his true rank. He was beneath *her,* not the other way around. Why, almost single handedly, she had gotten him elected. Donated thousands for new police uniforms. Even organized home delivered meals when his wife Sara birthed their first child. Moreover, Constance had anonymously donated a new cruiser in exchange for expanding the department by hiring Finn.

The audacity of Sam insisting she address him by his title! And how utterly humiliating that he had implied she might need two million from Juliette's life insurance policy. *Need?* Did he not realize that amount was mere pocket change? The absolute nerve.

Her decision had solidified during their interview.

Life, after all, was nothing more than a largescale pageant, and she was and aways would be…the winner.

If Constance were to draw in the public by playing the sympathy card, and if she planned, as she did, to capitalize on that emotional momentum to emerge as an influencer (more persuasive than ever before), then she certainly could not risk negative undercurrents— whispers that she might be a child killer. Of her own daughter, no less. Heavens no!

Therefore, she would add fuel to the fire during the investigation, engulfing those around her and attracting suspicions in their direction. Besides, her current inner circle, excluding Deanna Mae, deserved retribution. She had been watching them closely. How dare they underestimate her prowess. How dare they attempt to make her authority a mockery!

Indeed, they could all burn in hell because the only person rising from the flames and ashes like a phoenix would be Constance Isabel Reyes Parker.

Sam's insults had ignited scorching anger and she would make him look like an incompetent fool.

Stewing turned to planning and Constance had plenty of options available. Thankfully, she had cultivated moles throughout the geographic area. That is how Constance knew Mindi had dropped off a lover's note at the station, asking darling Finn for a lunchtime soirée at his pathetic watering hole, the Bistro. Had she not known, she certainly would not have approved her personal assistant's request to dine in town. Constance was rich, not foolishly generous.

The time was 5:00 p.m.

Surely Brock had fulfilled his orders by now.

In the foulest of moods, she speed-dialed him on her cellphone.

"Yes, Ma'am," he answered before the first ring had completed.

"Did you collect anything helpful on camera? Something on video I could use?"

"Definitely."

"Perfect. I will come by your place tomorrow night. You can show me then."

"*My* place?"

"No need for embarrassment," she consoled. "Loyalty is the most valued currency. Which means, you will afford much more than a double wide in the near future. Prepare to say goodbye to trailer parks."

"Whatever you need, Constance. I'm your guy."

"You are, indeed, indispensable, darling."

35

Wednesday, August 18, 2027
The Scarboroughs' Residence: Rock Hall, Maryland
(Three Days *after* Juliette's Death)

TRUITT FELT AWKWARD being in a girl's bedroom at night, unexpected and unannounced.

When he and Jules materialized beside Lila's bed, she was sleeping on her back. An army of stuffed animals flanked her, holding their positions on both sides of her pillow. A nearby nightlight cast shadows on the walls overcrowded with posters of former Miss America title holders, including Mrs. Parker. Some of the crowns in the pictures had been foil stamped in gold, allowing them to glisten despite the meager lighting.

The door to Lila's bedroom was ajar, allowing soft brightness to stream in from the hallway. Looped from one bedpost to the other, a string of dreamcatchers hung across Lila's headboard. Silver rosary beads lay on her nightstand.

If Truitt had to guess, Lila "Lovelace" Scarborough was afraid of the dark. Or, perhaps, she was scared of paranormal visitors who frequented the night.

Although the room had felt pleasantly airconditioned, after their arrival, a frosty mist began to billow from Lila's mouth. Releasing a moan while asleep, she grasped her blanket, pulling the thin fleece up and over her neck.

"Wake up!" Jules said, shaking the bed.

A stuffed unicorn toppled to the floor.

Lila's eyes fluttered open. Gasping, she pushed herself into a sitting position, pressing her back against the headboard, trying to gain distance between herself and what she no doubt saw: ghosts.

"Juliette Parker?" she asked, blinking as if her vision might be a lingering nightmare. "You're not here to…to hurt me, are you?"

"Have I ever done one bad thing to you, Lila?"

The girl shook her head, still clutching her covers like a security blanket. Her eyes wandered to him. "Who's that?"

"My best friend. Truitt," Jules said, sounding proud of her declaration.

"Thought you weren't allowed to have friends."

Lila clearly wasn't the smartest tool in the shed. Seemed obvious rules changed after death.

"Yeah, well, death has its perks," Jules said, using her sassy tone on someone other than him. "Mind if I sit on the edge of your mattress?"

"Go ahead."

"Have you always been able to see ghosts?" Jules asked her.

"Yes, but I've never told anyone," Lila admitted. "I see spirits when I'm awake and in my dreams. So I better ask: Is this real or am I asleep?"

Jules looked at the door as it closed shut without anybody touching it.

For eight months, Truitt had been a ghost. He had never considered himself a slow learner. But Jules…she had already mastered energy manipulation in three short days.

"Okay, real," Lila declared. "So if you're not here to hurt me, what do you want?"

"To figure out who murdered Jules," Truitt said. "Your name popped into our minds."

"Why is everybody pointing fingers at me and Mom?"

"The *Beauty World* interview for starters," Jules answered. "You shared my secrets with your mother. She used them against me on live television. Next day? I'm at the bottom of our pool. Dead."

"Backup for a sec. Did you say *everybody?*" he asked Lila. "Who else considers you a suspect?"

"Two detectives from Rock Hall stopped by today."

"What did you tell them?" Jules asked.

"The truth. My Mom goes to AA meetings on Sundays when everyone else is at Mass. No one knows she's a recovering alcoholic. She started drinking during the divorce. Not going to lie: She couldn't accept when my Dad ran off with the housekeeper. Anyway, that's where she was when you died, Juliette; she was at Alcoholics Anonymous.

"And in terms of *me,*" Lila continued, "I've always liked you. Not to mention, even though I want to win every title but never do, I wouldn't hurt my opponents, let alone *kill* them. Besides, I'm too young to drive, so I was here on Sunday. At noon, my neighbor brought over low-fat snickerdoodles. Officers checked everything out."

"Let me get this straight," Jules said. "Your mother has heaps of secrets (like being an alcoholic and a divorcee who still uses Mrs., the very *same* person who doesn't want to advertise she has a daughter in pageantry), but she's more than willing to spill the beans on a live broadcast about the private health issues of someone *else's* daughter? Namely, me?"

"I know. Horrible," Lila said. "Truth is, I didn't know my Mom was going to blab about what I'd told her. Swear I didn't. Apparently, Mom's boss had warned her, right before the show started, that ratings were down. He expected the interview to be much more *dramatic* and *uncomfortable* than originally planned—or things at TBC were going to get ugly fast. I'm sorry, Juliette."

Jules turned away from Lila and locked eyes with him. "Flushing out my murderer isn't going to be easy." She sighed. "So many lies and deflections from the people around me. Finding the one *innocent* person would be a lot easier."

"I hear you." Truitt nodded. "It'll be like looking for a murderer on death row."

"Maybe your Dad could help you guys," Lila suggested. "He's a police detective, right?"

"At the very least," Truitt echoed, "sharing information would be more efficient if we worked with him. Right, Jules?"

"Except my Dad never takes a stand on anything. He's the poster boy for noncommittal."

"We'll convince him," he said. "Peyton Manning used to say...*The most valuable player is the one who makes the most players valuable.* Your father would add value to our team, and I'll be effective at making him realize that. Of course, if he refuses to help, we'll haunt the hell out of him."

"I doubt my Dad will be able to see us," Jules said.

"One play at a time."

"Worse, what if he's guilty?"

"We'll figure it out."

"Who's Peyton Manning anyway?" Jules asked. "Your coach? A teammate?"

"Give me your hand," he said, rolling his eyes. "We can talk famous quarterbacks later. Let's visit your Dad at the station and move this ball down the field."

36

Wednesday, August 18, 2027
The Rock Hall Police Department: Rock Hall, Maryland
(Three Days *after* Juliette's Death)

UPON ARRIVING AT the police station, Jules observed a bottle of bourbon perched near the edge of Dad's desk, cap off, with a moist but empty shot glass beside it. His laptop was open. A small lamp cast a yellow spotlight on the desktop, a warm contrast to the cool charcoal shadows insulating the room. With numbers glowing in red, a digital clock hung on the wall. The time was 11:13 p.m.

Pacing behind his desk, Dad fingered his hair as if he might start yanking at it.

Jules, with Truitt beside her, stood quietly in a darkened corner of the office. Watching. Listening.

"What have I done?" Dad said aloud. Stopping, he poured another shot before downing the amber liquid. "I keep fucking up." He briefly squeezed his eyes shut. "I'm sorry, Jules."

Filled with worry, she looked at Truitt. Her heart literally ached even though the pain, like the rest of her, was a remnant of energy. "Could his words be a...*confession?*"

"We'll try to find out before we leave," Truitt assured her.

"Who's there?" Dad asked, hovering his right hand over his holster while scanning the room. "Now is *not* a good time to play cat and mouse."

The phone rang.

Dad flinched. A bead of sweat dripped off his forehead.

159

"Collect yourself, damn it," he said out loud to himself, before pressing the speakerphone button. "Detective Parker, Rock Hall Police Department. Is this an emergency?"

"Not unless the rabbit dies," a female voice giggled through the speaker.

Jules was shocked. Confused. The voice belonged to Mindi, talking in nonsensical riddles.

"I'm working," Dad barked. "What do you want?"

"To say thank you for a mouthwatering lunch."

"You bought."

"Yes, and you tipped. Quite generously, I might add."

Was Mindi flirting? Jules never doubted the money monger had an infatuation for her father. But hearing her woo him was disgusting. While he was at work, even!

"We'll talk another time," he said. "Don't call here again."

He hung up.

"Weird," Jules whispered, mostly to herself.

"I said...Who's. There?" Dad demanded, close to shouting.

A white mist escaped from his mouth with each spoken word. After pouring and swallowing another shot of bourbon, he stomped to the thermostat on the wall near the door.

"Your father clearly knows something atmospheric has changed in his office, but you were right, he isn't seeing or hearing us. Any suggestions on how to communicate?"

"Follow me," she said to Truitt, tilting her head toward the desk.

Using the laptop's mouse and keyboard, she opened a word processing app and typed.

> This is Jules. Don't freak out, Dad. I'm in the room with Truitt Windsor. Guess you could call us ghosts. We want to talk. Please try and see us. We need you.

When Dad returned to his desk and read the message, his eyes darted around the room. "Who's playing this sick joke? I swear. I'll kill you. Right here. Right now."

The whites of his eyes grew as he watched additional words form on his laptop screen.

You have to believe me. Watch...

Dispatching her energy, she slowly slid the shot glass off the edge of the desk. Dad held his breath as the glass fell and bounced once it hit the floor.

"Am I drunk?" Dad asked out loud. "Is this real?"

We're real, Dad. And we need your help.

He lowered himself in his desk chair, his hands trembling as he clutched the armrests.

"Ghosts? Seriously?" Deliberately blinking, Dad looked around the room. "I can't see you, Jules. I'm trying. I am. All I feel is cold. Are you...*safe* where you are? How can I help?"

Jules typed that she and Truitt were fine; they just hadn't passed over yet. They had things to do first, like working with him to solve her murder.

Dad quickly delivered his standard noncommittal song and dance.

The man would never change. Disengaging was a bad habit, an addiction to nothing and no one, including his daughter. Perhaps that reality crushed her more than anything else that had gone wrong in her short life. Dad had never put her first, had never wanted to help her. He was more comfortable ignoring her lonely hell and caving to the Queen Mother who ruled over it.

Truitt followed her lead, using his energy to type.

Truitt here. Think good cop, bad cop. I'm the latter. See, you don't have a choice, Mr. Parker. We need you to join your department's investigative team so you can keep us updated on Jules's case.

But before you join us in solving your daughter's murder, I have one question: DID YOU KILL JULES?

161

"That's ridiculous," Dad snapped, pounding the desktop with his fist. "I loved my daughter more than anyone in my life! How dare you imply otherwise."

Jules keyboarded:

> Mother insinuated to Chief Keller that you needed money, that the life insurance payout on me would benefit you and your financial problems.

"That's preposterous, and you know it," he snarled. "She's filthy rich, and I'm her husband."

> New subject. Why was Mindi calling you?

"She asked to have lunch with me at the Bistro today. I was curious. Turns out, she wanted to make sure I was okay. You know, after your death." He gave a weak smile. "I think you're right, kiddo. She might have a crush on me. No worries, though. I'll handle it."

Jules typed that Truitt had seen a man help Mother into the house after she'd sprained her ankle in the garden. In response, Dad claimed he didn't know who that could be.

> We're going to find out who he is.

"You've got me interested, too," Dad said. "On this end, we found an unidentified set of fingerprints on the pool skimmer. I'll let you know if our Maryland system finds a match."

> Bad cop again. So you're agreeing to join your department's investigative team, right?

"I'll share what I know, but no, I'm not officially getting involved in the case."

Jules had enough. Throughout her life, she had asked for hardly anything while accommodating her parents' every whim. Time to finally express herself.

Racing to the wall, she yanked hard on the hanging print of a sailboat on the Chester River, pulling out the nail and picture hook from the wall. When the frame hit the floor, the protective glass shattered.

"Was that you, Truitt? Mr. Bad Cop? I swear…," Dad growled.

I did it, Dad. Me, Jules. Your daughter.

"Okay, okay," Dad said. "Christ Almighty. I'll talk to the chief."

A female officer showed up at the door, holding a McDonald's bag and smelling of warm French fries. "What the hell's going on in here, Parker?"

Jules reached for Truitt's hand. When they locked fingers, they vanished from the station.

37

Wednesday, August 18, 2027
The Parkers' G&G Estate: Hickory Thicket, Maryland
(Three Days *after* Juliette's Death)

WHEN JULES MATERIALIZED, sitting next to Truitt on a concrete bench beside the fountain in her garden, she was still holding his hand. Crickets and cicadas welcomed them with their nighttime chorus, complemented by the steady sound of water splashing into the fountain's lower basin.

The waxing moon cast its yellow glow. Searching for insects, several bats swooped and dove under the starry skies. A brackish breeze rustled the sculpted shrubs.

For the first time since her death, Jules realized how much she'd miss her garden sanctuary if she ever passed on. She had planted and nurtured many of the fruits and vegetables herself. Having made life possible for them, she was thrilled by their growth and wondered if that's how loving mothers felt about their children.

Jules enjoyed Truitt's fingers intertwined with hers. Without him, being a ghost would've been lonely and she had already lived a lifetime of feeling alone.

"Must be close to midnight," she said. "Shouldn't I feel tired?"

"Not necessarily," Truitt said. "We don't get tired in the same ways. More like drained of energy. Similar to a light dimmer slowly powering off. I call it *the fade.*" He locked eyes with her. "I was terrified the first time I faded. I kept feeling weaker and weaker. Suddenly, I found myself in a black void. Sometimes I stayed in limbo for hours. Sometimes days. I never knew if I'd be able to power up again." Smiling, his cheek dimples deepened. "Thankfully, my sunny disposition has always rekindled."

"Is fading the same as a blackout?"

"Same destination," he said, "but the reasons for getting there are different. Blackouts are stress induced. They can happen anytime if you're not careful. If you can't calm yourself."

"I'll try and remember that. So what do you miss most about your former life? Seriously. Besides your parents since you can still see them?"

"Huddles on the field. My guys counted on me for clear, effective directions. I loved pulling through for them. Loved executing a perfect play. Their respect made me happy."

"Doesn't sound self-centered to me," Jules said.

"Guess I was my best on the field." He gave her hand a little squeeze which felt like a *thank you for noticing*. "Off the turf, though, I was a self-absorbed brat. I felt I had earned it."

"Let's huddle now, figure out our next move. Show me your stuff, number seven."

"Prepare to be impressed," he said, letting go of her hand and rubbing his together. "Before every game, I would determine where everybody's head was at. Since you're my team now, tell me: What can you remember about your drowning? What happened after I left you to check on my Mom?"

"I fell asleep right where I was, on the recliner, under the pool house awning. And when I woke, I was burning up and nauseous."

"That damn tea is to blame."

"I remember the pool looked so inviting. I thought the water could cool me off, make me feel better."

"And then?" he pressed.

"Then I was sitting on the edge of the pool trying to figure out who Garth was trying to save. Turned out to be me."

"You can't recall anything in between?"

She shook her head. "I feel like I used to remember more."

"No worries," Truitt said. "My thoughts get foggy, too. Memories come and go. Eventually, they'll stick. Let's move on to the possible suspects in your murder."

They agreed the Scarboroughs were innocent; both had alibis.

Next was Garth. Jules wholeheartedly believed he couldn't have killed her, given she'd watched his determination to revive her.

"That leaves Mindi," Jules said. "I can see now that she clearly wants Dad. Why wouldn't she make sure he has some money if he leaves Mother? I guarantee Mother made him sign one of those prenuptial agreements because she makes sure everyone knows their wealth belongs to her. And Mindi knew my parents, plural, had a life insurance policy on me. His two-million-dollar 'reward' assures he'll be able to move her up on the socioeconomic ladder. Not to mention, Mindi wasn't aware, but I watched her rummage through my drawers. She was looking for something."

"Guilty of the same. Remember?" Truitt asked. "I thought maybe you had a diary. So this morning, I searched in your loft, hoping to find entries with clues. Instead, I found you."

"I never kept anything Mother might use against me, especially in written form. Anyway, I doubt Mindi has any interest in solving the mystery behind my death. She's more of a cover-her-own-ass opportunist. Or a what-can-she-gain (from murdering Jules) type."

"Definitely need to keep an eye on her, but she's not the only woman in question."

"You truly believe my mother could've killed me?" Jules asked. "Her own daughter?"

"In huddles, we explore every option. Emotions remain on the sidelines."

Jules listened as Truitt shared what information he had collected or overheard about Mother and how it might connect to her death.

In terms of the unclear directions Mother wrote on preparing Jules's morning *stea,* he wondered: Was her mother intentionally vague, *hoping* Mindi would add the pills from the pill box like usual? Did the woman suffer from a form of psychosis? Wanting her daughter to become sick while she was away to prove *she* was the only one who could properly care for her?

Or was her mother attempting to throw another powerplay in her daughter's face? Like…*Continue to disobey me and here's what can happen.* But then, tragically, the powerplay had accidentally backfired?

His suspicions didn't stop there.

They continued with Mother's unlikely alibi on the day of Jules's death. Truitt didn't believe she *ever* had an in-person meeting with Orin Yates in D.C. (which the man had supposedly canceled last minute). Why would Mr. Yates have agreed to a meeting in the first place? On a Sunday no less, just one day after the *Beauty World* interview had taken place? As unprofessional as Mrs. Scarborough had been and as horrible as Jules's asthma attack had become, Mr. Yates likely wouldn't have felt the urgency to interrupt his weekend for a time consuming face-to-face with Constance Parker.

Truitt also didn't believe Mother had kept her plans to go shopping and lunching with her best friend, Deanna Mae. To him, the story sounded too perfectly crafted when in truth, life was rarely seamless. That's why he thought her mother had built a colony of lies…to hide something.

His precise words: *Lies are like ants: there's never just one.*

Jules wasn't ready to accept that Mother was responsible for her death.

"You're not crazy about my mother, are you?"

"Should I be?"

"No, she isn't nice."

"I know that's hard for you to say," Truitt acknowledged. "One more thing. About the mystery man who carried your mother into the house after she sprained her ankle in the garden. Like your Dad implied: He might be the same person who left prints on the skimmer. Finding this guy may lead to multiple answers."

"Maybe he'll come to my funeral service on Saturday. Think you could pick him out?"

He shook his head. "Too dark that night for details other than the basics. I know he's white and drives a light-colored truck, but I couldn't tell the make or model."

"Then we have our first play, Quarterback." She loved having a friend, especially Truitt. "Let's see if we can learn more about this mystery man. Enough to identify him."

"Checkmark. That brings us to your father—the next person in our playbook."

"Dad? You saw how he reacted to your insinuation he might be my murderer!"

Truitt tilted his head and raised his eyebrows. "Could be a play action. That's when a quarterback fakes a handoff to his running back, drawing the defensive line's attention. Meanwhile, his receivers get open. The quarterback passes the ball nobody knows he has."

"In other words," Jules said, catching on, "Dad could be faking us out. Trying to buy time for himself."

"Your father seems like a guy who's gotten comfortable playing the victim to your mother. He's never accepted his power to turn things around. I worry about people like that. Sometimes, they snap. Sometimes, they end up proving they have control in all the wrong ways."

His words struck hard, whether or not he intended them to.

"What did I say?" he asked, his forehead creasing.

"Your description sounds like me."

"Sorry, Jules. Didn't mean to make that connection. Anyway, you're turning things around now. As Coach Fields always said: Now is the only time change occurs."

She nodded. "You're right. Keep going."

He didn't hesitate, focusing on the fact that Mother had suggested her father's finances were less than stellar. What did her father need money for anyway? As he himself had stated, he was married to an extremely rich woman. Unless, Truitt guessed, their marriage was actually heading for a crash and burn.

"Wouldn't surprise me if they were divorcing," Jules admitted. "I can't remember them ever acting like they loved each other, not that I honestly know what love looks like. However, Dad would *not* kill me to gain financial security. I'm not denying he lies. He told Chief Keller the locks on my loft were there because the space was a former storage attic. Totally not true. Adding to his deceptions, he called himself and Mother *typical* parents. *Bah!* Even still, Dad adored me—as much as he's capable of loving another person."

"I hear you, but it couldn't hurt to have a heart to heart with him, using his laptop," Truitt said. "Why not press him on what's happening in his life? He might open up to you."

"Speaking of communicating, we're not only here for me. Let's visit your parents. Do they have a laptop we can use?"

"My parents rarely turn it on. They only got their laptop to google football stats, but now, they avoid anything football since the game triggers grief. I'm guessing their device is collecting dust somewhere."

"What about cellphones?"

"Nope. Where did you think I got my love for nostalgic devices?" He winked. "The truth is: When I was alive, they forced themselves to be *connected*. Now that I'm dead, they've cut the cord so to speak."

"We'll have to problem solve from a different angle. Game to hear what I have in mind?"

"Do quarterbacks wear helmets?"

"*Umm…*"

"Yes, Jules. Yes, they do." He rolled his eyes. "Go ahead. Call our next play."

"When does your Dad shower in the morning?"

"Wait. What does hygiene have to do with it?"

38

Thursday, August 19, 2027
The Windsors' Residence: Hickory Thicket, Maryland
(Four Days *after* Juliette's Death)

TRUITT COULD NOT believe he had agreed to invade his Dad's privacy as he showered, though the risk of him and Jules getting in trouble was non-existent. Ghosts didn't get grounded, didn't get their car keys taken away for two weeks. Parents couldn't force them to hand over their cellphones or smartwatches. And human nudity no longer mattered. Besides, Jules had promised him she had a plan that would make their amateur sleuthing pay off. He was beyond curious.

When he and Jules materialized in his parents' master bathroom early Thursday morning, his Dad was singing his favorite church hymn under the double showerheads. Back in Bishopville, no doubt their neighbors would've heard him hit the high notes.

Before the chorus, his Dad stopped singing. "Is that you, Abby?"

"Wait for it," Jules said, looking at Truitt and smiling.

As they absorbed heat from the bathroom, the temperature plummeted. And with warm water flowing from the showerheads, a dense mist quickly formed.

"Bet you thought you were the only nerdy scientist in Hickory Thicket," she teased.

"I stand corrected. Now where are we going with this?"

"So impatient, Quarterback."

"The clock is always ticking."

She smirked. "Except on your wrist."

"Ouch."

The shower turned off.

"What the heck is going on here?" his Dad said aloud. "Abby?" he shouted.

The mist reminded Truitt of Friday the 13th, the foggy night Jules first noticed him.

His Dad grabbed a towel and wrapped it around his waist, knotting two ends. He stepped onto the tiled flooring and stood motionless, like he was assessing his surroundings, perhaps wondering why he was in the middle of a cloud.

"Son? Is that you?"

Truitt glanced at Jules. "My parents have mastered feeling my presence, though my Mom still finds it upsetting that I'm not in Heaven. The thought of a ghost freaks her out."

"Go stand in front of the misty glass," she said. "Use your energy to write what I tell you."

"Good to know you haven't lost your bossy queen vibe."

He walked to the large wall mirror over the vanity and wrote as she dictated.

We need to talk, Dad. Please hire a psychic medium.

"Sign your name," she added.

Truitt wrote: *Love, T.*

His parents referred to him as T when they were being sentimental because prior to entering middle school, that's what they called him.

The bathroom door flew open, and the fog began to evaporate.

"You called me," his Mom said, sounding confused and swatting at the mist. "My gosh, Darren. You're supposed to use the fan."

"Look." His Dad pointed at the glass.

The words were dripping now. Dripping like blood.

39

Thursday, August 19, 2027
The Parkers' G&G Estate to Hidden Creek Trailer Park
(Four Days *after* Juliette's Death)

GARTH USUALLY RESERVED Thursday nights for his high school buddies. They still met at the Bistro's bar to catch up for an hour or two. Before 2025, the tradition took place on Fridays, but now most of the guys had partners or spouses, even kids, so the informal get together switched to Thursdays at 9:00 p.m. to prevent conflicts with family obligations.

At 27, he and his friends were in the throes of adulthood.

Tonight, Garth had to bail out from his weekly outing. Another weed had sprouted at the G&G's jungle of perpetual cray-cray.

Instead of laughing with friends while downing micro-brews, he sat in the pitch black, in his truck, backed up in a driveway across and slightly north of the electronic gate leading to the Parkers' estate.

He waited in silence. No music. No navigating on his cellphone.

Yesterday evening, after Garth had unclogged the sink's trap in one of the mansion's first floor bathrooms, he had overheard Mrs. Parker talking on her cellphone as she sat in the sunroom, unaware he was in the nearby hallway. If he had to guess, Mrs. Parker had been conversing with a man. With women, she tended to sound curt and blunt, obsessed with flexing her authority. With most men, however, she emoted feminine suave with a hint of intelligent sexy, often referring to them as *darling*.

The person on the other end of her cell yesterday was a *darling*.

What caught Garth's attention in the conversation was Mrs. Parker's inquiry. She had asked: *Did you collect anything helpful on camera? Something on video I could use?*

The woman loved her cameras, hiding them in nooks and crannies like Easter eggs.

Exceedingly strange was that Mrs. Parker had already submitted captured footage (from inside the mansion), to the Rock Hall Police Department in the event that it might help with the investigation into Jules's drowning. So what video was she referring to? And what did she mean when she said…*video I could use?* Use for what?

The *whats* were multiplying like a nasty virus.

Any other time, Garth would've ignored the conversation. However, since Jules's suspicious death had only been four days ago, he was paying attention.

During his eavesdropping, Mrs. Parker insisted she wanted to review the footage at the darling's double wide—even more peculiar. Going to trailer parks wasn't exactly her style.

If anyone considered him foolish or overreaching, Garth didn't care. No one was going to stop him from following his boss, from learning who she was visiting. It was a free country.

Anyway, the address of her destination would lead to a name. A name, to a connection. A connection, to a possible match with the mystery prints found on the pool skimmer.

Bottomline, he felt super guilty about letting Jules down while she was alive. He knew the kid's parents weren't treating her right and yet, he had turned the other cheek and let things ride out. Now, the sweetest, brightest, most beautiful girl he had known was dead.

He'd made up his mind he would learn from his mistakes. Bringing Jules back wasn't an option, but the least he could do was help find out who had taken her life.

Headlights appeared in the distance, coming down the Parkers' long driveway, growing larger as they neared. The darkness didn't allow him to immediately identify the make and model. Stopping until the gate fully opened, the vehicle continued through the entrance and turned north onto Eastern Neck Road.

Garth's heart pounded in his chest.

The car was a Maserati sedan: Mrs. Parker's.

He started his engine and inched forward in the dark, turning on his headlights once he was on the road. Hardly any traffic was heading in or out of Hickory Thicket, which made following her easy. On the downside, if he got too close, she might become suspicious. That would be disastrous. She didn't take kindly to intrusions into her privacy.

Beyond the town sign of New Yarmouth, Mrs. Parker turned right into Hidden Creek Trailer Park. Good thing her Maserati would be easy to spot.

Pulling over on the shoulder before the community's entrance, he parked, wanting to give her time to reach her destination. Being overly eager might blow his cover.

Gripping the steering wheel, Garth deeply inhaled.

He could do this.

After five minutes, he resumed his quest and entered into the trailer park which had gravel roads. It didn't take long to find Mrs. Parker's car. Problem was, she hadn't pulled into a driveway which meant he couldn't be 100-percent sure which home she was visiting.

As he drove toward the closest driveway to her vehicle (the nicest double wide to his right, set on top of a slight elevation), he slowed and read the mailbox number. Once past the home, he switched his headlights from automatic to fog lights. Driving to the cul-de-sac at the end of the lane, he turned around and parked on the other side of the road from Mrs. Parker, about seven car-lengths down from her sedan.

Thankfully, there were no streetlights. Knowing his boss and her compulsion to be efficient, she'd probably use the driveway closest to her car to back up and turn around. Anyway, he needed to be close enough to see which trailer she exited while being far enough away that his truck didn't catch her attention.

Maybe he should've borrowed Pete's coupe.

Oh well. Too late for that.

Garth turned off his ignition. In the dark, he googled the address he thought was accurate, learning the double wide belonged to a Brock Nolan. The name meant nothing, so he did another search on his cellphone. The guy, five years younger than Garth, was a former lacrosse star at Kent County High School. He must've graduated with

Mindi since she attended the same high school and was the same age.

Was there some sort of a triangle between Mrs. Parker, Mindi, and this Brock Nolan?

He'd stay put and wait for Mrs. Parker to leave. If his boss took all night, so be it.

Garth would unearth her secrets. Even if the effort spanned a lifetime.

After all, rich people always kept a secret or two...*thousand.*

40

Thursday, August 19, 2027
Hidden Creek Trailer Park: New Yarmouth, Maryland
(Four Days *after* Juliette's Death)

FIVE MINUTES AGO, Constance had plodded up the dirt and stone driveway leading to Brock's trailer. Wearing Dolce and Gabbana sandals had proved to be a miscalculation. She could scarcely *walk like a queen* on rutted soil covered with gravel, especially nursing a healing ankle.

Adding insult to injury, her sedan would require washing now. Arriving at Juliette's service in a filthy vehicle was out of the question! Not surprising that in this gritty neighborhood, dusty dirt clung to her Maserati like cheap lint on couture slacks.

Constance had stepped around Brock's gargantuan silver truck, raised ridiculously high off the ground. Her first thought: Was the young man compensating for his own inadequacies?

The front door had opened before she even knocked.

Brock stood in the doorway in tan chinos (skinny fit) and an even tighter V-neck T-shirt. At least the cotton material of his shirt looked to be Egyptian Pima. He had tousled his blond hair in an orchestrated way—fashionable like torn knees on designer jeans. Bulging biceps reminded her of his athleticism.

He had smiled wide, donning straight white teeth. "Constance, please come in."

"Thank you, darling," she cooed.

Brock had closed the door behind her.

Constance's first order of business had been to inspect her surroundings. Home décor spoke volumes about a person.

Inside and to the left, the elongated space included a living room and kitchen. Clear plastic covers sealed the couch and chair cushions. Against one wall was a desk with a large computer monitor which was on. Near the kitchen, two filled-to-the-brim wine glasses were on a tiny table topped with laminate. A vase of fresh carnations was beside the glasses.

Two dozen candles glowed throughout the space—one placed here, one there, one everywhere. They cast flickering shadows on vinyl walls which were far from plumb.

In a mere second, she had concluded the young man was far from adept at imitating class. How far? Diving into the Chesapeake with plans of swimming to Europe, far.

Being tasteful was completely out of his reach.

The crunch of tires on gravel distracted her musings as she stood in Brock's living room. From his bay window, she glanced outside into the darkness.

"That's the problem with stone," he said in response. "The whole neighborhood hears you coming and going."

Rushing to the table, Brock snatched up the glasses and jogged to her, handing one over without spilling a drop. Lacrosse had its benefits, she supposed.

Constance did not bother swirling the wine to admire its legs before taking a sip. Not only was the glass inappropriately full, but her expectations were appropriately low. She had made a wise choice. The wine tasted of vinegar. Vinegar, that had gone bad.

He held his glass up for a toast. "Here's to working together."

Together? Poor child. Brock was light years out of her league and apparently was unaware. Yet, she needed him...for now. Which meant, Constance had to promise him something he obviously craved but would fail to acquire: *her*.

Leave them wanting more did not mean suitors would *get* more.

They clinked glasses and she took another horrid sip.

"You have my undivided attention," she said. "Show me what my camera filmed."

Brock asked if she preferred that he mute the audio.

177

After she declined, he clicked play on his computer. Freezing her features to mask her emotions, she watched and listened to her darling husband having aggressive sex with her whore of a personal assistant.

The ungrateful bitch.

Hidden deep within her, Constance felt a pang of sadness. Finn used to be such a fervent lover. Always creative. Attentive. Robust. And now their fairytale had struck midnight, only with reversed roles. Constance was the wealthy princess. Finn, the penniless forsaken.

Not even a custom-crafted Swarovski crystal boot could bring them back together.

Unintentionally, she glanced down and noticed Brock's crotch. "May I recommend wearing loose sweatpants, preferably black, to watch pornography? They are less…revealing."

"How embarrassing." His neck turned crimson. "I'm so sorry."

"Not another thought. So, is that all you have? I was hoping for more. Much more."

Brock tightened his eyebrows as if no one had ever expressed disappointment before.

"I am referring to *evidence,* of course," she clarified.

The young man's shoulders relaxed.

Perhaps relieved that impressing her was still in his reach, he exhaled and pulled up several photographs on his computer, those snapped of pages in Mindi's journal—the entries which revealed her nefarious motives toward Juliette. Some excerpts were very damaging, especially the one written two days before her daughter's death:

The only reason Finn and Constance are together is because of Beauty Brat. If only BB Jules would go away. Forever might be nice. Then Finn could divorce the dreadful Queen Mother and I'd have my sexy hunk of blue all to myself. Mark my word: I'm going to put my plan into action. Mindi Parker sounds deliciously like nirvana. And everyone else in Castle Privileged can burn in bloody hell.

"These entries are perfect, Brock. When did you find her journal?"

"When you told me to discretely search her apartment, back before you hired her. I found the journal then, only her entries weren't incriminating. I kept my eyes on the book, though, and snapped new photos every time I snuck into her apartment to 'monitor' her." He cleared his throat and looked down at the matted carpet. "I should've mentioned them sooner. But at least I already had a collection of photos before she burned the journal."

"Yes, I am pleased. Did you save these on a thumb drive for me? Along with the video?"

Nodding, he handed her the device.

"About the fingerprints on the skimmer..." she started.

"Not gonna lie..." He coughed. "I mean, truthfully, I've been worried."

"Put your concerns aside. If they even make a match with yours, I will admit that I have been contemplating adding another groundskeeper to the Glitz and Glamour staff. Better construct a resumé to make everything look official. Email it to me." She nodded as another idea solidified. "Remember the foggy conditions on Friday the thirteenth? Juliette had retired early to her loft and Mindi had served her dinner before leaving the property several hours later. You arrived after she was gone. *That* is when you cleaned the pool for me. No one was at the estate to discredit my claim." She raised her glass. "Here's to contingencies."

"Amen." He guzzled the rest of his red vinegar.

Constance put her glass down, unable to stomach another sip.

Reaching into her purse, she retrieved an envelope and handed it to Brock. He started eagerly tearing open the paper. Gently placing a hand on top of his, she effectively stopped him.

"Trust and obey your handler," she said. "Count the bonus after I leave. Otherwise, you will look desperate. And that, darling, is never attractive."

He dropped the envelope on the kitchen table like the paper was about to ignite.

"I must return home to rehearse my eulogy for Juliette." Placing the thumb drive into her purse, she expressed her goodbye by lightly kissing him on each cheek, European style.

His skin immediately flushed red.

She enjoyed the power she had over him.

After gingerly walking down the god-awful driveway, she got into her sedan. Although she thought about backing up in Brock's driveway, she decided to avoid the ruts. Instead, she drove to the cul-de-sac and turned around.

She was about to shower herself with praise over the successful meeting with Brock when her heart jolted. Parked in the neighborhood, down the lane from Brock's, was a white truck. One with dual rear tires on each side.

Garth Harris. The truck belonged to her groundskeeper.

Highly unlikely their individual visits to the trailer park were a coincidence. Garth lived in Rock Hall, in an apartment. Not to say he had no friends in Hidden Creek. Still, it was more probable that the nosy bastard had followed her. That he was spying on her.

Slowing, her Maserati inched past the truck.

The cabin appeared to be empty.

Would she ever get a break from cleaning up messes?

Whether Garth was at the trailer park legitimately or tailing her, he would have recognized her Maserati. After all, his truck had not been present when she arrived.

"Garth Harris: Prepare to burn," she uttered between gritted teeth.

41

JULES LINGERED IN the garden with her best friend for the entire night, chatting about every subject under the moon. She was especially interested in Truitt's views on current events.

In her former life at the G&G, Mother had rationed television and the Internet, as well as selected the books she could read. Not to mention, Jules never had any friends with whom to exchange ideas in order to form her own viewpoints. Hence, Queen Mother had always told Jules what her opinions would be.

Predictably, Jules's positions on issues had always aligned with the majority of the pageantry judges.

Rule number 12: *Be whom others expect you to be.*

Listening to Truitt, she admired his thoughtful compassion regarding possible solutions to humanity's challenges. He led with his heart while being practical, trying to avoid hypocrisy. Best of all, he wanted to hear her thoughts even when they were different from his.

If he had been self-centered in life, he had made remarkable progress over the eight months following his death. Which meant, there was hope that Jules could become her own person rather than a ghostly puppet still victimized by her mother's narcissism.

Before sunrise, she and Truitt climbed the garden's eastern-facing brick wall and sat on the ledge, dangling their legs over the front. Alive, Jules would've needed a ladder.

Mosquitos buzzed around them, only they had no flesh to bite.

As the sun crested the marshes and the skies brightened to a tapestry of oranges and pinks, she was in awe. Earth was a miraculous place. She could see that now. Could feel its natural beauty. If only she had opened her eyes when she was alive and focused on the surrounding splendor. Instead, the craziness of her life had always held her attention.

Staring at Gibson Island at night had been different. She was escaping, not appreciating.

A carpet of mist covered the backyard of the G&G. Overhead, a flock of geese squawked.

"Fall is coming," she said. "I wonder if we'll still be here when the leaves turn."

"To everything there is a season." He winked.

"Ahh, you attended Sunday School, I bet."

"Yuppers. You?"

"A time to plant and a time to harvest. Ecclesiastes. My church had three members: me, myself, and I. Just so happens that *I* read the Bible three times. Me and myself took notes."

As the morning matured, they continued to talk and laugh.

Truitt froze. "Someone's calling me. I don't recognize the voice."

"Where's it coming from?"

Truitt tilted his head. Concentration tensed his features. "From my house, I think."

Jules reached for his hand and clasped it. *"There's a time to every purpose.* Let's find out what's going on. Who knows? Your parents might've already found a psychic medium."

"I'm nervous," he admitted.

"Leave emotions on the sidelines. Explore every option."

"Dang, Jules. Not only were you a queen, but you could've been a good quarterback. You catch on quickly."

She and Truitt vanished and materialized in the Windsors' den.

"I feel his presence," a woman announced to Truitt's parents.

The woman wore flared jeans and a light blue tunic embellished with small teardrop mirrors, each sewed on with white yarn. Her red hair was long and wild, abundant with curls. Above her freckled cheeks, she wore large glasses framed in blue.

"Hello, Truitt. My name is India Cloud," she said, frosty mist already escaping with every exhale. "I'm a medium who hears what spirits have to say. Your parents asked me here to fulfill your wish. I understand you want to speak with them." She paused. "I'm sensing you're not alone. Someone travels with you. A female. Who is it?"

"Jules Parker, my friend from next door," Truitt said. "Actually, it was her idea for a medium."

Mrs. Windsor's lower lip quivered. Then she bobbed her head while leaning forward, a nonverbal insistence for the medium to share her son's answer.

"Truitt is with the spirit of the girl next door," the medium said. "A...Jules Parker?"

"She died five days ago," Mr. Windsor confirmed. "Tragically. Possibly murdered."

"I'm so sorry, Jules," India Cloud said. "Is this what we're going to talk about? Your death?"

"No," Jules answered. "Truitt wants to talk with his parents."

"Okay. This meeting is for him and his parents." The medium glanced around the room, perhaps not knowing where she and Truitt were standing. "About the process: When I raise my hand, talking stops so I can share what Truitt has said. Anyone can start."

"It's Mom. I miss you, son. Dad and I miss you. Each and every minute, our hearts ache." She reached for Mr. Windsor's hand and clasped it. "As desperately as we wish the accident had never happened, that our lives had never changed, we've finally accepted we can't turn back time. Which means we worry terribly about you. We've felt your presence from the beginning. Since your death. We know you haven't passed on."

With her free hand, his mother dabbed her eyes with a tissue.

"We thought moving here might bring you peace," she continued. "Might convince you it was okay to leave the past behind. Now we're not sure we made the right decision. You're still here. And even more...restless."

Jules squeezed Truitt's hand more tightly.

"I miss you both, too. More than you know," he said, his voice cracking with emotion. "Honestly, at my death, I wasn't so sure paradise was my destination."

To Jules, Truitt looked uncharacteristically nervous as he ran his teeth over his bottom lip and wiped tears from his eyes.

"At home," he continued, "I wasn't exactly the easiest kid. I pushed the limits all the time. Off the field, out of the game, I had trouble putting anything before myself. I preferred getting what I wanted. I admit that now. Don't get me wrong, I'm not saying I don't believe in grace and forgiveness—you know, everything Sunday School taught me, but I've got to be due for some consequences and that scares me. Big time."

India raised her hand and shared what Truitt had said.

"Son," his father responded, "family life is a dynamic, just like a football team. You didn't create your hardheadedness in a vacuum. We nurtured it."

Mr. Windsor looked at his wife and she nodded. They had clearly talked about this before.

"We focused on your accomplishments," Truitt's Dad continued. "We didn't want conflict to sour any of them. But if we hadn't given in so much, if we had set firm boundaries and stuck to them, then maybe you would've understood your limitations better. We made you feel invincible. In hindsight, we regret some of our parenting choices. Your Mom and I are on the same page about this."

Truitt disclosed he had overheard them speaking one night about their relationship, about *not* being on the same page. He worried they were heading for a divorce because of his death.

"People grieve at different speeds," Mr. Windsor said. "Your mother and I found ourselves on opposite ends of the field. That was difficult, albeit normal. And even though we didn't arrive at the same time, we've both reached acceptance now."

"No need to worry about us, son," he assured. "You can pass on knowing we're working through it. Together. We've even agreed to speak with a counselor to make sure we stay in sync as a team."

The conversation continued, with the medium relaying what Truitt had to say. He confessed that at first, moving to Hickory Thicket had affected him. Then he realized no matter where his spirit was, the circumstances wouldn't change. He had died on that snowy road last December.

"The past never changes," his Dad said. "No do-overs."

Truitt went on to explain he would be staying on Earth to help Jules unravel the mystery of her drowning. And after she prodded him not to forget, he also asked his parents if they'd keep their laptop on, so he could reach out to them.

The Windsors eagerly agreed.

"Before you leave the house today, I have to know, T," his mother said softly. "We prayed you didn't suffer during the accident. Did you pass quickly? Without pain?"

He looked at Jules with wide eyes. She saw his fear, his uncertainty about how to answer.

Jules nodded, indicating what his answer should be, but knowing if she spoke aloud to explain herself, the medium would hear her.

"Yes. I died quickly, Mom," he said, rubbing his neck. "No pain."

Rule number 17: *White lies are the desired truth; use them wisely.*

What made Jules proud was that no one had forced her to apply that rule. Mother wasn't threatening retribution if she didn't. Instead, Jules thought for herself. She understood in her heart, that in this instance, a white lie would bring Mrs. Windsor comfort.

His Mom released a long exhale. Her shoulders relaxed. Stress eased from her face.

Truitt smiled, looking pleased he had followed Jules's advice.

Without warning, she began to feel a pull, like someone had unplugged a drain from a basin full of water. She blinked rapidly, trying to assess what was happening. Although the feeling wasn't painful, nor was it pleasant. It was a heavy, sinking feeling. Maybe similar to what she had likely felt while drowning in her parents' pool.

Truitt must have noticed the change in her.

"We've been in ghost form for a long time," he said. "Our candles have been burning on both ends. Are you feeling like your light is about to extinguish?"

She nodded, too scared to talk. Tears welled in her eyes.

"Don't be afraid, Jules," he said. "Sometimes the fade is more pronounced. I'm feeling a strong one, too. Keep holding my hand and we'll go together. It'll be okay. Promise."

Using his analogy, the dimmer had finished its slide.

She and Truitt blipped to off.

42

Friday, August 20, 2027
The Rock Hall Police Department: Rock Hall, Maryland
(Five Days *after* Juliette's Death)

FINN SAT BEHIND his office desk staring at his laptop screen, preoccupied with its blinking cursor. Beads of sweat moistened his forehead and dampened his underarms.

The time was 10:28 a.m. In two minutes, Chief Keller would walk through his door for a meeting. As Finn had promised his daughter's spirit and her obnoxious sidekick, he'd request reinstatement onto the team investigating Jules's suspicious drowning.

Maybe his boss would flat out refuse him. Help keep it easy.

Then again, a tiny part of Finn knew getting involved was the right thing to do, especially since it meant so much to Jules.

In the moment, what he hoped for the most was having his meeting with the chief remain private, without any paranormal eavesdropping. He had no clue what information Chief might throw at him and some things he still didn't want Jules—dead, alive, or in between—to know about.

Besides, with his boss, Finn couldn't afford distractions. He had to be sharp. On his game.

About a half-hour ago, he had keyboarded:

Jules, are you here? Type if you are.

The cursor had done nothing but blink. No response.

Antsy, he stood and marched to the thermostat. More promising news. The temperature held steady at 74-degrees and his exhales were still mist-free. And even though he was brand spanking new to the whole ghost phenomenon, he *felt* alone.

As Finn returned to his desk and lowered himself in the chair, Chief Keller appeared in the doorway. Wearing a dorky grin that resembled boyhood naivety, Keller walked in, shut the door, approached him while taking off his uniform-issued brim hat, and laid it on Finn's desktop.

Beginning to rise from his chair, Finn extended his hand for a shake. His boss motioned for him to remain seated as if good friends could forgo conventional formalities. Mid-motion, Finn froze, uncertain if Chief was testing his resolve for respecting superiors.

"You're fine. Relax," Chief said, continuing to wave him down while sitting in the chair in front of Finn's desk. "Thanks for understanding I couldn't meet with you yesterday. A few issues came up requiring my attention."

Finn knew his boss's ammo. He played the jovial dumb guy, but Sam Keller was neither. Chief knew exactly how to trap his opponent into checkmate without the poor soul even realizing the chief had outsmarted him from the very first move.

Crossing his legs, Chief twiddled his thumbs as if he hadn't a care in the world.

Fixated on the wall behind Finn, Chief had to be gazing at the hanging print of the sailboat.

"Walker tells me there was quite a ruckus in here two nights ago. On Wednesday, I think she said," he started. "Something about shattered glass?"

"The frame fell. I rehung the print yesterday using screw anchors this time."

"Weird, isn't it?" Chief asked, ahead of his real question. "How things seem perfectly stable for so long and then in one second, they come unhinged?"

Finn caught the implication; after all, Walker had probably told Chief about the bottle of bourbon, too. Alcohol was prohibited at the station. Yeah, she was a brown-nosing office snitch.

"Falling down is part of life," Finn countered. "Recovery is the real measure of something's worth." He looked over his shoulder at the print. "Looks even sturdier now."

"So what's on your mind, Detective?"

"I initially declined your offer to join the team assigned to Jules's case, but I've reconsidered and would like to be included. Not only do I know my daughter and the property better than anyone, being involved would be therapeutic, in terms of grieving, especially if I can solve the unanswered questions surrounding my daughter's death. And you said before that you'd make an exception regarding my conflict of interest as Jules's father."

Planting his elbows on the armrests, Chief raised his hands to his face, rubbing his chin's stubble. His eyes shifted to his lap as if thinking about something awkward. He slowly exhaled.

"What?" Finn sounded more defensive than intended.

"See, Constance planted this nasty seed that you might be in financial straits. Naturally, I had to check out her assertion as part of the investigation. Any idea what I found?"

Christ Almighty. There it was: checkmate.

Chief had trapped Finn, forcing *him* to decide how to handle his secrets. If, for example, Keller had learned about the condo and Finn didn't disclose this fact or worse, lied about it, everything Finn had worked for in the department would be in jeopardy. His job, his reputation.

Of course, Chief could be bluffing.

Maybe Keller hadn't looked into anything.

Either way, his boss was well aware of the weight attached to his simple question. Not to mention, even if Chief didn't know *now,* he certainly could learn the truth later.

Chief had placed the burden of the next move squarely on Finn.

Fuck.

Finn glanced at his laptop screen. Thankfully, still no response from Jules. The coast was clear.

"I consider my finances a personal matter," he started, "but I can appreciate your curiosity, given Connie and I had a life insurance policy on our daughter."

Clearing his throat, Finn hoped he wouldn't choke on his words as he spoke the truth out loud. "The unflattering facts…I want to divorce my wife, though I haven't told her yet. Then again, she has moles everywhere—people who keep tabs on me. Maybe she already knows. Anyway, I have no money and a prenup will keep it that way. To fly under the radar, I used Jules's name to purchase a condo in Chestertown, for my life after Connie. My daughter's assets are collateral only, in order to satisfy the bank that I can make the mortgage payments." He paused. "Sometimes the truth isn't pretty."

Pretty, no. Liberating, yes.

Chief raised his eyebrows. "I take it Jules had consented to purchasing the condo?"

Finn shook his head. That was the best he could do. The words were too damn ugly.

"Got it," Chief said. "Contracts usually require a down payment. How about this one?"

Jesus. His boss *had* done his homework.

"I borrowed seventy-five grand from a private lender. That's not a crime, Sam."

"How were you planning to pay back this...lender? I mean, before your daughter died? Before her death gave you access to two million from the life insurance policy?"

"I hear your accusation, but thought you were a bright man."

His boss's hands stopped fidgeting. "Excuse me?"

"If I were the murdering type and was willing to risk my freedom by drowning someone in my pool, who would I choose? The daughter whom I adored? For a measly two million? Or the wife whom I loathe for a hefty half-billion? If Connie is dead, the prenup dies with her since it only addresses *divorce*. Her Will, on the other hand, kicks in with her death and would benefit me just fine."

"Point noted," Chief said. "And to be clear, I certainly believe you loved Jules. Ease my mind, though. Are you in some sort of trouble with this lender? Maybe late in paying up? Should we be looking in that direction?"

Finn avoided telling his boss that Rip had pressured him, maybe even threatened him, before his daughter's death. Nor would he mention that he had missed the first deadline on August 16th for $37.5 grand. Thankfully, Rip had left him alone after Jules's death, which meant the guy wasn't totally ruthless.

The second payment, due on August 23rd, might be a different story. Rip would probably expect Finn to satisfy the entire balance. But he'd share none of this with his boss. He'd figure things out *after* Chief reinstated him on the investigative team.

"The situation is under control," Finn said instead. "I'm going to hock my wedding band and cufflinks to pay back the loan. My lender, by the way. You know him. Rip Riley. We all went to high school together. He's a prick, but strongly doubt he's capable of murder."

"I remember him. Yeah, a guy with an overgrown ego. And what about Constance? Anything odd happening on her end?"

Finn wanted to mention that Truitt had witnessed a strange man carrying Connie from the garden but throwing ghosts into the mix would also defeat his attempt to appear ready and able (and of sound mind) to join the team. So rather than blathering on about ghosts, he bit his tongue. He'd get Jules and Truitt to discover the man's identity for him. Afterwards, Finn would vet the guy. Find out if the mystery man was a suspect or merely one of Connie's playthings.

"Connie and odd?" Finn grinned. "You mean, over and above the standard fare? Believe me, I'll find out what my dear wife has been up to. Will you reassign me to the case?"

"Don't make me regret this, Detective. Anywhere else, your personal connection to the victim would preclude you from getting involved. But this is Rock Hall and we're family. Nevertheless, I'll have you work independently of the others. Report directly to me."

Chief leaned forward and continued. "However, you're not off the hook on this condo fiasco. When the case wraps up, I'll insist you clean up that mess—the right way. Mortgage fraud is a crime, Finn, and detectives are not above the law. Not in my department."

Standing, Keller picked up his hat from the desktop. "For now, though, I'll agree to keep your financial affairs on the downlow. But you and I both know…once Constance finds out, they'll be little anyone can do to save your sorry ass."

Staring at the hanging sailboat, he added, "In the meantime, my friend, I do believe there's hope for that print. New starts are possible."

43

MINDI'S STOMACH RUMBLED, and she wasn't even close to being hungry. The unsettled churning had everything to do with her nerves—a combo of being angry and scared shitless.

The smug reception by the Bistro's hostess, the one named Heather, had only served to agitate Mindi further.

Sitting in the back corner of the restaurant, at Finn's table, Mindi sipped her third sweet tea. She hadn't been in the mood for alcohol. Thinking clearly was paramount. Her plans weren't going as expected and she struggled with what her next move should be.

One thing was certain: Talking with Finn was crucial. That's why she had come to the Bistro at lunchtime, hoping her sexy hunk of blue would show up.

Unfortunately, over the last 36 hours, he hadn't returned any of her calls or texts. Had he blocked her? Or was he sending her a message to back off until he figured things out?

No lie. Wednesday had been the best day of her life.

She had connected with the man of her dreams, sharing an epic fuck. One she'd never forget. But during their last exchange, when she had playfully called him at the station to thank him, Finn had been cold and distant, perhaps even mean—treating her more like a nuisance than an extraordinary promise for the near future.

Momma's saying came to mind again: *Skunks don't stink to smell themselves.* Something foul was happening, and she was taking the brunt of the spray. This morning proved it.

Fifteen-minutes before Mindi regularly left her apartment to head for the G&G, the Queen Mother texted her, urging her to look at her email inbox prior to leaving.

She placed a copy of the visceral notification on the table, reading it again.

Ms. Maxwell:

Please be informed that I no longer require your services at the Glitz and Glamour Estate, effective immediately (August 20, 2027). This letter serves as official notice of your termination as my Personal Assistant due to incompatibility and behavior detrimental to the wellbeing of my family.

As a reminder, your signed nondisclosure agreement remains on file and is binding.

I forbid you on estate property. In addition, return the estate-issued sedan to the Volvo dealership by Monday (8/23) at 5 p.m. (Any damages to the vehicle will be your responsibility.)

Constance Isabel Reyes Parker

The email was CC'ed to Constance's cutthroat lawyer.

Just thinking about the letter made Mindi sick to her stomach. So much for managing their secrets together. And how convenient for Constance to dispose of Mindi after she had helped organize tomorrow's funeral service.

The hostess approached the table and Mindi quickly turned the letter face down.

"Detective Parker is rarely late," Heather said, like she was intimate with Finn's every move. "He's probably not coming in for lunch today. Want your check?"

No way was Mindi going to give this bitch the upper hand. "Bring me another iced tea."

The woman huffed away.

Finn needed to fix Mindi's situation, or she'd play hardball, depending on where his heart was. Because, if his heart *didn't* beat for her, she'd threaten to tell his wife about their sexcapade. What did Mindi have to lose? If she was out of a good paying job and her sexy hunk of blue wasn't interested in her, then Finn deserved to feel gut-wrenching pain, too.

The hostess delivered the tea *and* a check, quickly walking away.

Cunt.

Mindi texted Brock. Go figure. He hadn't returned any of her communications either.

Hey. What gives? I need to talk to you. Urgently.

Five minutes ticked by. No response.

Dialing Brock's number, she let the call ring 20 times since he had intentionally avoided setting up voicemail. She hung up when it was clear he wasn't picking up.

Fucking fireballs to hell.

Everyone was ghosting her.

44

Friday, August 20, 2027
The Rock Hall Police Department: Rock Hall, Maryland
(Five Days *after* Juliette's Death)

IF JULES WAS comprised of tiny particles of energy, each of them began to vibrate and hum. The light dimmer was sliding upwards, releasing her from the dark limbo where nothing happened.

Her memory was foggy, except for recalling the horrible feeling which had consumed her as she and Truitt faded into nothingness after talking with the medium. Truitt had described the destination as a void or temporary oblivion, and he was spot on.

When she reappeared as a ghost on Earth, she was still holding Truitt's hand. Relief overwhelmed her because during her fade, she had feared that time and space might separate them. Maybe he'd reappear at his childhood home back in Bishopville while she popped into her loft. How would they know where the other had ended up?

The thought of losing him was unnerving.

Alive, Jules had gotten comfortable being alone. She had known no other option. But after experiencing a friend's support, she never wanted to feel completely on her own again.

Pulling him to her, Jules threw her arms around his waist, squeezing him tightly. The side of her face pressed against his chest.

"Hello to you, too," Truitt teased, gliding his hand over her back.

"When the fade hits," she said, "promise we'll hold hands to stay together. Promise."

"Your bossy queen vibe is growing on me." He looked down at

her and smiled. "Of course. Promise. One-hundred percent."

Jules heard a drawer open behind her.

She'd been so focused on Truitt that she hadn't noticed where they had materialized. The room was familiar. They were standing in the corner of Dad's office at the station.

Releasing her embrace with Truitt, she scanned the room. Dad was rummaging through drawers and lifting papers.

"Where in the hell are my car keys?" he griped. "I'm late for lunch at the Bistro."

She and Truitt walked to the desk.

Already powered up, his laptop was opened to a word processing page. Dad had keyboarded a message, asking her to type when she had arrived.

Truitt and I are here, Dad. What's up?

Dad glanced at the screen, but he didn't have time to answer. A deputy appeared at his door with Garth standing beside her. Their groundskeeper was holding a book.

"Mr. Harris would like a word with you," the female deputy announced.

"Sure. Thank you, Walker," Dad said. "Come on in, Garth. Close the door and take a seat."

After shaking hands, Dad motioned for Garth to sit in the chair in front of his desk.

"This is unexpected." Her father sat. "What's on your mind?"

"Wanted to stop by before reporting to work at the G&G." Garth shivered. "It's cold in here, sir."

"Yeah, the thermostat is on the fritz every now and then. Well?"

Their groundskeeper shared how he had unintentionally eavesdropped on Mother. He had overheard her request a meeting with someone in Hidden Creek Trailer Park to review some "collected" video. Maybe he shouldn't have followed her, but Garth admitted he had, along with googling the address of the home Mother had visited.

"Do you know Brock Nolan?" Garth asked.

"I don't. Should I?"

Garth opened the book and placed it on Dad's desk.

"I stopped by the library and signed out this yearbook," Garth said. "The photo is of Nolan and Mindi Maxwell. Turns out, they were high school sweethearts."

Along with Dad, she and Truitt stared at the photograph. Brock Nolan was slender and muscular: strength without the bulk. He had blond hair and blue eyes. Attractive. His smirk made him look cocky and his tight T-shirt displayed the words: *Defend and Attack, Baby.*

Mindi hadn't changed much, though back then, she had sported shoulder length hair instead of long. Her facial features truly resembled Mother's. They could pull off being sisters.

"I thought maybe with a name," Garth said, "you might be able to determine if the mystery prints on the skimmer belong to this guy...this Brock Nolan. You know, process of elimination."

Garth lifted the yearbook from the desk and closed it. "Guess I find it weird that there's a triangle between Mrs. Parker, Mindi, and Nolan. Seems strange, is all. But maybe it's nothing." He cleared his throat. "Hope you're not angry, sir. I overreached quite a bit."

"Don't be sorry," Dad said. "My daughter is dead, and every stone should be overturned to find out who's responsible. I appreciate what you did. You have guts."

With her ghostly heart racing, Jules used her energy to type on the laptop.

Ask if Mother spotted him following her.

Dad asked the question.

"There was a moment," Garth answered, "that Mrs. Parker drove past my truck. I ducked so she couldn't see me. Frankly, I don't think she pays much attention to my vehicle. Good thing white trucks are a dime a dozen around here. Pretty sure I wasn't detected."

Jules hoped not because if Queen Mother had recognized his truck, she would unleash retribution on him.

"Any idea what might have been *on* the video she was referring to?" Dad asked, probably knowing it had to be something significant for Mother to venture into a trailer park.

"I don't. But I'm extremely curious."

"Me, too." Dad said, standing.

Garth followed his lead. They walked toward the door.

"I'll keep this information between us," Dad continued. "The name helps. If I have anything to do with it, we'll pay this Brock Nolan a visit and slap him with a warrant, allowing us to collect his fingerprints for exclusionary purposes. Meanwhile, if anything else comes up, please call me or stop back in."

He patted Garth on his shoulder before their groundskeeper stepped into the hallway. "You did the right thing. Thank you."

"Sir, please let me know if you'd like me to check out your HVAC unit," Garth said, rubbing the chill from his biceps as he left. "You may need a new thermostat, too."

Dad closed the door and returned to his desk. "Could Brock Nolan be the mystery guy who carried your mother from the garden into the house?"

Truitt responded on the laptop.

> Truitt here. It was dark and rainy that night. Like I told Jules, all I know for sure is the man was white skinned and drove a truck painted a light color. White, tan, silver? Couldn't tell.

"*Hmm*. Lots of trucks in this area. Even our groundskeeper drives a white one. Still, every observation helps. I'll find out what this Nolan guy drives," Dad said. "Speaking of gathering information. Jules: Are you interested in popping in on your mother? Maybe you could overhear what she's up to. Meantime, I'll work on obtaining a warrant on Nolan. Sometimes they can take days to obtain."

> Sounds like a plan, Dad.

"Hey, kiddo. Do you and Truitt plan on coming to your memorial service tomorrow?"

> It'll be strange, but we'll be there.

"Won't be easy for any of us. Least we'll be there together."

Dad picked up his office phone.

"Right now," he added, "I'm starving. Instead of heading to the Bistro for lunch, pizza delivery sounds good." He winked. "Don't tell anyone, but I'm about to order extra pepperoni."

45

Friday, August 20, 2027
The Parkers' G&G Estate: Hickory Thicket, Maryland
(Five Days *after* Juliette's Death)

TRUITT HAD OBSERVED daily routines at the G&G enough to predict Mrs. Parker would be lounging under the pool awning, sipping a Bloody Mary or sweet tea, while reading a book on influencing others or manipulating perceptions. That's what she did on most sunny weekdays.

If Jules had still been alive, she would've been studying in her loft, door locked, forbidden to enjoy the outdoors, even in the summer. A timer would've been ticking away on a homeschool assignment until her alarm signaled that she was to move on to the next task.

In his opinion, a book on parenting should've been tops on Mrs. Parker's to-be-read list.

He and Jules materialized near her mother.

Their timing couldn't have been any better. Mrs. Parker had just dialed someone on her cellphone. Of course, they wouldn't be able to hear the person on the other end unless she activated the speaker. Either way, Mrs. Parker might say something helpful. Something that could matter in the investigation.

"I miss you," Jules's mother said, holding the cell to her ear.

Pause.

"Losing an only child is simply dreadful." She sipped her drink.

Pause.

"Rehearsing the eulogy. My homage is quite brilliant: poignant, classy, with a splash of drama. Paxton (the minister) projects attendance will burst at the seams during the service. And I dare anyone in the church to have dry eyes. If you see someone, take names. You are coming, right?"

Pause.

"Perfect. Please sit in the farthest-back pew, in the seat marked *reserved.* And wear your red tie, my favorite."

Pause.

"Best not to let Finn spot you. And why don't we give him the weekend before pressuring him. After all, I am not an ogre." She giggled and sipped simultaneously. "Let him have two more days to grieve. Monday will be an excellent night to commence provocations. Finn has night duty at the station, and I will be at Deanna Mae's for wine and cheese—a mourn and reborn session with my girls. Do not worry about the cameras at the mansion; they will be off. I will keep the kitchen door unlocked. Nine o'clock works best."

Pause.

"Excellent." Mrs. Parker placed her half-full Bloody Mary on a small round table beside her recliner. "Before I forget. I have decided to have a tennis bracelet custom-made to include the diamond—an exquisite focal point. My jeweler will be hearing from me next week."

Pause.

"Always my rock." She disconnected.

"I've heard your mother call someone that before," Truitt said to Jules. "I remember. It's how she referred to the guy who carried her from the garden. She had whispered...*always my rock.* Now we know where the mystery man will be sitting in church tomorrow. We'll be able to see if he and Brock Nolan are one and the same. If not, we'll find a way to learn the man's name and what he's up to."

"Our first huddle priority."

"Your memory's getting stronger."

"Wonder why Mother and this man want to pressure my father," she said. "Strange, right?"

"One thing's for sure. We need to be at the G&G Monday night. To learn what *provocations* mean, what purpose they have. And your Dad won't even be home."

Jules stared off into space. "Mother seems close to this person."

The Bloody Mary glass flew off the table, shattering on the pavers, launching the celery stick. Sending the red mix splashing on the deck.

"What the hell?" Mrs. Parker exclaimed. *"Ev-ell-lynnn?"* she hollered at the top of her lungs. "Come here this damn minute!"

"Sorry, Jules. This all has to be heart wrenching to hear," he said, realizing she had unleashed her energy to hurl the glass. "Is the hardest part finding out your mother might be having an affair?"

Jules shook her head, her eyes cast downward. "What's worse is that the closer we get to the truth about my death, the more signs point in Mother's direction."

46

Saturday, August 21, 2027
Mariner's United Methodist Church: Rock Hall, Maryland
(Six Days *after* Juliette's Death)

ATTENDANCE SHOCKED JULES, especially since she didn't have any friends to speak of. The gathered crowd at her memorial service resembled packed sardines. None of the shiny fish shared camaraderie; they simply swam in the same circles. Where a few darted, the masses turned and followed, having little emotional connection to each other or to where they were going.

People occupied every pew in the 300-capacity sanctuary, except for one seat—the space Mother had referenced to the mystery man. A taped sheet of paper displayed "reserved."

No one had claimed the spot as yet.

In the aisles running along the sides of the sanctuary, attendees without a seat stood, fanning themselves with programs while leaning against the wall or stained-glass windows. Two television stations had setup their camera equipment in the transepts—the square shaped nooks to the right and left of the pulpit and chancel. On the opposite end of the church, near the entrance, people (four rows deep) stood and bumped arms in the foyer-like narthex. Only the center aisle (the nave) was clear of people.

Jules smiled. Truitt was right: Her memory continued to improve.

Mother had made her memorize, from books, the formal names of designated areas within a church's floorplan, since learning firsthand by attending Sunday services was out—too much of a "distraction." Regardless, Jules had never expected the names to be remotely useful. She certainly never counted on *remembering* them.

Despite Mother's own rare attendance at Mariner's UMC, she knew the minister on a first name basis. Pastor Paxton Engle apparently granted informal privileges to annual donors landing on the highest tier of financial stewardship: *The Shepherd.* Singular. Mother made sure of that.

A glossy mahogany coffin was positioned at the "crossing," the intersection between the long nave, the arms of the transepts, and the top chancel. In other words, it was located at the center of the cross-shaped floorplan. The closed casket was blanketed with an over-the-top collection of white flowers (roses, lilies, and peonies). Displayed prominently on the flower arrangement was Jules's most recent jeweled tiara. The gems cast tiny rainbows on the ceiling and floor, depending on where the light hit them.

To the right of her coffin, a full-length poster of Jules stood—made sturdy, free standing, and lifelike by foamboard backing. In the photo, she wore her sequined gown, 2027 National Miss Junior Teen sash, and crown. Her image displayed her winning smile.

Another surreal experience.

In fact, she wanted to pause, to decipher her emotions, but her and Truitt's purpose for being there was more pressing: to learn the identity of Mother's mystery man.

For the best view of the empty seat, she and Truitt stood in the nave, near the back. Why not? Almost no one saw ghosts in the middle of the day. If they did, who was going to announce it? Ghosts were still taboo, especially in a place of worship. Nonsensical, of course, since one of the Trinity was none other than the Holy *Ghost.*

She and Truitt held hands, fearing the fade or a blackout might strike them like a light switch instead of a dimmer. They had talked about it briefly and agreed: The closer they became emotionally, the more unsettled they grew about getting separated, like if one of them passed on and they never found each other again.

An idea popped into her thoughts. A solution to their fears.

All she and Truitt needed to do was pick a spot where they could reconnect if they were still on Earth. She started to say something to him when the escalating noise distracted her.

Chatter in the church sounded like buzzing bees, squawking birds, and a humming engine jumbled together. The pitch was getting sharper, louder. People still clamored to find a space to sit or stand.

Not even the organist's playing was hushing the crowd.

"Weird, right?" Truitt said, close to her ear. "To be present at your own memorial service?"

"Weird on steroids. Thank goodness my casket isn't open. Seeing myself poolside, shortly after I died, was freaky enough. Not sure I could handle looking at my body's shell, all dolled up, with people gawking at me. Most of whom, I wouldn't even know." She turned toward Truitt. "Did you have a viewing at your service?" Instantly regretting the question, she quickly added, "Sorry. I wasn't thinking about how you died."

"No worries. Have you spotted your parents yet?"

Nodding, she pointed toward each of them.

Dad was near her coffin, facing away from them, chatting with Chief Keller. Outfitted in his ceremonial police uniform, he matched all the other law enforcement personnel in attendance.

Standing a dozen yards from Dad's left was Mother. Busy, busy, busy. Talking to a videographer, her hands were moving and pointing—emphasizing each demand, no doubt.

Wearing long white gloves and a sleeveless, tightly fitted black cocktail dress with a square neckline, Mother had accessorized her chic look with a black woven hat, trimmed in white around the brim. The hat included black and white ribbons and decorative feathers and pearls that accentuated the bow. Adorning her neck was a thick choker collar comprised of five strands of pearls, one row resting on top of another.

Jules remembered the necklace; it had belonged to Nana Bea.

The necklace threw Jules into a flashback.

On the day of her death, she remembered catching Mindi trying on Nana Bea's necklace, the one with the pendant featuring a two carat, heart-shaped diamond. It was Jules's favorite, especially since Nana Bea had willed the heirloom to her.

An unpleasant exchange with Mother's personal assistant had followed. To protect the necklace from Mindi's greedy fingers, Jules recalled clasping it around her own neck. But after consuming the concentrated *stea,* she had forgotten to take the special jewelry off before resting under the pool house awning.

"What's wrong?" Truitt asked.

"Do you remember me wearing a diamond necklace by the pool? On the day I died?"

"Hard to forget. I'd never seen a 3D heart-shaped diamond before. Not that I would've let on. Guess I figured wearing unique diamonds to the pool was typical for a queen of your stature. You know, *royal is as royal does."* He winked. "What made you think of it?"

"When Garth pulled my body from the pool, the necklace wasn't on me. I watched him trying to resuscitate me. The only thing around my neck was a thin abrasion. My murderer must have taken it."

"Wow. This sounds significant."

"Hey," a female whispered behind them. "I wondered if I'd see you guys here."

They turned to find Lila Lovelace Scarborough standing in the center aisle, dressed in a fashionable, three-quarter-length navy dress.

"I can't talk long," Lila said softly, barely moving her lips like a ventriloquist. "Wouldn't want people to think I'd gone bonkers and was talking to myself." She smiled. "By the way, everything looks lovely, Juliette. Your mother spared no expense."

Lila pointed across the pews to a woman slowly walking up the outer aisle as she shuffled in front of those leaning against the wall. "Oh. Look. There's Ms. Underhill. Haven't seen her in a while. You recognize her, don't you?"

Jules did. Ms. Underhill was a former librarian in Rock Hall who occasionally judged local pageants when Jules was much younger. Now the woman looked dazed. In a fog.

"Wait. Didn't she *die* a while ago?" Jules asked. "From a murder suicide? I heard about it at one of our competitions."

"That's right," Lila said. "Her boyfriend shot her, then himself. Before my Mom started going to Sunday AA meetings, I'd see Ms. Underhill walking up and down that very same aisle during the service. Sad. I thought she would've found her white light by now."

"You know, you really did have a lot in common with Jules," Truitt said. "Before her death, she could also see ghosts as if they were still living. That's how we met. She saw me like I used to be."

"And you?" Lila cleared her throat, as if her question to Truitt might be awkward. "When you were alive. Could you see ghosts?"

"No, not me. I could only see endzones," he said, winking.

"Who are you talking to, Lila Lovelace?" Mrs. Scarborough barked at her daughter from behind her.

Jules flinched; her heartrate spiked.

That woman triggered instant anxiety.

"You're making an unsightly spectacle—pointing and talking to yourself." Lila's mother huffed. "Never mind the cameras are rolling. Now go sit with your handler. This minute."

As Lila shrugged and walked away to comply with her mother's orders, Jules glanced back at the reserved seat.

Still empty.

In between the greeting, opening prayer, and hymn of comfort, Jules remained watchful of the back pew, waiting for her mother's mystery man to enter the sanctuary and sit.

The minister read scriptures from the pulpit.

Finally, Queen Mother stood behind the lectern and delivered her dramatic performance. Jules felt embarrassment's sting with every exaggerated sob, sniffle, or quiver of Mother's red lips.

"He's finally here," Truitt said, nodding toward the reserved seat. "Definitely not Brock Nolan."

The man nudging people to move out of his way was six feet tall, plus several more inches of burly. Decked out in black, he wore leather pants, cowboy boots, and a leather tunic-styled jacket. His tie was candy apple red.

With short, black curly hair, he also donned a closely shaven beard. His badass image exemplified money with a threat of danger.

"I don't recognize him," Jules said. "How can we find out who he is? Follow him?"

"He probably drove. If we get his license plate number, we can give it to your Dad. He can access a database and identify the man."

"I doubt he's going to stick around after the service."

"Yeah, he seems like a *last in, first out* kind of guy," Truitt said while rubbing his neck injury. "Let's wait outside to make sure we don't miss him."

As they exited the sanctuary, she stared at the man.

His eyes hadn't moved off Mother.

Outside, standing on the church lawn, Jules heard the choir singing. The service was winding down.

One of the church's double doors opened and the mystery man stepped out. As she observed him this time, he raised his head and seemed to lock eyes with her for a brief second.

He smirked, ever so slightly, and a shiver raced up her spine.

With a brisk pace, the man strutted across the street toward a futuristic, sleek, red and black motorcycle.

She had never seen anything like it.

"Unbelievable," Truitt said, his eyes wide.

"That's a special motorcycle, isn't it? I mean, it looks fancy enough."

"Fancy? Lace is fancy, Jules. That there is an MTT Turbine Streetfighter. Four-hundred-and-twenty turbine-powered H.P.'s."

She rolled her eyes. "You're drooling."

"They only make five of them," he said. "A year."

"That many? Because there's only *one* miss junior teen champion. A year."

Chuckling, Jules raced across the street and passed the man.

Standing behind the motorcycle, she froze.

If she had ever doubted that her mother was having an affair, she didn't anymore.

The license plate read: QueenRock.

47

Saturday, August 21, 2027
The Rock Hall Police Department: Rock Hall, Maryland
(Six Days *after* Juliette's Death)

ATOP FINN'S DESK at the station, the laptop's cursor blinked on an empty page.

As the sun lowered beyond his windows, Finn's eyes had dried. Sitting behind his desk, hoping beyond hope that words would appear on the computer screen, his chapped cheeks still stung like sunburn. He had wept like a baby at Jules's service, but not during Connie's melodramatic performance; *that* fiasco had only ignited a panic attack. Instead, his tears had flowed when he saw Jules's coffin for the first time. Despite the care his wife had undeniably taken to select the finest casket, topped with lovely floral trimmings, the image was bleak. Cruel, even.

Cruel, because Finn understood that if he had lifted the head panel, he would've found his beautiful daughter, reduced to an empty vessel—one destined for decay.

Morbid? Of course.

Realistic? Without a doubt.

Delivered peacefully or in violence, with acceptance or denial, converted to ashes or an embalmed corpse: death was never easy for the living. No matter the combination of variables, death generated the same devastating outcome: Dead was dead.

Not to mention, American culture regarding death did nothing (as in zero) to help those grieving focus *less* on the tragic loss and *more* on positive thoughts, such as celebrating the life of the deceased and lauding the comforting belief that spirits had a heavenly destination in which to rest—an eternal spring.

In Finn's mind, a victim's death (even when murder was involved) should not eclipse their life. Why not treat every death like its own little Easter?

But no. With Connie theatrically sobbing at the lectern, nothing positive could've risen.

The abbreviated version of his wife's message: *Juliette Annabella is dead. Taken too young. Too innocent. How unfair. Her parents will grieve forever. Thanks for coming.*

While he sat in the pew nearest Jules's coffin, his wife's words had collided with his fears. Sweat beaded on his skin; his heart pounded. He had become short of breath. Panicking, he remembered frantically scanning the pews behind him, as if that would've helped. Bottomline, he couldn't see Jules to know if she had come to the service as she'd promised. And it wasn't like he could've brought his laptop to ask her. No one would've understood the optics if he had.

The questions assaulting him during his moment of panic: Would his daughter's ghost vanish after her body's interment? What if he could never converse with her again?

The possibilities had struck Finn with blunt force, and he felt a magnetic pull to run from the church and return to his office. He hoped like hell Jules would reach out to him on his laptop. He needed to learn if her spirit was still around. God, he hoped so. How stupid of him not to consider that his visit with her yesterday might have been his last.

Maybe this was death's cruelest inevitability: Most people never acknowledged that each and every goodbye with their loved one, spoken or not, could be their final interaction.

The cursor moved and typing began.

His pulse accelerated.

Truitt and I are here, Dad. We overheard Mother talking to the mystery man yesterday. He was at my service; Mother had reserved a seat for him.

And he's not Brock Nolan. Anyway, we saw his motorcycle's license plate. Can you search "QueenRock" and tell us his name?

"Thank God you're still here, Jules," he said aloud, overflowing with gratitude that she hadn't disappeared. "I panicked I had lost you. That I would never see you again."

Finn felt better when Jules urged him not to worry, assuring him she'd tell him if and when passing-on seemed like a possibility.

Entering the personalized license into the database, he wondered what kind of guy would request "QueenRock" on his plate. Was the combination a tribute to Freddie Mercury and the rock band *Queen?* Or a variation of the singer *Kid Rock*, a.k.a. Robert Ritchie?

When the search produced a name, Finn could only stare at his screen. Dumbfounded.

Registrant: Ripley Rock Riley
DOB: 09/24/1988
SSN: XXX-XX-2173
Address: P.O. Box 1549, Chestertown, MD.

"Are you kidding me?" Finn banged his fist on the desk, jolting his laptop.

The whole damn point of using Rip as his financier was to keep the down-payment transaction hidden from Connie. Turns out that his dear, queen of a wife was having *an affair* with the bastard.

How fucking perfect.

What is it, Dad? Do you know him?

"Went to high school together. That's all," he snarled. "The guy's a bona fide jerk. A total A-hole."

No way would he confess his true connection with the slimeball. Maybe he'd never have to. Maybe his daughter would find peace before that nasty tidbit of truth surfaced. He just couldn't handle telling her what he'd done to secure the condo and its mortgage.

Could the fingerprints on the skimmer be his?

"No. Rip Riley has a criminal record. Our database would've made a match."

Previously, Rip had handled his own "motivational" tactics aimed at his slow paying clients. However, after losing a civil case for slashing someone's tires and knocking out a few teeth, Rip began hiring grunts to do his dirty work, though his fingerprints remained in the system.

Can you find out Mr. Riley's street address? Truitt and I want to pay him a visit to learn more about his association with Mother.

Christ Almighty.

Finn needed Jules and Truitt to stay far, far away from Connie's *rock*. Clearly, the queen got a kick out of her duplicitous scheme to make Finn's loan shark her lover.

Why couldn't Connie have been the one found at the bottom of the pool?

"If we know Rip Riley's fingerprints aren't on the skimmer," Finn said, trying to sound calm, "why not stay focused on your case? Why bother with this guy?"

Jules keyboarded she had been wearing her heart-shaped diamond necklace at the time of her drowning. When Garth recovered her body from the deep end, the necklace was missing. And when she and Truitt had eavesdropped on Connie's conversation with Rip Riley yesterday, Connie had mentioned she'd be going to their jeweler to have them custom make a tennis bracelet featuring "the" diamond. Jules wanted to know if her missing diamond was one and the same.

Someone, his daughter concluded, had clearly ripped the necklace off her neck, either during the struggle or at the time of her death.

"As much as your mother and I are struggling to get along—and we are, Jules—she has heaps of money to buy her own diamonds. At any cost. She has no need to steal one from you."

Finn hated Connie but she wasn't a murderer or thief. *Right?*

"Any chance," he continued, "that Garth might have taken your necklace during his attempted rescue? He had opportunity. And we all know he's trying to afford college."

Jules was adamant: Garth was a good guy.

Yeah, so was Finn and look what he had done for money.

The necklace was a curious development. He remembered their jeweler had appraised Jules's necklace at $28 grand—a healthy chunk of change.

Truitt, the annoying "bad cop" in the ghostly partnership, started giving him shit: *Why was he hesitant in sharing Mr. Riley's address? Was there a problem they should know about?*

No way around it. He couldn't avoid giving them Rip's address unless he wanted to raise suspicions. Besides, Jules had found the medical examiner's office on her own, hadn't she?

After sharing the street location of Rip's penthouse, he read Jules's next entry on his laptop:

> One more thing, Dad. Mother and Mr. Riley spoke of pressuring you. Mother suggested "commencing provocations" on Monday night at our house, around 9 p.m., when no one will be home. What could that mean?

Finn knew exactly what that meant. His wife was a vindictive bitch who was out for blood.

Obviously, Connie knew he had borrowed the condo's down-payment from her lover. No doubt she was also aware he was late in paying the loan recall. He had missed the first payback installment entirely, and the second (the total balance) was due, in fact, on Monday the 23rd.

What he couldn't quite figure out was why Connie would want to stick around and watch him feel the squeeze. What was the point? If she had already moved on with Rip, why not slap Finn with divorce papers instead? His financial ruin was coming no matter what.

Unless…Connie loved Finn's pain more than her prick of a rock.

Bottomline, Finn no longer had a reason to hang on to the marriage while he secretly prepared to leave his wife. She already knew everything.

"I'm not sure what provocations mean, Jules," he said. "But I plan on surprising whoever comes to the house. I'll find out why they're there. What they want. Don't either of you worry."

> You won't be alone. Truitt and I will be there with you, Dad. We're in this together.

Fuck.
The walls around his secrets were crumbling.

48

JULES FELT CONFLICTED about the collapse of her parents' marriage. For one thing, she had always desperately wanted the oil painting in the formal living room to reflect the truth.

Depicted in the portrait, framed in wood and coated in gold enamel, was Dad holding Mother's hand and smiling warmly. Mother's other hand rested on Jules's shoulder, like she was emphasizing the love for her daughter. Ten-years-old at the time, Jules was raising her chin and glancing up at her parents like God had blessed her with the perfect family.

Each paint stroke had been a white lie.

In fact, the artist had encouraged Dad to hold Mother's hand and gaze at her lovingly. Jules remembered her father making several attempts to display that emotion. He hadn't stopped trying until finally, his expression pleased the artist.

Also a vivid memory, Mother had occasionally dug her fingernails into Jules's shoulder in an attempt to stop her from fidgeting.

Maybe apart, her parents would find their own truth. Perhaps authenticity could lead them each to a genuine happiness.

No misleading family portrait required.

As she and Truitt traversed through time and space, destined for Mr. Riley's penthouse, Jules wondered what type of man had attracted her mother. How would he compare with Dad?

They materialized in a great room with a cathedral ceiling that had to be 24-feet high. The room's décor was masculine and minimalistic. There were no trinkets or knickknacks cluttering surfaces. The man's preferences were stark, smooth, and glossy in shades of black and gray, accentuated with designer cement flooring, stainless steel, and splashes of red. A tinted glass wall overlooked the Chester River.

One piece of artwork dominated the space: A larger than life, impressionistic painting of Mother's face hung over the obscenely large gas fireplace. The painting had to be at least eight-feet tall and five-foot wide. A spotlight illuminated her likeness as if she were a goddess.

"I don't know how to feel about my mother," Jules whispered.

Truitt answered with a hug. No words.

There wasn't anything he could've said to dilute Jules's disappointment anyway. Support was all she needed, especially today since it marked the one-week anniversary of her death. Truitt's embrace delivered a comfort she had rarely felt alive; it made her feel loved, made her feel as though her needs mattered to someone else.

Mr. Riley's cellphone rang. He answered on the first ring.

His eyes seemed to linger on her and Truitt, making her heart jackhammer in her chest. This man gave her the creeps.

"Hey. Listen carefully," he told someone on the other end. "Like I mentioned before, you'll be roughing up the master suite. Tomorrow night. Get there at nine. You'll find the backdoor by the kitchen unlocked. All security cameras and alarm systems will be off."

Pause.

"Have I ever, even once, hinted you could question me? If I tell you security cameras will be off, that's what they'll be: off."

Pause.

"We have no partnership here; no give and take. I am your boss. Period. Do what the fuck I say, when and how I say it, or you'll be breathing water or dirt instead of air. Capisce?"

Pause.

"Accepted." Mr. Riley paused. "Where was I? Oh, right: Remember to wear latex gloves. The master is on the left side of the house. Tear things up. After the room looks like shit, you're done. Make sure you leave by ten. Understood?"

Pause.

"No, don't take anything. I'm sending him a message; that's all. He'll recognize my calling card. Contact me after you're back home. Do not forget."

Mr. Riley disconnected.

"Fucking amateurs," he muttered, walking with swagger into his kitchen.

Truitt raised his eyebrows. "Not only are we going to find out why this Mr. Riley and your mother are harassing your Dad," he said to her, "we'll learn who his puppet is."

"Could any of this actually be associated with my death?"

"To find a fox, you have to follow the feathers."

She elbowed his ribs. "Sounds annoyingly similar to a rule."

"I hear you. My bad!" He unleashed his dimples before looking toward the kitchen. *"Now* what's this jerk doing?"

In the open-styled kitchen, Mr. Riley was pouring red wine into two empty goblets on the countertop. A wedge of cheese and a line of crackers were on a serving plate.

"Queen?" Mr. Riley said out loud to seemingly no one.

"Yes, Rock?" answered a voice that sounded like Mother's.

Clearly, Mr. Riley had a smart-home equipped with sophisticated artificial intelligence.

"Dim the lights," he ordered. "Start the fireplace and play my favorite music track. And while you're at it, raise the room temperature. The AC is freezing my freaking nuts."

His instructions were immediately executed. Simultaneously.

The cement floor vibrated.

Jules glanced at the elevator to the right of the great room. Each button on the display panel lit up as the elevator reached that level. The penthouse was on the fifth level (top floor) and already, the third-floor button was glowing.

A wave of anxiety struck her in the stomach.

"Quick!" Jules said. "We need to get out of here. Now!"

"Don't you want to see who's coming?" Truitt asked.

"I already know." She pointed to the wine bottle. "That's Mother's favorite: a 2018 Schrader RBS Cabernet Sauvignon."

"But if the visitor is your mother, maybe they'll talk about the diamond. Right?"

She squeezed Truitt's hand to convey her urgency in leaving. "I'm not ready to see her with another man. Not yet. Anyway, stress is making me feel like I might black out."

"Say no more. Let's blow this pop stand."

The phrase must have been as nostalgic as his wristwatch.

As the elevator door began to slide open, she and Truitt vanished.

49

Monday, August 23, 2027
The Rock Hall Police Department to Garth Harris's Apartment
(Eight Days *after* Juliette's Death)

FINN'S THOUGHTS WERE laser focused on the upcoming night when he planned to surprise Rip's grunt at the G&G. If only time wasn't moving like a slug on flypaper.

Sitting behind his desk at the station, he glanced at the wall clock. Almost noon. He wondered if he'd ever return to his normal routine of eating lunch in town at the Bistro. Anyway, he appreciated avoiding Mindi. His loyal hostess, Heather O'Brian, had texted him that Mindi was making a habit of lunching there, sitting at his table "like a dog waiting for a treat."

His and Mindi's sexual encounter had been a mistake. He regretted his loss of restraint.

In front of him was his open laptop.

Once again, the cursor blinked on an empty page.

Staring blankly at the screen, Finn hadn't noticed that the chief had entered and sat down in the chair in front of his desk.

"Am I interrupting something, Detective?" Chief Keller asked. "You've been glued to that laptop for several days now. Need an intervention for technology addiction?"

"Sorry, Chief." Finn's heart raced. "I've had a lot on my mind. What can I do for you?"

"The analysis of that broken teacup we found in your kitchen on the day of Jules's death came back from the lab."

"Anything?"

"Nothing we didn't already know," Chief said. "Three different fingerprints were recovered: your wife's, Mindi Maxwell's, and your daughter's. Also picked up traces of alcohol and zolpidem. Aligns with the toxicology report."

"We sure could use a break in the case," Finn said.

"Might've gotten one. An anonymous tip came in about your groundskeeper."

"Garth Harris? What kind of tip?"

"Walker listened to a recorded message on our crime hotline. The caller claims there's evidence in Harris's apartment that may be pertinent in your daughter's investigation."

"Seriously? Can I hear the message? Maybe I'll recognize the caller's voice."

"The male voice was intentionally altered," Chief said. "Made from the only payphone in Rock Hall, from the library, at ten-fifteen this morning. No one saw the individual making the call. We already checked. And the caller left no prints." He scratched his chin. "The caller said to act quickly. Out of curiosity, what time does your groundskeeper report to work at the estate?"

"Usually at one o'clock. But I saw a note on the kitchen counter this morning. Connie changed his shift today. He's to report at nine a.m. and work until four this afternoon."

"Interesting. So tell me your thoughts about this guy."

Finn shared he had considered Garth innocent of any wrongdoing associated with Jules's death, especially since he had tried to revive his daughter and had also furnished the tip about Brock Nolan. But recently, as in *very*, a few doubts had surfaced. Finn remembered Jules had been wearing a diamond necklace on the day of her death. A necklace that had gone missing.

"Who knows?" Finn said. "Maybe Garth had sticky fingers in hopes of financing his college tuition."

"You're just telling me this…*now*? About the necklace?"

"You mean, after eight short days since my daughter was found dead? My God! I buried my daughter this weekend. Sorry if my stress overshadowed my recollection of some details."

In Finn's mind, being defensive was a far better approach than admitting his daughter's ghost was experiencing some brain fog and had suddenly remembered this important fact.

"Curious. Was her necklace pictured on the video Constance submitted as evidence?" Chief asked.

"No. I looked. Jules's back was to the camera, or I would've remembered earlier."

"Got it. Notation made." Chief placed a paper on his desk. "Back to your groundskeeper. I have a warrant to search Harris's apartment. Seems like a good time, especially since he's at the G&G. Let's check out his place together. *If* I can pull you from that laptop."

Finn stood. "How'd you get a warrant so quickly? I'm still waiting on one for Nolan."

Smirking, Chief tapped his badge as fast as hummingbird wings.

On the drive over in the chief's cruiser, Finn wondered if they'd find the necklace in Garth's apartment. He agreed with Jules on one point: He didn't peg their groundskeeper as a murderer. But financial hardship and stealing went together like coffee and glazed donuts.

In lean times, diamonds were like sprinkles; they demanded consumption.

Although Rock Hall wasn't a mecca for crime, Finn had seen his fill of the grotesque over his 16-year stint with the force. Probably the worst was the murder suicide of quiet Ginny Underhill, the town librarian originally from the UK. Her jacked up boyfriend, who consumed steroids like jellybeans, had a problem with jealousy. Not at all rational since the only thing Ginny had ever loved were books. Still, he shot her in the head with a KEL-TEC combat shotgun before blowing off his own. Brain guts splattered the bathroom walls. The freak had shot her while she was sitting on the "loo."

Finn anticipated that their search of Garth's living quarters would be extremely tame in comparison, though he felt some trepidation. This was official business associated with his daughter's drowning.

Uneasiness soured his underarms.

As expected, no one answered when Finn, Chief, and the landlord knocked on Garth's apartment. After unlocking the door, Finn and his boss entered while the landlord remained outside.

The living room and attached kitchen looked normal. Tidy. No dishes in the sink. No smells of mold or a clogged garbage disposal.

Not surprising, Garth was clean.

The kid had setup a desk where a dining table could've been. Tablets and pens, still in their packaging, sat on top. A nearly empty bookcase loomed behind it. He was preparing for his collegiate studies, no doubt.

While Finn was rummaging through drawers, looking for anything suspicious like a heart-shaped diamond necklace, Chief Keller walked down the hallway toward the only bedroom and bathroom in the apartment.

"Shit," Chief hissed.

Cursing on duty was a rarity for his boss, so the exclamation got Finn's attention. He marched to meet Keller at the bedroom door, which his boss had closed.

"What'd you find?" Finn asked, his heart already accelerating.

Chief ignored his question and kept his hand firmly on the doorknob so Finn couldn't open it. Using his two-way radio clipped on his uniform, his boss pressed the push-to-talk button. "Chief here. Ten twenty-five for Lopez and Smith. At the Harris apartment. Pronto. They'll be collecting evidence. Over."

Finn's head felt like it might explode.

What the hell was behind that door?

Overwhelmed by an uncontrollable burst of adrenaline, he kicked in the door. Apparently, Chief hadn't expected that move. The door flew open and banged against the wall.

Without breathing or blinking, Finn stood and stared, trying to process what he saw. On every wall were posters of naked women. Some were being sodomized. Others were spread eagle with unspeakable objects being inserted. Handcuffs or rope restrained most. In every horrid poster, Garth had replaced the woman's face with an enlarged photo of Jules's.

The bed was disheveled.

Women's underwear were strewn on top of the sheets.

A wave a nausea overwhelmed him, and Finn darted to the bathroom, barely making it before his stomach contents landed in the toilet bowl. After retching, Finn washed his face with cold water.

His boss stood in the hallway, having closed the bedroom door behind him.

"I'm going to kill the son of a bitch, Sam," Finn said, clenching his fists. "I'll castrate him first."

"Hold on," Chief said. "Justice will work. Remember our oath. Let's not jump the gun. The evidence will lead us to the truth. We'll figure this out."

"Figure this out? The freak has been in our home! Fantasizing about this filth! And now my daughter is dead. Maybe she refused to play along. Maybe she threatened to expose him. And maybe he drowned Jules to keep her quiet, and she just can't remember it yet."

"She just can't remember it yet? What does that mean?"

Fuck.

The images were so jarring that he had let his filters down.

"Nothing. Nothing," Finn said, shaking his head, trying to buy time to formulate a logical response. "I...I had a dream about Jules; that's all. And in my dream, she told me she couldn't remember the details of her death. My mind shorted for a second."

"Listen. I'm going to drive you back to the station. You'll stay put there—that's an order. I'll help Lopez and Smith secure this scene and then we'll head over to your estate. We'll arrest Harris. Everything will be by the book. Got it?"

Finn nodded as tears streamed from his eyes.

Deep down, he knew following procedure was the only way to achieve true justice, even when dealing with a disgusting, loathsome pervert like Garth Harris.

Twenty minutes later, Finn was back at the station, seated behind his desk.

Chief reminded him again. "Trust in the system, Detective. And don't leave here until you hear from me. After we arrest Harris, I'll contact you. Then why not call it an early day? Forget the nightshift. Watch the sunset with a cold beer."

"I'll be okay," Finn said. "I've got paperwork to take care of and I'll make myself scarce when you bring him in. Anyway, I plan to leave here before nine. Thank you for understanding."

"Through thick or thin, we're family. Remember that."

50

CONSTANCE LOUNGED UNDER the pool house awning, sipping her sweet tea as she watched Garth work the pool vacuum, shirtless. A colorful tattoo of an American eagle decorated his back. Inked strands of barbed wire encircled his pronounced biceps.

Such a shame the young man could not keep his nose out of her business. He was eye candy, and she would miss the sweet view.

Not that she was a science buff, but even Garth should have known that every action generated an equal and opposite reaction. Retribution was, after all, an earned reaction. It was balanced justice for a wrong.

Garth Harris would not be spared from his comeuppance.

Someday soon, he would regret interfering in the personal matters of Constance Isabel Reyes Parker. Following her to Brock Nolan's trailer last Thursday night was obscenely reckless.

And unforgivable.

She heard vehicles, plural, traveling up her driveway.

Minutes later, three police officers came around the corner of her mansion, walking on the lawn. One was Sam Keller. They approached Garth as he placed the vacuum pole down on the deck.

In order to hear the exchange, Constance rose from her recliner and strolled toward the group. As she neared, Sam eyed her body which was on full display in her four-inch sandals and scant bikini.

223

Her long, unbuttoned sheer-tunic flapped behind her with each step.

The chief could never resist beauty.

"Gentlemen," she cooed, locking eyes with Sam. "What brings you to the Glitz and Glamour today? If I had known of your visit, I would have asked my chef to prepare a tray of iced tea and freshly baked cookies."

"No bother, Ma'am," Sam said, tipping his hat with his hand. "We have a personal matter with Mr. Harris. We'd like to bring him to the station and have a chat. Why don't you go on inside, Mrs. Parker?"

"Are you arresting him?" she asked.

"Arresting *me?*" Garth questioned, his face turning crimson as he glanced from one officer to another. "Seriously?" He took a step back from the group. "No way!"

The officers countered by taking an equal step toward him. A marvelous dance, indeed!

"They should be arresting *you,* Mrs. Parker!" Garth blurted while pointing at her with a shaky finger. "You locked Jules in her loft like a caged animal. You overdosed her! And now you've orchestrated something. Something to discredit me. So when I spill the truth about *your* secrets, no one will believe me. Bitch!"

"Oh my goodness," Constance said, hoping to sound shocked and hurt. "What has gotten into you, Garth? More and more, you are becoming two different people! And this side of you is most disturbing." Glaring at Sam, she stomped her right foot. "Garth has been acting strangely for the past month. I demand to know if your interest in him has anything to do with my Juliette Annabella."

"Detective Lopez," the chief barked. "Escort Mrs. Parker inside the house. This second."

Bastard. She had wanted to watch as they cuffed Garth and loaded him into a cruiser's backseat. Fine. Have it their way. But this year's Christmas donation to the department? Slashed in half.

As she and Lopez walked inside, he held her arm and insisted she sit on one of her stools at the kitchen island, as if she needed permission. Her house. Her stool. And now? Her anger.

Ten minutes later, Sam Keller opened the kitchen door and walked in. "Head back to the station, Lopez. I'll finish up here," the chief said.

After Detective Lopez left, Sam stood on the other side of the island and stared at her without words. She imagined he was trying to magically breakthrough her filters. Please.

"What's this about you locking Jules in the loft?" Sam pressed.

"I find it interesting that you obviously have culpatory evidence which warranted you coming here, on my private property, to remove that lunatic against his will. And yet, you use *his* accusations to question *me?* As if he were a pillar of righteousness? Is he, *Chief?* Is Garth Harris virtuous and decent? I am eager to hear your response."

"You didn't answer me about locking the loft," Sam said. "May I remind you: This is official police work. I'll wait if you feel you need a lawyer to be present."

Sam Keller was no pushover. That is precisely why she had always had a soft spot for the man.

"Juliette's loft was formerly a storage closet. My darling husband affirmed that fact."

"Garth claims you visited a guy by the name of Brock Nolan. He wonders if the unknown fingerprints on the skimmer might be his. What business do you have with this Nolan character anyway?"

"I have absolutely no obligation to explain *why* I visit whom I visit," Constance snapped. "However, for the sake of my beloved daughter, I will share that Garth has been acting strangely over the last month. Before my daughter's...murder, I caught him staring inappropriately at her."

"Inappropriately?"

"Yes, similar to how you are staring at my breasts. *Lustfully* might be a more accurate word."

"Shut up, Connie. I hate when you get like this."

She almost smiled. She had effectively needled through his armored façade. He only called her Connie when he was "the man" and not Rock Hall's Chief of Police.

"Why, Chief," she purred. "Thou doth protest too much."

"Answer the damn question." Sam's face was red. "What about this Nolan guy?"

"Oh, all right," she said, beginning to tire of the game. "I was contemplating adding another groundskeeper to our staff. I had Brock Nolan out here on Friday the 13th after Garth had gone for the day, for a demonstration of Brock's abilities, if you will. The young man cleaned the pool. Did some odds and ends around the property until the fog became too dense."

The truth was much simpler, of course.

On Saturday night (after the horrid *Beauty World* interview and just 12 hours before Garth had found Juliette dead in the pool), Constance had asked Brock to stop by the mansion at midnight. They met poolside, in the dark. It was then she had asked him to report any and all information he could unearth about her husband. During their talk, Brock had picked up the skimmer, as if he needed to find something to do with his hands.

At the time, wiping the skimmer clean of fingerprints had not crossed Constance's mind. Regardless, her explanation would quell any suspicions regarding Brock Nolan.

"And?" Sam pressed.

"I thought the answer was obvious," she said. "The mysterious fingerprints on the skimmer will be Brock's. And because the young man's work was impressive, I went to his trailer to discuss next steps, in terms of timing. Only, with Garth's unsettling behavior of late, I offered him Garth's position, as I had made up my mind to terminate Mr. Harris."

"Did your husband know about any of this?"

"On matters relating to *my* estate, I do not confer with Finn. This is old news."

"You have an answer for everything," Sam said.

"Truth flows easily off the tongue."

"Got it." He ran his hand over his smooth scalp. "Garth claims you have other secrets. Care to fill me in on any of them?"

She slid her fingers into her left bikini cup as if she might caress her nipple as foreplay, though she had no intention. She was in love with her rock.

"You mean," she said, "like those filthy nothings I whispered in your ear as you penetrated me several years ago, while your wife was pregnant and refused to satisfy you? Of course, I have been envious ever since. Sara is fortunate to have such a creative lover at her disposal. Maybe she and I should compare notes sometime. She might find mine…naughty."

"You really are a slut, Connie."

"Yet men with similar thirsts are called suave and debonair. Players, I believe."

Sam stormed from her kitchen.

"So pleased we are on a first name basis again, darling!" she hollered as she stood in the doorway.

51

Monday, August 23, 2027
The Parkers' G&G Estate: Hickory Thicket, Maryland
(Eight Days *after* Juliette's Death)

EXITING MR. RILEY'S penthouse last evening, Jules had faded into a dark void while holding Truitt's hand.

Neither had resisted since both of them welcomed the opportunity to restore their energy ahead of this moment: the night when she might learn why Mother and her *boyfriend* had tasked someone with vandalizing her parents' bedroom. An act meant to pressure her father; for reasons, they hoped to find out.

When she and Truitt materialized, the master suite was pitch black. The mansion, quiet. Lightning across the bay strobed through the French doors connecting to the balcony.

Minutes later, Jules heard someone's footsteps advancing on the west wing's stairway, the one leading to her parents' private quarters. Every fifth step or so, the person paused, no doubt assessing if anyone was home.

Outside the suite's opened double doors, a flashlight's beam darted from wall to wall.

The hired intruder was almost to the bedroom.

Jules's heart accelerated and she squeezed Truitt's hand.

"We've got this," he whispered to her. "And if we need to, we can always scare the bejesus out of the person."

A rumble of thunder rattled the windows.

"Great balls of fire," a male voice exclaimed from the doorway.

The intruder shined his flashlight throughout the suite. "The rich spare no expense, even for freaking shut-eye." He walked closer to the bed. "Someday, this'll be *my* hoity toity life. With all the secrets I know, I'll make sure of it."

Another flash of lightning lit the room.

"Nolan," Truitt announced. "Another triangle: Your mother, Mr. Riley, and him."

Wearing latex gloves, Brock Nolan wasted no time inflicting carnage on the suite using a hunter's knife with a nine-inch blade. If the original oil painting over the bed could've bled, it would've hemorrhaged. He sliced at the bedspread and pillows until the silk fabric was in shreds. Feathers from the pillows took flight. Moving to the chairs, he inflicted the same level of destruction: stabbing, slicing, and pulling stuffing from each fatal wound.

What could Dad have done to warrant this level of "provocation," as Mother called it?

Eyeing his work, Brock smiled. "Fast and furious, baby."

He headed for the walk-in closet.

"Where's my father?" Jules asked, not expecting Truitt to have the answer. "He should've been here by now. This guy is obliterating my parents' room."

"Let's follow him into the closet." He pointed to himself and smiled. "This Casper is about to show some attitude."

Inside the walk-in, Truitt flung shoes from the wall rack.

She rattled hangers.

Brock was too busy slashing Dad's wardrobe to notice.

When a steady stream of mist billowed with every exhale, Brock finally paused his assault.

"Who's there?" Circling in place, he used his flashlight to scan the large space. "Don't fuck with me or I swear I'll gut you."

A clap of thunder pierced the air and Brock flinched.

The storm was almost on top of the mansion. Rain pelted the metal roof. Gusts howled around the exterior walls.

With a click, light from the bedroom fanned into the closet.

Dad. Dad had arrived!

With eyes wide, Brock quickly tucked himself into a corner, the one to the left of the walk-in's entrance. He hid behind Mother's hanging garments.

"This is Detective Parker." Dad's voice boomed from the bedroom. "Rock Hall PD. I have my firearm deployed," he continued, using what Jules called his police voice—calm yet commanding. "Come out with your hands raised and no one gets hurt. Let's do this peacefully."

Brock didn't budge from his hiding spot.

"If Dad comes into the closet, he could get stabbed," Jules said, feeling a wave of panic. "I can't let that happen."

Discharging her energy, she slid the hanging garments to the side, exposing Brock. He must have thought Dad had done it because he stabbed the air as a defensive response, looking like a crazed animal.

Knowing he wasn't going to surrender without a fight caused Jules's electrical charge to surge and crackle. Applying all the energy she could muster, she pulled Brock toward her and forcefully pushed him out from the closet and into the bedroom.

Extending his arms in front of him, Brock looked like he was struggling to stay upright despite his uncontrolled forward momentum. His right hand still brandished the knife.

Two pops of gunfire blasted over the thunder.

Brock fell face down onto the floor. On impact, his hand released the hunting knife.

A lump formed in Jules's throat. She hadn't considered her father might shoot him.

"Fuck," Dad said while holstering his pistol and kneeling beside Brock. He turned him on his back and unzipped his black hoodie. Underneath, Brock's gray T-shirt showed two massive splotches of red indicating where the bullets had entered his abdomen.

The stains were rapidly growing. Blood blanketed the words on Brock's shirt: *Defend and Attack, Baby.*

"Why didn't you just surrender?" Dad asked. "Damn it."

Brock's eyes moved wildly in their sockets as if mentally assessing the severity of his injuries. Color had already drained from his face. He was ashen. His fingers trembled.

"Hang in there, son. I'll get help."

Pressing his two-way radio, Dad reported the shooting and requested an ambulance.

With a creased forehead, Brock clutched Dad's uniform as he attempted to breathe.

"Try and relax," Dad coaxed. "I'll stay with you. Help is coming."

"I didn't mean for this to happen," she said to Truitt.

"It's not your fault, Jules. Your Dad encouraged him to surrender, and Nolan wasn't going to." He placed his arm around her waist and drew her closer. "You were protecting your Dad and then he protected himself. You both had every right."

"I've seen you before. Brock Nolan," Dad mumbled, no doubt recognizing him from the yearbook Garth had shown. "Did you have anything to do with my daughter's death? Anything at all?"

A gurgle released from Brock's mouth. His eyes stopped moving. His chest deflated.

Dad pressed his fingers against Brock's neck artery. "That's fucking wonderful."

Somewhere close, a stick of lightning bolted to the ground.

The lights flickered before the room went dark.

Sirens in the distance competed with the thunder.

Unclipping a flashlight from his holster, Dad left the room and headed downstairs, most likely to meet the emergency responders who were about to arrive out front.

Jules started toward the doorway, wanting to follow her father. She felt Truitt squeeze her waist. His feet seemed frozen in place.

"It's happening," he told her, still looking at Brock. "Watch."

Rising from Brock's body was his spirit. His ghost stared down at his own bloody corpse.

Jules and Truitt each took a step back. Brock Nolan wasn't exactly a nice person.

Noticing Jules, Brock snarled, "Fucking bitch. Thanks for pushing me out of the closet. By the way, I didn't drown you, but if I got the chance again, I wouldn't hesitate. An eye for an eye."

She believed his every word. Why would he lie? He was dead!

Stepping toward her, anger contorted his face. His ghostly T-shirt dripped blood.

Jules's heart pounded in her chest. Could his ghost hurt hers? Or Truitt's? Were they in danger?

"We're not afraid of you," she announced, standing firmly in place to mask her fear.

"Not my fault you're stupid," he said, continuing to advance.

"Don't come closer," Truitt warned.

Stopping abruptly, Brock looked at his ankles with a confused expression. "Get off me."

Jules hadn't done anything.

"What the fuck?" Brock tried to lift his feet but acted like he had stepped in bay mud.

A black mist had seeped up from the floorboards and swirled around Brock's sneakers. Translucent hands formed and long fingers gripped his ankles.

Brock looked panicked.

"What's happening?" He reached out to her. "Help me."

Not moving her feet, Jules stretched her arm toward him.

"Won't do any good," Truitt said. "I've seen this before. His pathway has already been decided and there's nothing we can do to change it."

"Pathway?" she asked, lowering her arm.

Gasping, Brock was in full blown hysteria now.

"Do something!" he shouted. "Hurry!" He reached down and frantically scratched at his ankles, trying to free himself.

Hands morphed into smokey, pulsating vines, circling his calves and working their way up toward each thigh. When the vines' ascension stopped, Brock exhaled as if relieved. Like maybe whatever force had taken hold of him had decided to spare him instead.

He locked eyes with Jules and smirked. "Nothing stops a middie."

His reprieve was short lived.

Without releasing their catch, the ghostly vines began returning underground. Brock's feet sunk below the planks. His descent picked up speed. When only his torso remained above the floor, he grasped at a throw rug, but it didn't help.

"No, No!" he cried. "Please, no!"

In one final tug, the vines pulled Brock below the floor.

He was gone.

"Now you know why I'm afraid of where I could go," Truitt said.

52

Tuesday, August 24, 2027
The Parkers' G&G Estate: Hickory Thicket, Maryland
(Nine Days *after* Juliette's Death)

SITTING IN THE sunroom, Finn felt mentally and physically exhausted. Not to mention, on administrative leave while his law enforcement agency, along with assistance from the Annapolis Police Department, investigated the shooting and death of Brock Nolan.

Worse than being drained, a nagging sense of impending doom overwhelmed him.

Throughout most of the night, detectives had interviewed him while another forensics team scoured his master suite, taking photographs, documenting measurements, and collecting evidence. The room had been a ghastly sight even after detectives had finished with the crime scene and the coroner had removed the body.

Connie hadn't seen the carnage. His dear wife had never come home from Deanna Mae's.

Christ Almighty. Just when he thought he had hit rock bottom, the floor collapsed again, sending him into a freefall.

At least early this morning, he had contracted with an emergency cleaning service which immediately responded on site, as had Connie's personal interior decorator. Three hours later, no one could've imagined that Finn had gunned down a 22-year-old former lacrosse star, in the Parkers' master suite, after the young criminal had lunged at him with a knife when caught in the act of carrying out illegal activities ordered by his wife and her lover.

Adept professionals had restored the bedroom to pre-vandalism condition. Concurrently, the department had towed and impounded Nolan's truck.

Finn could almost pretend the tragedy had never happened.

When the news aired on television, however, everyone would know. No doubt, reporters would cluster at the end of the G&G's gated entrance. Police shootings weren't exactly common in Hickory Thicket. Add to that: two deaths in less than two weeks at a posh estate called the Glitz and Glamour? That combo would be too tantalizing for the press to resist.

For now anyway, he had a minute to chill and collect his thoughts. Apparently, Brock Nolan's father lived in the same trailer park as his son but didn't have a telephone. Detectives would pay him a visit soon. After notification, Finn's momentary reprieve would be over.

In the sunroom sipping his coffee, he gazed at the Chesapeake Bay. How could such natural beauty disguise the depressing reality of his life? No wife. No daughter. No job. No money.

Jules's life insurance policy didn't count. He had no clue how long Transnational would take to conduct their own inquiry into his daughter's death. Certainly, there would be no payouts until Finn's department closed the case. That wasn't happening anytime soon.

If only Brock Nolan could've answered some questions.

Chef Evelyn appeared at the entrance to the sunroom. Standing beside her was Chief.

After an awkward greeting, Sam Keller helped himself to coffee and sat at the dining table. Finn joined him. His boss wasn't visiting to bring great news; that was obvious. The creases on Keller's forehead were more pronounced than usual and his lips had thinned.

"You can't be serious," Finn said, jumping the gun on what he thought Chief was about to tell him. "I'm not getting slapped with criminal charges, am I?"

"No. The review board has declined to file. You shot in self-defense. Plenty of evidence at the scene to justify your actions."

"Then why the grim face?" Finn pressed.

Chief twiddled his thumbs. Definitely not a good sign.

"Pretty certain you're holding back on me," Chief said. "I told you we were family. I can't help you if you don't tell me everything.

Thought that was crystal clear."

Sam Keller knew something. But what?

Before speaking openly, Finn assessed the sunroom's temperature. His confession wouldn't be for Jules's ears.

According to his senses, she and her sidekick weren't around.

With the coast clear of ghosts, Finn unloaded the information he had chosen to conceal the last time he and Chief had a heart to heart. At this point, there was no reason to hide that Finn had missed the first installment to Rip Riley for his down-payment loan on the condo. And Rip had designated yesterday as the due date for the balance of the payoff (another missed deadline)—the very day Brock Nolan had inflicted property damage in the mansion's master suite, threatened Finn's life, and had gotten himself killed.

The obvious stuff led to the disclosure of more compelling tidbits. Nolan worked for both Connie *and* Rip. And oh by the way, Connie and Rip were lovers.

"Jesus, Finn," Chief said. "Haven't you ever heard the expression: *Oh what a tangled web we weave?* I mean, you've got a cluster of spiders at work here."

"I know. I know. Now you can appreciate why I'm desperate to get the hell out of all this."

Chief shook his head as if trying to dispel the craziness. "FYI, the unknown fingerprints on the skimmer were Nolan's. Surprised?"

"Not really. The kid clearly knew his way around here. I mean, he didn't vandalize the first room he entered. He chose the master suite. Knew how to get to it and this isn't exactly a small mansion. Like I told detectives last night, I asked the kid if he had anything to do with Jules's death. He died before he could answer."

"Your wife told me Brock had participated in a hands-on interview for Garth's job, which included cleaning the pool. That was eleven days ago."

"She has an answer for everything."

"Huh. That's what I told her."

"What about Garth? Any clarity on his involvement?"

"We've been a little busy handling your shit, Finn," Chief snapped, not holding back on cursing. "And you're not giving us any breaks. Everywhere we turn, you're at the center of a new problem.

Makes it tough to focus on Jules's case."

"Is there *another* problem, Sam?" Finn's heart accelerated.

Chief handed him a printout of handwriting, apparently from Mindi's journal.

Finn read the entry as a lump formed in his throat. Sweat beaded on his skin. His chest tightened to the point of pain as he read: *If only BB Jules would go away. Forever might be nice.* Mindi also documented her hope that Finn would divorce and marry…*her!*

Fuck.

"Where did you get this?" Finn asked.

"An anonymous envelope. Hell, maybe we can sit back and let informants solve this case. Anyway," Chief continued, "we've analyzed the handwriting. It's Mindi Maxwell's, all right."

His boss took the paper back and waved it at him. "See what I mean about a cluster of spiders? Their webs are forming a cocoon around you, my friend. Like maybe you and Mindi made a pact to kill Jules, collect the two mill from insurance, and start over. Together."

"Bullshit!" Finn shouted. "I would never hurt my daughter, not a hair on her head, let alone *kill* her. Come on! You know this. And I don't even like Mindi Maxwell. That woman is nothing but trouble."

"Let me get this straight," Chief said. "You don't care for your wife's former personal assistant. Not one bit. Is that what you want me to believe?"

"I loathe her."

"We're done." Chief stood. "I'm pulling you from your daughter's case. Don't report to work until I contact you. I'm through coddling you while you pull things over on me."

"What did I say?" Finn was in danger of hyperventilating. "All I said was I didn't like Mindi. And that's one-hundred percent true."

Chief's eyes narrowed. "I forgot to mention: We also received a video of you fucking Ms. Maxwell at her apartment, while on duty—seemingly under the influence of alcohol. Hell of a way to express your dislike. Even more abhorrent, you disrespected your badge."

His boss stormed from the room.

The mansion's front door slammed.

Finn was on the wrong side of checkmate all over again.

53

MINDI WAS IN route to Brock's double wide, driving a cheap-ass rental car. She missed her Volvo. Not only that, but she was also mad as hell and planned to rip Brock a new one. How dare he avoid her phone calls and texts! Every time he had asked for *her* help, she had pulled through. What did he do when she needed him? Ghosted her.

Seething, she pulled into his driveway around noon.

Odd, his truck wasn't there.

From experience, Mindi knew he usually rolled out of bed midday. Where had he gone so early? Didn't really matter. She knew where he hid the key for the backdoor. She'd wait for him inside. Wasn't as though she had someplace to be.

His key was under the backdoor mat. For a creative criminal mind, Brock had failed in the key hiding category. Tucked under mats or potted plants were everyone's go-to spots.

Inside the kitchen, the sink looked as it always had: stacked high with dirty dishes. Included in the pile were two used wine glasses. Lipstick marked one of the rims. A vase of wilted carnations was on the small dining table.

Brock was clearly keeping secrets from her.

Mindi heard his computer ding, the same sound her computer made when she received emails. What harm could come from looking? Maybe she'd learn what he was up to.

Screen saving bubbles bounced around the large monitor screen. When she moved the mouse, the desktop appeared, projecting Brock's email inbox. Mindi blinked her eyes to make sure they weren't deceiving her. The newest email was from none other than Constance Parker. The email's subject read: *Groundskeeper Position*.

Mindi didn't even know the position was open, but since there was no love lost between her and Garth Harris, she could care less. However, Brock working for the enemy? She'd have something to say about that.

Her curiosity was off the charts. Clicking on the email, she read it.

> You were to call our mutual friend when you returned home last night. Contact me this minute. As in, NOW.

Weird. *Returned home last night* from where? And who was their *mutual friend?*

Brock never mentioned he had any connection whatsoever to the Parkers, especially to the vile Queen Mother.

Something didn't feel right.

After minimizing the email program, she noticed a file folder icon on his screen's desktop labeled "Mindi." Why would Brock keep a folder on her? Once again, she couldn't resist her curiosity. Besides, with her name as the title, she had every right to investigate.

She double clicked on the folder.

The first file catching her attention was a jpeg titled, "Journal #1." There were nine similar files, each numbered.

Wait...*journal?*

When Mindi had come over to Brock's to burn her private journal, she had never let the book out of her sight. How could Brock possibly have photograph files of her entries?

Mindi's heart began to palpitate. She felt out of breath. Lightheaded. Like she might faint and never wake up.

Opening the first file, her eyes widened; her anxiety mushroomed. The file captured the journal entry where she professed her eternal love for Finn and vowed to get Beauty Brat out of the picture.

Forever. She had also mentioned "a plan" to actualize her goals.

The stench of duplicity wafted in the double wide. She knew Brock. He would never retain files of her written musings unless he had his own deviant "plans" for them.

Fucking fireballs to hell.

Mindi scanned the other files in the folder. A video file read: *Extracurricular, Rated X.*

Please, God…no.

She played the video.

Her sexual seduction of Finn displayed in living color. Every detail. Every sound.

Tears streamed down her cheeks. Her fingers trembled.

Her only friend in the whole world had betrayed her. Brock must have hidden a camera in her apartment and lied that her living spaces were clean. Bastard!

Connections began fitting together like pieces of a horror puzzle.

Constance had a grunt who was responsible for installing some of the hidden cameras at the G&G. The mystery person came at night, after Mindi had left for the day. Not even Garth or BB Jules had known the grunt's identity. Finn was completely clueless that a grunt even existed.

Clearly, the Queen Mother's loyal douchebag was Brock Nolan.

Why hadn't Mindi put two and two together?

No doubt her former boss had learned of Mindi's sexcapade with her husband. Probably why the Queen Mother had fired her. Probably why Mindi had lost everything, including access to her sexy hunk of blue. Maybe now, she'd even lose her freedom.

The police had already established a link between Beauty Brat's death and Mindi's mishap involving her tea. If Brock handed these files and video over to authorities, she'd rise as the prime suspect in BB Jules's death.

No lottery ticket was going to save her, and Brock knew it. What a pathetic joke, one directed at her.

Screwed, that's what Mindi was.

Except, she wouldn't go down without a fight.

What she needed first was more time.

Moving the folder to the Recycle Bin on his desktop, Mindi

trashed the entire folder and emptied the bin. She knew with some techno-wizardry, Brock could retrieve it. Most likely, the jerk had also saved the folder to his Cloud. At least he would realize someone was on to him.

In the meantime, wouldn't it be divine to make Constance Parker sweat in her silk slacks?

As if Mindi were Brock, she replied to the Queen Mother's email.

> I decided against the groundskeeper position. Go fuck yourself. I can make more money selling your secrets...

Smiling, she pressed the send button and then left the double wide, not even bothering to close the backdoor.

Fuck Brock Nolan.

Driving out of the trailer park, still on Brock's road, two police cruisers passed Mindi as they drove in the opposite direction.

Slowing to a crawl, she watched in her rearview mirror, curious about their destination. They stopped two trailers down from Brock's, at his father's hoarding pigsty.

Maybe the old geezer had croaked.

She'd shed no tears.

From here on out, having less Nolans in the world was a good thing. They could all burn in hell for she cared.

54

Tuesday, August 24, 2027
Detention Center: Rock Hall, Maryland
(Nine Days *after* Juliette's Death)

JULES'S SUBCONSCIOUS CLEARLY knew where she and Truitt needed to visit next.

Once recharged in their black void, she experienced an unexplainable magnetic pull to speak with Garth. She didn't know where he was or why she needed to speak with him. Only that she felt compelled to.

Three unknowns had emerged since the last time she and Truitt had seen Garth in Dad's office at the station: Why had Mother and Mr. Riley sent Brock Nolan to trash her parents' bedroom? Was the diamond Mother planned on adding to a custom-made bracelet the same as Jules's missing diamond? And did either answer have anything to do with her death?

Maybe Garth knew something. Maybe that something could shed light on the mysteries.

The challenge would be communicating with him. At the police station, although Garth had commented about the coldness of Dad's office, he was unable to see or hear her and Truitt. Hopefully, he would have an electronic device on hand—one they could access to type messages like they did with her father.

Holding hands, she and Truitt traveled and took shape inside a dimly lit space—a square cinderblock room with a concrete floor. Garth was sleeping on a rickety cot, covered by a thin blanket. With

241

every exhale, a white mist streamed from their groundskeeper's mouth. A toilet and tiny sink were to the right. Across from Garth was a wall of bars in place of the cinderblock.

Bars?

"I'm confused," she said to Truitt. "Garth is asleep in a prison cell. What could've happened since we last saw him?"

Shrugging, Truitt scanned the cell. "I sure hope he's one of those people who can interact with ghosts when he's in between sleep and being awake. Otherwise, we'll need a new play."

Jules released her energy to shake the cot, like she had in Lila's bedroom.

"Huh?" Garth mumbled. "What's going on?"

"It's me. Jules Parker. We need to talk."

His eyes fluttered open. Pushing himself into a sitting position, he wore a mixed expression of curiosity and fright. Masking his face with his hands, he rubbed his eyes as if to clear them.

"Can you see me?" she asked. "Me and my friend, Truitt?"

Uncovering his face, Garth blinked hard, several times. "I…I see a misty cloud of dust. Is the light playing tricks? Or could this be a dream?"

Although his vision of them was underdeveloped, at least Garth could hear them clearly.

"No, that's us," she said. "Tell me: Why are you jailed?"

Garth explained that Chief Keller had arrested him, that police claimed they had found unspeakable things in his bedroom. Things, he never would've thought about, let alone possessed. If Jules ever heard about the items police had confiscated, he begged her not to believe he had placed them in his apartment. The only truth she should accept was that he loved her as he would a younger sister. He didn't have a deviant bone in his body. Not a one.

"Your mother," he continued. "She's paying me back for following her to a trailer owned by Brock Nolan. I was wrong thinking she wouldn't recognize my truck. Obviously, she did. And her retaliation has been visceral."

Jules felt nauseous. She and Truitt were lost in a labyrinth of deceit with no way out.

"Did you hear me, Jules?" Garth asked. "Are you still here?"

"Sorry. I'm trying to reconcile the craziness which surrounded my life. It makes me sad. Forms a knot in my stomach."

Truitt squeezed her hand. Thank God for him.

"I totally get it, Jules," Garth said. "I'm sad, too."

Glaring at him, Truitt spoke slowly and with authority. "Are you hoping we'll believe that you didn't have anything to do with the craziness at the G&G? That *you* were just as much a victim as Jules?"

"No! That's not what I meant."

Garth lowered his eyes and admitted he shouldn't have stood idly by and done nothing about Jules's treatment at home. He immediately retracted his statement, probably realizing Truitt would've called him out again on the "done nothing" part.

As a correction, Garth confessed that he had contributed by installing the deadbolts on her door and by ignoring the emotional abuse. Installing and ignoring were *actions*. Bad ones at that.

"Believe me. I've got guilt about the role I played," Garth said. "I'm sorry. I failed you."

Jules wiped tears from her eyes.

With all her heart, she wanted to believe Garth. He had always been one of the best people in her life. It would crush her to learn he was as corrupt as the others. Except maybe for Dad. At least her father was coming around.

"Listen. Until I'm cleared," Garth said, "I've got plenty of time to think in here. Maybe I can help solve your murder. Is there anything you've learned about your death? Anything you remember, Jules?"

Most of her drowning was still a blur, she told him. Except she recalled wearing her Nana Bea's diamond necklace when she was killed. Her abrasion proved it. Now the jewelry was missing.

"I didn't see a necklace when I pulled you from the pool," Garth said. "Or when I moved you to the grass. I'm sure I would've noticed if you had been wearing one."

His answer seemed authentic enough.

"The person who drowned me," Jules said, "must have ripped it from my neck and taken it."

She didn't mention the bracelet Mother was going to have made at their jeweler. Why bother until she and Truitt had time to investigate "the diamond" in question?

243

However, Jules did disclose she had eavesdropped on Chief Keller while he was interviewing her mother for the first time at the house, just three days after her death. Mother claimed Dad needed money. But when Jules pressed her father about it later, trying to learn the truth, he had called the accusation "preposterous."

Garth acted as if he wanted to interject something, but Jules was on a roll. Her memories were crisp which wasn't always the case. She continued talking but picked up her pace.

Finally, Jules made her way to the events of last night at the G&G, explaining that Mother and her new love interest had sent Brock Nolan (the guy from the yearbook) to vandalize her parents' master suite for reasons unknown—to them anyway. Catching him in the act, her Dad had shot and killed him, at no fault of his own.

The news had already traveled to Garth. He'd heard about the shooting during mealtime.

"Something you said may have rung a bell," Garth said. "Can you describe your mother's new *companion?* That might help."

"He could've played ball," Truitt answered. "The guy's six-foot-four and buff."

"No, I mean, what'd his face look like?"

"Mr. Riley is white. Mother's age. Good looking," Jules said. "He has curly black hair and a close-to-the-face beard. Could double as a cowboy from Montana. You know, the rugged rancher type."

"This Mr. Riley may be a loan shark." Garth nodded at his own conclusion. "The night I installed new locks on your door, I observed a Skype conference between your Dad and a man matching your description. The virtual meeting occurred before you returned home from D.C., from the *Beauty World* interview.

"What I gathered," Garth continued, "was that Mr. Riley had loaned your Dad money for a down payment on a condo, but the guy wanted his cash back way earlier than expected. Like soon. And when your Dad said he didn't have it, the guy sort of threatened him."

"A down payment on a...*condo?*" Jules asked, feeling perplexed.

"Yeah. Your Dad asked me to keep everything secret. At the time, I didn't think your mother knew anything about the condo or the loan. Of course, now that you describe Mr. Riley as your mother's new love interest, who knows? Maybe they have been working together all along and we just haven't figured out their angle yet."

She locked eyes with Truitt. "Dad didn't mention anything about this! And when he identified Mr. Riley using his license plate, remember my father's reaction?"

"He banged his fist on the desk," Truitt answered. "When you asked if he knew the guy, your Dad only divulged that they'd gone to high school together and he was a jerk."

Unclasping her hand from Truitt's, she walked to the other side of the cell, staring at the cinderblock wall. She pulled at her hair in frustration. Why had God punished her by giving her the worst parents in the world? In the universe?

Her parents were liars and users and opportunists.

Why did she deserve having parents who were incapable of the most basic, instinctual emotion inherent in humankind's evolution: loving a child? Even animals loved their offspring!

Garth's revelation pointed the spotlight smack on her father, the man who *claimed* he was helping Truitt and her to solve her murder. The same man who lied about not needing money. The very one who would benefit from Jules's death by getting two-million dollars. Certainly that payout would remedy his loan delinquency with Mr. Riley.

"Jules," Truitt said. "Careful of your stress level. You're starting to blink in and out, to short circuit. Take a deep, calming breath."

"What?" She turned and looked at him, feeling tears race down her cheeks. "I don't know if I can take another disappointment like this. All I've ever wanted was to be loved. Loved by my parents."

"I love you, Jules," Truitt said, beginning to walk toward her. "Now hold my hand and we'll deal with this together. We'll form another huddle. Come on. Let's do this."

Her mind was mush.

Emotions swirled and collided inside her like a violent tornado. Energy was consuming her. Pressure in her chest was unbearable.

"Truitt, something's happening," she said. "Quick! Pick a place where we can reconnect…"

As he reached for her hand, her light switch flipped off.

Jules had blacked out into darkness. Into nothingness.

Alone.

55

Tuesday, August 24, 2027
The Parkers' G&G Estate: Hickory Thicket, Maryland
(Nine Days *after* Juliette's Death)

TRUITT WAS BEYOND furious when he arrived in Mr. Parker's home office. Despite his anger, the first thing he did was scan the large room hoping to find Jules. She wasn't there.

Absorbing more warmth from the room than Truitt needed, his temperature elevated several notches and energy flared from his body like tiny bolts of lightning.

A framed photo of Mr. Parker at his police academy graduation rattled loose from its nail on the wall and crashed to the floor, sending glass shards onto the oriental rug. At the same time, papers took flight from his desktop and the window shutters chattered. Books thudded against the back of the bookcase.

Jules's father jumped to his feet. The momentum sent his wheeled office chair rolling; it slammed into the workspace behind his formal desk. A large monitor blinked on impact.

"Who's there?" Mr. Parker hollered with mist escaping his lips.

A laptop was open on the desk. Releasing his energy, Truitt grabbed the mouse and commandeered the cursor.

Mr. Parker's eyes grew wide. "Jules? Is that you? What's wrong?"

Opening a blank word processing page, Truitt was going to give the man a piece of his mind. Jules's father must have sensed the negative energy because still standing, the man clutched the edge of the desk with trembling hands as Truitt keyboarded.

So many questions from someone who gives so little answers. YOU are what's wrong, Mr. Parker.

"Truitt? Don't play games with me, young man. Where's my daughter?"

Via typing, Truitt explained how he and Jules had visited Garth in jail. While talking, the groundskeeper had identified Rip Riley as Mr. Parker's loan shark. But back when Truitt and Jules had questioned Mr. Parker (about his current association with the guy), he had denied having one. Learning about the deception had jumpstarted Jules's panic attack which, for a ghost, was an instant trip to blackout city. Truitt blamed their separation on Jules's father. Blamed his lies.

"Where do you think she is?" Mr. Parker asked.

If I knew, do you really think I'd be here with you? She blacked out before she could tell me where to meet up with her.

"Damn it!" Mr. Parker pounded his desk. "And quit being unfairly harsh on me. More advice: Don't be so quick to take sides with Garth Harris. Do you know what disgusting, vile filth we found in his apartment?"

Right now, I'm not interested in that. Instead, I want to know if Garth was telling the truth about your relationship with Mr. Riley. So if I'm being "unfairly harsh," does that mean you DIDN'T take a loan from the man for a down payment on a condo?

"No. I mean, yes. Yes, I did take a loan." Muscles in Mr. Parker's jaw twitched. "It's just...I didn't want Jules to find out."

You do that a lot, Mr. Parker. You struggle with the truth. Haven't you figured out that lying and withholding information doesn't work? It can get people killed. And the facts eventually rise to the surface anyway. I mean, you're in law enforcement. Shouldn't that be way more obvious for someone in uniform?

"Christ Almighty, Truitt. I'm simply trying to get out of a bad marriage, to buy a condo and start over. Jesus." He pulled at his hair like Jules did when she was frustrated. "Forgive me for not being overly boisterous about Mrs. Parker and my irreconcilable differences. Regardless, it's not a crime to borrow money. And your implication is ridiculous. I did *not* hurt or kill my daughter."

Maybe not directly, but you'd better not be giving yourself a free pass. Did it ever occur to you that Mr. Riley might have retaliated against you for not paying him back? Like maybe he drowned your daughter to show you he meant business?

And by the way, you're still hurting Jules even after her death. Because of your lying, she's disappeared! I think the back of your uniform should display the words: "Because of me..."

"As far as retaliation," Mr. Parker sneered through clenched teeth, "in case you didn't know, Rip Riley and my...and Mrs. Parker are having an affair. Doubt killing Jules would make for good pillow talk." He banged his fist on his desktop. "Because of *me?* None of this is my fault!"

Dang. This guy had trouble taking responsibility for *his* actions. He was always whining about what someone else was doing wrong. Didn't Mr. Parker know that no one ever improved if they couldn't reflect on the only person they could control: themselves?

Not that Truitt was a saint. Saying so would be a bad joke. Still…

NOW is the only time change occurs. Grow up, Mr. Parker. I've had to. Believe me: Do it while you can.

The last thing Truitt wanted was to have translucent hands rising from the floor or ground to clasp his ankles, yanking him down to Earth's burning core for eternity. Thank you, but no thank you.

Somehow, Mr. Parker wasn't getting it.

Frustration melded with exhaustion and Truitt felt the fade. Without a struggle, he let the energy of "his body" disperse into nothingness. Lights out.

Longing to find Jules, maybe, just maybe, he'd find her when he arrived in his void.

Dark emptiness extinguished his hope.

Truitt was alone.

56

HEAT AND HUMIDITY plagued the otherwise tranquil dawn. The sun hid behind an overcast morning while leaves and grass were heavy with dew. Mosquitos swarmed. Forecasters had clearly forgotten to tell the weather that fall was less than a month away.

Recharged, Jules had materialized in her garden beside the heirloom tomatoes. She had hoped Truitt would be waiting for her in his favorite spot. No such luck.

Her heart sank. Why had she let go of his hand in Garth's prison cell? She knew the risks! And what if Truitt had passed on without her? What if she never saw him again?

With a churning stomach, she urged herself to calm down, to think things through.

First and foremost, Jules had to *believe* Truitt was coming back. Which meant, she had to wait for him and trust he knew she'd be by the heirlooms.

In the meantime, deep breaths might reduce her stress.

Laying down on a long and narrow swath of grass beside the tomatoes, Jules closed her eyes and filled her lungs before slowly exhaling. Even though breathing was a habit rather than necessity, the sensation felt real.

Jules listened to angry yellow jackets buzzing from one over-ripened tomato to another. Bees became ill tempered in late summer.

Regardless of the morning's heat and humidity, the insects instinctively knew cooler temperatures were on the way—probably by the position of the sun. Anyway, their days outside were winding down, and they weren't happy about it.

In a tree somewhere in her garden, she heard a Carolina chickadee and its upbeat melody.

Her heartrate accelerated. Beads of sweat erupted on her forehead.

A Carolina chickadee?

Why would the bird trigger a stress reaction?

As if someone had pressed the button on her memory's projector, her mind clicked into "play," forcing her to visually relive a flashback of her past.

Jules was wearing her favorite periwinkle bikini, lounging on a recliner under the pool awning, alone. She recognized the occasion. Her vision was replaying the moments before her death.

The wind blew, but she couldn't cool down. Her skin was blotchy. Hot. Jules felt sick. That's right: her stea. Mindi had spiked her tea with twice the prescribed zolpidem.

Jules had become nauseous, dizzy. And an asthma attack was brewing.

Noises sounded from the kitchen. A clank. Then something breaking.

She felt eyes staring at her, but she could only think of relief—the coolness of the pool and how the water could ease her growing discomfort.

After retrieving the inflatable lounger, she walked down the pool steps. The water was unusually chilly. Could she have a fever?

Before lifting herself onto the float and the purple towel she had draped over it, she touched her necklace, briefly. The tea had numbed rational thinking or the need to be cautious. All she remembered caring about was staying in the water long enough to cool down.

Floating, Jules had started to relax. Her wheezing subsided. She was so tired.

In her mental rewind, when Jules had closed her eyes while resting on her lounger, she heard a melody. A Carolina chickadee was singing in a nearby tree.

The joyful song lulled her to sleep.

Without warning, Jules was in the water, submerged. Confused and panicked.

Someone pressed on her head. Pushing her down. Forcing her deeper and deeper into the water!

She thrashed and fought.

Who was it? Who was drowning her? She had to know!

Her lungs burned. She couldn't breathe.

Below the pool's surface, she tried to open her eyes.

When she did, all she saw was darkness…

On the grass, Jules woke from her vision, her arms flailing.

"God!" she cried out loud, repeating the words of her past. "I don't want to die!"

Her flashback stopped, but her heartrate continued to gallop in her chest. She rolled onto her stomach and vomited water, smelling the chlorine.

Tears streamed down her cheeks. She was afraid. Her memories were coming back, but she didn't know if she wanted them to.

Looking up and down the garden's vegetable pathway, she saw no one. Jules continued to be by herself. Alone.

The only difference between *pre*-death and *post*-death was that she no longer accepted she had no choice. She wanted her friend by her side. She wanted Truitt Windsor.

"Find me!" she hollered in between sobs. "Please find me, Truitt!"

57

THE GRANDFATHER CLOCK in the foyer chimed nine times.

Sipping a mug of morning coffee in his home office, Finn heard the front door open and Chef Evelyn welcome Chief Keller into the mansion. What the fuck *now?* Every time his boss came to speak with him, he brought more bad news.

Finn couldn't deal with any more at the moment. For the time being, he was on worry overload. Where could Jules's ghost be?

Ever since Truitt had left him last night, Finn had sat in front of his laptop...waiting. Waiting for his daughter to keyboard she was all right, that her spirit was still on Earth.

He desperately wanted to explain why he hadn't told her about the condo and his loan from Rip Riley. Shame had been the culprit and he harbored plenty of it.

Despite his longing, the laptop's cursor continued to blink on an empty page. Blink, blink, blink.

Chief walked in and stared at Finn sitting behind his desk.

"You look like hell, my friend," Chief said.

"Astute as always."

Finn closed his laptop, wanting to avoid another lecture on technology addiction. He left his large monitor and computer on behind him; Jules had never used that device anyway.

"What brings you to the G&G this time?" he asked his boss. "Has another videotape surfaced? Like of me at my junior prom? Wearing a garish mullet? Or drinking spiked punch or something?"

Removing his brimmed hat, Chief sat in the chair in front of Finn's desk. Crossing his right leg over his left, his boss wore a neutral expression, ignoring Finn's sarcasm.

"I'll cut to the chase," Chief said. "Garth Harris's savings account had fifty thousand wired into it on August twentieth, five days after Jules's death."

Finn leaned forward. The information might be a break in the case, like pointing to a murder for hire.

"Do you know the source of the funds? The sender could be significant, Sam."

"That's the real interesting part. The wire came from an account in your name."

"What?" Finn's brain was about to explode.

While Finn tried to suppress the urge to bang his head against something injuriously hard, Chief explained that there was a banking account listed in Finn's name, opened 10 years ago in Switzerland. Authorities had traced authorization for the international transfer to his desktop computer's IP address, the one located behind him. After the withdrawal, the account balance still had 15 thousand in it.

Finn clutched at his hair.

When would his freefall into the abyss of sewer crap ever end?

Then again, perhaps his tumble from grace wasn't a freefall at all. Maybe someone was pushing him. Shoving him down the hole of stench. In fact, every surprise in his adult life *(the good, the bad, and the ugly)* had originated from one person: Connie.

"Would my wife happen to be a co-signer on the account by any chance?" Finn asked.

"Naturally."

"You see what's happening here, don't you?"

"I have my suspicions," Chief said, refusing to reveal any of them.

"If I knew I had sixty-five grand in an account, don't you think I would've used the cash for the condo's down payment? Certainly would've spared me from working with a prick named Rip Riley and all the trouble he's instigated." He pointed to the large Swarovski bald eagle sculpture on his desk. "Connie had that made for me.

Selling it could've brought me an additional ten grand, enough to cover the condo's entire down payment, all on my own."

"Does Constance know you've told me your financial woes?"

"Look around," Finn said. "Connie is AWOL. Our marriage is over. Any day now, she'll force me to move out. So to answer your question, I haven't shared a bloody thing with her. I will say, she thinks I'm predictable. Which means, she'll assume I won't disclose my dirty little secrets to anyone, especially to my boss."

"Between you and me, I never realized how cunning and vindictive she is."

Finn chuckled, but not because the comment was humorous. More for the irony that Connie had been able to blindside the king of checkmate.

"Precisely her goal," Finn said. "To have you think she's harmless. Pretty face; pretty character. Right? She even created a rule about it: Control the perception; control the outcome. Anyway, her whims constantly change. I've become boring to her. Even Jules's murder is old news." He sipped his cold coffee. "Not for me, though. I'd like to know what's next in the investigation."

"Unfortunately, nothing involving you. You still have orders to lay low. Can't bring you off administrative leave until we inventory some tangible proof clearing you of any suspicions involving your daughter's drowning."

"Aren't I cleared already? At the time of Jules's death, I was interviewing Daisy Smithhisler."

"Not enough. The optics suggest a possible murder for hire. Consider the circumstantial evidence: You were banging your wife's personal assistant who wanted to get rid of Jules (*forever,* she had written in her journal), in hopes of marrying you. Most will conclude that you and Ms. Maxwell were having an affair. You had satisfying sex, dined with her at the Bistro, even changed her car's oil. She left you notes. Made you brownies. Maybe you'd do *anything* for her."

"That's bullshit!"

"And *anything* leads to the money," Chief continued. "As a beneficiary on your daughter's insurance policy, you're slated to collect two million, more than enough to pay back your unsavory loan shark and start over with Mindi. Not to mention, you committed mortgage fraud on the condo's purchase, illegally representing your daughter and using her financial nest egg as collateral—without her consent. Not exactly what a loving father would do.

"And now," Chief said, "evidence has surfaced that a banking account, one in your name, wired money from this very office to the only person (a sexual predator by the looks of it) who was alone with Jules around her death. That person received what most will call a contract payment less than a week after her murder. Worst case scenario, say you were brought to trial on those talking points alone, how do you think a prosecutor and jury might perceive all that?"

"I'm royally fucked."

"I know I've been angry with you and still am," Chief said, "but if it's any consolation, I think you're innocent."

"Please, Sam. Tell me you have a plan."

"Yesterday, teams scoured Garth Harris's bedroom and Brock Nolan's double wide. They used every forensics tool available. Maybe your daughter's missing necklace showed up under a floorboard or in a hidden safe. Maybe a detective lifted unexpected fingerprints. Lopez and Smith will brief me this afternoon. How we move forward depends on what they found."

Although Finn was making progress on speaking the truth and coming clean on his secrets, he hadn't fully evolved. Chief would have to wait a bit longer for *the truth and nothing but the truth*. For now, Finn would bite his tongue about Jules's claim that Connie was going to have a tennis bracelet made, featuring a mysterious diamond that might have come from Jules's missing necklace. After all, he had just told his boss he wasn't talking to his wife. How else would he know? A *ghost* told him? Yeah, right.

On the other hand, Chief's reference to the necklace reminded him that even benched from duty, he could inquire about the bracelet with their jeweler. He had a right to know.

Chief returned his hat on his head. "FYI. Deputy Walker voluntarily disclosed that Constance regularly slipped her monetary bonuses for information about you: when you were at the station or out in the field, where you were dining, who called you, what notes you received. Seems Walker eventually developed a conscience, given Jules's unsolved murder. I've placed her on probation for an ethics violation. One more wrong move and she's out. At least she had the guts to confess. But she's made an ugly mess for herself."

Finn shook his head. He was so over Connie's control and manipulations.

"Sometimes the truth isn't pretty, Sam."

"Speaking of sordid, you're not having contact with Ms. Maxwell anymore, right?"

"I've blocked her from everything and haven't eaten at the Bistro in some time."

"Good," Chief said. "Now have you hocked that damn wedding ring yet? And those cufflinks?"

"On my to-do list."

"What are you waiting for? Walk away from your laptop and get it done. Don't count on any money from the Swiss account. The investigation will have that cash tied up for a while and you need to pay off that dick of a loan shark. Pronto." He scratched his facial stubble. "If you don't stop the hemorrhaging, my friend, there will be nothing left of you. Got it?"

His boss left the room.

Seconds later, Finn heard the front door close.

He opened his laptop and woke the device from its sleep mode.

The cursor continued to blink in place.

"Come on, Jules. Forgive me. Let me know you're okay."

Nothing.

His heart ached like he had never known.

Where was his daughter?

58

MINDI'S LIFE WAS as good as her coffee: stale and bitter.

As she sat on a stool at her small kitchen island, she admitted to herself that an emotional breakdown was percolating. That's why she had called her Momma, who had relocated to the mountains of West Virginia, begging her to let Mindi come "home" for some R&R over the upcoming weekend.

In her hour of need, being with her Momma was the only remedy that could quell Mindi's fear that her world was unraveling. Truth: With Brock gone, her mother was all she had.

What irked Mindi was that even dead, Beauty Brat was undoubtedly laughing at Mindi's misfortune. Bitch! BB Jules had always acted like she was better than her—prettier, smarter, richer. Not to mention, she was Daddy's little girl.

All of it was gag worthy to the nth degree.

Mindi could've kept her head above water if Brock was still alive. She was certain of it. His death, however, caused Mindi to lose her footing and plunge into the deep end.

For the first time, she realized she was out of her league. Way out.

Don't get her wrong: She was livid Brock had betrayed her. But the fact that Constance was able to persuade him to turn against "one of his own," was incomprehensible, demonstrating how remarkably powerful the Queen Mother actually was.

Just as shocking because she never would've guessed, Finn had gunned Brock down. The news reported the shooting as self-defense. Really? Finn could've shot Brock's leg. But no...he shot him twice. In the stomach. Which in her mind, was a deliberate execution.

Add to the twist, Brock had been following Constance's orders!

Clearly, the king and queen of Castle Privileged were lethal. They played for keeps and the carnage was piling up. Brock was dead. Garth, in jail. And now, her journal entries and that damn videotape threatened to guillotine her.

Mindi didn't need a rocket scientist to proclaim her neck was next on the chopping block.

Fucking fireballs to hell.

She knew what she needed to do.

Before the weekend.

59

EVERY TIME TRUITT was stuck in his dark void, he felt trapped underground, as though he were in a coffin, *alive*.

The feeling intensified without Jules by his side.

He had to resist the urge to panic—to pummel and thrash at his indistinct enclosure in an attempt to break free. Fighting did nothing. Freedom was an illusion in the realm of nothingness.

Instead of battling the sensation, he focused on steady breathing.

Thankfully, he had learned to accept his need to recharge, knowing the minute he recovered his energy, he'd find Jules. He wouldn't stop looking until he did.

His soul began to tingle.

Somewhere in the vastness of Earth, he heard Jules's plea. *Find me*, she was crying. *Please find me, Truitt!*

Her desperation tugged at his heartstrings. Big time.

Swirling and vibrating, the particles of his being moved faster and faster, forming into his image. His light switch slid to on and he was ready to search for her.

One thing was certain; Jules would steer clear of the pool. She had admitted she was scared to death of the water now.

Truitt understood. Wasn't like he'd ever climb into a car during a snowstorm again. That would forever remain a hard pass.

Would Jules choose to appear in her loft where she could stare out her window at the bay? Then again, there was a place she liked even better than her bedroom: the G&G's garden. Maybe she'd be by the fountain, the place where they first met on that foggy night. Or perhaps she'd go to *his* favorite place by the heirloom tomatoes. If she was also searching for him, she'd know that's where he'd be.

Truitt materialized among the cages and stakes supporting unruly vines laden with unpicked tomatoes. The bees attracted his attention as he acclimated. They were having a field day gorging on ruptured fruit dangling from vines.

His heart jackhammered.

Jules was nearby, kneeling on a swath of grass beside the path. Her cheeks were streaked pink, marking the streams of her tears.

Gazing up at him, she jumped to her feet, rushed over to him, and threw her arms around him. "Don't ever leave me again!"

Running his hands through her hair as she pressed against his chest, he acknowledged to himself that she embodied bliss. His bliss.

"I have no interest in leaving you. Trust me," he assured her, as she looked up at him, her blue eyes wide as saucers. "But let's get the record straight. An instant replay will show that you, Juliette Annabella Parker, left *me.*"

"I know. I'm sorry." She pressed her face against his football jersey again and he felt her tears seep through to his skin. "I tried to tell you to meet me here, only I blacked out first."

"At least you can't stump this quarterback for too long. I figured it out anyway."

Raising her chin so they could lock eyes, he explained that after she had disappeared, he'd gone to her father's home office looking for her. When he didn't find her, he basically unleashed a wrath of shit on her father for withholding information. For instigating her blackout. Thankfully, Truitt wasn't there long before he suffered his own fade, or he might have inflicted a lot more damage.

"You didn't hurt him, did you?" she asked.

"His office maybe, but not him. I kept my 'bad cop' persona in check even though I'm not a huge fan of your Dad's. One good thing. He seemed genuinely worried about your whereabouts."

"Not sure how much that means anymore. I'm so over my parents. Both of them."

"I hear you," Truitt said. "Just remember, we're probably still on Earth to change ourselves. And to find peace with the messes from our lives. Avoiding them might get us nowhere. Maybe you're meant to work things out with your father."

"Speaking of messes," Jules said, "I had a flashback of my drowning. It was terrifying."

"Did you see your attacker?"

"No. Everything turned dark before I could tell. Then I snapped out of it. Just like that."

"Don't be discouraged. Trust me, remembering takes time. But at least the portal to your memories is beginning to open. Each snapshot will add up. You'll see."

"In the meantime, do you really think I should talk to my Dad? To clear the air between us?"

"Yuppers. Why not help him grow into a more truthful adult?" He clapped his hands as if he'd just completed a huddle with the guys. "Let's do this! And hey, don't forget: His home office might be showing some...wear and tear. Broken glass could be involved."

"That's the thing about my parents. They hire other people to clean up their messes."

He held her hand and squeezed it. "Please don't let go, even if he stresses you out. Wherever we're heading, let's go together because separation from you is hell. Just saying."

A thought popped into his mind, and he tensed his eyebrows. "Except if misty hands grab my ankles and pull me under. Promise you'll let go before then. Promise, Jules. I'm serious."

"You're not going anywhere but up, T. You're an angel. Start believing it."

"No one has ever called me T before, except for my parents."

"Queens do what they want," she said, smirking.

60

Wednesday, August 25, 2027
The Parkers' G&G Estate: Hickory Thicket, Maryland
(Ten Days *after* Juliette's Death)

QUEENS COULD CHANGE their minds, and Jules needed a break. So instead of rushing over to Dad's home office, she convinced Truitt to spend the morning and most of the afternoon working in the garden which was sadly showing signs of disarray.

Thanks to a cooling breeze off the Chesapeake, the earlier heat and humidity had dissipated. Overcast skies had also broken up, allowing the sun to peek out from puffy clouds.

The day had blossomed into glorious.

Using their energy while never getting too far apart, she and Truitt spent hours plucking ripened vegetables and pulling weeds. As they worked early on, they talked.

Jules was amazed she never ran out of topics to discuss with him: Climate change, education, sports, animal rights, immigration, and green energy—the list was never ending. In fact, gardening and hanging out with her best friend (free from overbearing schedules, restrictive rules, and her maternal warden's pernicious oversight), gave rise to one of the best days of Jules's existence. Hands down.

As she and Truitt got deeper into a gardening rhythm, they both grew quiet. If Truitt was doing what she was, he was likely reflecting on what had been his life.

When Jules was alive, others claimed she was living a privileged life, yet gratitude was an emotion she had rarely felt. Having stuff didn't lessen the pain of her circumstances. But now, free from emotional abuse, gratitude was present in every particle of her being. Happiness was, too.

Death wasn't the catalyst for these new feelings. The source was *her.* Jules was changing—taking care of herself in ways she should have considered when she was living.

If she looked back at her life, excluding the fact that someone had drowned her, Jules admitted she might've fought harder for a better childhood. She just hadn't realized she deserved it. Or that she could've been her own advocate, could've insisted people listen to her and treat her well. People like her parents. And if they had refused to change and the abuse continued, she should've told the truth to someone. In a whisper, in a text. Maybe to Chef Evelyn, Lila, their housekeeper, or Chief Keller. Even a pageant judge.

As Jules reflected as she gardened, her pile of rotten tomatoes grew. With the weight of the decaying fruit removed, the vines had sprung upright.

Truitt was pulling weeds and there were plenty of them.

"I can tell Garth no longer works here." He wiped moisture from his forehead with the heel of his hand.

Tears instantly welled in her eyes at the mention of Garth. At the very least, she could've demanded *he* do more than buy her a window ladder for her locked loft. Had she insisted that he help her, Garth probably would've. Instead, she enabled him to pretend everything would be okay in time.

Jules was a victim, and she wasn't blaming herself. She was only acknowledging what she might've done differently. Everyone always said it took a village to raise a child and she should've called on hers, small as it was.

Secrets, after all, were the cornerstones of abuse.

"Time to head over to the mansion?" Truitt asked. "By the sun's position, I'm guessing it's late afternoon. Wouldn't want to run out of energy before we visit your Dad."

"See? A sundial would've shed light on the precise time, Mr. Quarterback with a peculiar tomato fetish and a broken, nostalgic wristwatch."

"Peculiar?" He flashed his pearly whites. "You mean…wise. Fresh

tomatoes contain lycopene which helps prevent cancer and high blood pressure. Even osteoarthritis."

"Silly me. Forgot you're also a nerdy scientist."

"Hey, if you've got the brains," he said, tapping his forehead with his index finger, "doesn't hurt to flaunt the knowledge." He reached for her hand. "Now let's see if your Dad is ready to turn over a new leaf. How about it? Anyway, I'm dehydrating." He winked.

Rolling her eyes at his dry humor, she clasped his hand. Moments later, they materialized in Dad's office, to the right of his chair.

Unshaven and wearing sweats and a crumpled T-shirt, he sat behind his desk, staring at an empty page on his laptop. Odd, some glass shards still littered the rug. Nothing had ever been out of place at the G&G. Mother was clearly not around.

"He looks awful," Jules said. "I've never seen him like this."

"Guilt is a bitch," he answered back.

Jules slid the laptop closer to her.

Dad jumped and clutched the armrests of his chair.

"He's so edgy," she said to Truitt. "What did you do to him?"

Shrugging, Truitt raised his eyebrows, trying to look innocent.

Jules keyboarded:

> Hey, Dad. We're back and I'm fine. When I learned the truth about you and Mr. Riley...that you took a loan from him for a condo, I freaked out and needed to recharge. Didn't mean to worry you.
>
> I'm not sure why you can't tell me the truth. I mean, I died. The worst thing ALREADY happened, right? From here on out, we need to change. We need to be honest.
>
> So...How do you plan on paying back Mr. Riley? Will you ask Mother for help?

"Thank God you're okay." Dad closed his eyes for a second. "I've been worried sick, Jules. Stayed up all night to hear from you."

"Cry me a river, man!" Truitt said, before looking at her. "Your Dad always brings everything back to himself, to his own pathetic pity party. Meanwhile, we're the ones dead."

"Hush," she scolded, highlighting her questions on the screen to draw attention to them.

"If you want the truth, here it is," Dad responded. "The only thing I'll be asking your mother for is a divorce, unless she asks me first. And to pay back her...her *lover,* I'm going to sell my wedding band and cufflinks. Seems apropos."

I'm hoping being honest felt good.

"Sometimes the truth isn't pretty, Jules. I've tried to spare you over the years, but now, I realize you can handle it." He paused. "I'm sorry."

"Sorry for what?" Chief Keller asked, standing in the doorway while taking off his hat.

Jules's heart acted like someone had shoved her on stage while the cameras were rolling.

She and Truitt had been so focused on their exchange with her father, they hadn't heard the chief enter the mansion. Dad must have been oblivious, too. Thank goodness Chief Keller hadn't heard the mention of her name or he probably would've questioned Dad's mental health.

"Never mind," Dad said. "I was talking out loud; that's all." He angled his laptop, no doubt trying to shield the chief's wandering eyes. "So to what do I owe the pleasure of your *second* visit in one day? Have you gotten the forensics report regarding the searches?"

"Sure did." The chief ran his hands over his biceps. "Chilly in here. Anyway, the news is good and bad. Which do you want first?"

"Hit me with the good; it'll be different than what I'm used to."

After sitting in the chair in front of Dad's desk, Chief Keller explained his forensics team had found fingerprints belonging to Brock Nolan in Garth Harris's apartment: at the front door, on the refrigerator handle, and on the doorknob leading into the bedroom. Clearly, Nolan wasn't wearing gloves until he got *inside* Harris's bedroom.

The chief shook his head. "Good for us that most two-bit criminals don't put a lot of energy into developing their smarts."

"Is that enough to prove Garth Harris *didn't* create those posters?"

Jules remembered Garth had begged her and Truitt not to believe that he had anything to do with what the police had found in his apartment. Turns out, they had confiscated…posters.

"One of Harris's friends (a Pete Rayburn)," the chief said, "claimed he had stopped by the apartment before Harris went to work at the G&G on Monday morning, the same day we found the posters and arrested him. The friend said he borrowed a tux for an event this weekend. When he went into the bedroom for the suit, he says there weren't any posters on the walls.

"Consistent with this guy's testimony," Chief Keller continued, "detectives found Rayburn's fingerprints in the bedroom. Also, security footage shows him parking his car in the lot for the apartment complex at eight o'clock in the morning. He was empty handed going in and was carrying a tux going out."

"Which means," Dad said, "Brock Nolan went to the apartment sometime *after* Garth left for his job and *before* we arrived at Garth's place, after receiving the tip."

"You got it. And there's a bit more. About the funds deposited into Harris's savings account: The Swiss bank, the one holding the account in your name, confirmed that Constance had opened it over a decade ago. They reported there was never any activity on the account until the recent transaction. This bodes well for your claim that you knew nothing about it."

Dad huffed. "Connie's damned rainy-day contingencies."

Jules shook her head. If her parents had spent half as much energy on positive endeavors as they did on their manipulations, her family life would've been different.

"Well, thank the Lord for small miracles," Dad continued. "Back to Brock. Did the team find any concrete evidence that he had created the posters in Garth Harris's bedroom?"

"In Nolan's double wide, the kid left a photo of Jules's face in his copier—the same photo used to bastardize the lewd posters. Obviously, he hadn't planned on dying or he might have disposed of the evidence."

"Anything else found that might link the kid to Jules's death?"

She didn't think the answer would be yes. As she'd told her father, Brock's spirit had denied killing her. Maybe Dad wanted to check if Brock's ghost could've been lying.

"Now we're heading into the bad news category," Chief Keller said. "Constance has explained away Nolan's fingerprints on the pool skimmer. Remember, she asserts he was applying for the groundskeeper position and had cleaned the pool as part of the interview. There were a bunch of emails discovered, corroborating that assertion. Makes it damn near impossible to prove he had grabbed the skimmer as a weapon against Jules.

"Speaking of Constance," the chief continued, "the forensics team lifted her fingerprints off a wine glass in the double wide. She was at Nolan's all right. We also confiscated the kid's computer but are still waiting to get a status report on recovering all the files. Maybe they'll find something useful."

"Any more bad news?" Dad asked.

"No necklace in either locale."

"Can I get back on the case, Sam? I need to be involved."

Dad had ignored the topic of her necklace. Most likely, he had already discussed Mother's mystery diamond with Chief Keller. Clearly, the issue still lingered as unresolved.

"I'm willing to go out on another limb," the chief said. "Clean yourself up and I'll lift your administrative leave. But I insist you remain low profile, working solo again. And stay clear of trouble. Though I must admit, somehow trouble sucks you in like a moth to a flame."

"Gee, thanks for the vote of confidence, boss."

Chief Keller placed his hat back on his head as Jules typed. Dad stared at the screen.

Dad...ask him who he thinks murdered me.

"You stare at that device like your life depends on it," Chief Keller said, as he stood. "Worries me, my friend. Told you before; they have interventions for this sort of thing. My Aunt Erma's kid had the addiction. Ruined his life. Consider getting help."

Dad verbalized Jules's question.

"I have trouble believing Constance would kill her own daughter. Or tolerate having a lover who was responsible. Just a hunch, but Mindi Maxwell is rising to the top of the suspect list. For starters, she wrote hateful things about your daughter in her journal. Then she overdosed her. Not to mention, detectives found her fingerprints in Nolan's double wide. Those are cold-blooded facts. We're keeping a close eye on that woman."

Decision made.

With Truitt beside her, Jules would pay Mindi a visit.

61

Thursday, August 26, 2027
Carat Patch Jewelers: Rock Hall, Maryland
(Eleven Days *after* Juliette's Death)

FINN DROVE TOWARD Rock Hall, heading to the jeweler with his wedding band and cufflinks stuffed in the pocket of his police uniform. He'd arrive as the Carat Patch opened its doors at 9:00 a.m., eager to strike a deal with owner Jacob Lawrence.

For the first time since his daughter's death, Finn felt some hope.

Even though he still harbored a few secrets, he had unveiled the majority of them, both willingly and unwillingly. Either way, the outcome was the same. Disclosing the truth had lifted the heavy burden of hiding his dirty laundry while trying to keep it properly sorted so that no one grew suspicious.

Jules had been right: Honesty felt damn good and was a whole lot easier to manage than lies.

Not even last night had ruffled his feathers. Connie had finally come home and insisted he sleep in the guest quarters. The Glitz and Glamour was *hers,* as if he needed reminding. Anyway, sleeping apart was the most honesty they had shared over the last five years.

After parking his cruiser curbside, he entered the store.

While salespeople finished wiping glass countertops, the owner stood behind a display case devoted to rare diamonds. Finn approached him. Jacob offered condolences as they shook hands.

Finn reached into his pocket and retrieved his jewelry, placing the band and cufflinks on the countertop.

Tilting his head, Jacob was undoubtedly curious.

"Sixteen years ago, Connie purchased these items from you," Finn said. "Their appraisals should be in your files. My question is: How much will you pay me to buy them back?"

"These are exquisite pieces, Detective. Rare, I might add."

"My thoughts exactly. Which means I'm expecting a competitive offer, or I'll see if Adelman's is interested in acquiring them."

Finn hated to play hardball right from the get-go, but he needed to get to the station. No time for beating around the bush. Either Jacob wanted to deal, or he didn't. The Carat Patch's competitor was two blocks away and Finn was more than willing to head to Adelman's next.

Jacob collected the jewelry with eager, trembling fingers. "Give me a few minutes to inspect them and review the files. Please, make yourself comfortable."

The owner seemed to take forever, and Finn began to lose his patience. At last, Jacob and an assistant entered the showroom. The woman laid a large velvet cloth on the counter and placed the jewelry on top of the midnight blue fabric. Admittedly, his pieces were breathtaking, but he refused to entertain the notion that he might miss them.

Jacob picked up the wedding band and held it up to the light. "This platinum band features five total carats of exquisite blue diamonds, each individually set. The appraisal is seventy thousand. I'm willing to offer fifty-six. Quite frankly, even the local market will shy from that price point, so I'll have to make connections in the California market."

Finn wouldn't strike a deal until he heard Jacob's offer for the cufflinks. After all, he had to collect enough from the buyback to pay off that prick of a loan shark.

"And the cufflinks?" Finn asked. "What about them?"

"The emerald-cut blue diamonds on these total four carats," he said. "Valued at fifty-two thousand, I'll offer forty-one. I can produce a check this minute. Bernie Adelman would need at least three days to pay you." He smirked at his assistant as if they were sharing a private joke.

Ninety-seven grand would be more than enough to pay Rip Riley back for the down payment on Finn's condo. He accepted the deal.

The assistant immediately handed Jacob a check made out to Finn for the amount, as if they had known he'd agree to the offer. Jacob slid the check across the glass countertop.

Finn placed the check in his pocket. "By the way, has Connie dropped by about having you design a tennis bracelet featuring a special diamond?"

Folding the velvet over the jewelry pieces, Jacob carefully handed the buddle off to his assistant like a swaddled baby. With a head bob, he motioned for her to take the collection away, perhaps so he and Finn could speak privately.

"Detective," Jacob started, "I don't make a habit of sharing details regarding individual orders or transactions. As you might suspect, some projects are not...*associated*...with spouses."

"Except, this is official police business." He tapped his badge for emphasis.

"In that case," Jacob said, "the answer is no. Constance has not placed such an order."

"If she does, call me right away, while she's still here at the store." He handed Jacob his business card and headed outside.

Before driving to the station, Finn stopped at Nationals Bank on Main Street. He opened an account and deposited his check.

Returning to his cruiser, he texted Rip while still parked.

> I have your money. How do you want the $81,000 ($75k + 8% interest)? Wired or in a check?

Finn saw the wave of dots in a speech bubble, indicating Rip was answering.

> Glad you finally made a deal with Constance, but the amount you owe me is off. – Rip

This guy was like The Joker: a freaking clown of psychopathic chaos. A deal with Connie? Why did Rip keep harping on that?

I don't need my wife to cover my personal loans. And what the hell do you mean by...the amount is off?

As his temperature rose, Finn's cheeks felt hot. He read Rip's reply.

You are three days late. That's an additional 6% each day. The balance is now $95.6 grand. Hand over a check to Constance. She'll give it to me. – Rip

Bastard. Rip was rubbing Finn's nose in the jerk's affair with Connie. Treating Finn like he was his dog who had just peed on his carpet. Fine. A fucking check handed to his dear Connie was perfect. What did he care? Their relationship was over.

The amount, however, was ridiculous. In the 16 days since he had accepted the cash from Rip, the loan shark was going to make over $20 thousand. Finn was in the wrong business.

He jumped when his cellphone pinged, indicating he had received another text. What did Rip want this time?

Only, the text was from Chief.

I need to meet with you at the station. Pronto.

Christ Almighty.

His morning positivity was taking a turn for the worse.

No doubt, another ax was about to fall.

62

Thursday, August 26, 2027
The Rock Hall Police Department: Rock Hall, Maryland
(Eleven Days *after* Juliette's Death)

THE NUMBER OF suspects in Jules's murder was narrowing.

Progress felt good. Helping to place her killer behind bars would be an immeasurable relief to her soul, not to mention, a protection for possible future victims. Still, a part of her was anxious. Learning who hated her enough to choke and drown her could break Jules's psyche, especially since law enforcement hadn't exactly exonerated Mother and her shady, loan shark boyfriend.

At least if Mindi turned out to be her killer, Jules would have an easier time dealing with it.

Refreshed for a new day after recharging, she and Truitt decided to visit Dad at the station, since Chief Keller had reinstated him to active duty. Besides, Truitt wanted to huddle and clarify their game plan to remain as efficient as possible. Always the quarterback managing his team for the win. In fact, because of him, she was beginning to understand football and decided she liked the game.

When they materialized in Dad's office, the digital clock on the wall read 11:03 a.m. Dad sat in his chair with his elbows anchored on the desktop, supporting his lowered head in his palms and rubbing his scalp with his fingers, disheveling his silver hair. The laptop was on and positioned in front of him, though his eyes were closed.

Jules moved the mouse, but Dad didn't notice.

Truitt and I are here. What's wrong, Dad?

No response. No doubt, Dad was deep in thought. "I'll make something fall off his desk," Truitt said. "That'll get his attention."

She watched as he used his energy to move a 3D wooden carving of Earth. The paperweight rolled off the desk and bounced when it hit the floor.

Dad jolted, releasing a plume of mist with his exhale. Focusing on his laptop, he read her comment.

"Morning, Jules. Truitt." He tried grooming his hair with his hands. "No worries, guys. I'm fine. Had a meeting with my boss. He told me something I didn't want to hear, that's all."

Whatever he and the chief had discussed, Dad clearly didn't want to talk about it either. Instead, he explained he had sold his jewelry and would be able to pay back Mr. Riley. To date, the jeweler hadn't heard from Mother about custom making a tennis bracelet, but Mr. Lawrence would monitor the situation and contact him if she came into the store.

We're starting to zero-in on the murderer, Dad. If I haven't thanked you recently, I'm sorry. Having you involved has made all the difference, especially because it shows you loved me.

"I've *always* loved you, Jules. Always will. And that sidekick of yours also helped impress upon me that getting involved was the right thing to do." He rubbed his chin and smiled. "You know, Truitt, I was curious and looked up your stats as a quarterback. Your record ranks third in the nation as an all-time high. I mean, did you really throw eighty-three touchdown passes in your last season, as a junior?"

Hell yeah, Mr. Parker. But I didn't do it alone.

"I would've liked to have been in the stands, watching you play."

Dad was beginning to feel how Jules already did. Truitt Windsor was remarkable and not just in football. He was someone who was inspiring her to become her best self.

Truitt lives Peyton Manning's truth, Dad. "The most valuable player is the one who makes the most players valuable."

Truitt looked at her with pride. "You remembered."
She nodded and smiled.
"Now that's a rule to live by," Dad said. "So where are you heading today, Jules?"

To pay a visit to the number one suspect.

"Mindi Maxwell," her father announced.
"One and the same," Chief Keller said at the doorway of Dad's office, with Mindi standing beside him. "She's come to the station to talk to us, Detective Parker. She promises we'll be real interested in what she has to say."

63

Thursday, August 26, 2027
The Rock Hall Police Department: Rock Hall, Maryland
(Eleven Days *after* Juliette's Death)

SEEING HER SEXY hunk of blue for the first time since their epic fuck eight days ago caused Mindi's heart to hammer in her chest.

Every nerve ending in her body began to vibrate and crackle.

Anxious and overwhelmed, Mindi swallowed hard to keep her morning smoothie from erupting onto the floor. At the same time, as much as she hated Finn for gunning down Brock and ghosting her as if she had been a whore not worthy of payment, she couldn't stop imagining his expert lips and fingers stimulating her body.

Mindi's emotions were straight up insane.

Finn directed her to sit in the chair in front of his desk. As she sat, Chief Keller took off his hat and pulled another chair beside hers. She felt a bit crowded. Thankfully, the office was chilly, which was good; the coolness might prevent perspiration.

Reaching into a drawer, Finn retrieved a recorder and placed it on top of his desk near his boss.

After pushing the play button, Chief Keller recited his spiel, emphasizing she had requested the meeting and was at the station of her own free will. He asked if she was declining legal representation for the interview and placed his open palm near his ear, indicating he wanted a verbal answer. She stated yes for the record.

"You have the floor, Ms. Maxwell," the chief said. "Whenever you're ready."

Proceeding chronologically seemed the safest. Otherwise, Mindi feared she might confuse herself trying to separate actual events from *contingencies*. She hated borrowing one of the Queen Mother's favorite words, but it captured the deceptive strategy so perfectly.

"Okay," Mindi said, swallowing hard again. "Right off the bat, I want to establish that I'm *not* your murderer. I didn't like Beauty...excuse me, Juliette...but I didn't kill her."

"Got it." Chief Keller rubbed his chin. "Why not tell us what you *did* do? I'm guessing that's why you're here."

"Sure, but if you don't mind, I'll start at the beginning." She cleared her throat. "After just two days on the job at the G&G, I felt attracted to Finn. And since I'm a goal oriented woman, naturally, I wasted no time developing a plan to have my interest reciprocated."

Finn's eyes grew wide, and he awkwardly shifted in his chair.

"My plan was simple," Mindi continued. "Since I thought the only person holding Constance and Finn together in their marriage was Juliette, I wanted to catch her being a problem child. If I reported enough rule infractions (like she stole a knife, snuck out at night—that sort of thing), then maybe I could convince Constance to send Juliette off to boarding school. The move wouldn't affect pageantry; she could've come home on weekends. And without his daughter hanging around during the week, I fantasized Finn might have time to notice me. To...reciprocate.

"My desires, my dreams," Mindi said, "were noted in my private journal, which I've since destroyed. As suspicious as it sounds, when I wrote that I wanted Juliette to 'go away forever,' I was referring to boarding school."

Pausing after referencing her journal, she hoped to detect a reaction (like a nod) suggesting the men already knew about her entries, thus confirming they had received the computer files from Brock.

Finn and the chief remained frozen. Stone faced.

Talking about the day of Beauty Brat's death was next, since that's probably what Finn and Chief Keller were most interested in. Placing her receipt for the sports drink on the desk, she reminded them that Rock Hall's convenience store was her first stop after leaving the G&G at 10:04 a.m. She knew the time because she had looked at the

Volvo's dashboard. From there, she went home to her apartment.

"Can anyone verify you stopped by there?" Chief Keller asked.

She put a notecard on the desk. "I said hello to Mrs. Cravats, apartment twenty-six, on the way in, and Mr. Ellington complained to me about the overflowing trash dumpster on my way out. Their names and phone numbers are on that paper. Afterwards, I came here to the station to deliver a note for Finn. I spoke with Deputy Walker at the front desk. I left right before noon."

"In your last statement, taken on the day of Jules's death," Finn said, "you told us that from here, you did the following: purchased a lottery ticket, went back to your apartment, and then stopped by the convenience store for a third time to get feminine products before returning to the estate. Anything to add? Or does that itinerary still stand?"

Good thing Mindi wasn't expecting any special treatment or even a sign that she and Finn had shared a connection between them. He was cold and detached. Business only.

Taking a deep breath, she disclosed her lottery ticket and menstruation schemes which sounded pathetically amateurish when spoken out loud. Stupid as they now seemed, they were merely contingencies designed to mask where she really was: at Brock Nolan's trailer.

"With Mr. Nolan…deceased," the chief said, "how can you prove you were there?"

"I'm sure you found my fingerprints in his double wide," she stated. "But to be more specific, on the day of Juliette's death, I pulled over when I was leaving Hidden Creek Trailer Park. A woman with long, curly hair was walking her brown poodle. I bet she'd remember my G&G Volvo because she wasn't happy that I had parked in her way. Unfortunately, I don't have her name, but it can't be too difficult to find out who she is. The trailer park is small."

Finn wrote a few notes on a sheet of paper and using the intercom on his phone, he asked a detective named Smith to come into his office. When the guy arrived, Finn handed him the notes. No doubt, he wanted Detective Smith to check out her claims.

After the cop named Smith left and closed the door, Mindi backtracked, as she'd forgotten to mention that Constance had cameras everywhere in the mansion. Juliette had known about them. In fact, on the morning of her death, before Mindi ever left the G&G, she and Juliette had a brief disagreement which the loft's hidden camera had recorded. To avoid Constance's fury over their argument, they worked together to erase the footage. The editing took place in Constance's communications central: her walk-in security closet.

Raising his eyebrows, Finn looked as though he hadn't known about the camera in BB Jules's loft or about Constance's command center in the security closet. Not going to lie, the man should've been more aware of what was happening in his own home.

She decided not to mention the locked doors to BB Jules's loft. After all, first and foremost, she was at the station to protect her own ass. Nothing else mattered.

Mindi went on to explain that she and Juliette had developed a plan together (off camera) so Mindi could leave the G&G for a few hours and Juliette could get a break from having a babysitter. Their contingency around buying a sports drink seemed perfect. Not to mention, the two of them were on good terms when they acted for the kitchen camera as Juliette drank her potent tea, which was an awful mistake—one Mindi blamed on Constance's faulty directions.

"Her death shocked me," Mindi said. "Surely, I didn't want anyone to think *I* had killed her, so I bolstered my whereabouts to strengthen my alibi and to distance myself from Brock's place, at his insistence. And if I'm being frank, Juliette's death made my goal easier to achieve. A few days later at the Bistro, I seduced Finn by getting him drunk and taking him back to my apartment."

Neither of them reacted, *at all*, which meant the chief knew of their affair. She'd bet they had already seen the video or at least, Finn had told his boss about their filmed sexcapade. Otherwise, there would have been a hint of shock on both their faces. On Finn's because she shared their dirty little secret. On Chief's because her confession proved she could be blatantly sleazy.

Loud bangs, coming from behind her, assaulted her ears.

Everyone flinched.

Mindi turned to see what had caused the racket. Three different blinds had released from their down, locked position. All of them had fully retracted and smacked against the rods installed across the top of each window. *At the same time?* Weird.

"Sorry," Finn said. "I've been meaning to get them fixed. You were saying?"

"I didn't know we had been recorded, Finn," she said, before looking at the chief. "Not until I went to Brock's double wide. See, I was angry he was ignoring my calls. Without knowing he was dead, I stopped by his place on Tuesday, around noon, and found the graphic footage on his computer, as well as print screens of my journal—those that sounded incriminating when taken out of context. Turns out, Brock was Constance's loyal grunt who did unsavory jobs for her like hiding a camera in my bedroom. That woman turned my best friend against me."

"What proof do you have regarding your claims?" the chief asked.

She mentioned the email from Constance to Brock which Mindi had intercepted on Brock's computer and had responded to, out of anger. The email would show the date and time she sent it. Brock was already dead. In addition, she admitted to trashing the computer file labeled "Mindi" by dragging the folder into his recycle bin and emptying it.

After Mindi left the double wide, she had seen two cruisers pulling up to Mr. Nolan senior's trailer. How would she know all that if she hadn't been there on Tuesday, around noon?

"Do you mind if we search your apartment, Ms. Maxwell?" Chief Keller asked. "While you're still here at the station?"

"I don't mind at all. But you won't find the necklace."

"Excuse me?" the chief asked, as Finn's face lost color.

Finally, Mindi had gotten a rise out of them. They genuinely looked surprised.

She confessed that the disagreement she had with Juliette on the morning of her death had been about the necklace. She had tried it on without permission. As a safeguard from envious fingers, namely Mindi's, Juliette had put the necklace back on. She was wearing the heirloom, in fact, when she had gone to lay down under the pool awning. Earlier kitchen footage couldn't verify this because Juliette had her back facing the camera, but Mindi was telling the truth.

"Whoever has that necklace is the murderer," Mindi announced.

"And who do you think that is?" Finn asked, baiting her.

"Your dear wife," Mindi answered. "You really think she went to Washington D.C. on August fifteenth? Have you interviewed Deanna Mae Anderson? Anyone close to Constance knows she coordinates elaborate 'contingencies' (her word) to make people think she's in one place instead of her actual location. Brock wasn't the only one who taught me how to be at two places at the same time."

"Interesting," Chief Keller said.

"Getting back to Jules's necklace. Why would Connie want it?" Finn questioned. "Or want our daughter dead, for that matter?"

"Maybe the Queen Mother thought she could garner more attention playing the sympathy card than counting on Juliette's future victories." She locked eyes with Finn. "I mean, your daughter would have been moving up to the 'miss teen' age group soon, where Jonelle Benét is dominating. No one's even close.

"And about Constance *wanting* the necklace?" Mindi continued. "I'm not a killer, so who knows. Perhaps she kept it as some kind of sick token? Like: *Look how much power and control I have?* Let's face it: Constance is an obsessive control freak with bouts of paranoia and extreme narcissism. My unprofessional analysis, of course, but I did take psychology in college."

Above them, the lightbulb inside the pendant's domed shade burst, as if a power surge had been too much for the filaments.

Chief Keller jumped to his feet, his right hand hovering over his holster. In contrast, Finn appeared unaffected. Cool as a cucumber.

If not for the blindless windows, the room might've turned dark.

Mindi noticed mist with her every exhale.

The police station was freak central.

"Let's wrap up this meeting," the chief said, sounding anxious. "I'll have you wait in the front office while we search your apartment. It'll be warmer there, with less…disruptions."

Fucking fireballs to hell. As long as waiting didn't involve Finn's creepy-ass office, she'd agree to anywhere, including the basement.

In the pitch black.

64

Thursday, August 26, 2027
Rock Hall Police Department to Carat Patch Jewelers
(Eleven Days *after* Juliette's Death)

WHILE DAD AND Chief Keller searched Mindi's apartment, Jules and Truitt had waited in her father's office.

Unusual "disruptions" within the room weren't an issue for them since her energy had caused the blinds to roll up and the lightbulb to shatter. Bottomline, Jules was gaining more confidence in expressing agitation, an emotion Mindi evoked. Not to mention, being dramatic came naturally for a ghost who had formerly been a beauty queen.

Five minutes ago, Dad had returned and closed his office door. He shared what he and the chief had found. As Mindi claimed, Jules's necklace wasn't in her apartment or, for that matter, was any incriminating evidence, including the camera used to record Mindi and Dad. Detectives had already discovered *that* device in Brock Nolan's double wide.

"We sent Mindi home," Dad told her. "Listen, it's one o'clock and I'm starved. Mind if I order take-out and delivery from the Bistro? Eating will boost my energy. We need to talk about our next steps now that Mindi's not a prime suspect."

Jules enjoyed her father's improving attitude. He wasn't standing on the sidelines hoping someone else would take charge and do the right thing. Dad was becoming that "someone."

Forty minutes after he had ordered lunch, there was a knock on Dad's door. He invited the person in—a woman in her mid to late twenties, carrying Dad's order from the Bistro. Her hair was platinum blonde, cut in a pixie: a petite hairstyle for a petite physique. The back of her neck donned a colorful rose tattoo.

"Oh. Hey, Heather," Dad said, smiling. "Since when does the hostess make deliveries?"

Her cheeks flushed crimson to match her rose petals. "I volunteered. You haven't been around much, so I wanted to check on you. Make sure you were doing well."

She exchanged the bag of food for his payment.

"It's good to see you," Dad said. "And I'm hanging in there. Thanks for your concern. As soon as we solve my daughter's case, I'll be back. Will I be able to reserve my special table?"

"I've practically carved your name in it." Winking, she headed toward the door. Before walking down the hallway, she turned for a final glance. "See you soon, okay?"

Jules couldn't help herself. She had to comment via his laptop.

> She likes you, Dad. I can tell.

"Not this again," he countered. "You predicted the same about Mindi. And since you heard her testimony, you know what a disaster I made out of her infatuation. No relationships with anyone until I'm divorced, which is a rule I should've followed in the first place."

> I agree. Because having someone who likes you doesn't mean you need to ACT on it.

"Always the wisest, most mature person in the room, Jules."

The phone on Dad's desk rang and he pressed the speaker button. "Detective Parker."

"This is Jacob Lawrence at the Carat Patch," he whispered. "Mrs. Parker has come to the store in reference to that tennis bracelet you mentioned this morning. I slipped away from our conference to let you know. I can't say how long our meeting will last."

"Please stall her. We'll be there soon. And thank you."

Dad disconnected and immediately called Chief Keller, asking his boss to join him by driving to the jewelry store while Finn brought him up to speed on the way over.

Hanging up the phone, Dad stood. "Why don't you and Truitt head on over there now? See what you can see and report back here regardless of what transpires. Sound good?"

We're on it, Mr. Parker. Jules and I won't let you down.

Holding hands, she and Truitt vanished and materialized in the jewelry store.

Mother was sitting at a table nestled in the back corner of the store. A portable partition created an atmosphere of privacy. On the table was a rectangular midnight-blue cloth made of velvet. Sitting on top of the velvet was what looked like a smooth cutting board made of white plastic. And resting on top of it were tweezers, a magnifying tool, and a black velvet bag with a silk ribbon drawstring. Beside a note pad and pen was a desk light which lit the entire tabletop.

Wearing a silk sundress patterned with bold fuchsia flowers, with her black hair pulled in a bun accessorized with a bow matching her dress, Mother looked fashionable as always.

Jules hadn't seen her for five days, not since the funeral; and honestly, as she stared at her mother, she didn't feel an ache or longing in her heart. That's what made Jules sad.

Mother impatiently tapped her fingers on the table until Mr. Lawrence returned.

"Good heavens, Jacob. Are we conferencing or not? I have important places to be."

He sat across from her. "I promise; you have my undivided attention from here on out."

Mother explained what she wanted: a platinum tennis bracelet that featured a special diamond. She opened the black bag and carefully emptied its contents onto the white board.

Jules's heart pounded in her chest until she realized the diamonds (all 24 of them) appeared the same. Each had a rectangular shape with a radiant cut.

Mr. Lawrence studied them one by one, picking them up with his tweezers and inspecting each through his magnifying tool, before placing them face down on the white plastic. He made notes after each examination.

"These diamonds are colorless and flawless," Mr. Lawrence said. "They are of the highest quality, indeed. Yet, curiously, I detected no differences between them. I apologize, Constance. I am unable to determine which one is your designated 'special' diamond."

Rolling her eyes, Mother huffed. "Honestly. You really need to get out more."

The bell attached to the store's front door jingled as someone entered. Mr. Lawrence nearly gasped. His fingers began to tremble.

"Are you all right, Jacob?" Mother asked.

Truitt looked at Jules. "If Mr. Lawrence doesn't get a grip, he might alarm your mother."

"Except it doesn't matter. Our suspicions are unfounded," Jules said. "You've seen my diamond, so you know. None of these are the one from my necklace."

Mr. Lawrence deeply exhaled. "Yes. Yes, of course, I'm fine," he assured Mother. "But help me understand what you meant by a *special* diamond. Which one is it?"

Mother reached into her handbag and retrieved a small jewelry box. Smiling, she slowly opened the top. Inside was a brilliant, three dimensional heart-shaped diamond.

Jules's diamond.

She clutched Truitt's arm to steady herself. "I think I hate my mother."

"I hear you," he said. "Remember, we'll deal with this together. You're not alone. But right now, your Dad is expecting our help. We both need to think. What can we do?"

If Truitt was trying to distract her, it was a good strategy.

Mr. Lawrence looked as if he might begin to drool as he cooed over the exquisiteness of the diamond. He and Mother were fully engaged, keeping their eyes locked on the gem.

"I know. I'll text my Dad," she told Truitt, eyeing Mother's cellphone on the table.

Using her energy, she composed and sent a text to her father.

This is Jules, Dad. I'm using Mother's cellphone. The diamond is the one from my necklace. It's Nana Bea's heart-shaped diamond. If you can, try to get to the store before she leaves.

The cellphone pinged when Dad responded. Mother ignored it.

We're on our way, Jules. Just had to make sure our paperwork was in order.

"I expect an estimate tomorrow, Jacob." Mother stood. "Feel free to call or email."

Picking up her cellphone, she sauntered through the store and out the door. When she heard another ping on her cell, she stopped on the sidewalk.

Jules and Truitt read the text at the same time she did.

We're turning the corner now, Jules. Be there in a sec. Keep her there if you can.

After reading the entire texting exchange, Mother became pale. She frantically looked up and down the street. Trying to take a step, her legs failed her. As Dad's cruiser approached, Mother fainted and slumped onto the concrete.

Constance Isabel Reyes Parker, the Queen Mother, was out cold.

65

Thursday, August 26, 2027
The Rock Hall Police Department: Rock Hall, Maryland
(Eleven Days *after* Juliette's Death)

TRUITT WAS BEYOND relieved that Jules hadn't blacked out after seeing her mother present Jules's missing diamond to the jewelry store owner. Dang. Mrs. Parker had to be one of the most selfish, cruelest mothers on Earth.

Jules deserved so much better. Life could be viciously unfair.

EMTs had arrived at the Carat Patch as Mrs. Parker was recovering from fainting. The medical technicians determined she was fine, giving Mr. Parker and the chief a green light to transport her to the station for questioning.

Surprisingly, Mrs. Parker's lips had remained sealed about the texts, even as she got inside the back seat of the cruiser.

Truitt was glad he and Jules decided not to ride along with Mr. Parker and Chief Keller. By now, Mrs. Parker had probably ripped them each a new one. Double ouch.

When the vehicle arrived at the Rock Hall Police Department, he and Jules were already there. They listened and observed as her Dad insisted that Chief Keller allow him to place Mrs. Parker in a private waiting room, one without cameras turned on until the interview started. He wanted an unrecorded minute "alone" with her.

The chief agreed to his request.

After Mrs. Parker entered the room and Mr. Parker closed the door to give them privacy, she morphed into a Medusa lookalike, dripping with venom and ready to strike.

Sitting at the table, she placed her cellphone on the tabletop. "Why are you playing this sick joke on me, Finn? What is wrong with you? How demented of you to make it seem as if you were conversing with our dead daughter! You need help."

Mr. Parker calmly explained that Jules's spirit hadn't passed on after her tragic death. Her ghost was helping him solve her murder.

"Absolute rubbish!" she snapped. "You are mad. I forbid you to use our loss in an attempt to ensnare me on *your* personal journey to psychosis." She rubbed her arms. "Why exactly am I here, damn it? And why is this pitiful room so cold?"

"We need to ask you some questions, Connie. You can call a lawyer if you want. But if I were you, I'd get off your high horse and listen to what I'm saying. You may never get the chance again. Take a minute to talk with Jules and make peace with her. Or don't. The choice is yours."

"I've never heard Dad talk to her like that," Jules admitted to him.

"He should've started a long time ago," Truitt said. "If ever a person needed firm boundaries, it's your mother. She's beyond spoiled. Trust me, I know what that looks like."

Mother stood up. "I am leaving. My lawyer will be in touch."

Truitt used his energy to slide her cellphone across the table.

Mrs. Parker stared at the moving device in horror.

"Sit down, Connie," Jules's father said. "Speak out loud and one of them will text a response in the thread we were using. The comment will be sent to my phone, but you'll see it."

Mrs. Parker's cheeks reddened. "What do you mean *one of them?*"

"Jules is with Truitt Windsor," Dad answered.

She plopped into the chair, looking defeated. "The dead kid from next door?"

The phone violently shuddered on the table, thanks to him.

Mrs. Parker flinched.

Dad smiled. "I'd be respectful. Ghosts have a way of calling you out. Anyway, I've grown fond of Truitt."

Using Mrs. Parker's cellphone, Truitt wanted to reciprocate the sentiment.

Back at you, Mr. Parker :)

With trembling lips, Mrs. Parker asked her husband, "How do you know they are here? I mean, in this very room? That the typing is not from some hacker tricking us?"

"Can't you feel them?" Jules's Dad asked. "They need to harness energy to interact with the living; that's why it gets so cold when they're around." He got up and opened the door. "Talk to them, Connie. Sam and I will return in a few."

The door closed. He and Jules were alone with her mother.

"Juliette? Are you still here?" Mrs. Parker asked.

Yes, Ma'am. We were at the jewelry store, too. How did you get my heart-shaped diamond? We've always thought the person who had it would be my murderer because I was wearing Nana Bea's necklace when I went into the pool the day someone drowned me.

"First of all, young lady, I forbade you to swim that day. You disobeyed me. And secondly, I had instructed you to return the necklace to your wall safe. I hope you have regretted the negative consequences of your actions and the hellacious toll they have had on all of us."

Truitt hoped Jules wasn't going to let Mrs. Parker talk to her that way. Thankfully, when she responded, she stuck up for herself, even using all caps to text shout.

Are you seriously going to spend this time lecturing me? I'm dead, Mother. Your control over me died along with my body. SO HOW DID YOU GET MY DIAMOND?

"Your attitude is appalling, Juliette Annabella. And your implication is quite hurtful. A close friend gave me the diamond in question. It is not *yours*. End of discussion. Do you understand?"

Truitt here. Was this close friend...Rip Riley...by any
chance? And might your boyfriend have murdered
your daughter and stolen the diamond? Only to give
it back to you as a gift?

"Considering your extreme rudeness, I do not believe I will ever
warm to you, Truitt Windsor." She glanced at her nails as if they
suddenly required an inspection. "The diamond resembles Juliette's;
that is accurate. Mr. Riley wants me to think of my daughter every
time I wear the tennis bracelet. However, the diamond gifted to me is
three-and-a-half carats, young man. Juliette's was only two."

Law enforcement could easily check out her claim.

Mrs. Parker looked up at the ceiling, as if Jules might be floating
above her instead of standing beside her. "Juliette: changing subjects.
Do you remember the details of your drowning?"

I'm slowly remembering some, but not all.
Unfortunately, I snap out of my flashback before I
can see my murderer. Why?

"The first part of rule number eighteen comes to mind," her
mother started.

Sorry, but I loathe your stupid rules.

"Suppress the negativity, young lady. Hear me out. Rule number
eighteen starts with 'the truth is in you.' Have you gone back to the
pool? Allowed the location of your death to trigger your memories?
As your handler, I insist you take my advice."

You are no longer my handler.

"Let's consider her suggestion." Truitt rubbed Jules's back. "We
can recognize the value of what your mother just said while still being
disappointed in her as a person. Right?"

Jules locked eyes with him. "I'm not following."

"We've been avoiding the actual pool, but maybe going into the water will help release the truth that's inside of you. I'm thinking it's an idea worth trying."

"Juliette Annabella Parker," her mother barked. "Are you listening to me?"

"Because it's you," Jules said to him, ignoring Mrs. Parker. "I'll try it, but only because it's you."

They vanished.

Destiny: the Glitz and Glamour pool.

66

Thursday, August 26, 2027
The Parkers' G&G Estate: Hickory Thicket, Maryland
(Eleven Days *after* Juliette's Death)

THE WEATHER RESEMBLED the day of Jules's death. *That,* she could remember in detail.

Blowing across the Chesapeake from the west, a steady wind caused the flags at the G&G to be on active duty, flapping and saluting toward the mansion. The pool house awning fluttered. Sunshine glistened off the pool's surface, still reminding Jules of miniature glowing fairies surfing the ripples. And on the other side of the bay, a wall of thunderheads was building on the horizon.

Standing beside the pool's shallow end while clutching Truitt's hand, Jules couldn't believe their subconscious minds hadn't missed a beat. Her best friend sported royal blue swimming trunks which featured an osprey logo and the name of his high school. She wore her periwinkle bikini—the one she had worn when she died nearly two weeks ago.

In her ears, her heart sounded like a construction team hammering nails into wood.

"Okay," Jules said, hearing her voice quiver from nerves. "We're poolside and nothing's happened. No tell-all flashbacks like Mother predicted. I'm only remembering that the weather was similar. Let's head back to the station. This pool gives me the creeps."

"Before we go," he started, delivering his crooked smile that now made her swoon. "Have I reminded you that you're beautiful?"

"You mean for a dead girl?"

"Stop!" Shaking his head, he widened his smile. "I meant, you're beautiful because you're as pretty on the inside as you are on the outside."

Her eyes lingered on his chiseled six pack. "Is that how your body really looked alive? Or is your creative ghostly-self hoping to impress? Hoping to qualify for The Beauty Channel?"

"Just saying, I was hot. Probably didn't help me, given my whole attitude thing."

"Well," she said, "now you're hot *and* thoughtful. Clearly, you're gifted at multitasking."

"I also helped you relax, right?"

"Always the quarterback. But sorry to disappoint; I'm still not remembering anything."

He nudged her shoulder. "Let's get closer to the deep end."

Instantly spinning its wheels, Jules's heart left burnt rubber in her chest. If her sternum hadn't been a barrier, her racing heart might've launched through her chest.

She grasped Truitt's arm, trying to steady herself from a wave of dizziness. She filled her lungs with air.

Although Jules desperately wanted to learn who had killed her, she understood that reliving her death would be terrifying. Partial flashbacks had already proved that. Which is likely why her memories were slow to surface.

She leaned against Truitt as they inched closer to where Garth had found her drowned body.

Standing on the concrete edge beside the deep end, she stared at the drain positioned at the deepest point in the rectangular lap pool, 12.5 feet down. A small cloud cast a shadow over the pool but when the sun poked out again, a sparkle caught her attention.

"Did you see that?" Jules asked.

"Something glimmered. Couldn't hurt to take a look. Why don't you check it out?"

"*Swim* down there? By *myself*? Are you kidding? No way."

"Fear no one and no thing," Truitt recited.

"The last thing I need," Jules snapped, instantly annoyed, "is a ridiculous rule. You should know that by now."

"Not all the rules are the enemy," Truitt said calmly, not backing off. "The people who forced you to use them, whether you agreed with the rule or not, *they* are the culprits—the bad guys. But now you have freedom. Now you can choose rules for yourself, ones that make sense."

"But I *am* afraid."

"Of what?" he asked. "Name your fear."

"Learning the truth, for starters."

"The truth already exists. The question is: Do you want to find out what it is?"

"What if I black out because what I find out is too painful?"

"We already know where to reconnect if that happens."

Truitt sat down on the edge of the pool, letting his feet and calves submerge into the water. He tapped the concrete beside him with his hand, signaling he hoped she'd join him.

"I'm not a great swimmer," she admitted, sitting down next to him. "So come with me. We can swim down there together."

"This strikes me as something you need to do on your own," Truitt said. "A quarterback helps his receiver get to the right spot, but when the ball is thrown, the receiver does his part; he catches the ball himself."

"I may not be able to do this."

"You're ready to conquer your insecurities, Jules. To prove you don't need someone else to control you, to determine your self-worth. You are *not* self-less." He squeezed her hand. "The good news is that you've got someone on your team. I'm not leaving. I promise."

She closed her eyes. Tears escaped down her cheeks.

"Don't let anyone convince you, ever again," he said, "that you're nothing without them."

Jules lowered herself into the water and swam underwater toward the drain. Toward the truth she deserved to know.

67

AS JULES SWAM underwater, she reminded herself she didn't *need* air. She was already dead even though the urge to breathe remained.

Holding her breath simply required a mind over matter discipline.

Plenty of times during pageant competitions, she had to coax herself to apply the strategy. Doing so, she overcame physical challenges (like anxiety) by countering them with sheer willpower.

If she was being 100-percent honest, though, her determination never stemmed from self-confidence, a desire to win, or even helping herself. Her fierceness came from being afraid of failing, of facing Mother's retaliation for doing so.

Truitt was right when he told her the truth already existed.

The difference was that today, versus any other day in Jules's existence, she felt strong enough to deal with it, in this case, to discover who was responsible for her death. Conquering her insecurities and fears by facing the truth might be the first step to letting go of her pain. Afterwards, maybe she'd find acceptance.

Bottomline, she wanted peace and longed for a restful soul.

Now is the only time change occurs, she recited to herself.

Reaching the drain, she saw strands of long hair (*her* hair) anchored to the cover as they swayed like bay grass. Wedging her fingertips in between the grates, she used her energy to tug at the lid, hoping to lift it. The drain cover wasn't budging.

She stopped struggling and let the water settle. Maybe all she needed to spark a flashback was to identify what had glimmered.

Jules felt something. One of her fingertips touched a chain.

To avoid drifting to the surface, she kicked her legs above her while facing downwards toward the drain. She tried freeing the chain, but one end had tangled around a grate. Jiggling it caused the other end to move, enough for Jules to see what hid under the drain cover.

The source of the sparkle was her heart-shaped diamond. Still on the chain. The clasp had prevented the pendant from slipping off.

Panicked, she twisted and flailed while holding her breath.

A flashback began to play in her mind as if she were holding a camera to capture the best angle.

Her vision advanced in slow motion.

In her drugged condition, Jules floated on her lounger in the pool. Spread out beneath her, an oversized, purple towel had soaked up the cool water and lowered her body temperature. A nearby Carolina chickadee practically lulled her to sleep.

Her viewpoint recalculated as if she looked down from above.

When her lounger drifted under the skimmer which Truitt had balanced half on the deck and half over the water, the net brushed against her face and disturbed her rest. Disoriented, Jules rolled onto her side as an involuntary reflex.

The underinflated lounger couldn't support her, and Jules toppled into the water. When her float capsized, her soaked towel landed on top of her, covering her head and upper body. It was heavy, and she was so tired from the zolpidem.

What had felt like angry hands was the towel's weight, pushing and forcing her toward the bottom.

Her perspective shifted again, giving her an underwater view.

Finally able to thrash her arms, she pulled down on the towel to remove it, but it clung over her head and body. She resisted releasing any air or trying to breathe. Opening her eyes, Jules saw nothing but darkness. Her towel had entombed her. Why wasn't it floating off her?

Her legs kicked against something. A person. It was the only conclusion she had remembered. But now, in this unfiltered rerun, she could see that the physical contact which was cold and hard like metal was actually the skimmer sinking to the bottom with her.

At that moment, Jules realized she was drowning. She had to free herself from the towel and kick to the surface for air. She didn't want to die!

She reached under her towel. Maybe she could lift it off her. But when her hands got near her neck, she found why her towel was stuck to her: the fibers had snagged with her necklace. Breaking her chain might free her. When she tried, her right hand tangled with her hair and chain. She yanked and pulled from every angle, feeling the burn of the thick chain digging into the skin on her neck.

Jules thought someone had been choking her, but the horrible sensation was being self-inflicted. One final tug. She had to get free!

The necklace finally broke and detached from the towel and her hair, the heirloom falling and sinking to the bottom. The diamond landed under the drain cover, held there by part of the chain which had wrapped around a grate.

Jules's chest burned. She needed a breath. And she took one.

Water rushed in, filling her lungs. Her feet touched the bottom of the pool.

She tried a few more thrashes. Tried to push off the bottom.

At last, her towel drifted off her like a magic carpet.

Even though her struggle took only 24 seconds, it was too late. The overdose of zolpidem had clearly affected her ability to fight for her life.

Her body stilled as she hovered near the drain.

Three minutes later, her soul released itself from her corpse.

Jules panicked from her flashback and kicked to the surface.

When her face broke through the water, she gasped for air.

Truitt grabbed her hand and pulled her to the side of the pool where he had been waiting for her in the water. He pressed her body against his as she coughed up water and reclaimed her lungs.

With one hand clutching the edge and his other arm wrapped around her, she felt safe. Truitt had kept his promise.

Jules wasn't alone. She had his love. His support.

"Can you talk about it?" he asked. "Any memories come back?"

She looked up at him. His eyes were the color of a wheat field. Gazing deeply into them, she shared every detail of her flashback.

"My drowning was an accident," she concluded. "No one killed me, Truitt. I died because one mistake compounded another."

Thunder rumbled as a storm neared the bay from the west.

When Truitt kissed the top of her head, every particle of her spirit tingled with hope.

68

Thursday, August 26, 2027
The Rock Hall Police Department: Rock Hall, Maryland
(Eleven Days *after* Juliette's Death)

FINN REQUESTED A momentary break during Connie's questioning to read an important email he had just received via his cellphone. He didn't disclose the sender because it was Jules.

What she wrote left his emotions jumbled.

When his daughter and Truitt went to the G&G's pool, she found her missing necklace under the drain. Jules wrote that her discovery sparked a vivid flashback of her drowning. Afterwards, she had used Finn's desktop computer in his home office to email him the details, as well as her conclusion that her death had been an accident: a series of missteps which had ended tragically.

Part of his reaction was relief that her death wasn't intentional. Without a doubt, learning someone might have hated Jules enough to murder her or cared so little for human life that they had killed her, with a purpose or without, would have been a woeful legacy to bear.

On the other hand, having someone to blame might've been therapeutic. He and those who loved Jules would've known where to direct their anger and misery: at the murderer.

Accidents were more of a gray area. They created plenty of room for guilt because they gave rise to the dreaded *what-ifs*. What if Connie had never left the property on August 15th for her supposed D.C. shopping spree? What if Mindi had called Connie to clarify her directions for preparing Jules's tea? What if Mindi had done her job and stayed with Jules at the G&G? What if his daughter had obeyed her mother and never gone into the pool?

The big questions, the ones which haunted him the most: What if Finn had paid more attention to what was happening in his home? What if he had acted like a father and insisted on what was best for Jules…like no more spiked tea or locked doors? Would the outcome have been different?

Those ponderings would have to wait for another day.

Right now, he and Chief Keller were still in the private holding room at the station, interviewing Connie. The time was 3:00 p.m.

At some point soon, he had to find an opportunity to ask Detectives Lopez or Smith to investigate under the pool's drain cover at the G&G. Detectives hadn't known Jules was wearing a necklace when they originally examined the pool. All they removed was the skimmer and his daughter's towel. No way could he suddenly blurt out that his dead daughter's ghost had just found her necklace under the drain cover and figured out her death was accidental.

Instead, he had to lead detectives into finding the evidence.

The phone on the tabletop rang and Finn picked up the receiver. The caller was Lopez. He was at the Carat Patch, having been tasked with comparing the appraisals for Jules's heart-shaped diamond with the one Connie planned to use in her tennis bracelet.

As Connie had claimed, the diamonds were different. Not a surprise to Finn since he now knew where Jules's diamond was.

"Lopez," Finn said. "How about swinging by the G&G estate?"

Chief tilted his head. The request clearly surprised him.

"I've been thinking," Finn continued. "We never lifted the drain cover to see if my daughter's necklace might have fallen there, which might point to her death as accidental. Just a thought. Could you contact our forensics diver and check it out right away? It's urgent. Call me or Chief to let one of us know if he's found anything. Before the end of the day, if possible."

Lopez agreed and Finn hung up the receiver.

As if annoyed, Chief narrowed the gap between his brows.

During interviews, detectives weren't supposed to divulge any information; their only mission was to collect it. Fuck Sam. Finn had done what he needed to do. Besides, he and Sam were on thin ice.

"Undoubtedly," Connie started, wearing a smirk, "my jeweler confirmed the two diamonds are not one and the same, as I had stated, gentlemen."

When Finn shared what Lopez had reported about the appraisals, she gloated even more.

"Where were you, Constance, on the day of your daughter's death, on August fifteenth?" Chief asked. "Are you still claiming you were at the boutique in D.C. and ate at Le Diplomate? And before you answer, may I remind you, we've read you your Miranda Rights for this questioning, even though we haven't arrested you…yet. I suggest you tell the truth."

"I am growing weary," she said, retrieving a tissue from her handbag and dabbing her forehead. "Your relentless hounding is draining my energy."

"Answer the question," Chief snapped.

"No, Sam. I was not in D.C.," she blurted. "I was with Rip Riley at his penthouse for a sexual soirée. Are you satisfied or would you like me to furnish you with the details?"

"And your proof?" Finn asked. "About being there, I mean."

"Of course that is what you meant, darling. The details of our repeated frolics might be too much for you."

Connie went on to explain that Rip's condominium building had security cameras in its parking lot which his complex retained for two months. Rip's vehicles (his GMC Denali truck, Tesla Model S, and Streetfighter motorcycle) never left the premises that day. According to Connie, footage would show that her Maserati arrived at 9:21 a.m. and left at 3:05 p.m. so she could rendezvous with Deanna Mae. When she did, her best friend handed over receipts and merchandise as evidence of their contingency in D.C.

The temperature in the room dropped. Finn glanced at his phone.

We're back, Dad.

"Anyway," Connie continued, "it is not illegal to say you are having lunch in D.C. while you are actually sharing intimacies with your lover. Women have an equal right to be unfaithful. And to lie, for that matter. After all, men are not entitled to all the fun."

Apparently, Connie was also claiming her equal right to being a bona fide bitch.

"One of your rules comes to mind," Chief said to Connie.

"Oh?"

Finn could tell that Connie seemed surprised. And he was curious where Chief was going with the rule angle, as he sensed his boss was making his move toward checkmate.

"I think the rule is number eighteen," Chief said. "Yes, that's it: The truth is in you; sharing it is a choice."

"Your point?" Connie asked.

"That rule doesn't hold up in crime investigations. See, you don't have a choice to withhold information or to present misinformation (like your damn contingency), not for matters involving a homicide or suspicious death. In the legal world, Constance, that's called obstruction of justice. Which is a punishable crime."

Connie's face turned bright red.

From Finn's experience, when his wife got visibly angry, she would strike her foe like a viper: attacking, releasing her venom, and slithering away as her victim writhed in agony.

"Given you are an upstanding steward of righteousness and disclosure," Connie hissed at Chief, "I suppose you have already confessed to Finn about how we slept together when your wife was pregnant. Not once, but twice."

"This is a deflection," Chief countered. "But yes, I requested a private meeting with Finn this morning. That's when I told him. He wasn't happy with me, and I don't blame him. I expressed my sincere regret and asked for his forgiveness."

"I wonder how your wife will feel when I tell her."

"Sara learned the truth last night. She's hurt, but she isn't giving up on me. I'm not saying she doesn't know I'm a fool; however, she also knows I love her and only her." He tapped his index finger on the tabletop. "I should probably tell you something else. Sara and I, we're both relieved. See, you can no longer hold my unfortunate lapse in judgment against me. Manipulating me is over."

As Finn had suspected: checkmate.

69

CONSTANCE WOULD NOT let Sam Keller and her soon-to-be ex ruffle her feathers. No, indeed.

She did *not* kill Juliette. And everything Constance had done and said near and around her daughter's death were well within her rights as a private citizen.

Obstruction of justice was an unfounded threat. An intimidation. Besides, Sam would never do anything to risk her annual donation to the department.

The fact that Sara Keller now knew of Constance's "relations" with Sam would have minimal consequences. She and Sara did not frequent the same social circles. Heavens no!

Constance could not deny, however, that Sam had played her well, stripping her of leverage over him. Nevertheless, she would find other methods to manipulate him.

Another truth bubbled up from the fissures in her façade. Constance Isabel Reyes Parker was tiring of her charades. She had busied herself by creating one distraction after another; so many in fact, that she had forgotten how they all fit together to benefit her.

Purging might clean her slate so she could start over.

With her rock, life would be different. No need for contingencies. No need for retributions, not that she regretted any of them.

Especially retributions directed at her husband.

Finn had insulted her in every way possible, placing her reputation at risk. Adding to her utter frustration, he had become *un*predictable.

Then there was Mindi and her infatuation with her darling husband. How dare Mindi steal affections from the woman who paid and fed her? Submitting the sex tape and journal entries to law enforcement was fair play. Making it seem like Mindi harbored motivation to kill her daughter was an earned consequence due to her personal assistant's betrayals.

Garth was no less deserving. He had the audacity to overstep and follow her to Brock Nolan's trailer. Knowledge of her connection with Brock jeopardized her ability to use him as her undercover grunt. Constance had no choice but to punish Garth.

"Did you transfer fifty thousand from a Swiss bank account, one which listed your husband's name as the primary owner, into Garth Harris's account?" Sam asked. "Five days after Jules's death?"

"There is nothing illegal about issuing severance pay."

Constance smiled. She had rehearsed in the event of questioning.

The chief rubbed his stubble. "You and Mr. Riley hired Brock Nolan to rough up your master suite at the G&G. Didn't you?"

"This has nothing to do with my daughter's case," she answered.

"We have multiple investigations happening, Constance, and your hand seems to be in every one of them. Respond, please."

She admitted she gave Brock the order to commit the vandalism.

"I can destroy my own property," Constance added. "I paid for everything and can do as I please with my belongings."

"Nolan *died* following your orders," Sam said. "You really need to find a better lawyer to help school you on these matters."

"I had nothing to do with Brock's death." She glared at Finn for emphasis. "Your detective shot and killed him."

"We have this thing called manslaughter, Constance," Sam said, using a condescending tone she did not appreciate. "Manslaughter can arise when a defendant, *you* in this case, behaves recklessly and with negligence, resulting in the unintended death of someone—that would be Nolan. Sending the kid into your home at night to enact a crime clearly led to his death. Manslaughter may apply.

"You've also made it quite clear that you, and you alone, run your estate. That may be well and good for giving orders on bush sculpting, but you may find yourself in more legal hot water when it comes to tea concoctions and door locks. Yes. Finn has opened up about a few things, and we're looking into additional charges.

"Let me sum this situation up for you, Constance," Sam continued, looking smug as hell. "We're up to three criminal offenses: obstruction of justice, manslaughter, and child abuse."

Constance's heart sputtered. "I would like my lawyer present."

"Of course you would," Chief said.

Finn leaned toward her, perhaps trying to project sincerity. "I'd appreciate some answers, Connie. Off the record. Why go through all the trouble of pressuring me to pay back a small loan? Why didn't you just serve me divorce papers and let the lawyers hash everything out? Do you hate me that much?"

"So disappointing." She shook her head. "For the first time in our sixteen years of marriage, you decided *not* to be predictable."

"Go on…"

"I asked Rip to recall the loan because I knew you could not satisfy the debt on your own. After all, you knew nothing of the Swiss bank account. Rip and I…we were certain you would come to me, begging me to pay off the loan since you were unaware of my romantic connection with him. And then when you asked me for the money, we would strike a deal: the seventy-five thousand for a quick, uncontested divorce. A divorce that *I* had requested, of course."

"We have a prenup, Connie."

"Even still, you could drag out divorce proceedings, darling. And I have retained a decorator to give the Glitz and Glamour a fashionable overhaul. Tick, tock, as they say."

Finn ran his fingers through his hair, a clue he was frustrated.

"My God, Connie. If you had just asked me for a quick divorce, I would've given it to you. Instead, you tried to destroy so many lives…Brock, Mindi, and Garth. Not to mention, me and Jules."

"Look at you! Pretending to be a pillar of virtue." She glanced at the ceiling for dramatic effect since she was certain Jules was still hovering above them. "Forget about the down payment. Had you ever shared with our daughter how you were able to get bank approval for your condominium's mortgage?"

70

Thursday, August 26, 2027
The Rock Hall Police Department: Rock Hall, Maryland
(Eleven Days *after* Juliette's Death)

WITNESSING THE ARREST of a parent for a variety of charges was a milestone no child ever anticipated, especially when their father was the detective placing the handcuffs on their mother.

The event didn't sadden Jules, though; it actually gave her hope.

If Mother had any chance of changing for the better, she needed to accept that her money didn't afford her different rules from the rest of society. Laws were for everyone, even the rich.

Mr. Riley would bail Mother out of jail. An absolute given. Even still, contingencies weren't going to get her out of the legal messes she had created with lies and manipulations. The justice system would hold her accountable this time. Jules was certain of it.

She and Truitt had followed Dad back into his office after the arrest. The wall clock read 5:14 p.m. No doubt a fade would begin to dim their energies. Before that happened, she had to make sense of Mother's last comment. She keyboarded her father on his laptop.

> What did Mother mean when she said... Have you ever shared with me how you were able to get bank approval for your condo's mortgage?
>
> Is this another one of your secrets, Dad?

306

Jules's heart sank as her father explained how he had forged her signature and committed mortgage fraud without her ever knowing it.

Why-oh-why did her Dad find it so easy to lie?

"I'm different now," he assured her. "You hoped I'd become the best man I could be. With your help, Jules, I've grown. I have. Please say you can see the changes in me."

She wrote nothing.

"I'm starting to take responsibility for my life," Dad continued. "No more turning a blind eye or ignoring the truth. Or waiting for someone else to do the right thing. I only wish I could've learned sooner. So I could've been the best *father* possible." He wiped moisture from his eyes. "Your validation would mean so much, Jules. I'm sorry I failed you when you were alive."

Tears escaped from her eyes. Truitt was crying, too.

Dad *was* beginning to change.

> I see the changes, Dad. And I forgive you for the past. Please don't forget, though: Your future will be so different if you work on problems instead of ignoring them.

"I'm done with secrets," he continued. "In fact, Chief Keller knows about my mortgage fraud. Everything else, too. I'll face charges as soon as your case is closed."

> You won't go to jail, will you?

"Chief promised this morning to seek leniency on my behalf. I should get probation, but the justice system will decide. I'll accept whatever a judge thinks I deserve."

Chief Keller opened the door and Dad flinched.

"Quick rundown, my friend," the chief said. "Detective Lopez reported that the diver found Jules's necklace. Good catch. Glad you suggested looking there.

"Now about Constance's claim that she had been at Riley's penthouse on the day Jules died: Security video from the parking lot corroborates her timeline. And her best friend, Deanna Mae Anderson, finally admitted to participating in their D.C. *contingency.*"

"Curious," Dad said. "Did Mindi's alibi flesh out? That a woman saw her at the trailer park on the day my daughter drowned? Because if Mindi's still lying, I'll push forward with a civil lawsuit. I don't want to ruin her life; she's only twenty-two. But she made a lot of careless decisions and if she doesn't get it by now, I'll make the hard choices to hold her criminally accountable."

"Her story panned out," Chief Keller answered. "The woman's name is Rachel Green, and she remembers the Volvo and even the time. Guess Mindi really pissed her off."

"Today's been a productive day then. Can't imagine there's more."

"I also called Dr. Zappa, the medical examiner, to update him on everything," the chief said. "He stated that absent suspects, a motive, or any unexplained evidence remaining, he's going to switch Jules's manner of death from undetermined to accidental drowning while intoxicated. Now that he knows she was wearing a necklace and the department has retrieved it, he's concluded the chain caused the abrasion on her neck as she struggled to save herself.

"Which brings me to an important question," the chief continued. "Do you accept his opinion, or do you want me to push for the case to remain open?"

"After all we've learned, accidental drowning sounds accurate."

"We're on the same page."

"Is the case closed then?" Dad asked.

"Will be shortly. Just wanted to check with you before I finished the paperwork." The chief rubbed his scalp. "Hey, this has been really tough, my friend. Jules was a great kid. I'm guessing she would've been proud at how you handled yourself, how you pulled through even after some major bumps in the road."

"I'd like to think her spirit helped guide me."

The chief cleared his throat. "And I'm sorry again for what I did with Constance years back. I hope you'll forgive me. Not sure I deserve any redemption, but it would soothe my soul."

"I haven't exactly been a saint," Dad admitted. "Forgiveness needs to flow all the way around. I've been a real jerk, so let's forgive each other. I want to change."

Chief Keller looked at the hanging print of the sailboat. "If it means anything, I believe you're heading in a positive direction, with the wind at your back." He rubbed his arms. "By the way, I've scheduled your man Garth Harris to check out the HVAC unit here at the station. He's available for hire, as you might imagine. Anyway, our AC is cranking out frigid air. I'm sure our electric bill's going to be sky high."

"I have a feeling the temperature will be leveling off soon."

Jules agreed with her father. She might've even concluded the feeling was in her bones, but the expression no longer held up.

"Yeah? We'll see, I guess." The chief shrugged. "Not to hit you with unpleasantries, but with the case wrapped up, we're ready to process you for mortgage fraud."

"I need a second. Okay?"

"Got it." Chief Keller closed the door behind him.

"What are your plans now, Jules?" Dad asked her. "Will I see you and Truitt tomorrow? I'm planning to move out of the G&G around noon. Having you guys around would be nice. Would calm my nerves."

Truitt wants to say goodbye to his parents tomorrow. And then we're hoping to pass over. I'm not sure if we can ask for that sort of thing; it just feels like the time is nearing.

"I understand." Tears streamed down his cheeks. "Love you, kiddo. I'm going to miss you, but you deserve peace. Truitt, too."

I love you, Dad. Always and forever.

She felt a fade coming on.

"Want to say goodbye to your mother?" Truitt asked her.

"Mother's not ready to mean what she says, so there's no point."

She squeezed his hand as they vanished into their void.

309

71

Friday, August 27, 2027
The Windsors' Residence: Hickory Thicket, Maryland
(Twelve Days *after* Juliette's Death)

APPREHENSION WAS THE word which came to mind. Truitt could feel that he and Jules were on the cusp of change and the anticipation made him anxious.

In comparison, on the day of his accident, he was calm, cool, and collected. He had no clue he would die and wake up, standing beside his car in the snowstorm, as a ghost. One minute he was alive and sometime after the airbag deployed…*boom,* he wasn't.

His current predicament was definitely a one-eighty from death's past ensnarement because he had time to worry. And worry he did. Although he no longer believed translucent hands would clutch his ankles and yank him into the bowels of fire, he also wasn't certain about what he'd find on the other side. The mystery was unsettling.

There was another factor adding to his trepidation.

Truitt had been on Earth as a spirit for eight months. People, even as ghosts, were creatures of habit and he had gotten comfortable where he was, especially after he had gotten to know Jules. She had helped him rise out of his depression, out of his mental funk; so other than energy fades, his frequent blackouts had dissipated.

He felt like himself again.

His existence was "a known." Heaven was an unknown.

Maybe that's why some ghosts never passed on—ghosts like Ms. Underhill at the church. They were afraid to leave what they knew.

As his spirit powered up, Jules squeezed his hand.

"To your parents?" she asked.

He nodded and in a blink of an eye, he and Jules materialized in his parents' den. His Dad was sitting behind his desk. His mother lounged in her recliner. The wall clock read 8:10 p.m. which meant he and Jules had been recharging in their void for almost 24 hours.

"Still nothing, Abby," his Dad said, sounding somber.

"You can't keep staring at the computer screen, Darren. It's bad for your eyes. You need glasses with blue light protection."

"Look how the tables have turned! You're the calm one now."

"Truitt promised he wouldn't leave without a goodbye, and I believe him." His mother rubbed her biceps. "Wait. Do you feel that? That icy chill?" She looked around. "I think he might be here."

> You're right, Mom. Jules and I have come back. I'm sorry it's taken a week, but a lot has happened.

Continuing to keyboard as his Dad read aloud, Truitt recounted all that had transpired since he'd spoken to them last Friday via the psychic. The best news he shared was Jules had remembered the details of her drowning. She had figured out her death had been a tragic accident. That no one had murdered her.

"Glad you supported Jules as she learned the truth, son."

> I found out something, too, Dad. Remember our expression: The past never changes; no do-overs? It's only partially accurate. Turns out, we can change our futures. Remember Coach Fields' take on change?

"Wait. Need a second." His Dad closed his eyes. "He used to say it before every game. Was it: Now is the only time change occurs?"

> Yuppers. See, I'm a do-over. I've changed. Jules has, too. So have you and Mom. You've embraced a new start here in HT. You've adapted.

"This house *is* starting to feel homey," his mother admitted.

Her smile always warmed his soul.

"Guess the do-over expression only applies to throwing a football," his Dad said. "Then again, if you have a bad throw, you can make the next one better."

Exactly. It's never too late. Well, almost never...

After death, if you head down versus up, there isn't time for a do-over. It's too late, like when the clock in the fourth quarter runs out. Game over.

At least Jules and I got the chance to stay in between for a while. To work out what needed working out. Not sure why, but we were given an overtime.

"Are you and Jules ready for what's next, T?" his mother asked, always sensing what was at the heart of any conversation.

We're heading to the garden, hoping the light will come for us. Not sure if hope is enough to make it happen. Anyway, you need to know that I'll always be your T and you'll always be my heroes. I love you both. More than I could ever say with words.

"We love you, too. And this isn't goodbye, son," Dad said. "It's just halftime. Your mother and I will join you and Jules on the field in paradise sometime in the future. Count on it."

We'll do the Windsor huddle then. For sure!

As he and Jules disappeared for the garden, he heard his mother repeat a family saying that was more about burdens than suitcases.

She whispered, "Pack lightly and travel with ease."

72

Friday, August 27, 2027
The Parkers' G&G Estate: Hickory Thicket, Maryland
(Twelve Days *after* Juliette's Death)

JULES ARRIVED BESIDE the heirloom tomatoes with Truitt next to her. In the darkening skies, stars had illuminated. The moon was full and rising. As fireflies blinked with approval, crickets and cicadas sang their late summer melody. A salty breeze rustled the treetops which poked above the garden's brick walls.

No doubt the lights were twinkling on Gibson Island.

Everything teemed with life, an ironic contrast to the foggy night she'd first met Truitt in the garden.

Looking around, she shrugged. "The waiting begins…"

"Remember when you told me you were fifteen going on twenty?" Truitt asked. "In any of those years, did you ever attend a prom?"

"Since having friends is a prerequisite, that would be a no."

He donned what she thought would be his touchdown smile.

"Thank goodness times have changed," he said. "You have *me* now. And I can teach you how to dance. I've got moves. Just saying."

She rolled her eyes. "Just because I never went to a prom doesn't mean I can't dance. I was in pageantry, remember? Dancing and singing are considered basic, entry-level skills."

"Okay then. Would you join me in a *basic* dance?"

A surge of adrenaline raced to every perceived muscle in her being. Her heart could barely keep pace. Swooping and spiraling, her internal rollercoaster reached maximum velocity.

"Sure. I guess," she said, cringing at the shakiness of her voice.

Truitt clasped her right hand while placing his other hand on her waist. He drew her close to him and she nearly gasped from the sensation…his warm hand pulling their bodies together. His breath mingled with her hair. His chest pressed against hers.

"So tell me, Queen Juliette," he said softly near her ear. "Do you regret being in pageantry?"

As they swayed from side to side in dance, she was grateful for his question. It kept her mind off his body and the raging hormones coursing through her ghostly veins.

"No."

"A one word answer from the winningest junior teen in the nation? Someone who has mastered the art of hyperbole? The unrivaled star of The Beauty Channel?"

"Sorry, I'm distracted."

He looked down at her, winking. "Buff pecs and abs can do that."

"You helped me think differently about pageantry," she said, ignoring his comment, although it was 100-percent accurate.

"I did?"

"When you reminded me 'rules' weren't my blame-all enemy, I got to thinking about pageantry in the same light. The beauty circuit isn't pervasively bad; I actually learned great life skills from the experience. Instead, I'm now able to acknowledge that in every hobby, there are bad apples. But they don't make the *entire* hobby rotten. It's not okay to blame 'the whole' for the sordid behavior of a few."

"You earned a ten out of ten for that answer, Contestant Parker."

Gazing up at his eyes, she batted her eyelashes. "I always do. Now it's my turn to ask you a question, Contestant Windsor. What have you learned in your eight months as a ghost? Give me three lessons."

"*Hmm.*" Truitt looked at the starry skies for a second, as if thinking about his answer. "Here goes. I'm not 'all that' (I died, after all); there's more to life than football; and helping others improves the soul. The latter was my most important lesson. How about you? I mean, you only drowned twelve days ago, but you're a quick study."

"Easy. I learned how to fight for myself and insist I be treated well. Not to mention, to hold others accountable for their actions. Mostly, I learned how friendship works."

"You might have slipped on your math, though. See, quarterbacks are good with numbers. You mentioned four lessons, not three."

"Well, Mr. Number Seven. Perhaps *you* have forgotten that Common Core math allows variable approaches to the same problem. And my approach yielded four correct answers."

"I'll never tire of your bossy queen vibe."

He stopped dancing, their chests still touching, and lifted her chin so they could lock eyes. The full moon made their skin glow.

Her heart sputtered and her breath hitched.

"Jules," he started, sounding so serious. "If we had gone to high school together, or even met somewhere, I would've asked you to my prom. I've never known anyone like you."

"I learned something else…"

"You're adding a *fifth* lesson? That's bold. You've crossed the line into the overachiever endzone."

She didn't want to lose her courage. "I've learned what love looks like." She swallowed hard. "Love looks like you, Truitt Windsor."

Her words sounded foreign—like they had come from someone else because Jules had never uttered anything intimate before. At least, not anything which had reflected the truth.

A wave of fear swept over her.

Jules had finally gotten close to someone. *Fallen in love* if she had to label the feeling. Yet, her future with him was a mystery.

"Do you think there are couples in Heaven?" she asked.

"Probably not, but we won't know for sure until we get there." He tilted his head. "I picture a cloud of love, glowing in golden sunlight, where no one is left out. Everyone co-exists in harmony, for keeps."

Tears welled in her eyes. "I don't want to be separated, Truitt."

"I'm anxious about that, too. I guess we have to trust that everything is…in hands wiser than our own." He caressed her cheek with his thumb. "Remember when you told your Dad that just because somebody likes you, you don't have to act on their affection? So when *is* it okay? Because I feel love for you, too, Jules."

"Now seems like a good time."

Truitt slowly lowered his face as their eyes remained locked. His lips brushed lightly against hers and a hunger erupted in her swirls of energy. Pushing upwards on her tippy toes, she pressed her mouth against his. His lips were soft, yet confident.

Opening her mouth, she invited him in. Their kiss lasted for close to a minute and she felt dizzy with happiness.

"I see your truth, Juliette Annabella Parker. It's not hidden anymore," Truitt whispered. "I'm so glad you see mine."

A bright ray of light descended from the skies, casting a spotlight onto the pathway. Energy radiated from the light and nothing about it felt scary. In fact, the aura emitted love and acceptance. And she could hear a chorus of positive whispers waiting to welcome them.

Tears raced down her cheeks. Truitt had them, too.

Holding hands, they walked toward the bright beam.

"To everything there is a season," Jules said to him, smiling and continuing to gaze into his eyes.

"A time to every purpose," he added.

As they acclimated with the light, Jules knew in the core of her being that no matter what unknowns were ahead, one truth was certain: She would never be alone again.

The End

ACKNOWLEDGMENTS

BECAUSE I GREW up in a haunted house, writing ghost fiction was as natural as pouring salt in every corner of my childhood bedroom in hopes of warding off our ghosts' ability to appear. (Salt is believed to absorb negative energy, thus preventing ghostly manifestations.) Having them seek rest was preferred over competing for residency! Of course, Mrs. Pinkerton (who died in 1917) and her nebulous sidekicks helped me understand that restless spirits aren't easily dissuaded from their aspirations. Nevertheless, I should extend a thank you to them for inspiring MYSTIFIED. Not to mention, creating a ghost character was both cathartic and fun.

The depth of my gratitude, however, is extended to my amazing human team for MYSTIFIED. They are phenomenal, and their feedback was beyond valuable. Thank you, thank you, thank you!

Dena Baker (Beta Reader)
Damonza (Cover Design)
Kerrie Flanagan (Developmental Editor)
Mary Lee (Beta Reader)
Charlene Sharpe (Proofreader)
Diane Stulz (Beta Reader)

To my longtime developmental editor (Kerrie Flanagan)...given our mutual love for the mountains and hiking, I offer this pledge: If ever needed, I will "take a spider for you." Lol! This oath reflects my immense appreciation for Kerrie's expert guidance in developing solid storytelling.

To all my family, friends, readers, authors, bloggers, reviewers, librarians, bookstore owners/managers, Goodreads community, social media communities, book industry experts, and local news media, please know how very much I appreciate you, too. You are at the crème-de-la-crème level, as my character Jules Parker might say!

Until the next project...

ABOUT THE AUTHOR

JULIA ASH'S INSPIRATION for MYSTIFIED came from growing up in a haunted house in West Chester, Pennsylvania.

Julia has also authored a dark fantasy series: *The ELI Chronicles* which includes THE ONE AND ONLY (2018), THE TETHER (2019), and THE TURNING POINT (2020). THE TURNING POINT earned Honorable Mention from Writer's Digest in its 2020 Self-Published E-Book Awards and the paperback was a Semi-Finalist for the 2020 BookLife Prize competition, sponsored by Publishers Weekly.

She lives with her husband and pup on Maryland's Eastern Shore.

For a complete biography, please visit Julia's website. And don't forget to join her on social media!

Website:
https://juliaashbooks.wordpress.com

Facebook:
Facebook.com/JuliaAsh.Books

Twitter:
@Author_JuliaAsh

Instagram:
julia.ash.books

Goodreads:
Goodreads.com/julia_ash

Reviews

Please consider providing a star rating
(with or without a written review) of

Mystified
by Julia Ash

Vendors make it easy to give reviews
on the novel's detail page
(the online page where you purchased the book).

Authors appreciate reviews more than you know.

Thank you!

Made in the USA
Coppell, TX
08 November 2022